D1429324

533 867 00 3

THE WINTER DRESS

By Lauren Chater

The Lace Weaver

The Winter Dress

THE WINTER DRESS

Lauren Chater

Allison & Busby Limited
11 Wardour Mews
London W1F 8AN
allisonandbusby.com
First published in Great Britain by Allison & Busby in 2022

First Edition

ISBN 978-0-7490-2900-5
Typeset in 11.5 Sabon LT Pro by Allison & Busby Ltd.

FSC
www.fsc.org
MIX
Paper from
responsible sources
FSC® C171272

The paper used for this Allison & Busby publication
has been produced from trees that have been legally sourced
from well-managed and credibly certified forests.

Printed and bound by
CPI Group (UK) Ltd, Croydon, CR0 4YY

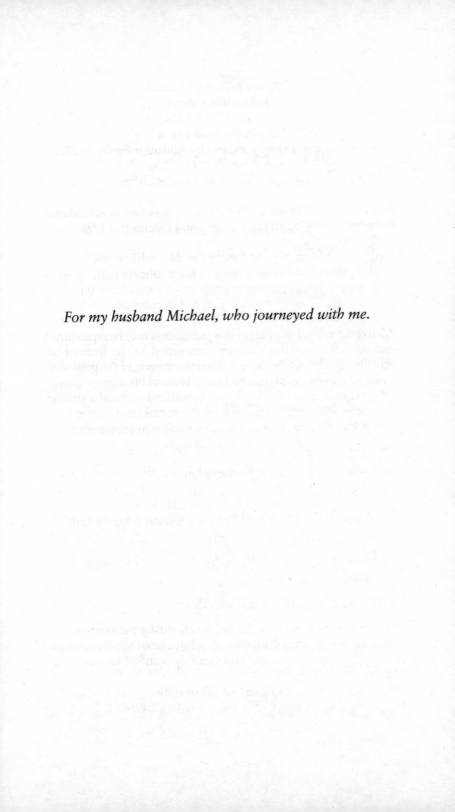

For my husband Michael, who journeyed with me.

AUTHOR'S NOTE

THE WINTER DRESS WAS INSPIRED BY A COLLECTION of seventeenth-century artefacts discovered off the coast of Texel, a small island in North Holland in 2014. The most unusual artefact retrieved by divers – a well-preserved seventeenth-century silk dress – was later identified by leading dress historians as one of the most significant and exciting discoveries in textiles history. The story of the dress's discovery spread to the Dutch mainland where it became an international sensation, attracting the attention of conservators and academics eager to unravel its mysterious origins. After reading an article about the dress published in *The New Yorker*, I instantly knew I wanted to write about it. Something about its ethereal, unearthly beauty captured my imagination and I was intrigued by the life of the woman who wore it as well as her fate.

In June 2019, I travelled to the Netherlands to interview the Texel divers who made the discovery as well as the historians and specialists charged with preserving the artefacts. Their theories formed the basis of *The Winter Dress*, however I have taken the liberty of inventing an entirely new cast of characters and fictionalising dramatic turning points to enhance the novel's themes. I'm indebted to the staff at the Kaap Skil Museum on Texel (particularly Alec Ewing and Corina Hordijk), as well as members of the Texel Diving Club, for showing me around the island and sharing their stories. Thanks also to Rob van Eerden for allowing me to view the dress – a spellbinding and unforgettable experience I drew on many times during the writing of this novel.

Introductory note for *The Winter Dress*
Alec Ewing, Head Curator, Kaap Skil Museum, Texel

In 2014, local divers from the Dutch island of Texel stumbled onto a unique discovery: a nearly complete satin gown, dating back to the seventeenth century. The gown was found in a broken chest, located near the main mast of a wrecked vessel. Remains of other textiles were found alongside it, while nearby chests held silverware and rich book bindings. Locals had already given it a name: the Palmwood Wreck, named after the previously discovered cargo of boxwood.

The existence of the wreck itself is not unusual. The seas surrounding Texel are in fact littered with shipwrecks. Historically, the island was strategically located in the middle of several trade routes, with the eastern coast serving as a busy roadstead during the seventeenth and eighteenth centuries. Several dozen wrecks have reappeared from beneath the sands in the last few decades. Due to their poor state, few can be historically identified. While parts of the rigging, weaponry and robust cargo can still be salvaged, textiles are a big exception. As organic material is usually the first to disintegrate, a decayed sock or sleeve is a rare discovery.

While all are heritage sites that yield important information about Dutch history, none have come close to matching the value of these discovered textiles. Remarkably, this gown has survived a nearly 400-year-long stay below the surface of the water rather well. While no undergarments remain, the gown itself is almost completely whole. Its silk still carries a shine and its floral patterning still clearly stands out. Its colours are reds, browns and cream, though it has clearly been contaminated by the dyes from other fabrics stored in the same chest. Parts of those other garments have been salvaged as well, though none are as complete.

Extensive research into the gown and the rest of the collection has been ongoing since 2016. Why did these textiles survive? Are they part of one wardrobe with a single owner? What was the ship's name, and how was it lost? Not all answers have been found, but an image is taking shape: of a well-armed Dutch merchantman returning from the Mediterranean between about 1650 and 1670. Whatever its name, that ship took several chests filled with valuable goods on board somewhere along the way. They are rich, worldly, personal, and often feminine. Some carry an English connection, others a Dutch one, and some are more exotic. The textiles and silverware would not look out of place in the highest social circles of Western Europe, but who in Holland would be wearing a kaftan?

Though much room is still left for speculation, the value of the collection is already hard to overstate. In many ways, it is shining new light onto fashion, travel and material culture in North-western Europe during the seventeenth century and is spurring on new insights and research initiatives. Highlights of the collection will be put on permanent display in Museum Kaap Skil on Texel in 2022.

1

Jo
2019

THE FIRST THING I RECALL ABOUT THAT DAY IS NOT the image of the dress nor Bram's phone call. It's the man's clothes, arranged in a neat pile halfway up the beach. A pair of shorts folded over canvas sneakers. A white shirt fluttering in the breeze. The stranger had removed his watch before he entered the water. In the gathering heat, its glass dial blazed like a second sun. Two grim-faced paramedics knelt on the sand packing up their equipment, while a uniformed cop directed curious onlookers away from the poor man's body, partially concealed under a plastic sheet.

I imagined the fleshy contours and rich, sun-tanned hues of the victim's face – not the blanched, sunken look he'd worn when the lifeguards dragged him out of the surf, but that earlier version of him, the living, breathing one that had escaped my notice. After arriving at Bondi Beach an hour ago, I'd run as quickly as I could towards the water, paddling hard until I felt the vertiginous pull of the current grip my legs and arms, the sandy shelf giving way to a bottomless blue. I floated, waiting for the sea to work its magic and ease the knotted tension in my neck.

I'd spent most of the previous day hunched over my laptop, attempting to finish writing my book. The past eight months had taught me that it was one thing to write a dissertation on cultural dress theory and quite another to convert it into a digestible piece of creative non-fiction people might actually want to read. Before leaving my job as a lecturer at the London Metropolitan University, I'd applied for, and been accepted into, a research fellowship program at Sydney University. I'd written most of the first draft of my textiles book in a tiny office over-looking the university quadrangle, knocking out twelve chapters within six months in a kind of frenzy. Then, for reasons I found hard to explain to the Dean and my colleagues, my progress had stalled.

I had started sleeping badly, my dreams brimming with voices speaking all at once, as if half a dozen radio frequencies had been spliced together to torture me. Some of the voices I recognised as belonging to people I knew but many of them remained stubbornly vague. They prattled on about the most mundane subjects – what they were planning to eat for dinner, what mischief their children got up to, the kind of house they hoped they could afford once the mortgage rates fell. I'd tried everything to tune them out – meditation before bed, half a Valium before dinner. I even banned caffeine from my diet, although my resolution lasted less than a fortnight (the coffee withdrawals made me so irritable that my aunt, Marieke, insisted I resume the habit). And then, just as suddenly as they had started, the bad dreams lifted. For the past few days, my head had been clear. No more voices, no more headaches. Just peace. The terms of the university fellowship stipulated that the book I was working on needed to be ready for publication within a year. Meeting the deadline would be challenging after my health issues but, if I worked hard, not impossible. I'd pushed myself yesterday to regain some momentum. Now I was paying for it.

My neck had felt poker-stiff, the tendons stretched as taut as piano wire. Every turn of my head sent a ripple of pain shooting down a labyrinth of nerve-endings into my spine. I could have arranged a massage but that would have meant putting my body in a stranger's hands and making the dreaded small talk, an ability I'd always admired in others since it was a skill I felt I lacked. The beach had seemed a far safer bet.

Marieke insisted the cure for any ailment was salt water. She swore by the restorative benefits of a good cry, vowing she always felt better afterwards. But crying had never affected me that way. I hadn't even cried the night two police arrived from the Dutch mainland on Texel, the small island where I lived, to tell me that my parents' bodies had been found in an isolated swamp in Southern Holland. Too numb and shocked to accept what they were trying to say, I assumed the tears would come later. I waited for them to arrive, the way I expected my parents to walk through the door again, their voices raised in perpetual argument over some slight committed years ago. But they never did.

When Marieke had showed up to make the funeral arrangements and organise the adoption paperwork so I could leave Holland and return to live with her in Australia, I'd asked if she thought it was odd I was yet to cry over my parents' deaths. What if I was one of those strange criminals you read about in the news – a person devoid of empathy who tortures others without remorse? But Marieke had assured me grief has its own timeline.

'Your parents died in a freak accident, Josefeine, something nobody could have predicted. It will take time for the shock to wear off. But one day, you will cry, and when that moment comes I'll be there to console you.'

I'd never quite worked up the courage to tell her she was wrong.

I let the ocean cradle me and, after half an hour's gentle rocking elapsed, raised my head and glanced back towards the shore. The southern end of the beach was already packed, although it was not yet nine. Teenagers splashed playfully in the shallows and a pod of surfers wove in and out of sight, their boards spearing the waves as neatly as needles through cloth. Bondi had been packed with tourists and locals for as long as I could remember. I could still recite the number of the bus that had conveyed me to the city interchange during the summer holidays, I could picture it wheezing to a stop outside Marieke's Marrickville terrace where she'd brought me to live. There was a particularly cranky bus driver on the 412 route who always shouted at me to hurry, then sighed as if greatly put upon when I fumbled the unfamiliar coins. I once heard him mimic my Dutch accent to another passenger, exaggerating the vowels like a toddler learning their first rhyme. I accepted his mocking without complaint but promised myself I would work hard to be rid of the accent, casting off the fragments of my old life like an ill-fitting shell.

How strange everything had seemed in those early months. Even the light was different. It stung my eyes if I stared too long at the waves and it painted glowing after-images of striped towels and beach umbrellas on the back of my eyelids. That particular kind of light – that bright, unforgiving Australian sunshine – was a stark contrast to the soft ambience of my Northern European childhood. It marked, distinctly, the two phases of my early existence and allowed me to press on without worrying too much about the past. Moving to Australia with the only person in my family brave enough to leave the island of Texel, where generations of Baakers had always lived, seemed like a wild adventure, the fulfilment of a destiny I'd always sensed waiting. I felt reborn, as if I'd been given a second chance. I knew I had to be tough to survive and I wasn't about to throw away my hard-won independence by dwelling on things that might have been.

I was still floating on my back when the screaming began. A woman's voice, shrill, panicked. I've never been scared of sharks – you can't be when you dive as regularly as I do. You've got more chance of being caught in a rip and washed out to sea than you do of ending up as a white pointer's lunch. But the screaming rattled my nerves so I started paddling in, using the current to propel me through the surf. As I neared the shore, two lifeguards emerged, hauling something wet and heavy between them, water streaming off their shoulders and necks as they fought the tide. Spectators standing in the shallows watched the drama unfold, their faces frozen as if turned to stone.

I staggered back onto the sand just as the lifeguards laid the man down and began performing CPR. By the time the paramedics arrived, it was obvious to everyone that the man was gone. His profile was a pallid sculpture carved from bleached bone, save for his nose and lips which were purple-tinged: classic signs of oxygen deprivation. A few months after my parents died, I became obsessed with drownings and near-drownings. It was a morbid fascination; something I'm now a little ashamed to admit, although in my defence, I was sixteen and my whole world had been upended by their unexpected passing.

When I had first arrived in Australia, Marieke was working as an administration assistant in a community art gallery. It was the summer holidays. I was yet to make any friends. Each morning, I followed Marieke into town and she dropped me at the State Library. I spent hours there poring over books and old newspapers and dog-eared magazines, indulging in my strange infatuation. I learned that there are five stages of drowning, that clinical death can occur after four minutes of complete submersion. I learned that even after successful resuscitation, some victims continue to experience breathing difficulties, hallucinations and confusion. Approximately ninety per cent of drownings occur in freshwater lakes, rivers and swimming pools. The remaining ten per cent take place in sea water.

People who have drowned and been brought back describe the experience as 'surreal'. They liken it to sitting in a darkened theatre, watching themselves as actors going through the motions on screen. First comes disbelief – the mind and body struggling for dominance, one refusing to acknowledge how serious the situation is while the other searches frantically for a source of oxygen, rapidly leading to a semi-conscious state. Doctors describe this as 'the breaking point' – the moment where chemical sensors inside the body trigger an involuntary breath that drags water into the windpipe. After that comes shock and then the grave acceptance of their inevitable fate: a kind of surrendering.

These accounts had made me shiver even as I devoured them. Was this what my parents experienced in their final moments? The enduring mystery – that I would never know their last thoughts – had haunted me well into adulthood. There was one thing I was sure of, though. When death had rushed headlong into the salt plains of Saeftinghe, flooding the sea asters and scurvy grass verging the isolated hiking trail where they'd chosen to walk that day without a guide, their last moments hadn't been spent worrying about what would happen to me. I was their burden. They'd always made that perfectly clear.

Swinging my bag over my shoulder, I walked towards the carpark, passing the small group keeping silent vigil over the man's body. There was nothing to be done. The police would check his identification and notify his next of kin as they had when my parents had passed. I had been spared the horror of having to identify them because my best friend's father offered to do it for me. I was grateful to him then, as I was grateful for a good many things Bram's family did for me, providing stability where none existed.

I opened my car door and sat in the driver's seat. As I lifted the key to the ignition, a great heaviness overcame me. My hand shook. I stabbed at the ignition, came up short. Tried again. Failed. Resigned, I let the key drop into my lap and took a few deep, steadying breaths, letting my mind wander to the images I'd been analysing yesterday. This kind of procedural sifting never failed to calm me. Thinking about clothes had always offered sanctuary, a safe place to retreat to when the harsh realities of life threatened to overwhelm. The chapter I'd been working on yesterday had focused on the impact of the English Civil War on seventeenth-century European fashion. I'd managed to track down a number of suitable examples of formal male dress, including some grisly images of the blood-stained shirt King Charles I had been wearing when he lost his head on the execution block outside the Banqueting Hall at Whitehall. There was also an exquisitely embroidered men's hunting jacket, wearer unknown. While little was known about the origins of the embroidered jacket, the King's shirt had become a relic after his death, understandably infused with the horrible import of deliberately killing the God-ordained English monarch: a kind of existential buyer's regret. What I needed now were real examples of gowns – not something painted, since portraits couldn't always be relied upon to convey the precise ways clothes sat on a person's figure, but tangible artefacts through which I could explore the complexities of women's lives. Unfortunately, few examples of clothing from that period existed now. The ones that did were housed in archives and museums far from Sydney. The Met in New York and the Musée de la mode et du textile in Paris held some extraordinary pieces of women's clothing in their collections but organising to view them or requesting permission to reprint the images taken by their official photographers would take time.

My phone buzzed in the bottom of my bag, snapping me out of my contemplation. I fished it out and unlocked a message from an unknown number and drew in a small breath as a photograph of a late Jacobean court dress flickered to life on the screen. The colour was striking: rich ox-blood, overlaid with burnished copper. The elaborately embroidered fabric patterned with pale florets, caterpillars and bees, a common motif signifying birth, death and fertility. There was some obvious damage. A dark stain had turned the laces black, indicating the corrupting presence of iron mordant. Once prized as a fixative that brought out the glorious shades of natural dye, the metal salts could weaken the chemical structure of fabric over time.

I had no doubt that close examination under a micro-scope would reveal tiny holes in the delicate fabric. The damage would inevitably worsen, spreading like spores of mould on cheese until the entire composition eventually broke down. For now though, the undamaged parts of the brocade shimmered like fish scales, illuminated by an arc of rainbow light as if someone had sponged the panels with water to bring out the peculiar, dazzling shine of gold thread ribboned throughout the weft. The hem and sleeves were fringed with yellow-starched reticella lace, very fine meshwork which must have taken hours of back-breaking labour to produce. Excitement bubbled through me.

Under the image on my phone, the sender had written in Dutch: *Wat denk je, Feine?*

What do you think, Feine?

Only a handful of people knew me from my Texel days and only one, apart from Marieke, was bold enough to use my childhood nickname. *Bram, is that you?*

It's me, he wrote back. *I've changed phones. Glad this is still your number! Did you get the photo?*

I did! What's the time there?

A little after 5 a.m.. I'm at the clubhouse in Oudeschild. Sem's here, too. He says congratulations on that piece you wrote for The New Yorker! *We bought three copies and had one framed for the display room. You're famous, Feine!*

The article, a watered-down version of my PhD, had been published five years ago to coincide with the opening of an exhibition on Tudor women hosted by a London gallery. I'd argued that the intimate items of Elizabeth Tudor's boudoir actually belonged to her lover, a woman. One of her ladies-in-waiting, to be precise, the daughter of a wealthy landowner who had made his fortune selling acres of oak forest cut down and repurposed into a fleet of naval ships. The story had been picked up by international media outlets and syndicated across the globe. It was the only article I'd ever written that had gone viral and, looking back, I was woefully unprepared for the fallout. For a few months, my phone was clogged with weekly messages from journalists demanding exclusive interviews or armchair historians wanting to discuss their own Tudor theories. Worst of all was the avalanche of hate mail I received from die-hard monarchists who despised the suggestion of homosexuality in any members of the institution, living or dead. The whole experience had left me wary of committing too early to a theory and espousing it publicly before I was mentally ready to deal with the outcome.

Tell me about the dress, I wrote.

We were diving a wreck yesterday out near De Ezei – a galleon, a big old grandmother ship. She's usually under a layer of mud but a storm uncovered her. Blew all the mud and sand away. Nearly blew us away! There was a sealed chest on the upper deck. We had to break it open with a knife. Then the wind picked up again and the visibility turned to shit so we grabbed everything we could and hauled it back to our boat. Sem unrolled the fabric and we

19

realised it was a dress. We couldn't decide what to do with it. Then somebody remembered your article. I haven't even shown you the other stuff yet. Stand by.

I watched three tiny circles revolve while more photos loaded. The first was a seventeenth-century lice comb on a black background, the blond wood purled with knots, the edges needled with sharp, uneven teeth. I'd handled a similar one years ago in a lab in Oxford, cleaning the wood with a fine sable paintbrush before prising the desiccated bodies of centuries-old lice out of the tines. Next came a four-sided drawstring purse, the exterior worn so thin that the hard leather scaffold showed through the patched velvet like exposed cartilage. A woman would have tied those purse strings around her waist and stored her personal items inside – a sewing kit, perhaps, or a herbal pomander, something to ward off the foul stench of the city streets. The final image revealed a scattering of crimson carpet fragments piled up beside a damp leather book cover. The book's pages had long since dissolved, leaving just the fragile bindings. A heraldic crest was stamped on the leather, but the camera had failed to capture the finer details so all I could make out was a blurred shape resembling a sword or a staff hemmed inside a scrolled cartouche.

I waited but there were no more photos, only a text message. *So? What do you think of our treasures?*

I hesitated for exactly ten seconds before pressing the tiny telephone logo. Bram picked up on the second ring. His voice was warm and familiar, despite the oceans and years separating us.

'Feine! Or should I call you Doctor Baaker?'

I could tell he was grinning. I pictured his sparkling eyes

and lopsided grin, the way his chipped right tooth always snagged on his bottom lip – the legacy of an adolescent encounter with a 40-pound scuba tank. I tried to remember when we'd last spoken. It must have been around four years ago. He'd called to invite me to a school reunion which I'd declined to attend, although I could have easily flown from London, where I was based, to Amsterdam and arranged a hire car. The reunion was to be held in the college gymnas-ium of our old high school on the Dutch mainland. When I'd lived on Texel, the student population was so insignificant that the local government didn't feel they could justify paying a teacher. Instead, each morning Bram and I had taken the ferry together, crossing the deep, cold waters of the Marsdiep, the tidal race that thundered between Texel and the coastal village Den Hoorn, providing the only access to the island except by air.

At sixteen, Bram had towered over the sixth-form boys and some of the teachers, too. He was smart, a joker, always ready to laugh at his own expense. In the summer holidays, he could be found in the backroom of the scuba-diving shop his father owned, filling air tanks and washing wetsuits and kitting out the tourists with snorkels and masks. We'd lost touch a bit after I moved away, eventually reconnecting in our mid-twenties when Bram tracked me down via the staff website of the V&A Museum where I was working. He'd sent a cautious email, wanting to know if I remembered him. He had recently opened a pizza shop in Den Burg with his brother and was quick to reassure me he understood if I preferred not to reply. It might be too painful, after everything I'd been through. But I'd replied almost at once. *Of course I remember you!* I'd written, before going on to describe my work sourcing a series of traditional masque gowns to be displayed alongside the museum's extensive collection of seventeenth-century Stuart furniture.

My enthusiastic response to Bram's email surprised me. It was like rediscovering a fragment of myself I thought I'd lost. We'd always joked about running away, escaping the island and carving out a life for ourselves in South America or, yes, even Australia. Somewhere hot, where the long winter months couldn't touch us. But somehow, despite the banter, I always knew he'd stay behind. Our friendship had been purely platonic and I'd trusted him with my life. We'd often dived together. Immersed between thirty metres of water and the ocean floor, we'd had only each other to rely on. The trust we'd built over our years of diving together had never faded, nor had the promise we'd once made never to lie to one another, if we could help it.

'It's just Jo,' I said. 'Not Doctor Baaker. Or Feine, if you prefer, although nobody's called me that in a long time. As for the artefacts, I think they're extraordinary. I'm not exaggerating when I say this could be a huge bloody deal, Bram. We're talking international coverage, the pick of the world's very best museums, the most outstanding textiles conservators and researchers.'

I paused to draw breath, aware of the budding excitement, the blood whooshing through my body, spurred on by my erratic, febrile pulse. I recovered myself enough to ask where the artefacts were.

'The purse and the comb are in the display room. The dress is hanging up in the bathroom. We hosed it down to get the mud off.'

'Hosed it down?' I sputtered, unable to conceal my shock. The idea of that fine silk surviving centuries of potential damage only to be blasted by chemically infused tap water and stuck on a wire coathanger to dry made me feel queasy. The temptation to scold burned. Mishandlings are common in the archaeological field. Any artefact dating back fifty years or more was bound to contain a litany of improperly applied conservation techniques, accidental mishaps and unsuitable storage methods. Sometimes there was a record, a series of notes kept alongside the item that could provide clues to its future management while telling the story of its past. But Bram and his brother were not conservators. They would not have known, for example, that the best way to store a dress retrieved from the bottom of the ocean was probably to keep it submerged in water for as long as possible, in a dark room. Oxygen, light and fluctuations in temperature were anathema to old fabrics.

As soon as that dress hit the surface, the process of deterioration would have begun. Invisible at first, the damage would eventually manifest as dark stains and tiny tears in the fibres of the fabric as the seams crumbled into a powdery dust. The leather book casing, already fragile, would probably suffer a similar fate. All too often, I'd taken possession of textiles that had warped due to high levels of humidity. Under such conditions, a fabric's surface could be permanently deformed mere months after exposure, leaving the artefact completely unrecognisable. Antique cellulose, once used to glue together fabric seams, was viewed by rapacious silverfish as a free meal, while an infestation of carpet beetles, prized by conservators for stripping skeleton specimens of hard-to-reach flesh, could destroy an entire collection of historical garments in less than a week. Carpet beetles were voracious eaters, chewing through silk, fur, wool and leather indiscriminately. The discovery of an outbreak within a museum was always met with a flurry of anxious activity as conservators and curators rushed around trying to ensure the affected clothing was quarantined and frozen to kill the bugs and prevent the damage spreading.

Bram knew none of this. While well intentioned, his expedition to retrieve items from the wreck was at best reckless, at worst deliberately provocative. I could have murdered him for being so foolish. But then I remembered all the times he'd shared his lunch with me in the schoolyard and the countless nights he'd slept on the floor of his bedroom, gifting me the comfortable bed so I'd be well rested when we rose at dawn the next day to go diving. I felt my frustration ebb. What was done was done. The important thing now was to ensure the artefacts were stabilised without subjecting them to further damage.

I explained to him that, based on what I could see, the items appeared to be early to mid-seventeenth century. The cargo had probably belonged to a merchant's ship, one of the many that had been lost on the famous Texel Roads during that period. The Roads had been a popular shipping route used by Dutch sailing vessels to import wood from Norway and grain from the Baltic. The fabric for the dress could have been woven in Holland by Amsterdam silk-weavers or a family of French Huguenots who'd fled to London to escape religious persecution after the Revocation of the Edict of Nantes. Or it could be Bursa silk, spun during the

Golden Age of the Ottoman Empire when Turkey and Syria competed with China and Persia to supply fine textiles for use in both clothing and household furnishings. Intricate floral patterns woven onto silk panels in gold and silver thread were just as likely to be found on dresses as on cenotaphs, the waxy pomegranates and delicate peony blossoms twined through Qur'anic verses honouring the dead. 'What you need,' I said, 'is a professional who'll be able to stabilise the artefacts and make a proper assessment.'

'Great. So, when are you available?'

'You want me to do it?'

'Of course! Why do you think I made contact?'

Ouch. That stung. Maybe my rejection of Bram's invitation had bothered him more than I thought. He'd asked me to visit the island on other occasions but I'd always found some excuse. It wasn't that I didn't want to see him; I valued our friendship possibly more now than when we were children. While memories of my parents were like vague shadows glimpsed through smoky glass, the ones I retained of Bram and his family were vividly clear. His occasional updates were a reminder that I hadn't sprung into the world fully formed at the age of sixteen. I had a past, a history, even if it was one I selectively chose not to think about. Cocooned in the cosy, protective warmth of Bram's family, of which I was an honorary member, I'd had no reason to delve deeper into those experiences I'd shared with my parents that were potentially unstable and served no good purpose. Occasionally, if I was exhausted, my mind would seek them out, returning to old hurts and bitter accusations, replaying them over and over like scenes

25

in a movie. Reprisal never brought relief. Bram had never harassed me to return to Texel. He had always accepted my excuses with mild diplomacy. Now I wondered whether the needle on his internal bullshit meter had been swinging wildly the whole time we were speaking, the current of my lies forcing the needle all the way to the right.

'I'm not a trained conservator,' I warned him. 'I can do the rudiments – stabilise the items, assess the damage. My specialty is illuminating the cultural significance of an article of clothing, tracking down its origins. With luck, I can unlock certain key aspects of the wearer's identity, the time and place where they were born, the things that shook their world – religious wars, revolutions, scientific advancements. I'd love to help, but we're going to need to get someone else on board with experience in other aspects of conservation, not just textiles.'

I paused, mentally sifting through the profiles of former colleagues. My contact list was a little rusty since I'd moved back to Australia to work on my book, but I could think of only one person who could fulfil all our requirements.

Liam Pinney was one of the best conservators around. We'd known each other since we were undergrads and had kept up our friendship all the way through our admittedly colourful careers. Six years ago, we'd been asked by the London Met, where we were both working, to assess a collection of sixteenth-century French tapestries and silk brocade nightgowns discovered by a wealthy octogenarian in the attic of her Cambridge castle. The woman had contacted the London Met to request an assessment and they'd sent Liam and me out to investigate the artefacts. We ended up publishing our findings at the same time, but the university chose to promote Liam's research into the tapestries, while my paper championing the delicate gowns as some of the earliest and best examples of royal dress was relegated to second and third-tier publications. This had resulted in a depressing lack of citations.

I'd confronted the Dean of Social Sciences, who'd said nightgowns simply weren't in the same league as priceless tapestries. His insinuation, that the study of women's fashion was unworthy of any real academic distinction, was one of the reasons I left academia shortly afterwards, vowing never to return.

Liam had rung me to apologise straight after I'd stormed out of the Dean's office.

'I'm so sorry. If I'd known what the university was planning, I'd have insisted on combining our research and publishing it together. You've got to believe me, Jo.'

He'd sounded so earnest, it was impossible not to forgive him. Last I'd heard, he'd been teaching at the Glasgow School of Art while working on his own research about the 'self-made man' and the rise of dandyism in early eighteenth-century Europe.

'I have someone in mind,' I told Bram. 'There may be some complications over ownership of the artefacts. You'll probably be asked to explain what you were doing down there, retrieving items from a known wreck.'

Bram sighed. 'We expected as much. But what were we supposed to do, Feine? Just leave those things down there? Let the storm wash them away?' His voice had risen an octave, fuelled by the force of his words.

There were no easy answers to his questions. They echoed

the complex relationship between world heritage committees and amateur collectors that had been going on since the dawn of time. In Texel, scavenging had always been a way of life. Ships broken apart by storms spilled their cargo into the sea and the tides washed their goods ashore where eager locals waited to take their pick of the spoils. Sometimes rare and useful items materialised. One year, a midnight squall sank a tanker carrying luxury fur coats. Everyone showed up at church the next day dressed like glamorous movie stars. Locals had a name for this unique beachcombing tradition. They called it *jutter*: what the sea gives, the finder keeps. But even a remote place like Texel couldn't escape regulation altogether. In 2007, the Netherlands had committed to an internationally binding agreement designed to protect sites of marine archaeological significance. If you found something valuable on Texel, you were supposed to report it to the *Strandvonderij* – the official beachcombing board – who would take possession of the goods, if they were valuable, and decide whether a finder's fee should be paid. Penalties for violating the agreement ranged from a slap on the wrist to extensive jail time. I tried to imagine Bram sharing a cell with hardened criminals, trading heroic diving adventures for tales of bikie vengeance and corporate greed. The image refused to stick.

'We'll sort it out when I get there,' I promised him.

2

AN HOUR LATER, I WAS BACK HOME AND PACKING when Marieke burst in. 'I've got tickets to a play tonight at the Sydney Theatre Company! Margaret was supposed to come along but her daughter's sick so she's watching the grandkids. I thought you might like to join me instead.'

Her gaze swept the room, taking in my documentation folders and the camera lenses cushioned in their fabric packing cubes. The wardrobe door stood ajar, revealing the gaps where clothes once hung. In the open duffle bag at my feet, a cross-section of jeans and jumpers was layered between the delicate paintbrushes and fragile fibre-optic lights to protect them from damage during the flight.

Marieke's smile faded.

'You're leaving,' she said, sinking onto the bed. She was wearing a tight, sleeveless shift dress patterned with purple hyacinths which showed off her tiny waist. A green sweater tied around her shoulders softened the sharp protrusion of collarbones.

'What about the university? I thought they were expecting you to stay on until the book's finished.'

'They are,' I said. 'But I've been offered an opportunity I can't really refuse.' I plucked a pair of copper pliers off a shelf, dropped them into a ziplock bag. 'Bram Lange called earlier. You remember Bram? He wants me to visit him on Texel. I agreed to go.'

Marieke pressed a palm against her thin chest.

'At last! What changed your mind?'

I told her briefly about Bram's phone call and the shipwrecked items. I didn't elaborate on the specifics of why Bram and his friends had been diving. If Marieke discovered there might be legal trouble looming on the horizon, she'd only come up with some unhelpful suggestion about putting things back where they belonged.

'So you understand why I have to go,' I concluded. 'I'll still be working on the book. In fact, if everything goes to plan, I might be able to use the research on the dress to write the final chapter.'

It was the first time all morning I'd let myself say those words aloud and, as soon as they were out, I knew they were true. I had the strangest sense of peering down through time, as though I was gazing into the ocean, trying to puzzle out sinuous patterns carved in sand. I wanted the dress for myself. Not to wear – I would never dream of committing such a sin – but simply to hold it and smell it, to experience first-hand its craftsmanship, its perfections as well as its flaws. There was something seductive about the way the silk fabric flowed, as if the dress, even on land, remembered an earlier version of itself. As if it were more fish than fabric. It would be the perfect example to support my argument that women's historical clothing was just as worthy of scholarship as men's. Women's dresses were less likely to survive because they laboured harder, making do with what they had, altering or selling their gowns to compensate for disasters like the death of a protective male figure, a father or husband. They lived their lives at the mercy of other people's whims. This dress was a survivor and I had the spookiest premonition that its owner had been, too.

Marieke could not possibly understand.

I went and sat beside her on the bed and held her hand. Up close, I could see the deep grooves her thick makeup hadn't been able to mask, the ropey tendons in her slender neck. Although she was barely sixty, she looked much older. I'd always assumed this was due to the psychological effects of having to raise a child not her own. She'd spent years trying to convince my mother to uproot our family and join her in Australia, but she had been wasting her breath. My parents would never have moved away from Texel. They were like the island, entrenched in their ways, shaped by winds and tides that had blown into existence long before I was born.

'It's good you're going back,' she said, quietly. 'It might bring you some closure. You know your parents loved you very much. They didn't always show it, but they did. They only wanted what was best for you. Your mother always said your favourite time of the day was dusk because that was when she'd take you down to the beach to look for shoes. You were obsessed with shoes! They used to wash up quite regularly, especially after a storm, but somehow you always found left shoes, never right ones. You'd beg her to take you, even when it was still storming outside and she

31

always let you convince her. She was soft-hearted like that.'

I stayed silent. There was no point arguing that, by the time my parents passed away, I was a stubborn sixteen-year-old who had long ago given up relying on them for either comfort or entertainment. I assumed the story about the shoes had come to Marieke via the long-distance phone calls my mother took at the same time each week at our kitchen table. Crouched on the other side of the door, I listened to Marieke espouse the wonderful freedoms of her new life in Australia, enamoured with the vision she painted of summer days and shiny, freckled faces, of the Opera House sails like shards of broken porcelain, gleaming against a Delft-blue harbour. I tried to convince my parents to let me visit but they refused to let me travel alone. Maybe they were afraid that I'd fall in love with the world beyond the island's borders. My aunt had returned to Texel just once when I was born, staying only long enough to hand over a christening gift before driving back to Schiphol Airport and taking the first available flight back to Australia. She told me years later that people had treated her differently after she left Texel. It made her feel uncomfortable, as if two versions of her existed, sharing the same body, but neither one was whole.

'Do you remember the lullaby?' she said now.

'No,' I said, flatly.

I sighed. That damned lullaby. We'd been sparring over it for years, dancing around each other like boxers looking for our opponent's weaknesses. The argument had gone on for so long, I could barely remember how it had started.

Marieke cleared her throat. I could tell she was getting worked up, assembling her reasons, laying strong defences in anticipation of my inevitable scorn.

'It started with a wooden shoe,' she sang, in a wobbly, off-key voice.

'Okay,' I said.

She waited for me to say more and when I didn't, continued. 'They sailed off, into the night, on a river of crystal light, into a sea of dew. "Where are you going?" the old moon asked. "To fish for herring," replied the three. "Nets of silver and gold have we." The old moon laughed and sang a song as they rocked in the wooden shoe, and the wind that sped them along that night ruffled the waves of dew. All night they threw the nets, to the stars in the twinkling foam, then down from the skies sailed the wooden shoe, bringing the little fishermen home: Wynken, Blynken, and Nod.'

She sang the last line again, softer this time, trailing off into uncomfortable silence.

'That was it,' she said, wiping her damp eyes. 'Your parents were Wynken and Blynken and you were Nod, the one who was always falling asleep. I can't believe you don't remember. It's simply not possible, Josefeine. How can you hear something every day of your life and not remember it?'

She was guilting me, expecting me to respond the way I always did. Truth be told, I didn't remember the lullaby. Maybe that was why I could refute her claims with such absolute conviction. There was a hollow emptiness where that memory should have been. If my parents *had* sung me the same lullaby every night without fail before I went to bed, wouldn't I have remembered it? According to Marieke, they'd stood outside my room crooning the song together, my father's booming tenor balanced by my mother's soft contralto. They'd met at an audition for the church choir when they were seventeen and married a few years later. I don't know when, precisely, things had soured, whether the rift occurred soon after the wedding or if some other event was the catalyst for the marital disruption. Had my birth been an accident or had they hoped it would save their foundering marriage? If so, the experiment was a failure.

Marieke insisted my recollections of that time were wrong, that I deliberately skipped over all the good things about my parents. She claimed we'd once been inseparable, like the three fishermen from the lullaby, sailing our shoe into the sky to catch falling stars. I didn't remember it that way. Even as a child, I knew I was different, a changeling belonging to another family. I wished I could give Marieke what she wanted. It would be so easy to lie and say I remembered only kindness and warmth, safety and protection. But it would not be true. And the truth was important to me. It was what drove me to uncover the stories woven into the clothing I was charged with preserving. Human history and textiles were inextricably linked; one could not exist without the other.

'It doesn't matter now.' Standing up, I jammed a pair of archival gloves into the suitcase, hoping she'd take the hint and leave me to finish packing. By some extraordinary stroke of luck, I'd managed to nab one of the last flights out of Sydney today. The plane didn't board till six, but I wanted to get there early so I could sit in the lounge and write out the contingency plan I was formulating – an emergency response to counteract damage inflicted on the improperly handled artefacts. I needed to try contacting Liam again, too. His

34

mobile had gone straight to voicemail. He was probably up to his elbows in lab work or stuck in some dusty archive.

Marieke sighed. 'I always thought Hilde would run off with you to the mainland,' she said. 'But she stayed on the island, against all the odds.'

I crossed the hallway to the bathroom to retrieve my toothbrush, 'Maybe you didn't know her as well as you thought.'

'It wasn't that. She met someone. They were together for years.'

I froze. 'Like . . . a boyfriend?'

I couldn't say lover. It didn't gel with the image I had retained of my mother in her stiff blouse and humble cotton skirt. At the same time, Marieke's declaration that she'd been carrying on an affair did not altogether shock me as it probably ought to have done. I'd known for years about my parents' extramarital dalliances. They loved to fight about – not the affairs themselves but the way my father went about it. He was often careless, forgetting to hide hotel and restaurant receipts or encouraging strange women to leave cryptic messages on our answering machine. One night, a particularly bold paramour showed up at the house. She parked her car, with its mainland numberplates, in the middle of the drive, the idling engine louder than a speedboat. From my bedroom window, I watched my mother cross the lawn and peer into the driver's side. I heard her knuckles rap the glass, the retort echoing like a gunshot through the cold night air. When the car drove off, I climbed back into bed and tried to sleep. But it was impossible to block out my parents' raised voices. When I came downstairs the next day, they were eating breakfast as if nothing had happened. Ignoring me, my mother handed my father the milk and asked what time he would be home so they could take their evening walk across the dunes. My father said he had some business to take care of in Horntje but he planned to be back no later than five. Everything was so calm and placid; if I hadn't caught the glare that passed between them, I might have convinced myself I dreamed the whole thing. I forgot all about it, although things between them grew increasingly cold.

They died a year later.

At the funeral, I half-expected a few strangers to come forward and lay claim to their affections. Nobody did. If my mother's suitor was in attendance, he was indistinguishable from the neighbours and colleagues who crowded into the packed churchyard, stamping their feet to shake the damp clods off their boots, hugging themselves to ward off the winter chill. In books, revelations always take place at weddings and funerals. Jane Eyre discovers Rochester's dark secret, Hamlet is driven mad with grief over Ophelia's suicide, Miss Havisham stops the clocks at twenty minutes to nine and spends the rest of her days eating rotten wedding cake and corrupting impressionable young minds. In real life, people take their secrets with them when they die.

I walked back into the bedroom and knelt beside Marieke.

'Who was he?'

'His first name was Gerrit. I don't know his surname. They met at a café in town, but he worked at the ranger station.'

'He was a scientist, then.'

Marieke shrugged. 'Maybe. Your mother never said.'

I tried to recall the faces of my mother's friends. Had this Gerrit been the reason for my mother's increasing distraction in the last few months of her life. She'd been even more closed off than usual. I was living almost permanently at Bram's, returning to my parents' house only on weekends.

Bram's mother Carlijn had taken me under her wing. With four boys and one husband to care for, I think she saw my presence as a way of counterbalancing the male energy within the household. She kept a bed made up for me in her craft room, her fortress of femininity – floral armchairs and chenille quilts and pressed flowers blooming in gilded frames. She loved to sit with me and talk about what I planned to do once I graduated high school. One summer, she taught me how to sew but, although I enjoyed the practice, I abandoned it quickly in favour of the much more thrilling hobby of scuba diving.

On land, Bram's father, Tomas, seemed awkward and reserved, but he transformed in the water. He was warm and effusive, eager to share the diving skills he'd spent a lifetime perfecting. Although he was careful never to endanger us, he consistently pushed us beyond our comfort zones, taking us to dive sites that even more experienced divers might have found challenging. We returned home happy but exhausted, eagerly anticipating the hot chocolate Bram's mother always had waiting for us. I doubt my own mother even noticed what I was up to. When I'd mentioned to her, the day before that ill-fated trip to Saeftinghe, that I planned to stay at Bram's so we could get up early to go diving, she blinked as if I were a stranger or someone whose face she recognised but whose name was now forgotten. She'd been fiddling with her wedding ring, twisting it this way and that, turning it so the metal caught the light from the kitchen windows and refracted it into a thousand tiny rainbows.

'Oh,' she said. 'Be careful.'

The lukewarm warning irritated me even more than the compulsive fidgeting with the ring. I remember shouting at her, accusing her of parental negligence (I would not, under normal circumstances, have chosen that phrase, but I'd overheard Carlijn say it and I liked the way it sounded, the irrefutable recrimination it implied). My mother only stared at me for a long moment, looking sad, before turning away.

My thoughts returned to the present at the sound of Marieke's voice. 'Gerrit wasn't from Texel, originally,' she said. 'He was a southerner, I think. Somewhere near Middleburg.'

I ran a damp palm along my thigh. 'Why didn't you tell me before?'

'You never asked. Besides, I wasn't sure it was my place. But since you're going back, I thought it best to warn you. If he's still there, you'll probably run into him. Texel isn't a big place. When are you planning on coming back to Sydney?'

It was my turn to shrug. 'I'll stay as long as I'm needed. Once the items are stabilised, there'll be some diplomatic stuff to negotiate with the Dutch government. The media will probably be involved, which will require some careful handling.'

She looked suddenly worried. 'I'm glad you're going. But what if there's an accident? A break-in?'

Her voice was edged with panic, but I was wise to her ways. Her anxiety was mostly performative – an unsubtle device designed to trap me into staying home. There was no malice attached to her behaviour. She couldn't help herself.

'You'll be fine,' I said, tryingto make my voice as soothing as possible. 'Call a friend, if you're worried.

Call Margaret; she's supposed to be your best friend. You managed on your own for years when I lived in London.'

'That's because you were only ever a phone call away. The reception's probably terrible on Texel. It took weeks sometimes for your mother to reply to my emails.'

'She was probably too busy flirting with Gerrit,' I said. 'I don't understand why two people who were clearly miser-able together didn't just get divorced.'

Marieke looked pained. 'It was a different time. And there was you ...' She touched my arm gently and I didn't react, even though my first instinct was to pull away. 'Isn't it time you let go of all those old hurts and just listened to me for once?'

Her gaze was pleading. I glanced away from her towards the bookshelves filled with beach-worn paperbacks, their spines bowed, their covers bleached from prolonged exposure to the noonday sun. Those books – mostly historical romances – had been my companions when I first arrived in Sydney. Although I'd loved the stories themselves, I often found myself perusing the badly Photoshopped images of medieval knights and coquettish Victorian mistresses on the covers, searching for hidden meanings about the lives of the characters between the pages. Only later did I realise it was the clothes themselves I found so irresistibly alluring. Clothing held the key to thousands of years of human history, everyone from anointed kings and queens to humble washerwomen and midwives. It was my duty to follow the clues, wherever they led.

3

Anna
Amsterdam, 1651

O
N THE LAST DAY OF HER OLD LIFE, ANNA TESSELTJE wakes to find the water in the washstand has frozen solid. She uses a knife to jam the blade against the porcelain until the ice breaks apart, the cracked halves glisten like oceans trapped inside a storm glass. After dropping to her knees to pray, she dresses quickly, eager to fashion a barrier between her skin and the frigid air, even if that obstacle is only the addition of a cloak. After a wet autumn, winter has finally settled over Amsterdam, bringing frost and wild winds and stinging sleet. She has learned to sleep in whatever clothing she can find, shivering as cold seeps through the windowpane. But she refuses to sleep in the cloak. The cloth reeks of the bleach her sister Lijsbeth rubbed into the worst of the stains as well as some lingering, unidentified malodour – the sweetness of rot. The sleeves hang past Anna's fingers. She folds them back, trying to ignore the spectre of the cloak's former inhabitant. The dame at the second-hand clothing market swore that the owner sold it to her on her way to her new situation to work as a maid at a grand house on the Golden Bend. She suggested the cloak would bring Anna luck, too. You can't put a price on

luck, Anna knew she should quibble over the cost. If Lijsbeth had been with her, she would have. Instead, she handed over three *stuivers* and prayed that, whatever the owner's real fate, she had not died of the plague.

Slipping the protective pattens over her thin-soled shoes, she tightens the leather straps and ties a freshly starched cap over her hair. There. She is ready, except for her face and hands. She runs a finger along the hard spine of half a frozen slab. Her once-white hands are now permanently stained with ashes, the nails cracked from all the lye Lijsbeth insists on pouring into the copper pans they use to launder other people's collars. Their friends have been kind, under the circumstances. There is always work for them. Not the kind of labour Anna once imagined, but what choice does she have? At least Cornelis de Witt, the successful engraver who lives on the Kalverstraat, doesn't look down on her when she arrives at his door clutching a bucket under one arm and a basket under the other. One of the city's favoured artisans, he once offered to tutor her – to show her how he made the engravings in their metal frames come alive, the shadowed planes of a woman's face, the caulked ceilings of a church. It would be a leisurely distraction, something to fill in the time before her inevitable engagement. It wasn't hard to convince her father, Lodewijk, to give his permission. Lijsbeth would need to be married first and they had not even begun entertaining suitors. Then Lodewijk had his first bad spell, the one that led to his rapid decline. Now her father is gone and, each week, instead of following Cornelis de Witt into his workshop, Anna follows his maid into the washroom to collect the household's soiled nightshirts and stained collars. Sometimes, as she's brushing down his shirts, a fine layer of copper shavings sifts like grains of sand onto the tiles. Sometimes, she shuts her eyes and imagines she is standing on a beach, watching ships battle a raging storm.

There is a story her father used to tell, a family legend about the night she was born.

Christmas Eve. Winter. In Holland's north, near the bust-ling port of Oudeschild, a tempest converged on the Texel anchorage where hundreds of ships, including eight of her father's galleons, had waited patiently for a strong westerly to stave off a lee shore and drive them out to sea. Lodewijk was a merchant whose ambitions for dynastic success had overcome the kind of humble origins that might have caused another man to doubt his place in the world.

The last child born to an overstretched family of Utrecht carpenters, he had established his own business through the strategic acquisition of ships whose owners had not anticipated the high cost of repairs required when their vessels returned from long, arduous voyages to sea. For the first year, Lodewijk repaired the damaged ships himself or begged his friends for small gifts of labour. He hired out the finished galleons to whaling crews or merchant captains whose suntanned faces and arms were even darker than his own and whose tales of life at sea swung wildly between amusing and outrageous.

When one man intimated that he expected to make a hefty profit on his next journey east by selling some inferior *peperduur* to an unsuspecting English trader – and asked

Lodewijk if he might consider taking a cut in exchange for incorrectly registering the name of the vessel in Texel's shipping records – Anna's father suddenly found himself in the enviable position of possessing more wealth than anyone else in his family ever had before. There was no real moral quandary since no Englishman deserved to be pitied and everybody was guilty of fudging Texel's shipping records at least once for his own benefit. The outcome meant that Anna's father had amassed a small fortune by the age of twenty-one. He was soon entertaining offers from the kind of wealthy Amsterdam merchants whose ranks he once aspired to join, including the family of gunpowder heiress Arabella Van de Berg. Their marriage seemed the inevitable fulfilment of God's plan and the fleet of ships that was once the foundation of his fledgling business quickly multiplied now he could afford to buy *fluyts* outright instead of repairing damaged ones.

But then came the storm. It appeared out of nowhere, the only clues a sudden smudging of sky and a subtle restlessness in the water as the waves bellied and writhed. Having no time to raise the alarm, twelve sailors belonging to one of Lodewijk's crews were swept overboard. They sank soundlessly, leaving nothing to mark their departure. Eight of his prized galleons were torn apart and the wreckage, combined with the debris belonging to the twenty other galleons which sank that night, was strewn across Texel's beaches for weeks following the fatal storm. When a messenger delivered the news to Lodewijk in his counting house on the Amsterdam Bourse, Anna's father sat stunned, and then he began to weep. He blamed himself for ordering the ship's captains not to parcel out the most valuable goods onto smaller vessels as soon as they arrived, but to wait until the cargo could be unloaded all together and fitted onto small barges capable of navigating the narrow waterways trapped between the canal houses of Amsterdam and Delft. The decision to save a few *stuivers* had cost twelve men their lives and decimated a third of Lodewijk's fleet. There was a message here, buried in these tragic losses. What was it? What was God trying to tell him?

Here the messenger, who had been watching in uncomfortable silence as his master wept, spoke again, eager to share the other news he had been dispatched to deliver: the safe arrival, an hour ago, of Lodewijk's second daughter. The confluence of the two disparate occasions left poor Lodewijk conflicted. On one hand, the partial destruction of his shipping empire. On the other, new life. When he made his way home and trudged up the stairs to greet his newborn daughter, he experienced a flash of divine inspiration. He would name her Anna Tesseltjeruineren – *Ruin on Texel*. God would surely approve of such pious nomenclature. Anna's name was the currency that would tip the spiritual scales in their family's favour. She was the bargain through which he would strike a deal with Almighty God and her name would serve as a reminder that worldly wealth could be snatched away by Him at any moment. Out of kindness to Arabella, he agreed to shorten the child's name to Anna Tesseltje. Now the name is a part of Anna, like the taste of her favourite dish, *appeltaerten*, like the waxy coolness of her dead mother's cheek, or the oozing fissures on her own ruined hands. She flexes her blistered fingers experimentally, wincing as a welt splits, the pink flesh gaping like a hungry mouth.

Wolfert lifts his head as Anna squeaks open a drawer and searches inside for her gloves. In the nested bedclothes, he resembles a beached seal rather than an old hound, his dark coat greasy and back-combed. Grey light bathes his stooped shoulders and his stale breath forms a wispy, lopsided crown over his crinkled forehead.

He stretches out his limbs and yawns, his yellowed teeth worn to nubs.

'Hush,' Anna says, throwing an anxious glance at the curtain dividing the bedroom she shares with her sister. If Lijsbeth discovers Wolfert upstairs, she will banish him to the kitchen. Each night, Anna listens for her sister's heavy snores before she sneaks downstairs to collect him. She loves to observe the careful spectacle of Wolfert's nightly ritual, the way he searches the corners of the room for stray crumbs and huffs explosively into the vaulted archways of old mouse-holes before dragging his arthritic body up the step-ladder and settling near her feet. Wolfert was her father's dog. They went everywhere together – the warehouses, the church, her father's favourite tavern in the Eastern Islands. He never touched the dice, preferring to donate any extra money he made to the church and the city orphanage where he felt the money could do some good. Anna hopes these moral kindnesses have brought him some small luxuries in the afterlife. She hopes he has found a measure of peace since she failed to ease his distress in his final months. His confusion was a blank void, terrifying in its nothingness. He kept calling her Arabella.

At every turn, Anna failed to convince him she was not the woman who died giving birth to a son all those years ago. Once, in a fit of delirium, her father gripped Anna's waist and pulled her to him, his voice sweetened with misplaced desire. Anna managed to free herself and slip past Lijsbeth who stood watching in the doorway, a frigid smile contorting her features, a bowl of broth cooling in her cupped hands. Later, Anna heard her sister in the *voorhuis,* sobbing over their father's enfeeblement. She thought about going down, but she knew Lijsbeth would reject any offer of comfort. She realised that until that moment, her sister had been able to ignore Lodewijk's wild fancies. There could be no pretence now that Anna, too, had witnessed his deterioration.

It was frightening to watch his memories scatter like fish, darting this way and that with no reason or logic to net them. To serve him a platter of food, only to return later to find the meal untouched. He refused to wash himself in the tepid water Anna hauled upstairs. Lijsbeth wouldn't let him leave the house in such a disordered state. Instead, she forced Anna to stand guard outside his door as if he were a common criminal. She sent all the servants away, insisting they could better care for him themselves. Things were left to fester. Enquiries went unanswered, invoices unpaid, goods which had been acquired months before sat gathering dust inside her father's warehouse.

One afternoon, while Anna was scrubbing dishes, she heard Master Honig, his overseer, pacing in the front room.

'The fish is rotting inside the barrels. The men need paying. What would you have me do? What's wrong with him? When will he be well again?'

'Soon,' Lijsbeth answered, stoutly. 'He's eaten some bad

cheese and cannot rise from his bed. Leave the invoices; I'll see that he gets them. Tell the men they must be patient. Remind them they are lucky to have employment in these hard times. Remind them what God says in the Bible.'

'God doesn't put food in hungry bellies, Lijsbeth. Has the doctor examined him?'

'Of course. What do you take me for? It is exactly as I tell you – a bad meal, improperly prepared.'

Anna imagined her sister's face settling into its familiar affectation of innocence. Lijsbeth had always been a proficient liar. When they were children, it was Lijsbeth who spoke up if a vase was shattered, knocked carelessly off a shelf while they played. Lijsbeth who stared down the maids and blamed the accident on the household cat. But Master Honig was a man of experience, not a servant teetering on the brink of exhaustion. He had not been around when Anna was born. If he had, it's unlikely the accident in Texel would have been allowed to happen. Anna heard him clear his throat. Her own throat hurt, as if she'd swallowed a flying insect. She wanted to creep to the door, but her arms were trapped in the greasy sink, stray cups and spoons escaping her witless grasp. Master Honig spoke forcefully, with the authority and self-assurance of someone who had weathered many storms. Anna pictured his hands clenched as if he clutched an invisible ship's wheel, a gesture she'd seen him make countless times when her father was in better health and the two men were engaged in heated debate over some business decision.

'This is not a game, Miss Lijsbeth. It's been months. If you do not pay the men, they will refuse to work. If the goods in the warehouse don't reach their destination soon, they'll be worthless. I implore you. Speak to your father. Tell him to hand over control of the business before it's too late. If you need help, you must ask for it. Haven't I proved my loyalty ten times over? Don't allow pride to stand in the way of business. I can protect you. I can—'

'Sir, you forget yourself.' Lijsbeth's voice had taken on a hard, strident edge. 'Only God can protect us. My father built this business from nothing. He had to beg my mother's family for money to buy his first ship. For years, he worked himself ragged, trying to keep you all alive. And you choose this moment, when he is temporarily weakened, to pounce on his fortunes. Oh, I see your plan. You are no better than those Catholics who worship at the feet of commerce. If it's riches you dream of, you'd best seek another master. My father does not need your counsel, and nor do I.'

A tense silence followed, then Anna heard Master Honig's footsteps retreat. The front door juddered in its frame and, moments later, Lijsbeth appeared, looking pale. Her black dress, usually spotless, was creased and she gripped a rough assortment of papers.

Anna lifted a dripping finger. 'What are those?'

Lijsbeth ignored her. Anna looked down as a cup bobbed to the surface and she caught her worried reflection in its shining cast. 'What did Master Honig want?' she persisted.

Her sister brushed an impatient hand across her damp face. 'Does it matter? He's gone. God willing, he will not disturb us again.'

Anna watched her cross to the fire and feed the pages slowly to the flames.

* * *

Behind the curtain, Lijsbeth begins to cough. Her breath rattles in her chest like smoke trapped inside a flue. The coughing spell seems to last a lifetime. As Anna waits for it to subside, she is caught between her desire to hustle Wolfert downstairs and her responsibility to help her sister. She glances at the window, at the dazzling light gilding the thick clouds. Downstairs, somebody is hammering, the rhythmic blows like a clock's weighted pendulum striking time. The sisters should be leaving for work soon, if not already be on their way out the door. Of late, Lijsbeth has been difficult to rouse. She slumbers past dawn, her energy depleted by fits of nocturnal coughing. Anna has learned to sleep through these disturbing interruptions, yet they often make their way into her dreams, taking on the nightmarish form of barking dogs or fiery explosions. In the worst ones, she watches Lijsbeth choking on poisoned fumes, expelling her final gasping breath while the room around her burns. Only she, Anna, is strangely immune from corporeal pain. Floating above the scene, she is curiously weightless, suspended in an invisible trench of water, her body, stripped of its earthly demands, requiring no air, no nourishment. Perhaps she is already dead and the cracked ceiling is the gateway to heaven, and she is simply waiting for Lijsbeth to join her before they take their last journey together. But this interpretation strikes her as false. Isn't it more likely she is the cause of her sister's ailment?

For a while now, she has begun to suspect her presence is the primary cause of their family's suffering. It started the night she was born when she somehow caused those ships to sink and her father's men to drown. Why else would he have given her that name, if not to warn everyone that she is bad luck? She cursed her mother's womb, too. Each subsequent child planted there after her birth withered and died before it could fruit. When they carried out her mother's corpse, she overheard the midwife tell the doctor that the birth had been monstrous. So ill-formed was her infant brother, his blackened head would not fit through the opening. The midwife had no choice but to remove him piece by piece. It was unsurprising that Anna's mother had not survived the procedure. She died in agony while twelve-year-old Anna slept on in a nearby bedroom, dreaming of selfish things – dolls and dresses and sliced apples drenched in sugary syrup. Anna hasn't confided her suspicions to Lijsbeth or the pastor of their new church. He is nothing at all like gentle Pastor Bruin. Pastor Van Leersun is a dour, taciturn man whose bleak sermons seem designed to punish the parishioners for circumstances beyond their control. She does not feel comfortable confessing her worries to a man like that, even though he is one of God's chosen apostles. Lijsbeth would frown at Anna's suggestion of superstitious mysticism. She would say that, despite their troubles, they are lucky God has seen fit to grant them a roof, four walls, enough food to survive. But how long can they go on like this, Anna wants to ask her. How long can this purgatory last?

She clears her throat. 'Can I help?'

Lijsbeth hawks and spits into a chamberpot. 'No,' she rasps, the sound of her laboured breathing partially muffled by the curtain.

'Perhaps you should stay home and rest,' Anna says.

'How nice to have the luxury,' Lijsbeth says, bitterly. 'And what excuse do you propose I send the van Vliets? They will never hire me again.'

'Why don't you take the de Witts, then?' Anna tries to make the suggestion sound as if it has only just occurred to her. 'The wife and sons are away so there's only him. Shirts and aprons.'

Lisbjeth grunts. 'And have him pity me? Thank you, no. You forget, I was his favourite before you came along. No, you must see to the de Witts. I'm heading to the van Vliets. They're hosting a supper party tonight for the goldsmiths' guild and their maid will need help cleaning the linen and sponging all the furniture. It's not a task they trust to just anybody, you know.'

There is a note of pride in her voice, reminiscent of the old Lijsbeth. If their father had survived, he would doubtless have married her off to a fellow merchant's son. Anna catches a vision of her sometimes – her sallow skin restored to brightness, her knotted hair brushed smooth, the very image of a wealthy Amsterdam bride standing stiffly beside her husband. In years to come, Lijsbeth's grandchildren will stand in front of their marriage portrait admiring the handsome couple, envying the rich feast of half-eaten lobster on display, the glass goblets filled with crimson wine. Perhaps Anna would be there, too, lurking in the background. She doesn't mind playing second fiddle to Lijsbeth. There are worse things in life than being overlooked.

'We should be going soon,' she says. 'We don't want to be late.'

Lijsbeth grunts. Anna hears panting, feet sliding on boards, then something heavy falling, a short, injured gasp.

Wrenching the curtain aside, she finds Lijsbeth lying on the floor, struggling to stand. One hand is thrust between her head and the hard boards to protect her face.

'I slipped,' she gasps, looking up at Anna as though daring her to contradict her version of events.

Anna helps her back onto the bed where she slumps her head bowed over her lap. She is so thin, Anna can see the knobs of her spine pressing through her thin shift. Her hair, the same straw-coloured shade as Anna's, is loosely plaited and the ends are frayed as if she has been chewing on them in her sleep. Anna's mother used to smack them if they chewed their hair. She told them she once knew a godless girl who swallowed so much hair it continued to grow inside her stomach, spreading through her body like the roots of a tree. Eventually, it strangled her from the inside out.

Lijsbeth raises her chin and fixes Anna with her watery gaze. 'Go on ahead,' she says. 'The van Vliets' maid will hardly notice if I'm a few minutes late. She's a lazy girl who dawdles out by the canal, throwing kisses to passing boatmen. I suspect she has a lover. I'm yet to catch him. I would report her and have her sent away in disgrace, if we were back in Father's house.'

'Can I fetch you anything before I go?'

She expects Lijsbeth to refuse, but her sister draws herself further up the bed and waves an imperious hand at the dresser. 'Lay out my clothes for me.'

Anna crosses the room and opens the second drawer. Inside are stored the familiar working day-gowns they traded at market in exchange for their good brocade silks and warm, fur-lined cloaks. The laundry was Lijsbeth's idea. 'Why not?' she said to Anna, a few hours after members of the city's civic guard marched out of their house carrying the best furniture and painted vases and china plates. 'We can do anything; we are young and strong. Why shouldn't we take on laundry to earn a living?' Anna admired her sister's courage. In that moment, she forgave her for refusing to act while their father's wits disintegrated and his business failed. If only Lijsbeth had set aside her pride earlier and accepted Master Honig's offer of help. But there was no use dwelling on what might have been. There was still hope for them, as Lijsbeth said. They were in charge of their own lives and destinies. Like a child, Anna believed her. The reality, of course, is very different.

She's about to lift out a starched apron when her hand encounters the unexpected coolness of silk. She blinks at the yellow gown that has been folded carelessly and shoved towards the back of the drawer. As she draws it out, the fabric shimmers and dazzles and flares, as though defying its rough treatment. The silk train slithers to the floor and the scent of faded perfume rises – oil of roses, their mother's favourite.

Lijsbeth eyes her from the bed. 'It belonged to Mother. Do you remember?'

Holding the gown against her body, Anna caresses the hem of a sleeve with her thumb, the lustrous fabric clinging to her waist and legs like a second skin.

'It looks well on you,' Lijsbeth observes. 'I should have sold it. It would have fed us for months. Mother intended for it to be part of my wedding gift.' She coughs. 'Even less of a reason to keep it.'

'Don't say that.' Anna begins to fold the dress, careful to avoid tearing the fragile silk with her ragged nails. 'You may yet be married.'

'Who will have me? Not even the baker's son would look twice.'

Anna places the dress carefully back in the drawer, even though it feels wrong to do so, like hiding the sun behind a cloud. A dress like that is meant to be looked at and admired. It's unusual for practical Lijsbeth to keep it, but Anna is so glad she did. Unlike the befouled cloak, the dress feels like a comforting omen, a message of hope from her departed mother. 'I don't know,' she says. 'A baker could be useful. At least we would have buns for Epiphany.'

Lijsbeth laughs. For a moment, it's like the old days, everything good between them. Her face transforms as she begins to cough. Her eyes bulge. And then she chokes, splutters. Anna watches on helplessly, feeling as useless as Wolfert, who begins to whine, his white-flecked muzzle appearing anxiously around the curtain. Anna waves him away and bends to retrieve the chamberpot, holding it out to her sister, trying to ignore the chunks of greasy mucus coating the bottom. Lijsbeth's cough is growing worse each day; she needs to see a doctor. But how will they pay? Anna thinks of her mother's dress. The gown is worth twenty doctor's visits at least, maybe more. It could buy medicine, too. Firewood and blankets, a warm cloak, ingredients for nourishing soup. Anna opens her mouth to insist that Lijsbeth sell it, but then she hesitates. It's not greed that stops her, but what the dress represents – the promise of a life of comfort that no longer exists. They have given up everything. Is it truly wicked to cling to this last link? Lijsbeth sits back at last, her face dripping, too exhausted to speak. As Anna smooths her damp hair off her forehead, it occurs to her that their positions are now reversed. She is the strong one, while

Lijsbeth is weak. How did this happen without her noticing? They haven't always been close, but Lijsbeth is all she has left. If anything were to happen, Anna would be all alone, orphaned in the truest sense of the word. She resolves to get up a little earlier each day to pray for Lijsbeth's health.

Outside the window, the sounds of voices and carts and horses have begun to build and Anna taps the edge of the chamberpot restlessly. Time is slipping. Maria, the de Witts' maid, loves to find fault with everything Anna does. She's probably annoyed at having to share the laundry duties, even though she herself asked Mr de Witt for extra assistance, complaining the load was too much. Anna suspects that Maria resents the favouritism she feels Mr de Witt extends to Anna's family, as someone formerly belonging to a similar rank. The maid will seize on any excuse to get Anna into trouble.

Lijsbeth senses Anna's consternation.

'Go,' she croaks, waving at the door. 'I don't need your help. I'm perfectly capable of dressing myself. I'll meet you back here later.'

Anna begins to apologise for Wolfert's presence.

'Oh, leave him,' her sister says, scowling. 'Honestly, Anna, did you think I didn't know? He is louder than a herd of elephants.'

Reaching for Anna's hand, she gives it a quick, hard squeeze. Anna returns the gesture absently, her mind already focused on the tasks ahead.

She has to knock three times on the de Witts' door before it finally opens.

To her surprise, the master himself stands on the threshold.

'Anna Tesseltje!' he cries, all smiles under his woollen cap. He is dressed for the workshop, a tunic tied over loose-fitting breeches, his long face smooth and hairless. More than once, she's heard him say that an engraver's first duty is to his face. If he cannot attend the lines on his own face, how can he master the ones on his plate?

'I'm here for the laundry, sir,' she says, in case he mistakes her presence for some other purpose.

He smiles. 'Of course you are. Come in, come in.'

She sidles cautiously past him into the main kitchen, a dim cavern crammed with painted plates and silverware. Where is Maria? The place is quiet, no harried footsteps or trumpeting bellows drifting down from the living quarters upstairs. She drags off her pattens and slips on the uncomfortable wooden wedges Maria insists on making her wear inside the house.

'Are you all alone, sir?'

Cornelis nods. 'Luke is at the guildhall, fetching some correspondence on my behalf. Maria's child is ill. I told her not to come back to the house until he improves. I don't want the pestilence running rampant through my family. How is your sister?'

Anna hesitates, thinking of Lijsbeth's wet, hacking cough. She clears her own throat experimentally, guarding against a tingling heat.

'She's working at the van Vliets' today,' she says, eying the overflowing pile of linen in the corner. Without the maid's assistance, there will be more to do and less time in which to do it. 'I should get to work, sir.'

For the next hour, she works methodically, building up

56

the fire in the washing kitchen until sweat breaks out on her skin and dampens her armpits. When she's sure the fire is hot enough, she pegs out shirts to dry on wooden racks and dumps the soiled collars into the tub. She uses a brush to scrape off the stains, biting her lip against the raw-knuckle pain. Most of the collars are the everyday kind, but a few, like the ones Cornelis de Witt wears to his meetings with the guild members of St Luke's, are made from finer stuff. Anna has never been inside the guildhall; she's only passed by it and heard Cornelis describe it to his young sons – the gable stone over the artists' entrance depicting the philosopher saint and the sacrificial ox, the pointed turrets housing not only the painters and engravers but the surgeons and anatomists, the masons and the blacksmiths, all of them crammed together like parishioners in a church vying for the attention of a visiting archbishop.

Luke returns as she is heating the iron. Cornelis' apprentice is a few years younger than Anna. His family own an apothecary on the Kalverstraat. They can easily absorb the apprentice fees. She glimpses him through the passageway, the bright gilt of his curly, shoulder-length hair, his well-cut clothes. Envy flares then fades.

She returns to the collar, pressing the hot metal into the fabric, inhaling the hissing steam.

A sudden tap on the doorframe.

'Master de Witt would like to see you.' The young man blushes, seemingly unable to meet her gaze. What a doe-eyed milksop! she thinks, then feels a stab of guilt. She follows him out of the kitchen. De Witt's workshop is a wonderment of coloured inks and half-finished sketches, wooden stamps and copperplates shining like mirrored suns. Somewhere under bundles of dried herbs and half-hatched tulip bulbs and hand-blown glass orbs, there is a desk. Cornelis sits behind it, holding an open letter. He strokes his thumb along the blackened edge.

'Do you fancy a change in situation?' he says.

Anna stares at him in confusion. 'Sir?'

He smooths out the letter. 'A gentleman of my acquaintance seeks a lady's companion for his sister. He wrote to me, asking if I knew anyone. I thought of you.'

'Me, sir?'

She wonders if this is some kind of joke. But Cornelis de Witt is not a man to whom humour comes easily or often and his face is as bland and open as ever, not even the shadow of a beard to hide a smirk behind.

'The lady lives at Sterrenwijck, a property outside The Hague. She's an artist. They call her the Tenth Muse, although her real name is Catharina van Shurman. You must have seen her work around, although you might not recognise it. She goes by a number of different monikers. It's part of her mystery. She was a child prodigy.' A grin splits his face. 'She must be nearing forty now. Her twin brother, too; he is the one who contacted me. His name is Crispijn. We haven't spoken in person for some time, only corresponded through letters, but I trust him whole-heartedly. He will pay your travel expenses and is offering a generous wage. You would live with them at Sterrenwijk. You've visited The Hague before?'

Anna shakes her head. Her father travelled there a

few times a year to pay his respects to the Stadholder and represent the family's business interests, but he always returned in a black mood, complaining about the late nights and uncomfortable tavern beds and the endless parade of foreign courtiers and nobles fleeing the English war for the safety of the United Provinces. Their English accents unnerved him. He could never grasp what they were saying and he always suspected they were laughing behind his back.

'Are there no better candidates?' Anna says.

Cornelis frowns.

'I don't mean to sound ungrateful,' she adds, quickly. 'But there must be others who are better suited. I have no training as a companion. I can't imagine I will be able to contribute much, unless Master van Shurman intends for me to assist with the laundry.'

Cornelis regards her silently. At last, he says, 'I should think he was convinced by your circumstances. You do not, you will forgive me, have the manners of a maid. You understand when to stay silent and when to speak and you can converse on a wide range of subjects. To move between worlds is a gift, Anna. Not many manage it. You like to read, if I remember correctly?'

'I enjoy it,' she admits. 'But I no longer have access to my father's books. They were all sold last year. We could not justify keeping them when there were more pressing concerns.'

'Catharina likes books, too. You would have the entire library at Sterrenwijck at your disposal, were you to go. Your duties would be to read aloud and assist in the portrait studio and run small errands. Catharina's brother reports that her spirits are sunk mighty low. She complains of headaches and a weak stomach. She's stopped painting and the commissions are starting to pile up. She says her creative spark appears to be dead. Her brother is worried. He wants someone to watch her, since he cannot always be home.'

'Like a nurse?' Anna suggests.

'No,' says Cornelis. 'Like a companion, someone who can help her re-engage with society and remind her there's still beauty in the world. I can't think of a better person to do that than yourself. This opportunity will open doors for you, Anna. One of them may lead to a better life.'

Anna pins her bottom lip with her teeth. He's right, of course. It will be an easier job than the one she has now, a more genteel kind of servitude. But can she do it? Her mother once hired a woman from Alkmaar to take on the role of lady's companion when their father was away on business. The woman's duties had not been onerous – dressing her mother, reading prayers aloud, chaperoning the girls to church and the market. Lijsbeth had given her a cruel nickname. She called her Lady Kikker, a reference to the way the maid gripped their hands firmly like a frog as they wove through the *vleeshal*, keeping them close, as if afraid the butchers in their bloody aprons were beasts who might snatch the girls and gobble them up. The next summer, when Kikker returned home, Anna's mother wept for days, not bothering to conceal her grief in front of the other servants. Young as she was, Anna realised that although Kikker had been the one paid for her services, it was her mother who more keenly felt the loss of their separation.

'Women are lonely creatures,' her mother confided in a

rare moment of maternal transparency. 'Husbands are all very well, but they cannot know our ways. They cannot understand loss and all the small pricks of hardships we must endure while smiling through our tears.'

Lijsbeth had smirked in a superior way. Later, when she and Anna were alone, she confessed that she found their mother's emotional outburst embarrassing. A merchant's wife should know her place. She should keep her feelings to herself, since it was highly improper and unbecoming for a woman to expose herself in front of the servants. Such indiscretions could lead to gossip and the potential loss of business. When Lijsbeth eventually married, she would set a good example for her own household. She was already practising, training herself not to cry no matter how much pain she felt. Rolling up her sleeve, she proudly displayed the small, fresh welt on her forearm where she scored herself each morning with a razor blade.

'I cried so much the first time because it hurt so much I thought I would die. After the third time, though, I no longer felt a thing. These are the hard lessons we must teach ourselves, Anna, so that we can be successful wives and mothers. You should follow my example. God made me the older sister so I could guide you.'

She asks now, 'What about Lijsbeth?'

Cornelis looks surprised. 'Surely your sister can manage her own affairs?'

Anna thinks of Lijsbeth's cough, her pallor and foul breath, and the way the bedclothes must be soaked for three days in order to expunge the stench of sweat. She thinks of her sister's slow, shuffling steps and of how, on the worst days, even lifting her arms to string wet collars across the drying racks leaves her trembling with exhaustion. Who will walk to the market to fetch their food? Who will sweep the cinders out of the grate and haul the wet linen from the tubs?

'I'm sorry, sir,' she hears herself say. 'I'm very grateful for the offer, but I'm afraid I cannot accept.'

Cornelis stares. A line appears between his brows and she knows he is trying to puzzle out the mystery of her refusal. But how can he ever truly understand? He will never know how it feels to be caught between a duty to your family and your own desires. Of course, he must support his children and his wife, since she cannot work, and the boys are too young to be apprenticed. But if an opportunity arose to take on an engraving commission in some foreign place, he would no doubt go without even a backward glance, without even consulting the boy's mother. It's a man's birthright to place himself above the needs of children. And Lijsbeth is now as helpless as a child, as helpless as she once pictured Anna to be. How can Anna abandon her?

Eventually, Cornelis shrugs and says, 'Very well. I will advise Crispijn of your decision.'

He takes up a quill and a piece of parchment.

At the doorway, she summons the courage to turn. 'Perhaps, in summer, I can find a replacement, someone to help Lijsbeth with the laundry.'

Cornelis smiles politely but his eyes convey the truth: by summer, the offer will be gone.

The rest of the day passes in a daze. Disappointment haunts a hollow space inside Anna's stomach. Refusing to acknowledge it, she scrubs and irons and sluices water across the tiles until her arms ache and her back protests. By the time darkness falls, the emptiness has been replaced by real hunger. Walking home, her thoughts are consumed by visions of the hard bread she will slather with cheese and devour in one swift bite.

The house is unlit and filled with an eerie silence. Lighting a lamp, she hears a faint whine and traces the sound to the stairwell where she discovers Wolfert stuck halfway between the floors. He whimpers when he sees her and turns a clumsy half-circle, trying to disguise the foetid evidence of the long hours of incarceration. She falls on him, whispering soothing comforts and although her back feels as if it might snap, manages to help him downstairs. Settling him before the hearth, she scatters a handful of crusts for his supper. A gentle scratching in the floor overhead makes her glance up. New mice in the walls? Or perhaps Lijsbeth returned early and took to her bed.

She climbs the stairs and pushes open the door.

At first, she thinks her sister is asleep. A lantern burns low beside the bed, illuminating Lijsbeth's sharp nose and wide eyes, her parted lips. In her fevered delirium, she has hooked the bedsheet up to her chin and it falls in creamy waves around her arms and legs. With her hands knotted in the folds, she looks like a ship's figurehead, destined for some distant sea. Anna rips the sheet away, exposing her sister's body, still clothed in the blood-stained nightdress she wore this morning. A sour smell erupts and Anna's legs begin to tremble. The shaking spreads, moving from her stomach into her chest until she is curled inwards, like a creature quaking in a storm-tossed shell.

4

Jo

I'D ALWAYS ASSUMED MY FIRST GLIMPSE OF TEXEL after so many years would be a significant moment. I pictured the island hovering above the Wadden Sea like a fabled mirage conjured from the mists of my imagination. I saw myself leaning against the rail, watching clumps of seafoam break apart in the ferry's wake as each rolling wave brought me closer to my old life. It turned out there was barely time to grab a drink in the cafeteria and find a seat before the captain's voice came over the loudspeaker, warning travellers to return to their vehicles and prepare to disembark. The glass atrium emptied as people shuffled towards the exits. I stayed where I was, draining the last dregs of lukewarm coffee from my paper cup. I was grateful for the caffeine, weak as it was. The train from Amsterdam to Den Hoorn had been packed with commuters but I'd managed to find a seat and catch some sleep. Bram had promised to collect me from the marina when the ferry docked, barring some delay like a big lunch order from the crew working on the new road between Oudeschild and Oosterend. He'd promised not to touch the dress or the other items again until I arrived and passed on my instructions to the others. If the items did need to be moved for some reason, they should use gloves. As Liam had said when he finally returned my call before I boarded my flight, even disposable ones from the supermarket were better than nothing.

'Sorry.' Liam had sounded slightly breathless, as if he'd just run up three flights of stairs. 'Just got back to Glasgow. I was in London. God, but it's grim here. The plane was delayed on the tarmac for hours, not even an announcement. You should see where I'm staying. They're renovating the staff living quarters so they've stuck me in a leaky flat just outside campus that hasn't seen daylight or fresh air in about ten years. But they've reallocated my teaching units for the rest of the year to allow me to work on the book so I suppose I can't complain. How are you, anyway? Keeping busy? And how's your book going? Any bites? The university publishers wanted to dumb mine down. They said the text was too dense and erudite for Joe Everyman to be able to understand. Bullshit. They were just looking for an excuse to mass-market it. Can you imagine my book on the Father's Day displays next to all those crime thrillers and biographies of Winston Churchill? I told them to get stuffed.'

'The book's fine,' I said. 'That wasn't why I called. I have a proposal for you. I'm looking for a business partner, someone who can collaborate with me on a potentially ground-breaking discovery.'

'You have my attention.' His voice had lost its teasing edge. Behind his glasses, his blue eyes would be hard and focused, alert to the possible acquisition of precious knowledge.

I was seized by a sudden, panicky desire to keep the knowledge of the artefacts to myself. But I couldn't do the work alone. Liam had the contacts and the experience. We were a good team, despite our differing approaches to conservatorship and curation. Liam preferred the quiet sanctity of the chem lab while I liked to fall down historical rabbit holes, pinpointing an artefact's origin story. From the moment we'd met, we had recognised in each other the same fierce ambition, a desire to achieve something truly unique with our time on earth. I just had to give myself permission to trust him.

I took a deep breath and launched into Bram's story.

'Wow,' he said, when I finished. 'That's some find. I can't think of any extant examples of textiles surviving in water for that long. This is so exciting!'

I could tell he meant it and I was suddenly glad I'd shared the story with him. The discovery felt real, not just something I'd dreamed up. With his impressive publication record, Liam could drum up funds from sponsors whose support I could only dream of securing. Relocating to Sydney to work on my book last year had also taken its toll on my freelance career and years of renting in one of London's flashiest suburbs meant my finances weren't as healthy as I'd have liked. I'd been thrilled when Sydney University emailed to advise that my application for a research fellowship had been successful. The offer, which included access to their extensive historical archives, also boasted a quiet office set back from the main teaching buildings with a private courtyard and a view of the lawn sloping down to the pond. Teaching an occasional class was required but a pretty standard condition, so I'd accepted the role gladly. It seemed idyllic, the perfect opportunity.

Soon after moving to Sydney, it had became apparent the role carried with it certain unspoken opportunities, at least for the right candidates. At the end of my first fortnight, the faculty head invited me for drinks at a dimly lit restaurant overlooking the harbour. Monica Rosetti was extremely flattering, laughing easily at my bad jokes, groaning when I described the situation at home with Marieke, how she drove me crazy with her cleansing rituals, her crystals and dried herbs, dwelling on the constant fears and anxieties that half a lifetime of my reassurances had been unable to extinguish.

'She sounds like a nightmare. Why don't you just get your own place?'

I told her it was complicated. Whenever I returned to Sydney, I always ended up back at Marieke's. All my research books were there as well the small but precious collection of vintage clothes and shoes I'd rescued from countless London flea markets and deceased estates. Also, I could never forget that although Marieke had never wanted children, she'd flown halfway across the world when my parents died to claim me as her own. She was utterly mad and could twist the meaning of things around until you were so tied up in knots you wanted to scream but she had a good heart and I couldn't very well leave her on her own if we were living in the same city.

'You should apply for a permanent teaching role once your book is written,' Monica said, flicking her dark hair out of her face and swirling the wine around her glass. 'There's a generous stipend on offer for the right person and the university has an exclusive arrangement with an off-campus agency that manages a pretty impressive real estate portfolio. Of course, we'd need you to commit for at least five years. And the university publishing arm would want an exclusive option to check out this manuscript and whatever you write next before anyone else gets a shot at it. From what you've said, it sounds as if the research angle is quite a unique one. Academic publishing is such a brutal affair, perhaps even more so now. Social media moves so fast. Whoever breaks a story first is the person everybody remembers. Think about it, won't you?'

As she shook her arm, her bracelet glittered in the downlights, a conspiracy of tiny winking jewels. Through the rosy haze of intoxication, I saw her intentions clearly. Settling down to an academic career and teaching meant giving up a life I loved as a textiles historian and freelance curator. It meant stepping away from meeting with ordinary people to discuss their clothes and giving lectures to theatres packed with historical costume enthusiasts. I hoped that the successful publication of my book might lead to other opportunities – television shows, radio interviews, the opportunity to work on extraordinary projects.

Liam had then asked me to send him the photos so he could view them while he still had me on the line. As I listened to his breath rasp softly through the speaker, the background noises of the airport lounge – hissing coffee machines, flight announcements – lost their sharpness and dropped away. I saw the dress in my mind and filled out the curves, imagining how the fabric would sit on hips and waist and torso, clinging in some places, falling in others. The person who'd worn the dress had been dead for over four hundred years, yet they had left this imprint of themselves behind, like one of John Herschel's ghostly cyanotypes of the 1800s.

'Who else knows about this?' Liam had asked.

'Just you and me. And the divers, of course.'

'Good.' There was an air of finality about the way he said it. 'I'm going to jump online now and check for flights. I probably can't leave until the day after tomorrow – I have a meeting with the vice-chancellor tomorrow afternoon and it's one of those in-person-only deals, I'm afraid. Sound okay?'

'Sure. I can hold the fort until you arrive. What's the meeting about?'

'Oh, nothing important. I won't bore you with the details. I'll wait until we're standing on some suitably desolate beach on windy old Texel to do that. I may have to drop some clues so that Glasgow School of Art will give me some funds to hire a lab. I won't tell them the specifics. I'll just say I've stumbled across something totally unique and extremely important.'

'Great. Just don't forget it's a partnership. We'll share the scholarship, yes?'

There was no answer.

'Liam? Hello?' My words echoed like stones thrown down a well.

The line went dead and I assumed Liam's connection had dropped out. I should have known, then, what was coming. But

I was still floating somewhere above the real world, intoxicated by the glorious potential of Bram's discovery. I'd forgotten the cautionary tale of Icarus in Ovid's *Metamorphoses*, the way the wax in his wings melted and the feathers swirled in snowy clumps towards the waves as he fell. I didn't realise then how dangerously close I'd drifted to the sun.

Through the ferry's windows silhouetted against the morning sun, I could see the outline of Texel's gravel dykes, the green hills rising above the jutting timber buildings that formed the marina. It hadn't changed much in all the years I'd been away. A few restaurants were plastered with large 'Open until winter' signs and a stand promoting day trips to the outlying islands was splashed with posters of frolicking seals and airborne terns. A small knot of people were waiting on the marina for the ferry to dock. I grabbed my bag and headed for the exit.

The wind whipped my hair into my mouth as I disembarked. I gripped my suitcase and duffel with one hand and stepped carefully down the gangplank. Below my feet, the water churned, sucking at the timber pylons. The Marsdiep was deceptive. Seen from the shore, it was a flat sheet of dark water, all its wrinkles ironed smooth. Viewed from above, its secret currents revealed themselves, its estuaries branching arterially through lung-shaped sandbanks and islands uninhabited by anyone but seals and seabirds. A thousand years ago, a catastrophic flood submerged a nearby forest and cut a path through Lake Flevo. The salt water pouring into the channel poisoned the lake's freshwater fish and gave birth to the Zuiderzee –

the lake was turned into a bay. Dutch villagers eventually reclaimed the land, creating the area's first waterwolf – a soggy, low-lying peat bog. Unlike the swamp in Saeftinghe, the one near the Zuiderzee was quickly drained and dykes installed in an effort to hold back the flood. Materials were chosen carefully. A dyke built on too much sand could collapse while one built on peat could quickly crumble during a hot, dry summer. Muskrats were – and still are – a source of torment, since they loved to chew through peat and make their burrows in the salt grass, compromising the integrity of any man-made water management structures. They were also prolific breeders. For the most part, though, the dykes around Texel held firm. There was only a small number of recorded breaches over the past century. The worst was caused by a terrible storm surge that struck Europe during the winter of 1953 and claimed over two thousand lives. In the aftermath, a national relief fund was established to help pay for the damage. The Dutch government commissioned the Delta Works, a series of construction projects to reinforce the dams and dykes around Holland as well as the creation of a large freshwater lake. On Texel, the solution had been to build more dykes, rather than risk the total loss of aquatic wildlife, which was the inevit-able outcome of installing extensive storm-surge barriers. My parents used to joke about it. They had a saying – 'new year, new dyke', meaning whenever the council ran out of ideas on how to hold back the rising sea level, they would add another dyke to the ones already rimming Texel's coastline. Beyond the black humour, there was an undercurrent of tension. An almost biblical foreboding surrounded the possibility that the rising waters might one day overcome Texel's defences and swallow up the land again, taking everyone and everything in its path.

As I stepped off the ramp, a bearded man rushed forward, seized my shoulders and kissed my cheeks. I put my bags down.

'Feine! You haven't changed at all.'

Bram wrapped his arms so tightly around my shoulders, I had no choice but to submit. The enthusiasm of his embrace took me off guard. After a moment's stiff hesitation, I relaxed. I hadn't realised just how much I'd missed him. This was how I imagined a reunion with family might feel – the warm sense of belonging, of rediscovering an old identity you thought you'd lost.

'You haven't changed either,' I said.

Bram lifted a hand nervously to his thinning scalp. 'You're being kind. I'm surprised you even recognised me without the hair.'

'Of course I did. Although I must admit the beard's a bit of a shock.'

He grinned, rubbing his hand along his jaw. His once-chipped bottom tooth was now whole. He must have had it capped during the intervening years. I wondered what other changes time had wrought in the people and places I'd once known. I knew Bram's mother, Carlijn, had died a few years ago and that his father had nursed her through her final days in their Texel home, rather than travelling back and forth to a mainland hospice. I wondered if Tomas Lange's old dive shop was still around and whether the fishing boats from the mainland still sailed into the harbour every Friday afternoon, ready to compete with the locals for the weekend catch. I thought about our old teenage haunts – the local milk bar, the camping grounds in Volharding, the beachcomber's museum housed inside an old shipping container. Did they still exist or had they been sacrificed in the name of progress?

Bram took my arm and steered me towards two other men waiting on the marina. 'The others are so excited to see you. You remember Sem?'

Bram's older brother pulled me into a one-armed hug. 'Feine! How the hell are you?' He wore a black T-shirt embroidered with an image of an anthropomorphic olive and the words 'Lange Brothers Pizza' stitched in purple letters. As he kissed my cheek, I inhaled the fragrant scent of garlic and rosemary infused in his clothing.

'Sem's our unofficial photographer,' Bram explained. 'He took the photos I sent you, as well as some video footage of the wreck. I'll show you later, if you're interested. And this is Nico, in charge of safety and navigation. If you ever find yourself lost in deep water, Nico is your man. He'll get you home safe.'

I guessed Nico was in his early thirties. He towered over the others. I had to crane my neck to look up at him. When I did, I discovered a friendly, tanned face and a pair of deep-set brown eyes.

'So, you're Jo Baaker. The famous Australian journalist.'

'Historian,' I corrected.

'Bram says you used to dive together. Do you still?'

Since he was smiling, I assumed he hadn't meant the question to come off like a challenge. I was wary all the same. Walking into a group who'd been diving together for a number of years could be intimidating. It was the same in academia and in countless museums and university archives all around the world. You had to prove yourself in order to gain acceptance and even when you did, there was always someone waiting to cast judgement or find out where your alliances lay.

'If we're talking internationally,' I said, 'I have a soft spot for the Great Blue Hole in Belize. I did a pretty amazing dive there a few years ago at thirty-five metres. If we're talking about Australia, you can't beat the Reef.'

His eyes glinted appreciatively. 'The Great Barrier Reef? I've always wanted to dive there.'

'Well, you'd better go soon. They say the coral bleaching's only going to get worse. In less than fifty years, the whole reef will be gone. It's the same everywhere. Warmer oceans killing off the marine wildlife, coastal erosion, algae blooms. You must have noticed the changes here.'

Nico's smile faded. 'It's true. We've been warning every-one who'd listen for years. But nobody really takes us seriously. Maybe they will now, assuming we've found something special.'

'Have you been back down?' I said.

Bram shook his head. 'Weather's too unpredictable. You remember what autumn's like here; the wind has teeth. We get more storms now, too. Worse than before. One minute it's sunny, the next you're getting pelted with hailstones as big as your fist.'

He squinted up at the blue sky, as if expecting the heavens to open up and drench us all.

'We should get moving,' said Nico. 'Doctor Baaker's probably feeling pretty washed out after her flight. And I promised Anneke I'd be back soon.'

His accent was a little more Frisian than the others. The Frisian accent always sounded to me like a curious cross between English and Scottish, harder than English but softer than German, the lack of fricative consonants like sea glass smoothed by the tide. Mainlanders often struggled to understand the dialect.

'It's just Jo,' I said. 'We don't go in for official titles much in Australia. And I'm not tired. I'd like to see the artefacts as soon as possible. Textiles are extremely fragile and sudden change in temperature or humidity can damage them. Liam will take over when he arrives tomorrow. He's much better at the conservation stuff than I am.'

'Liam's your colleague?' Nico asked.

'My partner, yes. With big discoveries like this, it's best to work with someone you can trust. You have to get all your ducks in a row before the media get word of it. There's less chance of someone leaking the story early and catching you off guard.'

Bram led Sem and I over to a dark green SUV, the boot stuffed with the kind of gear found in every dive enthusiast's vehicle – plastic tubs for waterlogged wetsuits, custom shelves filled with spanners and bolts, tightly wadded emergency kits and spare oxygen masks. I caught a strong whiff of grease and the familiar, damp-dog smell of mouldy beach towels.

'See you back at HQ,' Nico called, waving at us from a rusted orange ute.

Sem ushered me into the front of the SUV before stuffing

my bags into the boot and clambering into the backseat. Bram reversed the vehicle out of the carpark then steered us along a winding road, past a cluster of small service shops and a stationary bus raddled with peeling paint.

'How does it feel being back?' Bram said.

'Good. But a little weird. Like retracing your steps when you've forgotten why you left the room.'

'I can't believe it's been so long. I remember your aunt Mila.'

'Marieke.'

Bram nodded. 'She was a wild one. Dad used to talk about her. Said she once dared him to break into the lighthouse and climb all the way to the top. He was too chicken. So, she did it all by herself.'

I stared at his profile. 'Marieke? My Marieke? No way. You must be thinking of someone else. Marieke's afraid of her own shadow.'

'I think Dad had a crush on her,' Sem volunteered. 'They were in the same year in high school. He used to say she reminded him of that old seventies actress from Utrecht – Sylvia Kristel. He kept a copy of *Emmanuelle* hidden behind the Bible in the living room.'

Both brothers laughed at this recollection.

'How is your dad?' I said.

There was an uncomfortable pause.

'Dad passed away last year,' Bram said at last.

I stared at him, incredulous. 'Why didn't you tell me?'

'Ah, we didn't want to bother you.'

'Bother me?'

Bram winced at the sharpness in my tone.

'It all happened so fast. Sem went over to the house to

ask why Dad wasn't answering the phone and found him lying in bed. A heart attack. The doctor said he'd been gone a couple of hours. Probably for the best. He was pretty broken up after Mum died. It would have killed him to fight some long drawn-out battle of his own with cancer or something else. I just don't think he would have had the strength to try.'

The vehicle bounced over a pothole. Through the window, I could see a field of rippling pink and purple tulips, their blousy heads and pale stalks quivering. A tractor lumbered along the field's edge, harvesting the nodding flowers which were sold at the local markets or transported to mainland supermarkets. It was a bucolic scene, belonging to a bygone era, a different world entirely to the very modern one I'd inhabited until a few days ago.

'I wish you'd said something. You could have at least given me time to come back for the funeral.'

Bram sighed. 'Sorry, Feine. We thought about calling, but you're always so busy with work. We didn't want to interfere. Also, when I tried to convince you to come to the school reunion you said you'd need to have a damn good reason to come back. We know you loved Dad. But we didn't want to put you in a hard place. We thought it would be best if you didn't know.'

His words staunched my outrage. If he had called to tell me Tomas Lange had passed away in his sleep, would I have booked the first flight to Texel? Or would I have made excuses about getting caught up in work? Would I have sent my condolences and promised to light a candle in his honour, organised a floral wreath to be sent on my behalf? Perhaps the unpalatable truth was clearer to Bram than it was to me. A remarkably preserved silk dress that was nothing short of a modern textiles miracle and an appeal for help from my former best friend had been enough to convince me to return to the place which held so many memories, good and bad, of my past life. But I should have come back much earlier. In my mind, everything in Texel had stayed the same.

Nico was waiting outside the clubhouse when we arrived. Bram parked the car on a thin strip of gravel between two bright blue shipping containers. The clubhouse, a squat, grey building with a flat iron roof, was almost indistinguishable from the industrial offices pressed on either side of the narrow service road leading to the dry docks. The only clue giving away its true purpose was a faded purple sticker plastered to the window advertising Lange's Dive Shop in De Waal.

'Dad sold the shop when Mum got sick,' Bram said, following the direction of my gaze. 'Tourists seem to be more interested in seal-watching these days, anyway. They love pizza, though.'

Nico was talking on his mobile as we climbed out. I extracted my suitcase as he hung up and wandered over to join us.

'That was Flora, Cristof's wife,' he said, coming to join us. 'Cristof's knee is playing up. She's called the doctor to come around and take a look. Hopefully it's nothing serious. I'm afraid he won't be joining us today.'

'Ah, that's a pity,' Bram said. 'He was really looking

78

forward to meeting you, Jo. He's the oldest living member of the dive club. He was down there with us the day we found the wreck. I don't think I've ever seen him so excited after a dive.'

'How old is he?' I said.

Nico flashed me a grin. 'Eighty-three.'

Bram unlocked the door and held it open. 'Watch your step. The storm knocked out the lights in the foyer and we haven't got around to replacing them. The ones in the display room are still okay. They run on a different circuit board.'

The foyer was dark, but I could see scuba tanks stacked against a chair and a disconnected fridge hulking in the corner. Nico offered me his arm and I allowed him to guide me through to the next room where shelves held whitewashed clay pipes and shards of broken plate and a pair of ancient, threadbare stockings. Four desks had been pushed together in the centre of the room to form a large worktable. There, resting on them, was the dress and purse I had crossed half the world to see.

It was smaller than I'd expected, the waist narrower. The delicate laces knotted across the stomacher, a triangular front panel, darker and more frayed than Sem's camera had been able to record. Leaving my suitcase near the door, I edged around the table. I could sense the others crowding in, closely observing my expression. The atmosphere was charged. After years of pulling up broken plates and salt-rusted machetes, the divers hoped they'd finally found something whose value might extend beyond the humble confines of their display room. A discovery of this magnitude could put Texel on the map. It could make them famous, too.

79

Up close, the floral fabric was so thin in some places it was almost translucent. The sleeves had been carefully folded so they didn't hang over the table's edges, but the extra material suggested they would fall to the waist. The pattern appeared to have been handstitched into the copper fabric. The skirt split open along the back, almost to the waist. It would have been worn over a petticoat, each extra layer a display of wealth.

Pulling on the archival gloves I'd retrieved from the suitcase, I ran a finger lightly over the bodice. The black flecks peeling off the knotted laces as well as the tiny pinprick holes indicated the pervasive presence of iron mordant. Metal salts had once been used as a fixative, altering the chemical substance of natural dye and lending the fabric that lustrous just-been-spun appearance that elevated a gown from some-thing homely to something worthy of being seen at ceremonial occasions. I turned my attention to the velvet purse. The pile had dried in tufts, giving it the unkempt appearance of a scruffy, wild animal. Amazingly, a few seed pearls, attached by their silken threads, still clung like ivory spiders to the weft. I carefully picked it up and opened it. The inside was in better nick than the exterior. While the outer velvet had faded to a dull vermilion, the silk lining's original pattern of vibrant yellow mustard flowers remained intact. The purse must have pleased the owner because she'd taken the extra step of having a phrase embroidered into the fabric: *mon préféré*. My favourite.

The lice comb was in excellent condition. There was some ageing to the timber, as expected, and a certain brittleness to the fine-needled teeth that left sharp little indents when I tested them gently against my gloved thumb. Head lice are tough little buggers, as any parent will tell you. Body lice, once the scourge of army hospital wards, were worse. I once wrote a paper on their devastating proliferation throughout seventeenth-century Europe. The damage they inflicted on generations rivals any apocalyptic plagues referred to in the Bible. A rampant infestation of these microbial passengers once decimated one-third of Napoleon's half-a-million-strong army. The victims spent their last days writhing in agony on hospital stretchers, screaming for their wives or mothers before sinking into the dazed, listless stupor that had given the original Greek word *typhos* its meaning. Lice-hunting became a vital part of every grooming ritual in pre-modern Europe. Friends gave lice combs as tokens of affection and regularly searched each other's hair to track the parasites down and stop them taking hold. I detected no traces of eggs or lice on the comb. It didn't mean they weren't there, only that a laboratory microscope was needed to determine their presence.

Finally, I examined the leather book cover. As I'd requested, the divers had placed it in a cardboard box, cushioned by thick layers of tissue paper. The dark bindings had warped and hardened as they dried, but the rough shape was still evident. It was about the size of a modern coffee-table book. Embossed in gold leaf, the heraldic crest still shone, perhaps not as brightly as it had when it was pressed hundreds of years ago, but the exquisite craftsmanship was undeniable. The pages, of course, were gone. There was no telling what the original text might have said. Judging by the size of the book and the careful tooling on the front, I guessed it was intended to demonstrate and enhance the gilder's remarkable skill, just like the items found in modern display homes. If, however, the book had been filled with illustrations, it probably would have been the most valuable item out of the collection.

When I explained this to the divers, they looked surprised.

'We thought for sure it would be the dress,' Bram said. 'Nico says silk was very expensive.'

'Oh, it would have been,' I agreed. 'But a few illustrated manuscripts or a Bible tooled in lapis lazuli and gold leaf could be worth as much as a canal house on the Herengracht.'

'So, what now? What do you think will happen once word gets out? I assume we won't be in trouble?'

I detected a hint of nervousness beneath Bram's cheerful tone. 'We're going to have to let the authorities know as soon as we can,' I admitted. 'Liam will probably take care of it when he arrives. He's good at handling that sort of thing. You might need to sign a waiver, something that says you have no intention of profiteering off the discovery. UNESCO has a rescue archaeology unit. We can speak to them about the artefacts and the wreck and develop a case for extracting the rest of the items urgently before the next storm surge washes them away.'

Bram nodded, visibly relieved. 'Thanks, Feine.'

I spent the rest of the afternoon alone in the display room, stabilising the items and sending emails to my contacts at mainland universities, trying to ascertain the best person within the Dutch heritage department to speak to regarding the discovery. As far as I was aware, nobody in Holland had ever discovered a ship containing so many well-preserved artefacts. My mind was already leaping ahead, envisioning the spectacle of excavation, the remnants of the dripping ship hauled from the water, the timber guts exposed. It might never be possible to raise Bram's ship but, as a last resort, robotic cameras could be sent down. Fifteen metres is extremely shallow as wrecks go. The *Swan*, another seventeenth-century *fluyt*, was still suspended one hundred and thirty metres below Baltic sea level. At least the freezing cold temperatures and lack of oxygen discouraged salt-water-loving shipworms from destroying it, as they might have done if the vessel had sunk somewhere warmer. The archaeologists who'd discovered the ship had named it after the sculpture of a timber swan spotted in the wreckage. The pictures I'd seen were eerie – carved flowers and Dutch *hoekman* and sculpted birds materialising out of the green murk. Whatever they were guarding was still down there, its essence unaltered by the high-tech photographs and wood samples extracted by state-of-the-art ROVs. I wondered what other secrets Bram's ship was hiding? What clues might these items hold – the dress, the comb, the velvet purse, the book?

I was still working when Liam called at three to find out whether I'd reached the island and to ask how the artefacts looked. I reassured him that they were in the best condition they could be, considering their unorthodox journey to the surface.

'How did your meeting with the vice-chancellor go?'

'Okay,' he sighed. 'I mean, I still have a job.'

'It sounds serious.'

'I guess it is. But hey, I'm always in demand, as you know. And this discovery is going to launch us both into the academic stratosphere. Have you given any thought to how you want to announce this thing?'

I set down the brush I'd been using to sweep grains of sand away off the timber comb. 'Sort of. I want to hear what the government officials propose first, once we tell them. We should consult with the local community once word gets out. It might be a good idea to get them onside.'

'A soft launch, you mean? Round up the local history society and ask for suggestions?'

'Don't joke about it. I bet there is one.'

'Well, I'll be there to charm them tomorrow. Can you take some more photographs of the artefacts? I want to check a few details.'

I promised I would and we hung up. Steadying myself against the edge of a desk, I picked up the camera and peered at the room through the viewfinder and snapped close-ups of the sleeves, the bodice, the hem. Without professional lighting, the images would be dark, but it was better than risking further damage by exposing the silk to the flash. I continued photographing the dress and then the other artefacts, trying to capture each angle, until a sharp knock on the doorframe made me look up. Nico smiled as he shook a crumpled paper bag.

'Late Lunch. I bet you haven't eaten.'

I followed him outside, blinking in the bright sunshine. It was late afternoon. Long shadows stretched between the buildings and cast their reflections in the dirty windows of Nico's ute. I leaned against the hood and heard my stomach growl. I'd been so focused on learning as much as I could about the dress, I hadn't noticed the day slipping away. Inside the paper bag were thick slabs of white bread with pale slices of gouda nestled between them. Simple Dutch fare, but I devoured it in less than a few minutes.

'I have a teenage daughter. Her name is Anneke,' Nico said coming to stand beside me. 'I don't think I've ever seen her put food away that fast. Bram sends his apologies. He meant to bring it back himself, but he got stuck at the pizza shop. One of the staff is sick. He told me to lock up the clubhouse and take you to your accommodation whenever you're ready.'

Despite the grungy look of Nico's ute, the inside was spotless and smelled pleasantly of apple air freshener. An electric-blue scarf was coiled on the front passenger seat. Nico tossed it into the boot before lifting in my luggage. We drove in silence for a few minutes, weaving along the island's coastal road, past the dunes and saltmarshes, a patchwork of yellow and green.

'My daughter is very interested in your work,' he said, at last. 'At least, I think she is. She didn't bite my head off or tell me to get lost while I was telling her about it, so I can only assume she was intrigued.'

'How old is she?'

'Fifteen.'

'Ah.'

'I don't know what happened. We used to be so close. Then she changed. It was like someone flipped a switch and suddenly I went from being the person she most trusted to the person she couldn't stand to be in the same room with.'

He tucked a strand of hair behind his ear. His skin was

still smooth; he must have had his daughter when he was quite young.

'What did you tell her?' I said. 'About my work.'

I found myself hoping he hadn't gone for the fashion designer angle. As well as being inaccurate – fashion historians are not designers, and never will be – it gives people the impression that historians possess extraordinary personal clothing collections, which couldn't be further from the truth. Most museums are not-for-profit and there are never enough permanent university positions to go around. If Marieke hadn't arranged the prudent investment of the inheritance I had received from my parents, I would not have been able to travel the world, picking and choosing the assignments I found interesting.

To my relief, Nico said, 'Well, she loves clothes. They're kind of her thing. I told her about the article you wrote for *The New Yorker*. Then we had a lively discussion about the relationship between clothing and culture and what material objects could teach us about the past. Okay, if I'm being honest, it was less a lively discussion, more of a monologue.'

I laughed.

'Anyway,' he went on, 'she did seem interested. I didn't tell her exactly why you're here, of course. Just said you were back to help us out with verifying a collection from a previous dive. Would it be okay – I mean, say no if you feel this is inappropriate, but I would love her to meet you. She makes her own clothes on her mother's sewing machine. It was something they used to do together. It would be nice for her to know there's a future in it.'

86

'I'd be honoured,' I said. 'Where's her mother now?'

'She left the island last winter. We'd separated and she decided she'd rather go home to her parents in Antwerp than stay here. Anneke took the news pretty badly.'

'But they still see each other?'

He shook his head. 'Tess needs space from everyone, including Anneke. Her family has a history of depression. She decided it was better if she just left altogether, at least for the next little while. A clean break, she said. I tried to convince her to let Anneke visit – even offered to drive her down there myself so they could spend time together on the weekends. But . . .' His voice trailed off. 'Anyway, I don't know why I'm telling you this. You look like you can keep a secret, I guess. Is this how you get the clothes to give up all their stories? Are you some kind of dress-whisperer?'

He narrowed his eyes at me in mock suspicion. I smiled. I liked him and I felt sorry for Anneke. It couldn't be easy, losing your mother like that. I knew from experience how tragic circumstances could impact your whole world. My mother had done something much more final, charging into death with eyes wide open, abandoning me so fiercely there was no chance of ever tracking her down.

We reached a thicket of trees, their branches knitted together to form an arboreal archway. Nico made to turn left halfway down the archway which seemed odd, but an entrance revealed itself and he swung the car between two posts and down a short embankment. As the hill bottomed out, the trees opened up into a sparse clearing and there was the rental cottage, set like a marker between two purple, heather-dusted sand dunes. I couldn't hear the sea yet, but I could smell it, the unmistakable whiff of kelp, the sulphurous stench of brine. As Nico brought the car to a stop, I saw a flat expanse of blue water lapping behind a scrim of bushes.

'I didn't realise I'd be staying so close to the water,' I said.

'That was Bram's idea. He thought it might be nicer for you. You can walk down to the beach, if you've a mind to. It's usually packed with tourists, but should be quieter now since it's nearly autumn. We'll have to go up to the main house to get the key.'

He pointed back up the slope at a white-clad beach house perched on timber foundations I'd seen as the car descended the slope.

'The owner likes to greet all the guests personally. He's old-fashioned, a bit of a character. When he found out you were the one who was coming, he insisted on letting you stay for free.'

We got out and I followed Nico across the sand.

The owner must have been watching our progress from the window because, by the time we reached the house, the door stood open, a cool breeze blowing through the dim interior. I could see a combined kitchen and living space, an old sofa cocooned in blankets. A rough-hewn oak table had been pushed against the wall and hemmed in by mismatched timber chairs. Most of the furniture had a similar washed-up, weathered look, but something about the carefully arranged photo frames and trinkets grouped on the mantle suggested they'd been curated with care.

A tall man emerged as we reached the steps. He looked to be in his late fifties with sparse grey hair, deep-set blue eyes and a chevron moustache. We regarded each other, me in a tired way, he intensely alert, scanning my face as if it were a book of poems he was hoping to decipher.

'Gerrit Visser,' he said, at last. 'I knew your mother.'

'Gerrit?' I said. I swallowed. My cheeks flushed. It had to be him. How many Gerrits had my mother known? I tried to picture him standing next to her, holding her hand, but my father's image kept intruding.

Nico glanced at his watch. 'I'll leave you to it. I left Anneke in charge of my book shop and I don't trust her for longer than twenty minutes. Actually, I don't trust her for less than that. She's probably invited all her friends around for a party. I bet she's holding a seance right now between Plays and Poetry.'

He backed out of the open door, giving me a small wave that I half-heartedly returned. I wished he was staying. There was something solid and grounding about his presence.

I heard the ute start up outside, tyres churning the sand.

'So,' I said. 'You and my mother were good friends.'

'Marieke told you.' He lifted a nervous hand to stroke his hair. 'Well, this is awkward.'

'It doesn't have to be,' I said, only slightly stiffly. 'We're both adults.'

'You must hate me.'

'I don't. I might have resented you once,' I admitted. 'But to be honest, I didn't even know you existed until very recently. And relationships are messy. I didn't realise that until I was old enough to screw them up myself.'

The muscles in his face relaxed. It took years off him; I could see the handsome man he'd been, the quick, bright eyes, the flash of a hard-won smile. It must have been a pleasant change for my mother to gaze on this face after years of my father's barely repressed sighs and dark looks and mutterings.

'Shall I make us a cup of tea?' he said.

As the kettle boiled, we sat opposite each other in the soft armchairs pushed up beside the big window. Through the glass, the view down to the water was unobstructed, an airy seascape framed by tall pines.

'It's peaceful here,' I said.

His mouth quirked. 'Why do you think I never left?'

I said nothing but I could feel the unspoken phantom of my mother hovering somewhere over my shoulder.

'Marieke said you were born in Middleburg. Why did you come to Texel?'

'Oh, a number of reasons.' He frowned. 'Chief among them, I suppose, was the simple fact that I love the sea. The canals of Middleburg can't really hold a candle to the ocean.' The kettle began to whistle, and he held up a palm, signalling I should stay while he fetched the tea. When he returned he was carrying two mugs. Handing me one, he sat back down, lifted his mug to his lips and took a sip before continuing.

'I trained as a vet. Completed my doctorate at Leiden, and spent a few years working at a local practice. Then I heard about the seal colonies up here on Texel. A friend said they were looking for someone to take charge of the Seal Sanctuary. So I applied.'

'And that's when you met my mother?'

He blinked down into his tea. 'Hilde, yes. We tried – I tried – to keep away as much as possible. I didn't want to come between them, if I could help it. But . . .' He shrugged helplessly. 'Hans knew, of course. They had an arrangement. It was meant to operate in a way that ensured nobody got hurt. When they were with you, they'd be together. And when they were apart, they could lead separate lives. Nobody was to know. But nothing ever really works out the way we imagine it will, does it?'

I shook my head.

'I think my father took advantage of the deal,' I said, nursing my mug. 'He always had a few women chasing him. I think he encouraged it. Loved it, actually.'

Gerrit cleared his throat. 'It's not my place to say whether Hans behaved in a manner befitting your parents' agreement. I suspect he liked the thrill of finding something new, though. It was the potential that excited him. He was always searching for the next best, brightest thing.' He sipped his tea.

'Did you find all these on the beach?' I said, waving at the shelf cluttered with trinkets.

'Most of them. It's become a bit of an addiction. I'm usually there first thing in the morning and I always go down after a big storm. You never know what the sea's going to throw back. There are still dozens of wrecks on the Texel Roads there. Or so I've heard. I wouldn't know personally. I don't dive.' He grinned, a little sheepishly. 'It sounds stupid, but I have an irrational fear of the open water. I suppose beachcombing is my way of making up for being scared. There's a persistent rumour that some folks used to light fires to lure ships onto the shore when times were hard. We're talking eighteenth, nineteenth century, not modern times. They installed the lighthouse in 1863 and that supposedly put an end to all the wreckage. But, of course, things still found their way here.' He laughed. 'Anyway, it's not important. Tell me about you. You seem to have done very well for yourself. Are you married? Do you have a partner?'

'No. And I've no plans to find one, either. I have no kids and absolutely zero romantic prospects.'

'I'm sorry to hear that.'

'Don't be. I like my own company. My parents weren't exactly the best role models when it came to love.' I let that sit for a moment. Eventually, Gerrit nodded, put his mug down and stood up. 'I should take you down to the cottage and let you get settled. Bram said you'd be staying awhile. I told him not to worry about the rent. Selfishly, I wanted to meet you, and see how you turned out. Your mother always said you were the one thing she treasured more than anything else.'

I shook my head in disbelief. 'My mother? You must be thinking of someone else.'

Gerrit looked confused.

'You don't have to pretend,' I said. 'It's not your job to protect her memory out of some misguided loyalty. I can handle the truth.'

'What are you talking about?'

I was almost afraid to go on, but I knew this story off by heart. It was one I'd repeated to myself hundreds of times over the years. Saying it aloud to someone else only made it truer, not less. 'My parents didn't care about me. They were so wrapped up in their own lives, they couldn't wait to get away from me. That's why

92

they were never around when I was hurt or confused or needed guidance. I don't hold it against them. God knows, I'd probably be the worst parent in the world. I was just lucky I had my best friend Bram's mum and dad to turn to. They looked after me.'

'You're wrong,' Gerrit said. 'I'm sorry, but I must respectfully disagree.' He paused, and when he looked back down at me, his gaze was a little fiercer, more urgent. 'Your parents loved you. They knew you were highly intelligent. If they seemed a trifle distant, it was because they wanted you to have some degree of independence. I remember Hilde taking you to a university on the mainland when you were about eight to take part in a program for gifted children. I think they already knew you were going to be something pretty special. The professor in charge of the program told Hilde she needed to stop coddling you. You needed to be allowed to make mistakes. Your particular type is the kind that thrives best when you have something to strive for, when you don't have the fear of familial obligations holding you back. Hilde and Hans only wanted to create the kind of opportunities and conditions that might allow that to happen. I think you've proved their approach was the right one, don't you?'

Anger pulsed in my gut and I glared at him. My hand itched, as if it might strike on its own, aiming straight for his chin. In that moment, he was the embodiment of both my parents, their ability to deflect my hurt feelings almost second nature, shrinking my emotional response to the size of a pea, to something that could be managed, hidden away out of sight.

I stood suddenly and he took a step back, as though the movement had caught him off guard.

'I'd like to see the cottage now.'

'Of course.' He fumbled in his pocket and pulled out a tarnished key. He placed it in my palm and I turned and strode outside, heading in the direction of the cottage, aware that he was still standing, dumbstruck, watching me through the open door.

I didn't look back.

I couldn't summon the energy to do anything except crawl into bed. I slept almost the whole way through the night, waking only once to stare around the dark room in confusion. In that strange liminal space, temporally untethered, I waited for the bookshelves of my bedroom to materialise, for the old wooden dresser to appear. Then I heard the rhythmic crash of waves. Sinking back onto the mattress, I didn't stir again until it was morning. When I sat up, the sun was streaming through the curtains, painting the whitewashed wall a fiery orange. The clock beside the bed read eight o'clock.

An email and a message were waiting on my phone. I scanned them quickly.

There's no hot water! Marieke had written. *I think the tank's failed. I've tried phoning the plumber, but he won't return my calls. I can't run a bath. When will you be home to help?*

I was tempted to reply that the reason the plumber refused to speak to her was because the last time we'd called him out to the house, she'd asked for his opinion regarding the recent election then shouted at him for voting for the wrong person. Instead, I googled another local plumber and forwarded the details on.

The other message was from Liam. He'd sent it an hour ago, so I guessed he was in the air now, somewhere over the UK. He planned to drive straight from the airport, and out to the clubhouse on Texel where I'd be waiting for him to arrive in the late afternoon. He'd booked a room in a hotel on the mainland, Texel being perhaps too small and provincial for his city tastes.

I showered in the narrow bathroom, no bigger than a linen closet, then went hunting for food. There was fresh milk in the fridge and bread and eggs, as well as a strip of greasy bacon wrapped in wax paper. I found a blackened pan inside the weathered dresser and a lump of butter in the pantry sweating under its glass dome. The kitchen was soon full of the smell of sizzling bacon. After I'd finished eating, I felt more like myself. I washed up, then pulled on some clothes and walked down to the beach.

The day was warm. A light wind ruffled the surface of the water and the sky was a swathe of blue taffeta, shot through with silvery clouds. I stood on the shoreline and hugged my elbows, letting the wind tease my damp hair.

A shadow on the waves caught my attention. Too dark and mobile to be kelp, it moved with the rhythm of the ocean, slipping in and out of view, as hard to pin down as a broken reflection. A whiskery snout nudged the water's surface and two eyes like glossy marbles fringed by thick lashes regarded me with a mixture of amusement and curiosity. Without warning, the creature disappeared in a trail of bubbles. I felt its absence manifest as a hollow ache in my chest. I began to pace along the wrack line, picking my way between strands of slippery kelp and broken shells as I scanned the breakers, searching for a sign. A pulse beat in my throat, like the echo of some long-remembered grief. *Come back!*

As silently as it had vanished, the seal reappeared, popping up less than twenty metres away from where I stood, just the barrier of the ocean surging between us.

I laughed, delighted.

'That's Hilde.' Gerrit appeared beside me, wearing the same outfit as yesterday, although his trousers were more rumpled and a smear of egg stained his collar. He looked older, thinner. Dark shadows under bloodshot eyes.

'She comes back every year around this time. I like to think it's her, anyway. She isn't tagged so there's no real way of telling, except for the markings. She was one of my first.'

'First what?'

'First rescues.' He raised a hand. As if magnetised, the seal surged through the water, her nostrils flared. Up close, I could better appreciate her colouring, the lichen-like blooms mottling her grey fur. There was something of the hungry waif about her. She watched us carefully with dark liquid eyes. Her pungent smell wafted towards us, overwhelmingly fishy.

'I used to feed her,' Gerrit said. 'Stopped eventually. Not good for them to become too complacent. She's a ringed seal. In the Arctic, they have to fight to survive on their own. You don't usually find them this far south. A storm drove her into my arms when she was just a pup. She's lucky the sea delivered her to me instead of a polar bear or a hunter who might have taken her skin.'

'And you named her Hilde? Don't you think that's a bit morbid?'

I expected him to meet my surliness with a frown, but he only smiled. 'I thought it was sort of fitting. She showed up the year after Hilde died, almost as if she'd been sent. Something had taken a chunk out of her hind flipper and the wound had got infected. You should've smelled the rot! Thankfully, it healed fine. She stayed with us about a year, over at the Seal Sanctuary. When she was ready to go, she bit me, not hard, just enough to let me know she was feeling better and it was time for me to get lost so she could move on. Ringed seals are largely solitary. They don't go in for big families. Couldn't fit many seals in those narrow snow lairs they build to keep out predators.'

'Does she ever come ashore?'

He shook his head.

'You could wade out there,' I suggested. 'Check the flipper. Then you'd know for sure if it was really her.'

'Could do.'

'But you won't.'

He smiled, a little sadly. The seal continued watching us from the safety of the water, her body rocked by small waves. She was a plump little thing, her square-shaped head resting on a stumpy neck. Compared to the huge sea lions I'd seen back home zipping merrily around the warm waters near Newcastle and Port Macquarie, Hilde was small and stocky. All that precious fat protected her, I presumed, from freezing to death in the Arctic currents. I tried to imagine what my mother would have said after learning her name had been given to a fish-eating mammal. Would she have laughed or frowned? She had never been overly fond of animals. Not domestic pets, anyway. I'd once waged a summer-long campaign, hoping to convince her to let me buy a parrot from a bird breeder on the mainland. I must have been ten or eleven at the time and none of my earnest promises to clean up its mess and take care of it seemed to make any impression. In the end, worn down by my incessant whining, she snapped at me over breakfast, throwing down her spoon so it struck the edge of the plate, reanimating the toast crusts.

'Birds are meant to be wild, Josefiene. How would you like to be caged up all day? Shall I lock you in your room so you can try?'

'But I'll keep it in my bedroom! I'll let it fly every day. It can live on top of my cupboard. I can train it to do tricks.'

She rolled her eyes. 'It's just cruel. There are enough bars already in this life. Animals belong outside.'

Encouraged by her arguments, where before there had been only grunts of refusal, I decided to go all out and say something provocative. 'I'm so lonely,' I said. 'Why don't you have another baby? Why is it always just me?'

I remember how her face changed from pink to grey in a matter of seconds, becoming the same lumpy texture as the cereal growing cold in my bowl. She went quiet and pushed back her chair. As she stood up, I saw her eyes were filled with tears.

Ignoring me, she lurched towards the living room, her hunched shoulders shaking as if someone walked behind her brandishing an invisible whip.

Back on the beach, a crab poked a claw out of a hole, testing the air. Hilde the seal dived beneath the water. When she broke the surface again, she was almost close enough to touch. I felt Gerrit shift restlessly beside me, as if he had the same desire to know what her skin felt like – rough or smooth? Neither of us reached for her. The moment lengthened, suspended. Then with a flick of her flippers, she was gone.

As we walked back to the cottage, Gerrit offered to drop me off at the clubhouse on his way into town. He was heading out to the seal sanctuary to check on one of the seal pups that had fallen ill a few days before.

'It's meant to be my day off,' he said. 'And I know my assistant Marta can probably handle things. But I can't relax unless I know for sure that everything's fine. So I better go and check. I can never stay away for long, it seems.'

At his insistence, I hovered in the living area of the main house while he dressed and gathered up all the equipment he might need to treat the sick creature if its symptoms had worsened. I studied the cluttered bookshelves, running my gaze along the thin spines of yellowed Dutch paperbacks and the fragments of sea glass shaped like lost puzzle pieces, the crenulated shells and desiccated seed pods whose progeny were probably now as tall as this house. A handful of spotted photos sat languishing in tarnished silver frames. Most of the images were of Gerrit as a young man in the seventies, standing on beaches I didn't recognise. There were quite a few of him without his shirt on which reminded me of the way I'd always felt seeing photographs of my dad during the same period. I wasn't bothered by the near-nakedness but I found the idea of all that timelessness stretching out before I was born somehow unnerving, like seeing an image of the earth taken from space. The most modern photo seemed to have been taken at what I assumed was the seal sanctuary. Gerrit stood with his back to the camera addressing a group of spectators, a bucket in one hand and a microphone in the other. Four seals lay horizontally in the wading pool at his feet, waiting patiently for their meal. I looked for Hilde, but the seal was missing. The photograph must have been taken after she was released back into the wild.

'What are your plans this morning?' Gerrit called. I could hear the tap running, water splashing in the bathroom sink.

I replied with some vague suggestion about taking more photographs I needed to return to the cottage anyway to retrieve my equipment for my appointment with Liam. But I'd done that yesterday. The truth was more complex than I cared to admit. I knew that as soon as Liam showed up, the dress would no longer belong to me. Yesterday had been wonderful. I wanted to conjure the same sense of peace I'd briefly enjoyed, before hunger and exhaustion got the better of me, the stillness that comes from utter absorption in an artefact, allowing the layers of history to wrap themselves around me.

'I'll give you my number,' Gerrit was saying. 'If you let me know when you're done, I can take you around the island, show you some things you might remember. Places your parents liked. A sort of getting-to-know-you-again tour. What do you think?'

I didn't reply. I'd stopped listening, my attention caught by a photograph I'd missed before. Perched on a different shelf to the others, it sparkled as though recently dusted. It was a picture of my mother holding a baby seal. Her head was thrown back as she cupped the seal's slippery torso, and a glass bottle fitted with a plastic teat rested on the bench beside her. The seal's expression was almost comical. It appeared to be smiling, its black eyes dancing in its fur-covered face. But it must have been the person out of frame who had amused my mother, who had made her laugh while the camera flashed. Gerrit. I leaned closer, fascinated by this rare glimpse into their relationship. It was no longer an abstraction; here was the living proof.

Footsteps sounded on the boards and then Gerrit was beside me. I could smell his spicy aftershave.

'She was so happy that day,' he said. 'It was taken not long after the sanctuary opened. You must have been about six. I don't know if you remember all the details, but we planned for a grand opening – balloons, colouring kits. We even hired a professional photographer and a mascot. Hardly anyone showed up, but your mother insisted on bringing you. She said you'd never get another opportunity to cuddle an orphaned seal, to give it the love it deserved before it went back to the wild. She wanted you to have that experience. I tried to stay out of your way. I just took the photos and let you enjoy each other's company.'

I frowned. 'I don't remember any of that.'

Gerrit's eyebrows lifted. I watched him turn away and search through a drawer.

'I'm glad you could make her smile,' I said. 'I didn't hear

her laugh much in the last few months. Although I guess I wasn't around. Too busy diving and making a nuisance of myself at the local skate park. You must have told her a joke or something, right before that photo was taken. She loved jokes although she could never tell them properly. She'd started giggling before she reached the punchline.'

'I didn't take that photo,' he said. 'The professional photographer snapped it. I was too busy taking this.' He handed me a loose snapshot. The film's surface was tacky with age, but I could clearly make out the figures in the foreground. The professional photographer's back was turned to Gerrit's camera; he had captured my mother's expression, but not what inspired it: me. Seated on a plastic chair opposite my mother, I held my own seal pup and my mouth was open, in either shock or delight. I was wearing the smock my mother had sewn for my fifth birthday. She'd let me pick out the fabric myself. I remembered running my hand along the cotton bolts, searching through the prints for something with rosehips and blackberries and toadstools, like the illustrations in my favourite fairy book. I'd worn that dress until it fell apart. How funny; I hadn't thought of it for years. I could recall with almost perfect clarity the way it had made me feel when I put it on – safe and warm, like a hug. I'd given up dresses later, swapped them for denim shorts and oversized T-shirts, things that could mask my body's confusing abundance of hair and sticky fluids. But if I could reverse time, if I could stand in a room full of all the things I'd lost or discarded over the years and be given a second chance, that dress would be the first thing I'd reach for.

The grief rose swiftly, before I could stifle it. I felt my wrist grow limp. The photograph fluttered from my hand onto the rug.

Gerrit bent and scooped it up.

Dusting it off, he propped it up next to my mother's image, her silent laughter the only sound I longed to hear.

I hoped I wouldn't forget the way to the divers' headquarters after our journey through the twisted maze of service roads around Oudeschild, I needn't have worried.

'Bram always invites me to the club's annual Christmas get-together.' Gerrit eased the car to a stop outside the clubhouse. 'It's a pretty exclusive guest list but I did Bram a favour a few years ago. Saved his dog's life. The poor creature had a tick the size of my thumb attached to its belly. Must have picked it up running around the dunes. Since then, I've been a kind of unofficial club member. Sometimes we trade; I have more clay pipes than I know what to do with.' His gaze slid towards me. 'When he said they'd found something and you were coming out to take a look, I knew it must be pretty special. He hasn't told me any of the details. I don't suppose you'd care to give me a clue?'

I shook my head. 'You'll just have to wait and see.'

He watched me climb out, then reversed the car and drove off.

Hitching up the strap of my camera bag, I strode towards the clubhouse and tried the door handle. Locked. I glared at it. *You idiot,* I thought. Of course the place was locked. I'd told Bram to make sure the items were secured every night. Even the windows were shut tight. There was no way in or out.

Sighing, I pulled out my phone and found Bram's number. I was about to dial when a sudden movement inside caught my eye. Someone was sliding open one of the windows – a girl with long blue hair the same shade as a kingfisher's crest. I watched her climb up and drop onto the gravel, her scuffed boots stirring up the dust. The bag she'd slung across her back seemed bottom-heavy, in danger of slipping. She yanked it up higher on her shoulder and I heard the unmistakable rattling slosh of liquid-filled cans.

Dusting herself off, she turned and saw me watching. She started guiltily, looked around to see if I was alone, then drew herself up.

'Do I know you?'

She was wearing a black, home-dyed jumper and a dark skirt. Beneath the dark eyeliner drawn crookedly across her pale skin, her eyes were a deep, piercing blue that matched her azure hair.

'I don't think so,' I said. 'Unless you're a figment of my imagination.'

She frowned then laughed. 'You must be the Australian lady. I can tell from your weird accent.' She shifted her bag. 'I'm Anneke.'

'Pleased to meet you,' I said. 'I'm Jo. Does your dad know where you are? Don't you have school?'

She made a face. 'It's the holidays. No classes. I was picking up something I left behind the other day.

Bram always leaves one window open a crack in case of emergencies.'

A truck rolled past, the driver crunching the gears.

'Can I ask you for a favour?' I said. 'I need to get inside the clubhouse. Reckon you could scoot back inside and open the door for me?'

Anneke lifted her dimpled chin. I could see her weighing up the advantages and disadvantages of helping me. She was probably working out which option would annoy her father more. The tension between them sparked and hummed, crack-ling with its own force-field.

'If you help me,' I said, 'I'll show you how to dye that jumper properly.'

She eyed me suspiciously. 'What's wrong with it?'

'Well,' I said, 'for starters, if you use a bigger saucepan next time, you won't get such a splotchy result. You'll be giving the dye a chance to settle into the fabric nice and evenly. And you could probably let the clothes stay in a bit longer. I'd leave a cotton jumper like that in for no less than an hour and a half, minimum. It helps if you have a friend. I imagine that's how witches did it back in the old days. When they got tired of stirring their magical potions, they asked one of their coven-sisters to take over so they could give their arms a rest.'

I broke off, letting the idea sink in. It's always a risk, negotiating with teenagers. After a moment, Anneke smiled and I experienced a dizzying rush of triumph.

'Okay,' she said.

Lowering her pack to the ground, she heaved herself back up onto the windowsill and appeared in the open doorway a minute later. Thanking her, I picked up her bag and held it out. It was heavier than I thought; the strap slipped from my grasp. There was a crash as beer cans spilled from the bag's open neck and rolled away in every direction. Anneke swore and scrambled after them. I tried to help, but she snatched up the cans before I could touch them. Shoving them roughly back into the bag, she stood up to face me, her expression defiant.

'I guess it's too early for spirits,' I joked.

She didn't laugh.

'Just so you know,' I said, 'I can keep a secret. I'm famous for it, in fact. And I grew up on this island. I remember how boring it can be. I'm planning to stick around for a while. Your dad says you're good at sewing. I am, too. I could show you some things, if you want, some techniques I've learned over the years. Or we could just talk.'

'Why would I want to talk to you?' she said coldly. 'I don't even know you.'

I watched her stride away from me up the service road, turning at the hairpin bend at the top of the slope and disappearing around a stationary tractor. She was probably sneaking off to drink beer with some friends. I felt a pang of guilt; I *should* get in touch with Nico and tell him what was going on. But it wasn't really my business and I didn't want to make things worse between them.

Full power had been restored to the clubhouse. The downlights in the foyer glowed and the fridge hummed loudly, its door slightly ajar. I nudged it closed, after observing the rows of beer cans stacked on the shelves and noting the empty space at the bottom of the pyramid left by Anneke's sticky fingers.

The dress was spread out across the makeshift worktable, the sleeves folded carefully like the wings of a paper crane. I was struck again by its eerie beauty. This dress was a time-traveller. It had lain at the bottom of the ocean for years, possibly centuries, communing with the creatures of the deep, waiting for Bram and his friends to come along and rescue it and bring it up into the light. Possibilities whispered to me like myriad voices inside a seashell. Had its owner been the daughter of a Dutch merchant? Or a lady-in-waiting, employed by royalty? I tried to picture her again but she stayed stubbornly in the shadows, refusing to oblige me.

Although the blinds were still drawn, I could see a narrow wedge of sky, the last of the stars fading as the sun gathered strength. I could see Polaris – the North Star, a fixed point in a world that must have baffled the astronomers of seventeenth-century Holland. They had adhered strongly to the Calvinistic doctrine of predestination, to the idea that every event was willed by God. Salvation could be found in the teachings of the Reformed church, which was only too happy to confirm that true believers could look forward to enjoying God's bounty in heaven while the damned were destined to endure everlasting punishments in the firepits of hell. Against this theological backdrop, the everyday lives of Dutch citizens must have seemed almost inconsequential – and yet, it was their industry that had given the Church its power. Famine, war, illness, flood: these disruptions could upend a person's whole existence. They could wipe out a family's savings in a matter of hours. Only the stars offered any real comfort.

No wonder the field of astronomy had drawn so many Dutch scientists and philosophers into its orbit. The cosmos, with its planetary motions and influence on the tides, could be scrutinised and debated without the need to imperil one's immortal soul. Here, the paradox of free will and theological determinism could be conceptualised as a risk-free exploration on the influence of matter.

I wondered if the dress should have stayed where it was, destined to rot at the bottom of the seabed. What might we have gained in bringing it to the surface? And what might have been lost?

I shook myself. Liam would be arriving soon. He wouldn't let me to wallow in these morbid, philosophical fancies.

Slipping on a pair of archival gloves, I peeled back the skirt to examine the stitches. Some of them were crooked – not those of a trained seamstress. Interesting. I ran my finger along the seam, as I had yesterday. Like most historians, I loved broken objects. There was always more to be learned from the way something worked than how it appeared from the outside. As a dress historian, I found decorative beauty as useful as a book with blank pages is to a reader.

The seam running along the back of the skirt was rigid, the sleek boning resisting the gentle pressure of my thumb. I'd almost reached the waist when, underneath the bone, I felt two hard lumps. I paused, my fingers resting on the unexpected texture. Whatever it was had been disguised well under the padding, which explained why I hadn't noticed it yesterday. I extracted a slim scalpel from my bag. Liam would kill me for doing this without him, but I rationalised the act by promising him silently that I would undertake all the documentation for whatever ended up being tucked inside. Delicately, I slipped the blade under one stitch and pressed it into the wadding, forcing whatever was in there out of the gap. There was a gentle snick as two small accoutrements dropped into my hand. The glass baubles each had a twisted hook set in one end, the kind that could be slipped into a woman's pierced earlobes. Inside, pale liquid swirled, like sea-mist or the Milky Way, celestial bands of dust and light.

5

Anna
Amsterdam, Spring, 1651

T HE *TREKSCHUIT* IS DUE TO LEAVE AMSTERDAM AT nine, but at the last moment, the driver discovers one of the horses needed to pull the boat has lamed itself. Men in fur-lined cloaks gather to smoke and give the driver their opinions on the cause of the misadventure while the other passengers, Anna among them, climb out again. The cold envelops her like an old friend. Tucking her hands inside her own cloak, she stamps her feet to ward off the chill rising from the canal. The water moves sluggishly between the banks, floes of ice and chunks of human refuse swept along by the lazy current towards the River IJ. At least the bitter air masks the worst of the stink. In summer, you have to smother your nose with your hand as you walk along this stretch of water. Everyone in this district, from the tavern owner to the wool dyer to the man who plucks pig droppings off the street to be turned into fertiliser, uses the canal as their own personal dumping ground. Only a colossal downpour or a hard freeze can hide the worst of the area's effluvious sins. Anna can't recall whether the canals

110

smelled any better where she lived on the Herengracht. She suspects the lavender water the maids used to sponge their clothes was partially responsible for keeping the unappealing miasma at bay. The house had strong foundations, too, and the convenience of a cesspit on the lowest level which neither she nor Lijsbeth was ever allowed to enter. Out here near the city ramparts, the houses lean together like drunkards, lacking the stately symmetry and ventilation of their richer counterparts on the Golden Bend.

The soil on which they are pitched is boggy, badly drained and prone to flooding. Even the polders – great swathes of land reclaimed by the ingenious extraction of water from windmills and canals – can't protect them from every storm surge. Exposed to the air, the houses' wooden feet have rotted like the stems of over-watered plants. It's only God's grace that stops them tumbling into the bay. Anna imagines their tilted frontages ripped away in a sudden storm, the inhabitants' lives laid bare. Is this what God sees when he peers down from His heavenly throne? All the people scurrying about, pretending they are in control of their own destinies? These are the dark thoughts of someone who has lost her whole family. Anna whispers a prayer for her sister's soul.

One day, she and Lijsbeth will meet again.

A woman patting a swaddled infant catches her eye. 'Why is it that men prefer to congregate around a problem rather than fixing it?' she grumbles. 'The canals will freeze if they continue their useless pontificating. They'll have to bring back the icebreaker.'

A thin, high wail escapes the blankets and Anna sees

a tiny fist fly up, as if in triumph or protest. The woman turns away, crooning placations. She has another child, a daughter of about eight. The solemn-faced girl clutches a small dog with dark-fringed eyes and white fur the soft, curly texture of lambswool.

'His name is Amandel,' the child volunteers. She lowers the wriggling dog to the ground. 'He's always restless when there's snow about.'

Anna squints up at the sky. The snow has held off for days, but the threat of it remains, the sun diffused behind a thick layer of dense cloud, the unmistakable scent, like mint or cinnamon, pervading everything. The expectation of the snow's arrival has heightened the anxiety surrounding her departure. She has been both dreading and anticipating today's journey, aware that by leaving Amsterdam behind, she is, in a strange way, abandoning her sister. Lijsbeth is already in the churchyard, in the section set aside for the penniless poor. She was buried along with four others on a day selected by Pastor Van Leersun for its unseasonal warmth. Workers were still digging the grave when Anna arrived. She managed to slip them a *stuiver* so they would bury her sister last. At least Lijsbeth will spend eternity staring at the sky, not pressed facedown against the body of a widow who had expired weeks ago and begun to leak.

Amandel has short, dowelling legs. He wanders over to inspect the hem of Anna's skirt. She crouches and runs a firm hand from the crown of his head to the base of his spine. Squirming with pleasure, he rolls onto his side, exposing a tufted belly darkened by a single, almond-shaped spot.

'He likes you,' the child observes, and Anna's chest

tightens with guilt. Last week, she made the difficult decision to leave Wolfert behind. She'd pictured them strolling together through The Hague, Wolfert stopping to growl at the canal cats sunning themselves, teasing him with their long, bewitching tails. But it was soon clear he could not make the journey. Out of pity, Cornelis de Witt offered to take him in, and Maria promised to send her news.

'He can slaughter the rats for me when they return to make their nests in summer,' the maid said, shaking out the old, threadbare rug she planned to use for his bedding, beating out the lumps with the flat of her palm. Maria had been in a good mood since she learned of Anna's departure. It would just take over a week, Anna suspected, for her to start complaining again about being overworked. 'I had a dog just like him when I was young. He was the very best of *smoushonds* – a vicious creature, although you'd never know to look at him. The rats lived in terror of his shadow falling on them. Trust me, a diet of goose gizzards is what your old gentleman needs. It brings out their cruel nature.' She patted Wolfert's head and he gazed up at her adoringly, his cataracts glowing like crescent moons. He'd already transferred his affections to the maid, lured by her generous distribution of kitchen scraps. Anna thought it best not to tell her that the only thing the arthritic Wolfert had caught in the past few summers was fleas.

Amandel tips himself upright and runs back to the girl who scoops him up and parrots her mother by rocking him like a baby. Anna looks across the IJ towards the dun-coloured fields of Volewijck where, each month, criminals are rowed across the water to face their punishment. The location of the execution fields is no accident; the surface of the bay is clogged with barges and fishing vessels. Everyone who sails into Amsterdam's port must pass the bodies strung up on the poles, a grim reminder of where vice leads. She supposes there is no disputing the fact that the condemned deserve the fates they received – but she cannot forget a story she overheard once about a young foreign maid who had moved to the city after turning seventeen. Unable to find work, the maid could not afford to pay her rent and, after arguing with her landlady over the debt, she struck the woman a deadly blow with an axe and found herself pursued by an angry mob through Amsterdam's streets. Wishing for death, she threw herself into the Amstel, but some industrious passers-by dragged her out and marched her to the *Spinhuis*, the female correction house. She was imprisoned and eventually committed to stand trial for murder. The city magistrates ordered her to be hanged and her body was displayed in the execution fields for all to see along with the weapon used to commit the wicked deed.

There is a sudden commotion, the jingle of harnesses, a shouted instruction that echoes up and down the water. A fresh horse comes to join the others while a young boy leads the lame one away. The driver gestures at the waiting crowd, who begin shuffling towards the entrance.

'At last!' the mother cries. Anna picks up her bundle. The inside of the barge is damp, the boards slippery with bilge water and mud tramped in from numerous city quarters. There are no windows. The air feels close, as if with each inhalation Anna takes, the wood exudes a counter-breath, releasing the odours of sweaty bodies and stale pipe-smoke trapped for years inside the grain. She chooses the same seat as before, settling herself opposite the mother and her grizzling infant. The young girl has tucked Amandel into her cloak. His head pokes out of the girl's collar, his wet nose quivering. He and the girl blink in unison and Anna thinks of a painting that hung inside her father's study – Hercules slaying the Hydra, a beast controlled by one mind and one heart. Once the transport is full, they move off, the vessel swaying back and forth as the horses strain against the bit, their hooves churning up familiar towpaths cut through the grassy banks.

Goodbye, Anna thinks. Her throat aches and her eyes sting. She should have spent more time this morning memorising the room she and Lijsbeth shared. Instead, afraid of missing the barge, she hurried out the door without looking back. She sees again Lijsbeth's body laid out on the mattress, her flesh greased with unguents, her jaw tightly bound. The smell of laurel leaves haunted the corners of the room for weeks, a scent Anna used to appreciate for its clean medicinal properties, but which she will now forever associate with her sister's death. When she arrived home after Lijsbeth's funeral, she found one of her neighbours had wedged a handful of straw under a brick and jammed it against her door, an old ritual to stop the dead coming back to harass the living. Anna refused to acknowledge its existence. The dead can haunt you easily enough, she now knows. There's no need for straw and broken stones. A quiet moment is all it takes.

'Are you travelling alone?' the mother asks.

Anna blinks away the image of her sister's still face. 'Yes.'

The woman nods. 'We're on our way to Haarlem to join my husband, a clothmaker. We were due to leave a month ago, but we had to stay behind and wait for this little one to grace us with his presence.'

She frowns down at the blankets and clucks her tongue, as if the baby is responsible for delaying his birth.

'Are you staying in Haarlem, too?' The older child's voice is slightly muffled by the dog's fur.

'I'm going on to The Hague,' Anna says.

'What's there for you?' asks the mother.

Anna shifts on the hard seat. 'A favourable position in a good household.'

The mother frowns. 'You look too young to be a *kamermeid*.'

'I'll be nineteen next month.' Anna's thin face and long limbs have always lent the impression of youth, and weeks of skipping meals to pay for coal to heat their freezing room have not done her body any favours. The headaches were bad enough, but the sharp cramps in her abdomen were worse, a hot-poker pain, the first occurrence of which left her doubled over in the de Witts' washroom. She'd mistaken the cramps for the return of her monthly bloods. Later, she'd touched her tongue to her gums and found the tissue spongy, the teeth slightly loose, as if sewn on by inferior thread. The cruel fact that she's eaten better since Lijsbeth passed and there is only herself to feed is yet another source of guilt. Perhaps the curse she harbours inside her – the one that stole her father's wits and her sister's life – needs more nourishment in order to dilute its power. 'Anyway,' she goes on, 'I'm not travelling there to

116

be a *kamermeid*. I have a position as a lady's companion.'

The mother sucks in her cheeks and purses her lips. She strikes the squalling baby hard on the back, as if she can drive out the child's wind by force and, when the baby shrieks in shock, she comforts him, cutting off the need for further adult conversation.

Anna can tell the woman doesn't believe her. She regrets saying anything and, at the same time, wishes she were brave enough to argue her case. It should be enough that she knows the truth, but the woman's reaction causes her doubts to flare again.

What does she really know about her new mistress? The bookseller at the market had squinted thoughtfully when she asked him. 'Catharina van Shurman? The artist? Of course, I know of her. I thought everyone had heard of the Learned Maid of Utrecht.'

He'd pulled some soiled pamphlets from a box, the topmost one showing a reproduction of a woman's portrait, the face haughty, the mouth a thin line, eyes hard and unsmiling. Above the mouth were strong, high cheekbones framed by a shoulder-length hairstyle neither fashionable nor flattering. It was a face that did not seem very likeable and, in fact, the more time Anna had spent staring at it, the more convinced she'd grown that the person who had drawn it had borne some grudge against the sitter. The information below was complimentary enough, a scrolled plaque proclaiming: *Star of the North, Catharina van Shurman. A paragon of Christian virtue, beloved by Almighty God. A Maid and A Scholar; One can be Both! See the likeness depicted here? May your kindness perfect what art has failed.*

'You can keep them,' the bookseller had offered. 'They're barely worth a *penning*, stained as they are.'

Anna had thanked him and tucked the sheets into her pocket. When she'd reached home, she spread the papers out. One contained a lengthy summary of Catharina's achievements. According to the pamphlet, she'd penned half a dozen plays and twelve poems over the past four years. Her pastel miniatures had been so highly praised and admired by the members of the Guild of St Luke's in Utrecht that they'd admitted her to their ranks as an honorary member: a rare honour, for a woman. Jacob Cats, the Dutch Republic's best-loved author and poet, sang her literary praises in his famous treatise on marriage and predicted her career would span decades – which it surely would, now that he had offered his precious endorsement. Further back, there was a record of her official artistic training, conducted under the watchful gaze of Magdalena van de Passe, an artist and engraver. The daughter of Crispijn the Elder, a prominent engraver and publisher, Magdalena was famed for illustrating her father's translation of Ovid's *Metamorphoses*. Unusual, for one woman to train another. Yet Magdalena felt compelled to nurture Catharina's talents. She declared they were nothing short of a divine calling. God himself had bestowed his grace on Catharina's artistic spirit. It would have been foolish, even heretical, to deny His wish to see her skills blossom and bear fruit.

A small line on the reverse page had caught Anna's interest.

The words in this pamphlet were prepared at Sterrenwijck by Margriet Pieterson, Meisje van Shurman's apprentice.

So Catharina, after tasting success, had taken on an apprentice of her own. Not just any apprentice, either: a woman.

When Anna had pressed Cornelis for details, his answers were frustratingly vague.

'There was some dramatic exit. Nobody knows where she went. Her family would not say. They are Papists who disapproved of the apprenticeship in the first place, Margriet being somewhat old at twenty-six to be an artist. Perhaps Margriet herself was displeased with Catharina's treatment of her, although I can't imagine that to be the case. When she was younger, Catharina developed a reputation for always speaking her mind. She's softened little over the years. You would never describe her as a shrinking flower. However, I cannot imagine her being capable of actual cruelty.'

He'd returned to his etchings, humming a tune, leaving Anna to stew over the mystery of Margriet's sudden disappearance and to wonder if she'd made a mistake accepting the offer she'd initially refused.

The water coach reaches Haarlem at three and the passengers clamber out, stretching their stiff limbs, sucking mouthfuls of clean air. The grizzling infant, asleep at last, lolls against his mother's chest, arms and legs escaping the confines of the rough blanket. The woman grunts as she heaves him up, and turns her back pointedly when she catches Anna looking. Anna bids farewell to the daughter. She watches them trundle off towards the city, Amandel trotting along at the child's heels.

There is no connecting service between Haarlem and Leiden, so she takes a barge downstream, stowing her bundle safely in her lap where the swirling bilge water cannot reach it. The bundle contains the few items she could not part with – her least-stained petticoat, two white caps, the purse containing the last of her *stuivers*. Buried at the bottom is her mother's silk dress. Anna felt like a thief removing it from the drawer, in plain sight of the bed on which Lijsbeth had drawn her last breath. The brightness of silk in that dull room was like the heavens parting after a storm, like a dazzling sunset splashed across a grey sea. Anna wanted to lose herself in the richness of the cloth and puzzle out the names of the fruits and flowers sewn into the surface. She wanted to keep on staring until the desire to wear the dress became an unbearable weight – and then drag her fingers through the laces until they were loose enough for her to slip the gown over her head, the silk softer than the touch of a hand. She imagined the folds falling around her legs, the texture so sleek it required no bleaching or soaking to massage rough fibres. It would be like wearing nothing. This thought made her blush even as a wellspring of longing sent a stream of possibilities racing through her bloodstream. She saw herself remade, no longer a poor laundress but a woman with means. Perhaps one day, if she proved herself a good manager, she could find a role as a housekeeper. Or perhaps Crispijn and Catharina would keep her on at Sterrenwijck indefinitely. She will have to make herself indispensable. She will have to keep the curse buried, smothered by her devotion to God, protected by the purity and goodness of her mother's silk dress.

In the end, she didn't try on the dress. Instead, she parcelled it up in a cotton bedsheet, ready for the journey south. She will keep it close to her – a talisman. Lijsbeth will forgive her for not burying it with her. Her sister will understand.

Darkness has fallen by the time the next coach reaches The Hague. Anna follows the directions she has been sent and goes to wait for Catharina's carriage near a water pump outside the town square. It's freezing now, cold gusts shivering the surface of the water in the canals, nudging the lanterns strung from the trees. In their orb-like glow, she sees the Binnenhof's Gothic turrets sketched against the purple sky. Home to the Princes of Orange for almost a century, the palace is like a church that has been reformed so many times its true religion has been lost. Additional wings, constructed whenever a new Stadholder took control, have given the palace an odd, mis-matched quality, zigzagging bricks and timber frames built one on top of the other, the future crushed against the past.

A man wearing dark gloves looms out of the darkness. He is ancient, at least fifty, his grey hair flattened under a peaked cap.

'You are the new *dienstboten*?'

She nods, her tongue stuck fast from nerves.

'I'm Mr Hartog. My wife Susanna is the *hoofd van het huis-houden*; the head of the household. We've been expecting you.'

'The coach was delayed.'

'It would be good if there were a direct way of travelling from Amsterdam to The Hague. Alas, the water.'

He makes a sweeping gesture, as if to suggest that the water is to blame for everything, good or ill, that shapes their lives.

She follows him to the waiting carriage. The carriage is a

jewel-box, fitted with padded seats far finer than any cushion she or Lijsbeth ever embroidered, the interior decorated with a panoramic scene of a moody sunset filtering through a copse of oak trees. The figure of a young man haunts the foreground, painted in autumnal oils. On closer inspection, Anna sees it is the goddess Athena half-dressed for war, her oiled breastplate glinting in the sun's dying rays, auburn hair spilling from the helmet she has just removed. A pair of armoured boots lies abandoned at her feet. She could be an ordinary solider, except her shield bears the goddess's unmistakable symbol of the snake-haired Medusa. It's hard to tell if she's coming from battle or going to it. The only other creature, a horned owl perched on a nearby rock, has turned its head away from the deity as if it cannot bear to watch the intimacy of the unfolding scene. Anna, too, experiences an uncomfortable sensation of intrusion, as if she has glimpsed the goddess naked, stripped of her usual war-like pride. She fusses with the heated-brick footwarmer, thoughtfully wrapped in flannel and left on a seat for her comfort. Outside the window, the starry sky and dark roads blend together like wet paint. Resting her head against the seat, she shuts her eyes, only to jerk awake as the coach pulls up in front of a large gabled house. A lantern bobs along the drive. There is a low, inaudible discussion, the soft snicker of horses, before a woman's curious face, florid and apple-cheeked, appears at the carriage door.

'Meisje Tesseltje?' She doesn't wait for a reply but turns the handle. 'I'm Mrs Hartog, the housekeeper. Susanna. Welcome to Sterrenwijck.'

She holds the lantern aloft and guides Anna into the

house via the main entrance. As they step inside, Anna's heart begins to thrum. Compared to her father's property and even Cornelis de Witt's, the entrance hall of this house is an astonishment of riches. Her feet sink into a velvet rug and she gazes up at a phalanx of framed paintings dominating the space above a scrolled mantelpiece. Marble floors reflect the warm light from the beeswax pillars, smooth as sour cream, poured into silver candlesticks. An empty porcelain vase, the value of which she cannot even guess, rests on a finely turned hall-table, beautiful in its varnished nakedness. This is wealth beyond what Anna has ever experienced, wealth beyond the reach of most citizens. It is the work of two or three lifetimes, carried over into the next generation like water spilling from a golden cup. Everything speaks of taste and tradition and the proper maintenance of things – citrus oil on the stair-rail, wax polish rubbed into the marble floor until it gleams.

'It's late. You must be hungry.' The housekeeper turns to face her. 'The mistress is already abed. You'll meet her tomorrow.'

'And the gentleman? Will I meet him then, too?'

Susanna shakes her head. 'Master Crispijn was due home yesterday, but he sent a letter ahead to say he's been detained. You must be hungry. I'll have some bread and cheese sent up to your room. First, let's have a look at you.'

She forces Anna to stand before her, where puddles of light cast by her lantern overlap in buttery crescents.

'Young,' she mutters, but unlike the woman on the water barge, Anna senses it's not an insult. 'You have plenty of years left in you. But a lady's companion . . . You've no training?'

Anna shakes her head.

Susanna tilts her head. 'You will be quite the pair, then. My mistress has never had a companion before. An apprentice, yes, but that is a different thing. She never had want of a companion. If she needed anything, she sent for me or Lotte, the kitchen maid. Now she has you.'

Anna wants to ask why the sudden change, but she stays mute. Despite the housekeeper's kindness, she's afraid she will embarrass herself by babbling some foolish nonsense. She imagines her voice shattering the glittering illusion, the grand house vanishing in a swirl of candlelight and paintings and porcelain.

'You need some proper clothes.' The housekeeper pinches the edge of Anna's cloak and wrinkles her nose. 'Give me your measurements. I'll arrange for the family's seamstress to make them for you. The fee will be deducted from your wages. You cannot be seen at court and other occasions wearing a pauper's garments. In the meantime, you'll find some serviceable bodices and skirts in your room. Other small items, too. Pins and pattens. They belonged to Margriet but you might as well keep them.'

Anna's head flies up. 'Why? Isn't she coming back?'

The housekeeper's mouth curves into a horseshoe of disapproval.

Ignoring the question, she beckons Anna towards the stairs. They have almost reached the first step when a commanding voice rings out from above. 'Is that my new companion?'

Susanna tenses. The woman from the pamphlet advances down the staircase towards them, carrying a candle. The illustrator's eye saw truth when they translated Lady Catharina's features onto the page. It's all there – the strong jaw and unflattering hairstyle, the sharp, bird-bright eyes. Catharina's age is impossible to discern. Although Cornelis swore she must be almost forty, she looks closer to twenty, her skin unblemished except for two slight parentheses around her quirk of a mouth. She wears a red velvet housecoat over a white nightgown, bishop sleeves billowing around her slim wrists. Pushing the sleeves back impatiently, she thrusts one hand on her hip and peers at them. Her hand, Anna sees, is scored by dozens of deep scars that must have bled significantly before they healed. Her first instinct is to recoil but then she catches sight of her own hands, the nails stripped thin, the skin at her wrists creased and mottled as if it belongs to someone twice her age.

Catharina misses nothing. 'The engraving stele,' she says, dropping her arm and shaking out the sleeve. 'You have to make mistakes before you can achieve perfection. If you were an artist, you'd understand.' She turns to the housekeeper. 'Where is my brother? He hires a new servant and then cannot even get himself home in time to greet her. Must I do everything myself? Bring some food to the sitting room. I'd like to speak to Miss Tesseltje alone.'

The front room is a generously proportioned space. A coal fire crackles in the grate, casting its warm glow on the beechwood furniture. More paintings adorn the walls, too many for Anna to take in all at once although her fleeting impression is of specimens in a *kunstkammer* – her cabinet of curiosities containing a hodgepodge of half-peeled fruits and gauzy butterflies and striped caterpillars clinging to withered vines.

'You're even younger than I imagined,' Catharina says, sinking into an overstuffed chair, leaving Anna to stand. 'When Crispijn told me your age, and what happened to your family, I thought you must have done something quite wicked to deserve such punishment. But you look so innocent. By the time I was your age I was at university, studying with Descartes. I was writing poems in Latin and engraving my own portrait on bits of copperplate. What do you think of that?'

Anna doesn't know how to respond to these extraordinary claims. She presses her palms together, hoping to stop the nervous trembling giving her away. Catharina's cool gaze flicks up and down.

'Are you pleased to be here?' she says. 'You're to have your own room with a view overlooking the canal and the stables. It's very pretty during daylight hours. Cornelis tells me you were living on the Raamgracht, in the Jodenbuurt.'

'Yes,' Anna says.

'Didn't the stink of the dyer's woad bother you? The last time I was in Amsterdam, an artist friend insisted I go with him to see how the dyes were made. Once was more than enough for me. You'll find the water here at Sterrenwijck is clean enough to drink, although I wouldn't recommend it. When we were children, my brother dared me to try a spoonful. It didn't kill me, but then I have a constitution far stronger than most. You'll be provided with new clothes and whatever else you require to fulfil your duties comfortably. We will travel together to court.

I will introduce you as my companion or my chaperone. It's not unusual for a lady of my station to acquire such a person, although usually the roles are reversed. Not many *hofdames* would consider hiring someone so young and inexperienced. But my brother has no common sense.'

'I'm very grateful, Madam,' Anna says, awkwardly.

'Don't speak,' Catharina says. 'Not unless I address you directly. How is your English?'

'Acceptable enough, I hope.' Anna forces her mouth to form the strange English words; their rough syllables leave a bitter aftertaste. 'My father insisted we practise at home. He wanted us to learn, in case my sister married a merchant and needed to translate.'

'Good. Her Highness Mary, the Princess Royal likes to remind everyone of her family's sovereignty. Especially important, now that she has been left a widow, charged with protecting her infant son. I think she fears an imminent attack on his young life. The Stadholder's powers may have been redistributed among the states, but we must not give in to murderous vice like those faithless English parliamentarians and their evil General, Oliver Cromwell.' Catharina's expression darkens. She grips the armchair with her scarred hands. 'The man was born a farmer! Imagine naming yourself Elector, setting your sights so high, you would dare execute an ordained monarch and install yourself in his place. It is – what is that English word? *Disgusting*. Not that we are blind monarchists, in this house. We put our faith in God. But our support of the exiled English court keeps us all safe. The Princess Royal is an Englishwoman, after all, by birth. And Queen Elizabeth Stuart. My friend and patroness. She grew up in Coombe Abbey, which I understand is somewhere in the vicinity of Scotland. She spends every waking moment writing letters to friends, petitioning for her nephew to be allowed home to reclaim his birthright. What are your views on the English, Miss Tesseltje?'

Her sharp gaze pins Anna to the floor. She is saved from answering by Susanna who sails in bearing a tray of sweetmeats and a carafe of wine. Fetching a glass from a sideboard, the older woman sets it down in front of Catharina on a square table inlaid with mother-of-pearl and splashes wine into the goblet.

Raising the glass to her lips, Catharina drinks deeply.

'Sin loves vanity. Our pastor says so. It is our duty to show things just as they really are – unvarnished, free of elaboration. Have you read this?'

She pulls a pamphlet from her coat pocket. It is a copy of the one Anna has hidden in her bundle. Catharina holds the pamphlet up to her face as if it is a mirror.

'I drew this likeness myself.' She tilts the pamphlet one way then the other. 'It is an honest reproduction, don't you think? I am as God made me. The words are, I grant you, a little florid. But then, I did not write them.'

Her expression changes suddenly. She frowns, her gaze darkening, and Anna guesses she is thinking of Margriet. She is wise enough not to ask, although her insides burn with curiosity. It's a wicked sin to pry into other people's business. Her mother always said so. But Anna knows her mother was as guilty of listening to church gossip as the next parishioner. She stifles a yawn, thinking longingly of bed. Catharina, noticing, calls for Mrs Hartog to take

128

Anna upstairs and the woman appears in the doorway, clasping a guttering candle.

As Anna starts to say goodnight, Catharina interrupts her. 'You're not to disturb me when I am painting. If I need your help, I will ask for it. Although for what reason I would need the assistance of a poor orphan remains a mystery.'

Anna watches her pour her third cup of wine, her hand trembling on the handle of the carafe. Although surrounded by wealth, she cuts a lonely figure in front of the fire. Is this why I've been summoned? Anna thinks. To warm up this cold woman? To distract her from her melancholy?

What if she fails? Will they throw her out? How much time does she have to win Catharina over?

Stomach churning with nerves, she follows the housekeeper up the stairs to her new bedroom. The gabled room is more like a guest room than a servant's dwelling. There is a soft, feather bed and a set of combs on a polished vanity. The damask curtains are already drawn, blocking out the cold. In the hearth, a well-tended fire sends a plume of smoke up the bricked chimney, the smog sweetened by scented herbs. From the special touches and rich linens, it's clear Anna is not to be treated as a common chambermaid. She wishes the mother from the water coach could see her now.

Mrs Hartog insists on lingering in the doorway as if Anna is a child who cannot be trusted to undress herself. Placing her bundle of belongings on the floor, Anna strips off her soiled clothes and slips on the nightgown laid out for her on the bed. The clean nightgown smells of linseed oil, both woody and exotic. Anna wants to bury her face into its folds. Instead, she says her prayers and climbs onto the mattress.

The housekeeper leaves the candle burning in its plated holder by the bed.

'I've lived here most of my life,' she says. 'I joined the household when the old gentleman, Madam's father, was in his prime. I can find my way about in the dark.'

Anna watches her figure vanish, swallowed up by shadow. The candlelight flickers across the flocked wallpaper. Her head spins with images of Father and Lijsbeth, now safe in God's keeping. She thinks of Wolfert, imagines his gentle exhalation at the foot of her bed, his soft body, its comforting topography of lumps and bumps. Her head begins to nod on the pillow and then, just as the curtain of sleep descends, she hears a door slam somewhere in the house below. She sits bolt upright, straining to hear more. But the house is quiet, as if the deep silence of the woods outside has found its way indoors.

6

Jo

'YOU'RE ABSOLUTELY SURE YOU WON'T COME?'

Outside the divers' clubhouse, Liam leaned against the boot of his hire car, arms folded over his chest. The wind had whipped his uncombed hair into a tempest but I resisted the urge to flatten it with my hand. Only a few days ago, he'd accused me of mothering him. 'It was just a misunderstanding,' he said. When I raised my eyebrows, he turned away.

We'd been standing in almost the same spot we were at now. Five days had passed since we'd arrived on Texel to assess the dress and the other artefacts. Now, exhausted after hours of taking photographs and documenting their condition, we'd headed outside to get some fresh air and the conversation had turned to Liam's meeting with the vice-chancellor.

'I think the words you're looking for are "fucked" and "up"' I said. 'Making a pass at the vice-chancellor's niece? Have you lost your mind? It's completely inappropriate.'

'She's an adult. And she's not even enrolled there.'

'Either way, it's gross. You should have known better. What would you even talk about? Interdisciplinary approaches to material culture? An analysis of research methods? Anthropology versus ethnography?'

Liam's gaze narrowed. 'Not everyone is as obsessed with their work as you are, Jo.'

'I'm not obsessed.'

'Do you even have any other interests? You can't exactly claim diving as a hobby anymore. How long did you say it had been since you dived? A year? Longer?'

I bit my lip. I hadn't told him the real reason I'd stopped diving. The event had been so traumatic, I didn't like to be reminded of it.

'That's not the point,' I argued. But the fight had gone out of me.

'I can't wait to get that dress into the lab,' he said. 'I've started calling around, sounding out who's got a free schedule coming up. Subtly, of course. Once we get a proper team of experts on board, we'll have the dress to ourselves for a few weeks before the hordes descend. Hopefully we can get a head start on any breakthroughs.'

We had agreed that the other artefacts – the book cover, the lice comb and the velvet purse – would need to be analysed separately by specialists in their respective fields. The day after Liam's arrival, we'd called the provincial government of Noord-Holland to let them know what the divers had found. Nobody in the public-facing office seemed to know the best person to ask so the conversation had been challenging, at first. After a series of transfers, a deep voice appeared on the line. The man had identified himself as Rob Disijk, the local member of parliament for the province of Noord-Holland. Rob was surprised to hear about the find but eager to offer his department's help. He requested a video call with the divers, which Liam and I had facilitated, gathering the group together at the clubhouse.

Rob was an older, handsome man, white-haired with bright blue eyes that held your gaze, penetrating the laptop screen despite the shaky internet connection. After asking the divers to relate the story of the dress's discovery again, he explained the delicate nature of the situation. According to Dutch law, the dress and anything else of value found inside the wreck belonged to the Noord-Holland provincial government. There was no real question of ownership. The dress couldn't stay on Texel. Rob planned to send a group of divers over to the island during the coming week. Unlike Bram and his friends, the State Defence divers were employed by the Navy and they were qualified professionals who dived for a living, trained in extreme conditions and had extensive experience retrieving valuable artefacts while leaving underwater sites undisturbed. If Bram and the other members of the club agreed to provide the exact location of the wreck and provide assistance, Rob promised to smooth over any legal difficulties that might arise from their illegal scavenging.

A tense silence met his words and from the looks they cast each other, I got the impression the divers were unhappy. Perhaps they didn't trust the government to help them; after all, Bram had told me they'd spent years reporting shipwrecks that potentially contained a swathe of treasures to the authorities, only to be politely told their information was of no interest. In the end, though, they accepted Rob's terms, leaving Liam and me to discuss the transfer of the dress and the artefacts.

Rob had happily accepted our offer to undertake analysis of the dress, since we were already on the ground and could quickly arrange for the lab-work and conservation work to begin. Liam and I planned to pool our collective research together – he would perform the chemical analysis while I would investigate the dress's origins. We had given each other a tentative time frame of three weeks to consolidate our initial findings for a long-form essay we planned to pitch to a number of academic and literary journals. I already had a few publications in mind – the cultural editor of *The New Yorker* was an old friend – but Liam liked the idea of auctioning our story off to the highest bidder.

'It's the best option, a way of controlling the narrative. If we don't strike now while we have the power, word will get out and then every journalist will descend on the island hoping to get the inside scoop. All our offers will dry up.'

He went on to assure me that the Glasgow School of Art was happy to back his research. A hugely successful discovery like this could restore the vice-chancellor's broken trust.

'And you'll finally be able to finish your book. Don't you feel like you've just been writing with no end point? Maybe this dress is the destination, Jo. The thing you've been waiting for.'

Through the tinted car window, I could see the silk dress lying on the back seat, shrouded in non-acidic paper. We'd decided it was best if Liam drove the dress himself to a lab he had found on the Dutch mainland. Located in the small town of Castricum, the archaeological facility was maintained by a private investment fund and boasted a state-of-the-art lab as well as an archival storage system endorsed by Harvard University. He'd spent an hour this morning speaking to the archaeological team there going over last-minute preparations for the dress's arrival. I'd chosen to stay behind, promising to join him in a few days' time. I wanted to be on Texel when Rob's team of technical Defence divers arrived to explore the wreck. The other artefacts – the lice comb, the velvet purse, the book cover and the glass earrings – had been collected yesterday morning by an antiquities historian Liam knew who ran a research facility at Leiden University. The historian, a woman called Marien Smits, had an army of post-doc students and researchers at her disposal and she'd promised to share her findings with us as soon as they could be collated and checked. She was particularly interested in the glass earrings and she'd emailed me this morning with a link to an article about the process seventeenth-century Dutch artisans had used to create them. According to the article, the glass beads were so strong they could withstand a blow from a hammer or a bullet without breaking. People gave them to their friends as love tokens or curiosities, calling them glass buttons or Dutch tears. They were valuable, but more for their scientific interest than any monetary investment. Someone had considered them precious enough to sew into the seam of the silk dress. Perhaps the dress's owner had feared they would be stolen? But why, if they were mainly of sentimental value, had she decided to conceal them where they would not be discovered?

Bram, Nico, Sem and another man in a knitted vest pulled up in the carpark just as Liam was leaving. Bram introduced the stranger as Cristof.

'Look after our treasure, won't you?' he called. Liam returned his smile tightly. He wasn't comfortable talking to the divers. He saw them as reckless bounty hunters, clumsily destroying items of cultural value without considering the greater consequences. I'd tried to get him to understand that there were valid reasons why the divers had brought up the items, but it was no good.

Liam climbed into his hire car and drove off in the direction of the ferry.

'There's been a slight change of plans,' Bram said, gathering us all together in the reception area of the clubhouse. 'The state divers are due to arrive any minute. Before they get here, I want to know how you all feel about going down again to the wreck.'

A ripple of excitement ran though the group.

'I took a call from Emerens Ericsson early this morning,' Bram went on. 'He's the head diver in charge of the Defence Diving Group, based in Den Helder. Rob gave him my number. He wanted to know exactly who was there when we found the artefacts and where we all were, what positions, when the items were recovered. The boat's prepped and I refilled everyone's air tanks this morning. Conditions look good. We're looking at a slack tide with minimal surge. It's supposed to rain later, but we should be well and truly home by then.'

Nico caught my eye. 'What about Jo?'

Bram turned his assessing gaze on me. 'How about it, Jo?'

I was already shaking my head. 'I can't.'

'Why not? Your certification's current,' Nico said. 'Only yesterday, you were telling me how much you wished you could go down and take a look at the wreck yourself.'

'My skills are a bit rusty,' I said. 'And I wasn't on the original dive. I'd only get in the way.'

'Nonsense,' said Nico. 'I'll look after you. We all will.'

'The most important thing to remember is that we need to demonstrate our professionalism. We want the Defence divers to understand we're into preserving Dutch history and just as committed to the cause as they are.' A hint of a smile teased the corner of his mouth. 'We just have more fun doing it.'

'I'll stay on the boat,' I said. 'I'd like to take some notes about the location.'

Bram shrugged. 'Suit yourself. The offer's there, if you change your mind. There's an extra suit and tank.'

A sudden noise came from the water and we turned towards the marina. Through the window we saw a sleek yacht rounding the headland and speeding towards us, lights flashing. Bram led us outside for a closer look.

From my diving experience, I knew enough about boats to recognise that the vessel, a Dutch Craft 56 with twin engines, could easily accommodate the six crew members ranged along its oversized aft deck. It was a top of the line performance yacht, powerful enough to handle both rough seas and deceptive trenches of shallow water concealing dangerous coral reefs. Bram's boat, *Proteus*, was, by contrast, an older-style sports boat. In a voice tinged with pride, he'd described the worn wraparound lounges he'd removed to create more deck space between the transoms fixed across the sternpost and the large fibreglass tank racks he'd installed behind the pilot house so the divers could quickly access their gear. Despite these modifications, there was no comparison between the two vessels. When the Navy boat pulled in beside it, there was no disguising the *Proteus'* age nor the battered hull which gave it the appearance of a used fridge nearing the end of its life.

Sem whistled as the crew members secured the yacht to the marina and started alighting. 'That's one good-looking boat. Wasn't that the model you were thinking of getting, Bram? Until you saw the price. Too expensive, you said.'

Bram frowned at him, clearly unhappy to be reminded. 'You and I both know those boats aren't worth a damn cent if you can't drive them properly. Come on.'

A tall, serious-looking North Hollander with greying hair led the team over. Bram introduced us. 'This is Emerens Ericsson, Jo Baaker.' Emerens shook my hand politely enough, though I noticed he squinted over my shoulder as he spoke.

'You're the fashion designer,' he said.

'Textiles historian.'

'There's a difference?'

I accepted the barb gracefully. 'Bram says you're in charge of the Defence Diving Group.'

'That's right. These are my boys. We've been diving together for – what is it, six, seven years now?'

The six men murmured their assent. They were all reasonably young, fit and broad-chested, dressed in identical black wetsuits emblazoned with the Defence logo.

'We don't usually dive out this way, unless there's something big that needs our attention,' Emerens said. 'An accident, you know. Search and recovery.'

The back of my neck prickled.

'Of course,' he went on, 'now that we know what's out here is a matter of international significance, I expect we'll be visiting the island more frequently.'

'You've known about this site for years, Emerens,' Bram said.

'True,' the divemaster conceded. 'I guess I owe you an apology for not coming out sooner. No hard feelings?'

He extended his hand. Bram hesitated, then shook it, easing the tense mood.

'Bram, you mentioned something about an extra diving suit,' I said. 'I'd like to take you up on it, if it still stands. There are a few details I'd like to clear up about the wreck's location.'

Bram turned to me. 'Of course,' he said. He threw Emerens a sharp look. 'I assume that's okay with you, Divemaster?'

'Fine by me, as long as she can look after herself. So, the historian is a diver? At least you're willing to get your hands dirty. Today's goal is to establish what happened down there the day the artefacts were found and to see if there's anything else worth retrieving or if, due to deteriorating conditions, it's better to leave things as they are. Everyone stays safe, yes? Everyone looks out for their friends. We'll take our boat; you take yours.'

'What if we find something?' Nico said.

'Then you leave it be,' Emerens said. 'Don't touch anything. The boys and I will come back for it. Just point it out to one of us. Got it?'

Nico frowned then nodded.

As the teams dispersed – the divers to their clubhouse to

gear up, the Defence boys returning to their boat – I caught Bram's arm. 'Is this really a good idea?' I said, low enough that I hoped nobody else could hear us. 'Why not just let them go? Give them the coordinates of the site. Why do we have to be involved at all?'

'Jo, I know you care deeply about what you do. So you'll understand what I mean when I say that site is ours. It's in our waters. We discovered it first! If we don't go along and protect it, what purpose do we serve? How is that helping Texel? The people around here rely on us to protect our culture.' Seeing my anxious face, he patted my arm reassuringly. 'Don't worry. We'll behave ourselves, as long as they do. Come on. Let's get you suited up.'

He led me through the clubhouse to the wet room, a caged area housed outside the main building where the divers washed and dried their gear after every use. Fluoro buckets brimmed with weight vests, glass snorkels and plastic fins. Wetsuits crowded a clothes rack, nestled tightly together like animal pelts. I chose one that looked about the right fit and selected a mask from a tub, my world shrinking to the narrow vision glimpsed through the tempered glass lens.

'Stick close to me,' Nico said. 'The visibility should be pretty good today, but there are patches – especially if we end up under the bow – where it gets a little murky. I'll make sure you have a torch.'

He turned to help Cristof strap on his tank. The older man was encased in a blue wetsuit edged with bright pink flames along the arms and legs. 'Flora chose it,' he told me. 'She thought it might help in the event of an accident.

You can't miss me, she said.' He tapped the dive computer strapped to his wrist. 'Anniversary gift. Flora insisted on buying the best model around. You can set it in your sleep – but of course, Nico's the expert navigator.'

When everyone was ready, Bram led us outside and performed the final checks on the group's equipment.

'You're good to go,' he told me, patting my back which made a dull clanging sound on the air tank. It made the hairs rise on my neck. Of course, I was technically good to go. But what if I panicked? What if I forgot to breathe? There were so many things that could go wrong. Arterial gas embolism, where a nitrogen bubble trapped in the bloodstream travels to the heart and causes it to stop beating. Decompression sickness, better known as the bends, where a too-fast ascent results in a reduction in pressure, causing nitrogen bubbles to fill the body's blood tissues. At its worst, it could end in nerve damage or even death. Then there's nitrogen narcosis, a condition only experienced when diving at certain depths. Divers have all sorts of names for it: the Champagne Giggles, Nitrogen Euphoria, the Raptures of the Deep. I'd experienced it a few times – all divers inevitably would if they dived often, as I had in my twenties.

Symptoms vary between divers. Some people get all turned around, no longer able to tell up from down, or right from left. Others hallucinate, offering their regulator mouthpiece to fish or turtles. They have trouble concentrating, become confused and distracted, make rash, impulsive decisions like entering wrecks or caves without checking first to see if they're safe. In my case, the narcosis had infused me with a warm sense of peace, the kind I had been searching for all my life. There was only one time I was ever in real danger. Diving a wreck near the Philipines I'd imagined someone was following me, convinced that each time I turned around, the person disappeared behind a rotting timber beam. I drifted further and further from my dive group, searching the cabins for the mysterious person who was taunting me. I started to grow angry. Grabbing hold of a column, I managed to cut my hand on a sharp bit of metal. Blood clouded the water instantly. I watched its progress impassively, with only the mildest curiosity. There was no pain, only a dull sense of disappointment. Thankfully, another member of the group noticed my odd behaviour. They hauled me up and we returned to the surface safely.

Ahead of us, Emerens Ericsson's yacht glided gracefully along the waves, a bubbling foam churning in its wake. Bram had given Emerens the coordinates for the dive site, which lay quite close to a sheltered beach just around the south-west headland, about a ten-minute ride away.

Nobody spoke as our boat chugged along. A nervous tension hung in the air and the charged atmosphere only intensified the closer we got to the dive site where a slight wind whipped the sea's surface into a light foam. Cristof, sitting opposite me, next to Nico, removed his glasses and pulled on his scuba mask, then placed the spectacles securely in a case and tucked it under the seat. I gazed back the way we'd come. From afar, Texel looked small and insignificant. It had felt big when I arrived almost a week ago, but I knew it again now, was becoming refamiliar with its cliffs and paths.

Shrieking terns circled the sandbanks and I could see the lighthouse standing straight and slim as a needle, towering over the dunes on the western side of the island.

Bram and Sem stood at the helm, going over the coordinates again. I heard Bram say he wanted the coordinates to line up with the GPS so they'd know where to drop the granny line when the time came. Secured to the stern of the boat, the granny line's cordage would enable us to find the boat again while we were underwater, if visibility suddenly worsened.

Bram's voice boomed out over the slapping of waves. 'Nico, come over here!'

I watched Nico join Bram at the helm.

There was a low, muttered conference and after a minute or so, Nico nodded as if in agreement before returning to sit beside me.

'What was that about?' I asked. He opened his mouth, then closed it and began clipping on his fins. When we reached the dive site, Bram cut the boat's engine and Emerens eased the State boat to a stop some distance away. Walking out to the bow, he raised his hand in Bram's direction, beckoning us closer. Bram steered *Proteus* alongside the State vessel, until the two boats were nearly touching.

From the stern, Bram lowered the dive platform and we all scrambled onto it, moving clumsily, our fins turning us from capable land mammals into awkward amphibians. There came the sound of splashing bodies entering the water. I saw Cristof edge to the side of the boat then disappear in a backwards roll, his flippers vanishing in a fountain of bubbles, like a whale's flukes beneath the surface of the waves. Bram quickly followed, his grin visible through the glass diving mask. Nico helped me to the edge of the boat. We dangled for a moment and I felt a surge of adrenaline swoop up my chest into my throat. Then Nico let go of my hand and I dropped backwards into the ocean.

The sound of my own mechanical breath filled my ears. Weighted down by the lead bars in my vest, I fought the instinct to control my surroundings. All I could master was myself. I forced my legs and arms to relax, let them adjust to the buoyancy my gear provided and gave myself up to the ocean's currents. My heart rate slowed. I felt myself drop down with it, entering that strange liminal space where the self is forced to turn inwards. The closest thing I've ever found to it on land is meditation. In those moments, as in this one, I became an empty vessel. I was breath and tissue, heart and lungs, a cork bobbing on the tide, tethered nowhere, to nothing, my identity as ephemeral as a worn label on an old bottle. I could have floated away and washed up on a strange beach, reinventing myself as someone new. I shut my eyes, resisting the temptation to try. I'd remade myself once; I could do it again. Something touched my shoulder – a hand, soft as an octopus tentacle or a fragment of leafy kelp. I closed my eyes and sucked in a breath around the regulator mouthpiece, salt water stinging my lips and tongue. When I opened my eyes Nico was peering at me through his glass mask.

He tapped his forehead.

You feeling okay?

Yes, I signalled. It was strange, the loss of verbal language, the shift into kinetic motion. The only way to understand each other now was to use our hands and eyes.

Come on, he gestured.

Nearby, through dense floating particles, I could see Bram and the rest of the Texel team. Emerens' boys had swum further out, sleek, black shapes floating in the semi-dark. They circled back slowly towards us, Emerens at the head of the group gripping his torch – a flashy, sleek design lighter than the ones Bram had distributed to us before we descended. He tapped the GPS on his dive computer, pointed down. The seabed was still a good ten metres below us. He wanted us to sink lower. I felt the pull of gravity in my stomach and pelvis as bubbles rushed past, twisted shapes fizzing away from me, zooming up towards the light. The bottom of the ocean was an alien landscape. Seen from above, it had a shape and texture I could understand, but as we approached it, the shifting currents and murky shadows cast by the boats overhead tinged it green and it became a mirage. Even when we reached the bottom and I ran my fingers through the gritty sediment, it was hard to believe it was really there. I could have sworn the sea was nebulous, a hidden creature, camouflaged, concealing its true self.

When everyone had reached the bottom, Emerens indicated we should break into pairs and follow him. Together, we made our way across the ocean floor, carefully avoiding the waving fronds of kelp and seagrass with our fins. The wreck came slowly into view, emerging from the murk like a behemoth, a mountain seen through blue mist. A tall mast protruded from the silt and sand, listing slightly to the left, the deck around it partially obscured by dun-coloured mud. A gaping hole revealed the precise spot where currents stirred up by the recent storm had blown away hundreds of years' worth of mud and debris, opening up a passage into the ship's lower decks and allowing divers access to the cargo hold. Small creatures shied away from the glow of Emerens' torch as he tracked a bright path across the deck and down the hull where crenulated barnacles clung stubbornly to the wood, old hermits resisting the possibility of new places.

I shivered. The temperature was much colder now that our bodies were no longer protected by the pleasing warmth of the upper thermocline. My hands felt numb, my ears rang. A raw hollowness spread through my chest, as if my organs had been scooped clean and replaced with chunks of ice. I wriggled my fingers, brought them up to my face and pinched my nose, breathing through the discomfort. The pressure relieved, I followed the others closer towards the wreck. When Emerens reached the open door near the ship's helm, he held up his hand. We stopped. Treading water, I wondered if this was the moment we would all be ordered to turn around and ascend again, leaving the technical divers to get to work. Was this as close as we'd get to finding out if there were other items on board, things that might clue us in to the ship's owner, the dress's owner?

Emerens directed his team towards the hollowed-out ship. Bram moved to follow too, but Emerens held up his hand again, *Stay put.*

We watched him guide his team through the doorway into the dark shadows of the lower decks.

Time seemed to stretch. I checked the dive computer circling my wrist; three minutes had passed. I could sense

Bram growing restless. At last, he beckoned us over. The others finned towards him, formed a semi-circle. I hesitated, stayed where I was. Hadn't Emerens told us not to move unless instructed? Bram's gestures became exaggerated. He swept his arm through the water. *Come on, come here.* Pushing off, I kicked my legs, the group breaking off to make room for me, Nico on my left, Cristof on my right. Bram manoeuvred himself into the centre of the circle, like the heart of a compass. He seemed to be addressing Nico, Cristof and Sem one by one. I couldn't understand what he was saying. All I knew was that something had shifted. I wanted to ask Nico what was going on, but of course, I had no voice at my disposal. I was limited to gestures – a helpless shrug, the sweep of an arm, palms raised in frustration. At last, Bram turned to me. He pointed two fingers at Cristof and myself, brought them slowly together. *Pair up.* I nodded to let him know I understood. Cristof finned across to me. He seemed calm, blinking at me, his eyes huge and owlish, magnified by the tempered glass. Bram and Nico dispersed across the upper deck, swimming close to the rusted cannons. They were like birds, graceful in their movements, but determined as magpies searching for treasures. Their torch beams crisscrossed the deck, radiant columns of light piercing the dark. I saw them pause, watched Nico's arm come down as he pointed to something on the deck. Bram hooked himself to a cannon. I saw him reaching . . .

What was he doing?

My breath quickened. A strong current crested through the water, lifting us all a little higher. A wave of dizziness spun my thoughts about. With an effort, I fought back, clawing at the current. Panic churned in the base of my stomach.

Someone, somewhere, had miscalculated something. A storm was on its way.

I was about to signal to the others when a sharp movement caught my eye.

I've never worried about sharks, but the dark shape at the corner of my vision sent a chill down my spine. My lungs began to ache and I realised I was holding my breath. Something shot past me and I reared back, startled. But it wasn't a shark. It was a seal, sleek and graceful. The seal moved in a fluid motion, darting through the water, looping circles around the mast. My heart rate slowed again. For a moment, I forgot where I was, when I was. I imagined the seal's ancestors swimming in the same place, jetting through the water as galleons glided overhead.

Suddenly I saw Emerens' crew emerge from the wreck's lower deck. An angry burst of bubbles erupted around Emerens' mask as he spied Bram and the others. He appeared to be swearing or shouting. Swimming over to Bram, he grabbed his arm. Bram shook him off. Emerens' chest heaved as he struggled to control himself. Another surge sent us all spinning. Above us, the sky had darkened. Visibility was growing worse. Emerens gestured for us to make an emergency ascent.

Raising my arm, I partially inflated my vest, leaving gravity and pressure to do the rest, my lungs expanding as I broke through the surface. It was raining on the surface, storming, dark clouds above us. Foolishly, I spat out my regulator, took a gasping breath then slipped it back in, before a big wave could come through and drag me under again.

The other divers popped up around me. We hauled ourselves up the ladder, Emerens and his team following, all of us crammed together on *Proteus'* narrow deck.

'What the hell was that?' The Divemaster yanked off his mask.

Bram shook wet hair out of his eyes. 'You said not to touch anything.'

Emerens' eyes flashed as he yanked off his mask and slapped it down onto the deck.

'I also said to stay fucking put! What were you doing?'

Bram raised his hands in surrender. 'We meant no harm. We were searching for the bell. The ship's bell. It would have given us the name, at least. We weren't planning to touch it. We were going to leave it there for you to find.'

'Bullshit.' Emerens pushed out his chest. As he raised his finger to make a point, a big wave buffeted the boat. He staggered, almost lost his footing on a coiled rope, swore under his breath. 'You wanted that bell for yourselves. Don't lie.'

'How would we have got it up?' Bram scoffed. 'Those things weigh a hundred kilos, at least.'

'How the hell should I know? Maybe you were planning to come back for it,' Emerens said. 'Maybe you were going to hide it? And all your little friends would have backed you up.'

'We'd better head back,' I shouted, as the rain became a deluge.

Bram shielded his face with his arm. 'Jo's right. We can discuss this later.'

Sem's voice rang out suddenly. 'Where's Cristof? And Nico?'

I scanned the faces on board the *Proteus*; none of them belonged to either man. My heart began to thud in my chest, booming in time with the rhythm of the waves. Cristof had been with me; I'd seen him rise, along with the others, shoot his arm straight up and head for the surface in a cloud of bubbles. No, I corrected myself. I hadn't seen him since the seal zoomed past us, heading off into the deep.

A wave of nausea lifted and fell inside me. I clutched the rail as the boat listed to the right, buffeted by another wave.

'We have to go back,' I said, hearing the frantic edge in my voice, the tendrils of panic spiralling outwards.

'We'll find them,' Emerens shouted at Bram. 'You take the others and head back to shore.'

Bram shook his head. 'They're our friends. And Cristof is eighty-three. He might be injured. I'm not going to sit around and wait for help to arrive. Sem can take Jo back on *Proteus*. When we find the others, we can come back with you.'

'You'd need to change your tank,' Emerens said. 'It's too risky. There's no time.'

Bram was already fitting on his mask and checking his computer. 'I've still got over half a tank left. More than enough.'

Emerens seemed about to argue, his expression furious. He opened his mouth, but then the boat wavered, rolled by a surging tide, and the sky rumbled overhead. 'Fine,' he said.

150

'But you stay down there for half an hour max. Then you're up. No arguments. And you stick to the area around the wreck. They can't have drifted far. We work together down there. Agreed?'

Bram didn't answer. He was already halfway to the boat's edge. Reaching the edge, he slipped in his regulator and disappeared into the water. Emerens did the same, gesturing to his team to follow.

I stared down at the place where they'd vanished, at the dark waves throwing up a salty, bitter spray.

Then Sem's hand was on my arm, forcing me back into my seat. Turning the boat around, he drove us away from the spot where the water had closed over the men's heads, leaving nothing else behind.

As soon as *Proteus'* stern bumped against the jetty, we leaped into action, running together along the jetty, shielding our heads from the drenching downpour. The clubhouse was only a short distance from the jetty, thirty metres at most but the journey through the pummelling rain felt interminably long. A few fleecy towels were hanging on the back of a chair in the reception room. Peeling off my wetsuit I wrapped one around myself, rubbing my numb arms and legs to get the feeling back, grateful for respite. Sem did the same, although he looked worried. He dragged on his warm clothes, blinking water out of his eyes.

'What can I do to help?' I said.

Sem blinked water out of his eyes. 'Nothing. Dry off and get warm. I'm going to wait for Flora's taxi to arrive.'

I watched him disappear back outside. He'd called

Cristof's wife on the way back to let her know her husband was missing. He'd informed the coastguard and the doctor, too, since Flora's family had a history of heart problems and he was worried the stress and shock caused by the accident might cause her to fall ill.

For something to do, I went into the cramped kitchen and filled the kettle. The water gurgled and spat as the heat climbed, a font of steam spiralling from the kettle's spout. I scrounged up three mugs and filled them with instant coffee and sugar. There was no milk in the fridge, only beer. I carried the mugs of black coffee to the communal table.

The door banged open and Sem appeared, supporting an elderly woman on his arm.

'You must be Jo,' she said, wiping a film of rain off her forehead and holding out her hand. Her skin was warm and slightly damp. 'Thank God you're here.'

I didn't know what to say, so I said nothing, watching in silence as Sem settled her on a plastic chair.

'Did Cristof look unwell?' Flora said, turning to him. 'When he was down there? Was he showing signs of confusion or distress?'

'Not that I noticed,' Sem said. 'I wasn't closest to him. Jo was.'

'He seemed fine,' I said. 'He was – we were watching a seal right before the storm hit. It was swimming away from us.'

Flora's forehead wrinkled in confusion.

'A bit late in the season for seals, isn't it?'

I swallowed a scalding mouthful of coffee and waited for the burning to dissipate before I replied. 'I'm not sure. Seal migrations aren't really my forte. I can promise you that your husband wasn't distressed, Flora. He was swimming and breathing normally. I didn't notice he was missing until we got to the surface. It all happened so quickly.'

I stifled a sob. Flora put her hand over mine.

'Now then,' she said. 'You listen to me. I know Cristof. He's strong. He may not look it but he's a marvel underwater. His brain is sharp, and his reflexes are just as good as when he was twenty. We've seen three children through life's ups and downs, set two of them on the straight path and buried one. Oh, don't apologise, it was years ago. A car accident. Nobody's fault, just sheer dumb luck. But my husband knows how to keep his head in a crisis. Cristof will be okay. God will watch over him. He always does. What happened today was not your fault. Storms have always hit Texel pretty bad, often without warning. I should know – I've been the president of Texel's Historical Society for the past twelve years. I was one of its founding members, along with a few other interested parties. We can trace our families all the way back to the 1600s.'

She lifted her chin, her eyes gleaming with pride.

'Our first meeting was held in the basement of Texel's lighthouse thirty years ago. There was a whole lot of stuff crammed in there needing sorting – old property deeds and ledgers, diaries and letters. My daughter has taken over most of the archiving now but back then it was just me and the others, covered in centuries-old dust, trying to preserve everything we could before it all fell apart. Cristof used to say I came home smelling like one of those mothballed coats you find at the second-hand shop. Said I set off his allergies, he'd start sneezing before I even walked through the door—'

She broke off, her thin lips trembling.

'Flora, your coffee's getting cold,' Sem said, gently. Flora glanced down at the table, blinked slowly at the porcelain mug and its liquid contents. Her fingers curled around the handle and she screwed up her face in concentration as she raised the mug to her lips, as if the effort of focusing took every bit of strength she could muster.

The front door slammed. Turning, I saw Anneke, Nico's daughter, standing in the doorway, her blue hair a wet snarl, mascara smeared down her pale cheeks.

She didn't speak, but I held out my arms and she ran towards me. A thick strand of blue hair plastered itself to my face as we embraced. I fetched her a chair and the four of us – Sem, Anneke, Flora and myself – sat in silence until the doctor and the coastguard arrived. The local doctor, a thin man in his thirties who introduced himself as Steffen, crouched in front of Flora, murmuring in a low, calm voice. She shook her head in response to his questions, her silver hair glinting under the artificial lights. The coastguard was a white-haired man in his sixties. He shook himself as he stepped inside the reception area, a spray of droplets flying off the slick surface of his yellow raincoat and spattering the floor.

'Emerens' team has radioed to say they're heading back,' he told Sem. 'There's no sign of Cristof or Nico. Visibility is gone. We're going to send a fresh team tonight, when conditions have calmed down.'

Flora cried out suddenly, the sharp, pained sound of

a wounded animal. Splinters of shock ran up my legs and arms as she started to cry.

'Call the vicar,' she gasped. 'Someone needs to let him know! What if Cristof's soul ends up in purgatory? What if he ends up in the wrong place?'

'Flora, for God's sake, calm down. They're sending out another team of divers,' Sem said. 'Flora, are you listening? They're going to find him and bring him back. He's still alive. Nico, too,' he added, glancing at Anneke who nodded, tight-faced, and hugged her elbows. When I reached out to touch her shoulder, she shrugged off my hand stiffly, angling her rigid body away.

At that moment, the door flew open and Bram appeared, flanked by Emerens and his team. The men crowded inside, water pooling on the concrete at their feet as the storm rattled the windowpanes. Flora was almost hysterical now, her chest hitching, one arm flapping loose at her side. Bram, his eyes bloodshot, started shouting at the coastguard, demanding that he be allowed to go back, even though his lips were blue from the cold.

'Can't you give her something?' I said to the doctor, as Flora's sobs echoed shrilly through the small room. 'She's highly distressed. She's going to injure herself.'

Extracting a syringe from his bag, Steffen filled it with clear liquid from a tiny bottle. I held Flora's hand while he punctured her upper arm with the tip. Flora's skin was damp and clammy, but I felt the rigid muscles in her hand start to relax as the sedative worked its magic.

She went quiet. Her head drooped, chin circling her chest.

I let out a sigh. My own body felt numb, as if the sedative had flowed through our clasped palms.

'That's better,' Steffen said. 'Are you okay, Mrs Van Tassel? Do you feel calmer?'

Flora sniffed. Raising her chin, she squinted at me.

'Brechtje?'

'No,' I said. My mouth was dry. 'It's Jo. Remember? The Australian?'

Flora shook her head. 'You're the lady from the ship.' Her mouth pinched. 'You should never have been out in such a terrible storm. It's dangerous. They should have brought you back to shore. Selfish man, your husband. All for what? A dress, a few bolts of silk.'

'She's hallucinating,' the doctor said, quietly. 'She'll settle down soon. Sem, maybe we can move her to the lounge in the display room? Let her lie down for a bit. I know it's not very comfortable, but better to keep her here than take her home where's there's nobody to look after her.'

Sem looked upset. Holding her elbow gently, he and the doctor escorted her out, taking small, careful steps so she didn't trip.

Bram and Emerens were still involved in a heated discussion about whose responsibility it was for ensuring the safety of the Texel diving crew. Anneke was biting her fingernails, the chipped polish sticking to her teeth. I leaned against the wall and closed my eyes, trying not to imagine Nico's blue and bloated face. At last I stood up, unable to sit with my thoughts any longer, sick of circling the same scorched earth.

As I reached for the handle, the door flew open and a blast of cold rain hit me right in the face.

I gasped.

Cristof and Nico stood in the doorway, Nico propping Cristof up with one arm. Nico cradled his other arm carefully to his chest. A deep red gash ran the length of his forearm, peeking through a ragged tear in the wetsuit. Both men had removed their masks, but retained their flippers. They were shivering, dripping wet, but unmistakably alive.

For a moment there was silence and then a violent cheer erupted. The two men were quickly surrounded in a sea of black neoprene as Sem and Bram and even the Navy boys formed a tight circle. The noise was deafening, a raucous cacophony of unbridled joy. Bram kept yelping swear words into the air, shaking his fist at the ceiling as if the storm was an enemy he had somehow defeated.

Sem whooped as he pulled Nico in for a hug. I saw Nico wince as Sem crushed him against his chest and, when he pulled back, his skin was even whiter than before. Steffen hurried over to treat the cut on his arm. Meanwhile Cristof seemed a little bewildered by all the attention. He blinked around at us, looking confused. It wasn't until Flora suddenly appeared, her face blotched, tears running down her cheeks, that he seemed to stir and come to life.

'We thought you were dead,' she sobbed, clutching him tightly.

'Dead?' He rubbed water out of his eyes. 'I don't think so. I mean, unless somebody's forgotten to tell me. I got carried out by the current. Lost sight of the group. I had to trust you'd all made it back. Thought the best thing to do was to let the current carry me out all the way, then circle back. Luckily, Nico spotted me getting dragged out and followed me. He didn't have to time to tell Bram or Jo. We washed up on Westerslag Beach. Sorry it took us a while to get back. The rain was coming down hard and we had to carry our gear.'

'Did you find it?' Emerens' voice cut through the celebrations. Heads turned towards him. He stood with his arms folded over his chest. Nico, now grasping a beer in his left hand, eyed him coolly.

'Find what?'

'The bell. The ship's bell you were searching for.'

Nico glanced at Bram.

'It's okay,' Bram said. 'You can tell him.'

'We found it.' Nico's gaze was challenging. 'At least, we think we did. It was intact, only partially buried.'

'We would have recorded the location,' Bram added, 'but the storm came on so quickly we didn't have a chance. The bell was extremely rusty, as you can imagine. But there was a symbol and, from the words I could make out, a name. *La Dragon.*'

There was silence, an intake of breath. Emerens cleared his throat.

'Well. I suppose we should thank you, assuming you read the name correctly. And assuming it's from the same wreck.' He shook his head. '*La Dragon.* I've never heard of a boat called *La Dragon* before. It's distinctive, isn't it? Sounds terrifying. Wouldn't want to cross paths with a ship like that on a dark night.'

'Flora might be able to check the shipping dues paid around that time,' Nico suggested. 'Her family's records go all the way back to the 1600s.'

Flora seemed to have perked up, despite the tranquilising effects of the sedative.

'I'd be more than happy to,' she said, her glassy gaze slipping between me and Emerens. 'I'm sure we can find something about our mysterious wreck, now that we have a name.'

Emerens stroked his chin. 'Well, that depends on whether we take the matter entirely out of your hands.'

The convivial mood faded. Emerens' threat wasn't idle; he did have the power to remove access to the wreck, if he wanted to. The artefacts, too. I cast a look back at the display room where the dress, the comb, the leather book and the velvet purse had been stored.

'I'm sorry,' Bram said, roughly. 'It won't happen again. We're more than happy to work with your team. We want to.'

Emerens' mouth twitched. 'Are you sure? I mean, what happened today can't happen again. Risking the lives of my men, your own boys and the lady here is inexcusable.'

Bram hung his head.

'But,' Emerens said, 'if you promise to work together with us, I'm willing to give you another chance. We have the equipment and the know-how. You have the knowledge of the island and the weather and the location of the dive sites. Those items you brought up were retrieved unlawfully, but I think we can get around it if you'll all agree to be officially certified by the Defence Diving team. If you're happy to do that, then let's see how far we can take this thing.'

Bram's head jerked up. He looked around at Sem, Cristof and Nico, who nodded. 'It's a deal.'

* * *

Liam rang early the next day. I missed his call because I was too busy nursing a wicked hangover to notice my phone flashing. After seeing Flora and Cristof safely home, Bram, Nico, Sem and I had spent the night drinking together at the local pub. The near-death experience had made us all ridiculously giddy. By the time I'd showered and dressed and corralled my thoughts enough to call Liam back, sunshine was streaming through the windows of the cottage, making rainbows on the wall.

'Yes?' I said, when he picked up on the second ring.

'Why do you sound like that?' he said. 'Like you've got a really bad cold?'

'I went diving yesterday.'

'Did you see the wreck?'

'Yes, but a storm blew up out of nowhere and we had to abort the dive. We think we found the name of the ship. It needs to be verified, though.'

I thought of Flora and her shipping records. Last night, in a drunken stupor, I'd made plans with Nico to visit the office of the historical society today. Their archives were conveniently located across the road from the bookshop Nico owned. He'd made me promise to let him know when I arrived and I guessed those plans still stood, although right now my whole body was aching and my head throbbed as if someone had set off fireworks inside my skull. I needed coffee or a nap, preferably both. But Liam was still speaking and I knew I had to concentrate so I forced my mind away from pleasing thoughts of sleep and caffeine.

'I have some news for you, too, about the leather book casing. Marien rang through with some information about

160

the heraldic crest on the cover. Seems it belonged to a family called van Shurman. Does the name ring any bells? Here's what I know so far. In the early seventeenth century, the van Shurmans were pretty prosperous. They were a brother and sister who lived together on a property outside The Hague. The patriarch of the family had died, leaving the property in the brother's care. But it was Catharina, the sister, who did most of the heavy lifting. She was an artist, a true Renaissance woman. She wrote poetry and she was a whizz with numbers, a polymath.

'My contact at Leiden sent me some letters Catharina had written to Elisabeth of Bohemia, daughter of Frederick V and Elizabeth Stuart. In one of the letters, she mentions her former lady's companion, a woman called Anna Tesseltje. Anna was leaving Holland, via the Texel anchorage, heading to the East Indies with her new employer when tragedy struck. The ship she was on reportedly sank in a colossal storm that hit the anchorage in 1651. There's a death notice. I'll send it to you. Catharina wrote it herself, so they must have been close. At least thirty people lost their lives that night. According to my contact, Anna would have been twenty at the time.'

Twenty, I thought bleakly. Too young to die.

'Catharina's an absolutely fascinating character,' Liam said. 'Could you do some searching around there on Texel, see if you find anything else connecting Catharina to the island? And it would be helpful if we could find out more about the ship.'

'It might be worth exploring Anna's connection, too. The dress could have belonged to her.'

'Hmmm. A lady's companion owning a dress that sumptuous? It seems unlikely. It appears Catharina and Anna were quite close until there was some kind of disruption. Something about the brother's death. Anna drowned before she and Catharina had a chance to speak again, and Catharina never took on another companion.'

'Oh, that's so sad,' I said. I felt bad for Catharina. All that tragedy taking place over a couple of years under her watch. It must have felt like one long, interminable winter.

Liam sniffed dismissively. To him, these long-dead people were mere abstractions.

'How's the chemical analysis of the gown going? Any updates?' I asked.

'It's only been a day so I'll need a little more time to analyse the samples I've taken. I should have the results ready by tomorrow though, are you still planning to come over? I could really use the help. The lab has given me an assistant, but she's not anywhere near fast enough and she refuses to get my lunch for me.'

I rolled my eyes. Trust Liam to complain about conditions other researchers would kill for. When we'd collaborated on the tapestries and nightgowns project, he'd always expected me to pick up coffee and pastries on my way to our shared office. It was only a small thing but the presumption – that his time, and therefore his research, was more important – got on my nerves. When I'd eventually confronted him about it, he'd smirked and adopted a condescending tone.

'It's no big deal, Jo. You were going anyway, weren't you? I'll grab the coffee tomorrow, if it's such an issue.'

I'd forgotten all about the incident until now, how small it had made me feel, how all my hard-won degrees and scholarships and professional successes seemed somehow tarnished, the tired keepsakes of a second-rate career climber.

'This is the twenty-first century, Liam. Get your own damn lunch.'

I hung up before he could say another word.

Gerrit drove me to Nico's bookshop which occupied the ground floor of a neat two-storey building on the main drag in Den Burg. Peering at the display in the front window was like stepping back into my past. Wooden bookshelves lined with paperbacks and trinkets crowded a velvet armchair on which perched a stuffed parrot, its iridescent plumage shining under a film of dust. The display stirred in me a fleeting sense of recognition. My grandfather, a fisherman from Oosterend, had once had a study that was very similar. He'd saved enough money in his thirties to buy a fleet of drifters which he rented to local herring catchers, leading to a significant profit. After he died, his house was sold to a developer and his possessions divided between relatives and friends. I never learned what became of the treasures he'd amassed during his lifetime. In my mind, that study still existed somewhere, untouchable, looking just the way it had when I'd visited with my parents, trailing my fingers along a conch shell's spine, inhaling the scent of dried roses from a Delftware vase.

'Good luck, today,' Gerrit said, leaning out of the open car window. 'I hope you find what you're looking for.'

'Thanks,' I said. He was wearing his uniform – a blue

fleecy jacket embroidered with the sanctuary's insignia and waterproof pants. I was grateful to him for giving me a lift – and even more grateful for the strong takeaway coffee he'd bought me on the way – but I was glad to be out of the car. Although recently washed, his clothes still reeked of fish. 'Say hello to the seals for me.'

'They're still waiting for you to come and meet them properly,' he said.

I promised to visit soon. Gerrit pouted, pretending to be disappointed, then gave a friendly wave and drove off.

Nico was with a client when I stepped inside the shop. Catching my eye, he indicated I should look around while I waited. The books were mostly novels and travel guides, but there was a small corner dedicated to Dutch history. I picked up a book of seventeenth-century emblems, reprinted a few years earlier by an obscure Antwerp publishing house. The book's pages brimmed with illustrations of flowers and animals inspired by the works of Ovid and Petrarch, as well as popular Greek and Roman iconography. I knew from my studies that the genre had been enormously successful during its time, reinforcing the moralistic teachings of the Church while offering the writers and engravers who created them the opportunity to elevate themselves from working-class artists to card-carrying members of the literary elite. I lingered over an image of Cupid depicted as a cooper bent over an ale barrel – it wasn't love that made the world go around, but the powerful Dutch coopers' guilds.

I kept reading. Another scene lifted from a collection by Jacob Cats, one of the leading poets of the time, showed a middle-aged peasant couple strolling along a promenade, the woman clutching a string of peeled onions – a symbol of matrimonial love and constancy in hard times. How times had changed! Modern audiences would have a hard time reconciling the symbol of common onions with spousal devotion after years of being fed much more romantic images of roses, doves and swans. Led by Cats, emblems had shifted their focus from the idea of courtly love to middle class morality. Cats had, in his own words, finished Cupid off, replacing him with a kind of aspirational domesticity praised across the Republic by good Dutch housewives and their husbands. His moralising lingered well into the modern era. Look at the way my parents had behaved.

As I closed the book and replaced it on the shelf, I saw Anneke stride past, her blue hair gathered in a high ponytail, exposing pale blonde wisps at the nape of her neck.

I called out. Her face changed as she recognised me, softening in surprise before shifting into an alert wariness.

I greeted her brightly. 'Where are you off to?'

She frowned. 'Nowhere.'

Her hostility surprised me. 'I was just wondering. I remember you saying something last night about seeing a movie on the mainland with a friend.'

She folded her arms and screwed up her nose. 'I would never have said that.'

We regarded each other for a long moment. 'I'm sorry. I must have misheard,' I said, at last.

She nodded. I watched her turn away and head for the door, slamming it shut in her wake, making the glass rattle in the timber panes. I hadn't misheard, of course.

Anneke had waited until Bram and the others were safely engrossed in a game of darts before sliding into my booth where she peppered me with questions about my work – what were my favourite museum collections? Where had I trained and with whom? To my surprise, I enjoyed her company. She was charming and sweet, her brittle exterior masking an intense curiosity about the world of textiles and clothing. We were talking about natural methods for creating peace silk when, quite unexpectedly, the conversation turned to her mother.

Tess had taught her how to knit at five, sew at seven and bought Anneke her first sewing machine when she turned twelve. Anneke had helped her put together the costumes for the local community theatre group, copying old designs from library textbooks and vintage patterns sourced from all over the world. The patterns arrived in envelopes papered with interesting foreign stamps that Nico showed her how to steam off and stick in the scrapbook Tess kept where she recorded every blouse, skirt and pair of trousers she'd ever made. Tess had taken all the vintage patterns with her when she moved away but left the scrapbook behind. Anneke ordered another spider and leaned back in the booth, sucking up the dregs of her first one through a paper straw, swinging her legs so the toes of her combat boots scuffed the sticky floor.

'What about your dad?' I said. 'Does he like sewing?'

She snorted. 'He likes books and diving. He can't sew a button or hem a sleeve to save his life.'

'Maybe you could teach him?'

She offered me a crooked smile.

'I used to think my parents had a perfect marriage,' she said, leaning forward suddenly, wiping the back of her hand along her lips, pink-stained from all the creaming soda. 'Then one night they had this really big fight. They were screaming at each other, like really loud, like they just didn't care who heard them. That was when I knew all the Disney stuff they feed you is utter bullshit. There's no fairytale prince, no happy ending. Princesses have to rescue themselves and they do it alone. That's why I'm moving away as soon as I turn eighteen. As soon as I finish high school in three years, I'm going to straight to Antwerp to find my mum.'

She glared at me fiercely, challenging me to disagree.

'You'll need some funds in Antwerp,' I said, after a pause. 'I hear it's pretty expensive now, renting on your own. You'll need a job and to get one, you'll need some decent experience. Maybe you could come and work for me for a little while after school? It depends where the dress ends up, of course. If it does end up in an exhibition here, perhaps you could help out some afternoons. I need an assistant. It would be great to have someone to look after all my social media accounts and help out with the exhibition. And I'm hoping to publish a book soon, so there's the potential for some marketing and administration experience. Working for me, you'd at least be able to save enough for a ticket and your accommodation while you search for her.'

She hesitated, uncertain whether to trust me.

'Okay,' she'd said at last.

* * *

The bell on the door chimed as Nico's customer left.

He came over to greet me, kissing my cheeks as if we hadn't seen each other less than twenty-four hours earlier.

'You talked to Anneke,' he said.

'I don't know if talked is the right description. She barely said two words to me. I hope it wasn't something I said last night.'

'It wasn't.' He grimaced. 'We got a letter this morning from Anneke's grandparents. Anneke insisted on reading it. Her grandparents don't know where her mother is. She's taken off again and didn't bother to leave a forwarding address. It's very hard on them and Anneke, of course. She's angry with me, she thinks I should just drop everything and take her to Antwerp so she can see her mother. Obviously, that's impossible. I know she just needs some time to work through it. She was so happy when I drove her home from the pub last night. I haven't seen her in such a good mood for a while. It's just a shame this news had to go and spoil it all. Anyway,' he shook himself. 'Enough of my problems. Should we head on over to the historical society? I think Flora and Cristof's daughter is expecting us. Her name is Olivia.'

I followed him out onto the footpath and across the street to a three-storey, whitewashed building with high arched windows.

'It used to be a church,' Nico explained, holding open the door. 'A big storm blew through and gutted it and nobody had the funds to fix it up properly so the society bought it for their headquarters.'

The church's religious iconography had been stripped

back and the walls painted a deep navy. Clear glass cabinets arranged around the room held framed photographs, old shipping ledgers and laminated letters from soldiers stationed on the mainland during the Second World War. I was studying an intricately carved wooden ship inside a glass bottle when a woman's voice called out from downstairs. Olivia appeared moments later. A slim woman in her late forties, her hands were encased in white gloves and she was wearing a woollen cardigan secured by giant tortoiseshell buttons.

'It's so cold down there,' she said, peeling off a glove to shake my hand. 'We keep the basement cool so the papers don't go mouldy. A man came out from Leiden University last year – a professor, would you believe. He gave a presentation to the society and showed us how to preserve things properly. I had to convince the other board members to let me invest in an industrial humidifier. It was expensive, but Professor Eckert says it will be worth it in the long run.'

I was impressed and told her so. Most historical societies didn't understand the value of ensuring documents and artefacts were kept in a temperature-controlled environment. I wished Bram had been there for Professor Eckert's presentation, although maybe it wouldn't have made any difference. The divers had their own way of doing things.

Olivia must have read my mind for she grasped my arm suddenly, her gaze flicking between Nico and myself.

'I heard about the dress,' she whispered loudly. 'Mum and Dad told me last night. I think they were both a bit shaken by what happened. Thank God everyone got back safely. I can't believe it, though. A dress that old being found on our island? It must have belonged to one of the ladies-in-waiting who sailed with Queen Henrietta Maria from England, hoping to pawn the family jewels and save King Charles I's neck. One of her baggage ships went down nearby, you know. All the crew escaped, but the women's clothes were lost. We have a copy of a letter she sent her daughter; the original is at the university in Leiden. Imagine if we could confirm that the dress belonged to one of her attendants.'

Her eyes danced with possibilities. I glanced at Nico who shrugged as if to confirm that it was inevitable that the news would leak into the community sooner or later. At least we had the Defence divers on our side now.

'We think we know the name of the ship already,' I said. 'It was called *La Dragon*. I was hoping you might have a record of it – judging by the style of the dress and the wreck's position, it probably sank sometime between 1630 and 1660. The wreck you're referring to, the one that belonged to Queen Henrietta's envoy, is pretty well documented so I doubt the current could have shifted the dress and the other artefacts so far east. Bram says they were fastened quite securely to the deck when they were found. My colleague, Liam, who's doing some forensic work on the dress, has a theory that it might have belonged to an artist called Catharina van Shurman. Her former companion – a woman called Anna Tesseltje – was travelling to the East Indies with her new mistress.' I paused to allow a truck to rumble past on the street, the noisy bleating of sheep competing with the crunch of gears. 'Anna seems to have taken the dress along with her, as well as a book bearing the van Shurmans' heraldic crest. Possibly, they were given to her by Catharina – the two women were quite close. Your mother mentioned yesterday that some of the shipping ledgers date back to the mid-1600s. If I could find out a little more about *La Dragon* – who owned it, where it was headed, who was on board at the time it sank – it might help us pin down the time period and maybe even illuminate some hidden aspect of the island's history. Can you think of a connection between Texel and Catharina van Shurman?'

Olivia frowned. 'Not off the top of my head, no. But that isn't to say one doesn't exist. Plenty of artists came to Texel over the years. There's a very famous painting hanging in the Rijksmuseum depicting the great Christmas disaster of 1630 when a storm sank over a hundred ships in one night. I can show you a reproduction of it later. We have one hanging in the gallery upstairs. But let's look at the shipping records first.'

We followed her down into the basement. It was cold, as she'd warned, and a large portable humidifier hummed quietly in the corner, releasing a fine mist into the atmosphere through plastic vents to counteract the effects of potentially document-destroying heat. Dozens of archive boxes lined the metal shelves, organised by year and divided into categories.

'We've digitised some of our earliest records,' she told us, a trace of pride in her voice. 'They were so fragile they were in danger of crumbling into nothing. It's probably best if we search the database for the shipping records that correspond to the time you're looking for, rather than disturbing the originals.'

She led us over to a computer and flicked on the monitor. I watched her scroll through a long file of scanned documents.

'The first bailiff on Texel, Ambrosius Baas, kept quite haphazard records, unfortunately. There are lots of holes in his shipping accounts. He was related to Jan Huydecoper, one of the first mayors of Amsterdam and he accepted the post here thinking it would bring him a steady income and a good deal of respect. But his style of governing didn't suit the townspeople. He spent so much time away from the island he was eventually discharged of his duties altogether. After his disastrous turn as bailiff, the governors decided to split the record-keeping between the postmaster, the *dijkgraaf*, in charge of building and maintaining the island's dykes, and the *wegermaster*, who ensured that goods brought onto the island were weighed and taxed. The responsibility for keeping the shipping ledgers up to date was given to the shipping master and his clerks. That's helpful. It means we can narrow down the lists, rather than wading through all the cargo and passenger records. Give me a minute.'

We wandered the shelves while Olivia searched the database. Peering into open boxes, I saw stacks of old newspapers and local community magazines. The covers of the magazines had faded, their crisp edges curling like brittle leaves. It occurred to me that the story of my parents' accident was probably hidden inside one of those magazines. It might even have been a cover story. Within a few hours of the police coming to the house to tell me, a flock of journalists from the mainland had descended on our front lawn to shout questions and track my every movement. Their lenses captured things I never even noticed about myself – the way I styled my blonde hair, for instance, parted dead centre like Aimee Mann, a singer I loved for her daring fashion choices. It was strange to find myself the sudden focus of intense public scrutiny. I was still a child, I should have been grieving; instead, I poured all my energies into coming up with increasingly wild fashion combinations, daubing on my mother's electric-blue eyeshadow, raiding her closet for the faux-fur vests and handmade floral suits that retained the scent of her sweat and perfume.

Bram's parents had tried to shield me, rushing me past the cameras and hustling me into their car so they could drive me to the police station in Den Helder on the mainland where a coronial inquiry had been set up to investigate the circumstances leading to my parents' tragic deaths. They didn't understand that the adrenaline rush of dressing up and being noticed after a lifetime of parental rejection was what got me out of bed in the morning. It was a bizarre reaction, a memory I'd buried deep inside myself until this moment, too ashamed or confused about what it all meant to unpack it properly. The phase had lasted less than a week, just long enough for media interest to wane and for Marieke to reach the island and start taking care of me. Although exhausted after crossing six time zones, she quickly dispensed with any remaining reporters and ruthlessly excised my parents' effects. The morning before our departure for Australia, I woke to find their wardrobes stripped bare. Marieke had set aside anything valuable – my mother's wedding ring, my father's gold tie pin – but she'd thrown out all their clothes. Even their undergarments weren't spared. Everything they'd ever worn was gone, destined for landfill. It was as if they'd never existed.

Olivia called us over.

'*La Dragon*. Built in an Amsterdam shipyard in 1649 and purchased in 1650 by one Maarten Horst, a senior officer with the VOC – the Dutch East India Company. Maarten did very well for himself, by the sounds of it. Worked his way up the ranks, accumulating wealth and status until he was the Governor's right-hand man. It probably helped that he had a good deal of money to start with. His family owned a number of plantations in Sumatra. Like many others, their wealth was built on the slave trade – something a lot of contemporary audiences seem to forget. The Golden Age wasn't very golden for those who weren't colonialist traders or settlers. All this—' she swept her hand around the archive, 'all our modern conveniences, all our little luxuries have been paid for by the brutal labour of countless slaves. How do we reconcile that? How can we make reparations for something that is so inconceivably cruel and heartless that it's almost impossible to read about without weeping? People torn away from their families, locked up like cattle, transported to a place so far from home they couldn't hear the voices of their gods and ancestors for all the noise?'

'Australians face the same dilemma,' I said. 'It's almost a collective amnesia. Out of sight, out of mind. And then you read something that brings it all back – the destruction of a sacred Indigenous rock formation by a mining company, for example. Tens of thousands of years of culture blown up in one moment. And, for a while, everyone's pissed off because this isn't new. This erasure has actually been going on for centuries. It's not just the physical eradication of culture, but the intangible stuff: language, textiles, stories passed down, generation after generation. But time marches on. Companies perform public atonement, removing board members, pay fines, hope everyone will forget again. And they do. The cycle never ends. One of the reasons I chose to pursue dress history was because I wanted to bear witness to the creation of textiles that simply won't be around in fifty years. The garments deserve better and so do the people who wore them.'

Olivia stared at me a moment longer, nodding in agreement. When she turned back to the computer screen, she seemed to sit up straighter, more determined than ever to help. I felt as if I'd passed a test.

'There's a record here of *La Dragon*'s interactions on Texel. She made three journeys before that final, fatal berthing. Goods traded most often were cinnamon, mace, linen, palmwood, sugar and weapons.'

'Weapons?' asked Nico.

'Machetes,' Olivia clarified. 'They were used for cutting paths through the jungles in the colonies. The passengers' log for the last journey shows mostly crew. VOC *fluyts* didn't generally transport passengers unless they were important guests, like senior officers or the Governor and his family. I don't see any Catharina listed, but there's a Blanche Horst here. She was Maarten's wife. There's a note from her husband, instructing the crew to give Blanche and her companion their own private cabin. He refers to her companion as "Anna Tesseltjeruineren". Isn't that an odd name? Tesseltjeruineren. Ruin on Texel! Reminds me of those names the Puritans gave their children during the Restoration. Some of them were so cruel. "Helpless". "Credence". "Fear-of-Almighty-God". It's a wonder poor Anna didn't change it.'

Olivia pushed her glasses up her nose. 'There's some additional correspondence regarding the loss of the ship. The VOC weren't happy with Maarten when they learned that he wasn't with the ship when it went down. He was on the mainland in Den Hoorn overseeing some business on behalf of the Governor when it sank. According to his account, he planned to join *La Dragon* before it sailed, but the storm hit so quickly he couldn't reach Texel harbour in time. All the crew drowned, along with Blanche and Anna. The cargo couldn't be retrieved. What a terrible loss. But there were many similar tragedies in the area, unfortunately.' She clicked open a new document. 'Looks like Maarten lived a few years longer. He remarried and died in 1656 on one of the Javanese plantations his family owned. And according to his death notice, he never returned to Holland.'

'Oh,' I said, my spirits sinking. Poor Anna. She'd probably assumed she was safe with the Horsts. Instead, her decision to leave Catharina had led to her death.

Perhaps Olivia was thinking the same thing because she was quiet for a long time. Eventually, she swivelled around in her chair.

'I seem to recall a mention of Maarten Horst that may

or may not be relevant to your interests. It's upstairs. There are some exquisite old quilts up there. Why don't you take a look while I check some more records?'

'I might go back to the store,' Nico said, touching my arm. 'I don't like leaving it unattended for too long. You'll be fine with Olivia.'

The quilts in the display case upstairs were indeed beautiful, the intricate floral patterns suggestive of chintz palampore designs, crafted in eighteenth-century India and brought to the island by visiting merchants. My hand itched to reach through the glass and stroke the delicate fabric, but of course, I made no such transgressions.

'This is a reproduction of the painting I was telling you about.' Olivia beckoned me over to a large oil painting of a storm-tossed ship. Towering waves crested over the ship's bowsprit and its torn sails fluttered in the wind like shredded silk. The vessel had clearly foundered and the storm front had swept it onto a cluster of jagged rocks. The crew, imperilled, could do nothing but pray.

'It was painted in the seventeenth century by a local artist Aelbert Van Loo who went on to train under Pieter de Molijn,' Olivia said. 'He painted this extraordinary seascape when he was only seventeen. We're quite proud of the association. We'd much prefer to have the original, of course, but the Rijksmuseum acquired it years ago through a private sale so we have no legal claim.'

She grasped my arm suddenly.

'Forgive me for being so forward, Ms Baaker, but I must ask you for a favour on behalf of my mother and the other society members. We understand the political delicacy surrounding the dress and the unusual circumstances of its retrieval. We don't have the resources to preserve something so valuable for any extended length of time. It makes sense that the collection should be taken to the mainland for observation and restoration. But we were hoping you might be able to convince the Noord-Holland government to allow us to exhibit them here on Texel for a few weeks. We've already discussed it this morning over video phone. Eva van der Berg, the matriarch of one of Texel's oldest families, passed away last year and bequeathed a significant amount of money to the historical society for the preservation of local Texel culture. Her directives were a little vague so there's been some heated debate over the dispersal of the funds but everyone on the committee agreed that this is exactly what Eva would have wanted. She was a passionate woman and she would have loved everyone to see the dress for themselves. If everything goes to plan, we'd want you to do the conservation side of it, of course. We could host the exhibition here, in this room; it would only take us a month or so to move everything and install the proper equipment. Please consider it. It would mean so much to the community. We're proud of our heritage, and the presence of something so precious and unusual would strengthen our connection to the past and to each other. You understand, being an old Texeller yourself.'

Her gaze was so intense, I found it difficult to look away. That old Texel pride. I knew it well, or used to. Spending the past week in the company of Bram and his friends had brought it all back in vivid technicolour. Even Marieke possessed that streak of stubbornness, although Australia had replaced Texel in her affections. Marieke maintained she'd thrown away my parents' belongings without consulting me first because she hadn't wanted anyone going through their things. She was worried one of the reporters would find something incriminating, some gossip that could be used against them, tarnishing their memory. I'd accepted her reasons at the time, but now I found myself wondering about my childhood home, what had become of it, whether the wallpaper in my old bedroom was still there, and remembering the loose floorboard under my bed where I'd hidden a packet of cigarettes and a gemstone bracelet I'd stolen from the pharmacy, but hadn't had the guts to wear. Those memories were stronger now that I was back, as if I'd upended a puzzle inside my head and each turn revealed another piece of myself.

I promised Olivia that Liam and I would speak to the Noord-Holland government and try to ensure the dress was returned. She led me over to one last glass cabinet at the back of the room, unlocked the door and eased out a small leather-bound book.

'This is a transcription of a journal kept by one of my ancestors. Her name was Brechtje de Jong. She was a weather enthusiast, recorded every Texel storm, saw signs and symbols in the clouds. She married the harbour master in 1682. Her husband, Arend de Jong, was born here. He came from a long line of harbour masters. I'm guessing Mum might have mentioned that a couple of hundred times. Her long-term memory is good, but she forgets small details. Hopefully it doesn't get any worse.'

Olivia paused to scan a journal entry then nodded to herself and held it out for my inspection.

'This is what I was looking for. I knew the name sounded familiar.'

I looked down at the entry dated 23 December 1685.

Close air at dawn and a rank smell on the beach like rotting seal meat. A bloody circle rings the full moon. A storm is brewing, the clouds are thick serpents eating their own tails. As I walk along the seawall, a flock of crows takes flight, their cries like Dutch tears, clear as glass. Maarten Horst bears down on us from the east, eating the horizon. I run along the docks, shouting. Hoist the sails! Secure the cargo! See, how swiftly Great Maarten comes? I reach the cottage with seconds to spare and fling myself into the bed box while Maarten hammers the windows with windy fists and does his best to extinguish the fire, pouring water down the chimney into the sizzling grate. Knowing how I hate storms, Wolfert comes to comfort me, settling his paws over my whale-belly, protecting the precious life within. I sense my mother watching over us. As Maarten howls outside, I crawl to my knees to pray. Mother, grant me safe delivery. Give us Pure skies again and a Crispijn morning. I will search the Heavens for your sign, the Star of Utrecht, to guide us safely home.

The entry ended there. I looked up at Olivia.

'Maarten Horst? She named a storm after him?'

'She was an odd creature,' Olivia said. 'Some people thought she was touched in the head. Brechtje used to tell people her mother nearly drowned while she was pregnant with her and that the near-death experience had changed her somehow, as if the water got in and altered her very constitution. Brechtje had a lot of strange notions. We've

180

no record of her mother's name, but we know that she grew up in an orphanage on the island. She was something of a beauty. That entry was written right before her daughter was born on Christmas Eve. Brechtje called her Annemie. It means "bitter grace"'.

'Brechtje can't have known Maarten personally,' I said, mentally calculating the years between them. 'Why did she choose him? What was the significance?'

Olivia shrugged. 'Perhaps she learned about him from a village elder? Her journal entries vary wildly. Sometimes, her observations are clear, other times they're riddles. You could spend half your life trying to puzzle out the meaning. Believe me, I've tried.'

Placing the diary back inside the cabinet, Olivia showed me downstairs. As we said our goodbyes, she repeated her desire for the dress to be exhibited in Texel, promising in return to let me know if she found out anything more about Maarten Horst and his connection with Catharina van Shurman.

'Brechtje sounds like quite the eccentric,' Nico said. He stirred his coffee slowly, his spoon scraping against the sugary sediment in the cup. Striped tulips shivered in bright planter boxes outside the window of the café where we'd retired after my meeting with Olivia to discuss the morning's revelations.

'There's been quite a few on Texel. Relatives bring their diaries and journals to the bookshop, hoping I might know someone on the mainland who'd be interested in publishing them. It's a bit awkward having to explain that nobody outside the island is very interested in their observations. I usually pass them over to Flora. Better their reflections end up in a display at the historical society than languishing in a dusty attic somewhere.'

'Brechtje reminds me of Marieke,' I said. 'My aunt back in Sydney. She can be so stubborn and overprotective, but she has a streak of crazy in her. It drives me nuts living with her. I'm always worried I'll come home and find she's changed the locks on me.'

'Tess, too.' Nico set down his spoon and frowned into his cup. 'She was increasingly paranoid before she started on antidepressants. It used to frighten me, to be honest. She settled down eventually, but it's been a journey. I wish Anneke felt comfortable talking about it with me. She flat out refuses to discuss it. Her recollections of Tess don't seem to correlate with mine at all.'

'I've asked Anneke to work with me,' I said. 'She seemed keen last night when I suggested she could come and do some work experience, once she finishes high school in a few years. Of course, that was twelve hours ago and she gave me the cold shoulder this morning so maybe she's had a change of heart.'

Nico's face relaxed. 'It would be great, if you could. A good distraction from all the Tess stuff.'

I looked across the café at the fire flickering in the grate. Soon it would be too cold for diving, too cold for anything but staying indoors curled up in front of the fire with a good book. I thought of Brechtje and her fear of storms. The poor woman must have suffered often, living on one of the most storm-prone islands in the northern hemisphere. I wondered about her reference to Maarten Horst. Had they been related? Had Horst's death notice been wrong?

Perhaps he'd made an undocumented trip back to the island before he passed away in Sumatra. Maybe they'd met. An image popped into my head of a girl in an orphan's smock leaping across the dunes, running down to the marina to greet a tall figure wearing the VOC's distinctive red livery. But the scenario felt unstable. Brechtje had not been fond of Maarten, I theorised – she'd been afraid of him, so afraid she had named a storm front after him. What had their relationship been? And how did Catharina's dress link them?

7

Anna

DESCENDING THE STAIRCASE THE MORNING AFTER her arrival, Anna hears a man's voice coming from the dining room. Two faces turn as she enters — one her mistress's, the other its mirror, except for the nose which is slightly humped, as if it was once broken and healed badly. They break apart as she approaches, affecting an air of breezy nonchalance which doesn't quite dispel the conspiratorial atmosphere preceding Anna's arrival. Anna guesses she has been the subject of their conversation. She decides to pretend she has not noticed.

'*Goedemorgen*,' she mutters, moving towards the table where an abundant breakfast has been arranged, a loaf of bread resting beside a platter of shimmering haddock, another platter piled high with wedges of cheese and dried fruit. A thick Bible embossed with the van Shurmans' family crest rests on the table in front of Crispijn's setting. Anna slips into her own chair and lowers her head, waiting for grace to begin.

'Crispijn, this is my new companion, Anna Tesseltje,' Catharina says, when Crispijn has finished praying aloud. 'Anna, my brother Crispijn. My younger brother,' she adds.

'A difference of less than a minute,' Crispijn says drily. 'I hardly think it counts.'

He has Catharina's strong jaw and brown eyes, so dark as to be almost black, and thick copper hair which falls in loose waves around his shoulders. Anna's gaze travels along the tablecloth to his hands. Compared to Catharina's and her own, his are virtually unmarked. They are smooth and alabaster pale, as if carved from a stone slab, and clearly belong to a gentleman of leisure whose entire existence involves being waited on. For some reason, their purity bothers her. Even her father's hands were rougher, marred by his early merchant days, the calluses and blackened nailbeds standing testament to his daily inspection of goods in the company warehouse. The van Shurmans' wealth, by contrast, seems somehow ill-gotten, not the result of hard labour, but something far uglier – idleness, perhaps. An inheritance that has not been earned. Anna has heard tales about the glaring pretensions of Catholic families, their rooms shamelessly papered with tooled leather and gold leaf, their gardens overflowing with expensive water features and marble statues. But the van Shurmans are devoted Protestants. Perhaps this is simply how people live who have amassed so much wealth it can't be spent any faster.

Her father often railed against such excess. If money was the root of all evil, he used to say, then idleness and the worship of Papist idolatry were its bedfellows. Anna's family had been rich, but not this rich. They didn't eat to indulgence as though food was going out of fashion. The only luxuries Lodewijk permitted in their house on the Herengracht were clothes and books. Anna was always welcome to browse the volumes in Lodewijk's study. He might have cursed her by giving her a name nobody could forget, but he was generous where learning was concerned. Perhaps he felt guilty for saddling her with the lack of a future or perhaps it was simply the absence of any son to converse with that endeared Anna to him and helped him overlook any misgivings he might have had about women's education. In any case, she found herself returning often to the writings of Virgil and Ovid housed in the leather-bound volumes in his study. The memory of those books in their familiar bindings is both a balm to her now and a torment. She remembers once stumbling on a Dutch translation of Seneca's philosophies. That book, astonishingly, had been written by a Danish noblewoman, Birgitte Thott. There was a picture of the author in the frontispiece wearing a wimple and looking stern, although there was something about the way her almond-shaped eyes tilted at the corners that suggested to Anna a latent sense of humour. Women can be both successful and self-sufficient, her expression seemed to say. Anything was possible. Anna nursed this thought to herself for years. Now she thinks: what was all that learning actually good for? How did reading all those books in her father's study serve her in the laundering of other people's linens? How will it help her survive?

As if sensing her sour mood, Crispijn catches her eye and smiles. 'How was your journey?'

Anna swallows a forkful of herring. 'Good, sir, thank you, although the roads are bad this time of year. They had to call in the icebreaker twice before we left, the frost spread so fast. It has a habit of creeping back just when you think the path is clear.'

He nods. 'It's worse at sea, not that I've been recently.

Out there the pack ice makes it hard for the whalers to hunt. It crushes the ships and screens the beasts so they cannot be seen from the surface. Many sailors have already drowned this season, thanks to this brutal weather. I suppose we should consider ourselves lucky the cold is merely an inconvenience for us, not a matter of life and death.'

Anna drops her eyes to her plate, the mention of drowned sailors settling like a lead bar in her stomach.

'My brother has been travelling around the country this past week securing commissions.' Catharina levers a piece of fish onto her spotless plate, her knife gleaming in the wintry light. 'I cannot be trusted to see to my own affairs. I am smart enough, it seems, to wield a paintbrush, but not smart enough to negotiate portrait commissions with worldly guildsmen. So Crispijn does it for me.'

'Do you paint, too?' Anna asks him.

Crispijn laughs, a pleasant, musical sound that lightens the atmosphere in the room and calms her nerves. Even Catharina smiles, as if she finds the idea of her brother daubing paint onto a canvas highly amusing. Anna can't remember the last time she laughed like that, so careless and free. It must have been six months ago when she and Lijsbeth were preparing a water bath for some stained collars and a frog jumped out of the tub, startling them, causing Lijsbeth to flee the room. Her sister refused to return until the creature was gone. Shaking with laughter, Anna had scooped the tiny, soapy body up and carried it outside, its tiny heart beating erratically against her slippery palm.

'Alas, no.' Crispijn drags his knife through his food, dividing the scrambled mess of fish and breadcrumbs on his plate. 'I have no artistic talent. Thankfully, Catharina has enough for us both. I inherited our father's business sense. It comes in useful, at times. For example –' He sets down his knife and extracts a small leather journal from his pocket. 'On my travels, I secured the following commissions, to be completed within the next three months: The wife of a silk merchant in Groen has recently given birth to her first child – a son. She would like you to paint the infant in a similar style to Anthony van Dyck's portrait of the young Stadholder. Lady van der Helst of Delft wants another portrait with her parrots. She owns a good many parrots, so I think it best we travel to her estate or else we risk turning this house into a menagerie. Lastly, Jacob Huydecoper wants a painting he can display in his office. He felt the last one was not quite grand or impressive enough and has requested this one be . . . life-size. He's willing to come to us. I told him I would draw up the contract and send him word when the roads were open again for easy travel.'

A frosty silence greets these pronouncements. Crispijn places the notebook down, picks up his fork and begins to eat, his gaze fixed determinedly on his plate. The bread on Anna's tongue forms a hard, indigestible lump. Forcing herself to swallow, she glances at Catharina who sags low in her chair, as if the air is laden with a thick choking smog she is trying to avoid inhaling.

'I told you I would not be ready to paint anything new until summer,' she mutters.

Crispijn, reluctantly it seems, looks up. 'I know. But if we wait for summer, all the best commissions will be gone. We must seize the opportunities when they present themselves. Besides, you have a companion now. Someone to entertain you while you work, to help you and boost your spirits.' Turning to Anna, he says, 'Master de Witt tells me you're quite the reader, Miss Tesseltje. You're welcome to borrow any of the books in my study – it's the one opposite the parlour, behind the door covered in copper stars. Catharina is often rummaging through the trunks for new volumes. I've been meaning to have more shelves built, but I'm yet to find time. When it grows warmer, there will be entertainments, masques and ballets, musical soirees. You and Catharina can go together. And you'll enjoy walking the grounds of Sterrenwijck. I promise there is more to the place than you've seen so far. We had Father's old barren orchards torn up a few years ago and replanted with new fruit trees and fragrant roses. There's a ruined temple on the hill overlooking the river which is worth exploring – it dates all the way back to 1648.'

His mood is so jovial, Anna can't help grinning in return.

Catharina snaps suddenly. 'I don't need a companion,' she says, thumping her fist on the table. 'I don't need anyone else. Don't you understand? Without Griet, there is no point. We have a studio full of paintings. You were supposed to focus your energies on finding homes for them. How many of those did you sell?'

Anna senses the mood has turned. Crispijn closes his eyes. When he opens them again, she notices how long his lashes are, darkly fanned against his cheeks, as soft and delicate as a baby rabbit's.

'You must understand,' he says, quietly. 'People want

certainty. With the position of Stadholder abolished, they want to see themselves reflected in their paintings, just as they are. They don't want elaborate costumes and mythical allegory. Even with the endorsement of the painters' guild, it's a difficult time to sell your kind of art.'

Catharina gapes. '*My* kind of art?'

'Yes,' says her brother, and Anna hears the frustration creeping in, although he does his best to remain calm. 'The kind of art that pleases you alone. The kind of art you are *inspired* to create, which is not always compatible with what a buyer wants. A painting of Icarus sailing through the sky on wax wings? A fortune teller on horseback, predicting the future on a Frisian beach? Sister, I cannot sell these. You expect too much of me.'

'You could sell them,' Catharina counters. 'If I were a man.'

'But you aren't.' Crispijn adopts an air of negotiation. Lacing his fingers together on the tablecloth, he sits forward, his tunic straining across his chest. 'Take my advice and accept the commissions. Just try. They're saying this winter will be a long one and bitterly cold. We should take the opportunities given to us by God to—'

He falls silent as Catharina holds up a hand. She looks weary, like she did when Anna left her last night in the parlour, dark shadows circling her eyes.

'Spare me,' she says. 'You could never understand. You think art is only something to be bought and sold. You see my talent as a means to an end. But when I see a vision in my mind's eye, it's as if God has directed me. I must paint it. It is a compulsion, it cannot be tamed or rationalised. A man without money is like a ship without sails, isn't that right? And what would you be, Crispijn van Shurman, without all your fancy clothes and fine horses and your pendulums and telescopes. You would be nothing.' She pauses to draw breath. 'I do not want to paint a portrait of another rich burgher from Antwerp. I cannot do it. I will not.'

Her impassioned refusal bounces off the walls. Anna looks from sister to brother, holding her breath and wishing she had the power to make herself invisible so she could slink from the room and take refuge in the kitchen, leaving the siblings to their tempest. Crispijn's expression reflects Catharina's resolve. His jaw is tight, his brow creased with fine lines that make him look older, more like the old gentleman whose portrait hangs in the entrance hall. Anna wonders if this is how the twins always behave or if such stand-offs are rare, like wild storms glimpsed off the coast that blow themselves out before they reach the shore. She's always assumed that her deference to Lijsbeth was based on their personalities, but perhaps age was a factor, as Lijsbeth once suggested. If only a minute's difference exists between the birth of these siblings, which twin has authority over the other? Can they ever truly be equals or will one always trail behind?

Crispijn dabs his cheek with his napkin, then stands abruptly and drops it over his plate.

'Life is not fair,' he says. Turning to Anna, he bows. 'Miss Tesseltje, you'll have to forgive my rudeness. I'd hoped to ask you more about your family, but we will have to speak another time. If you'll excuse me, I have some correspondence to attend to upstairs.' As he passes

Catharina's chair on his way to the door, he gives her shoulder a brotherly squeeze. She shrugs it off, two spots of colour sitting high in her cheeks.

'Give me something I can sell,' he says, bluntly, when he reaches the door. 'Or resign yourself to a lifetime of painting old men.'

His words linger in the charged silence. Anna watches him disappear, wishing she, too, could be excused. She stays rooted to her chair, afraid Catharina will snap at her if she dares rise. The artist has turned her head resolutely towards the window, her gaze fixed outside as if the answers she seeks lie somewhere beyond the wet woodland glimpsed through the glass. A girl in a white cap and apron appears at the table to clear away the breakfast things. This must be the young servant Susanna mentioned last night – Lotte. The girl peers curiously at Anna as she piles the baskets and silverware together and sweeps up the crumbs. Catharina ignores her as well as Anna, seeming to prefer her own thoughts to any comfort or comment they might offer. Shooting Anna one last glance, Lotte vanishes into the corridor. In her absence, Anna's thoughts grow louder, the doubts circling like noisy crows inside her head. Should she have defended Catharina against Crispijn's attacks? What are the protocols? To whom does her loyalty lie – the man who employed her or the mistress she now serves? What if they are both displeased and order her gone? Where will she go?

Despair creeps under her skin and she shivers. Outside, it has begun at last to snow.

From the sitting room window, Anna watches the flakes

drift, hoping for softness, for pincushion hills and trees fringed like ladies' parasols. What sluices down from the sky is a sleeting rain that litters the drive with dirty white pellets. Catharina sits in a velvet chair beside the fire, reading a translation of Seneca's *Philologus* and taking furious notes for a treatise she plans to write on the education of modern women. The argument with her brother has put her in a dark mood. She refuses Anna's offer to scribe.

'Just stay within shouting distance,' she snaps when Anna works up the courage to offer. 'I will send for you if I require your services.'

Feeling miserable, Anna retreats to the far window of the sitting room to watch the furious wind thrashing the trees. Will it always be this way? Catharina, sullen and cross, Crispijn absent, Susanna ensconced in the kitchen while Mr Hartog runs back and forth between the stables, ensuring the horses are safe and dry, shielding himself from the downpour with the aid of a patched oilcloth. Last night as she escorted Anna to her bedroom upstairs, Susanna explained that the head servants would usually sleep up in the attic but Crispijn had given up his quarters on the second floor, since he preferred the attic with its pulleyed trapdoor, affording open access to the night sky. Catharina's brother, Anna was told, has a keen interest in all things stargazing and astronomy. Lotte, however, sleeps in a space no bigger than a broom closet behind the two kitchens. Catharina's extensive rooms occupy the entire west side of the house and include a summer studio and portrait workshop.

'He is so tiresome,' Catharina says suddenly into the sitting room's silence, interrupting Anna's recollection of

193

the night before. 'My brother, I mean. I have to rely on him for everything, at least publicly. If I were a man, I could take control of my own business interests. I could sell this house and move to Paris and paint whatever I liked. As it stands, I am stuck here, like a living statue trapped in a walled garden who can see and smell the beautiful forest beyond the gates but can never touch it. If I were free, I could pay someone to search for Griet. I'm sure they would find her and then we could . . .'

Anna waits for her to continue, but the artist seems to remember herself. Frowning, Catharina shakes her head and returns to her book, dismissing whatever else she intended to say. The fire crackles, sending out small sparks that flare and fizzle before they can endanger the rug. Anna longs to sit down but as Catharina has not given her permission, she continues to stand, rolling her ankles every now and then to encourage the blood flow to return to her feet. She distracts herself by imagining the proper snow that failed to materialise. She conjures the soft whump of powder falling from the house's eaves, the vast interior silence, her thoughts stilled like boats on a windless sea. She's always loved new snow for its purity, for the way it smothers the earth like a freshly starched sheet.

The winter that her mother's companion Kikker came to live with them, she told them a story about three white sisters, fairies who had been given names inspired by winter: *Gletsjer, Verkoudheid, Stof.* When they were old enough to be wed, the sisters were courted by the same fire giant. He visited so often and for so long that the girls melted, merging into one watery being. The sisters now one, being married

194

to the fire giant, gave birth to a son called Stoom who was a volatile, unpredictable element. No walls could contain him. He had a habit of exploding when he lost his temper, endangering sailors' lives. In time, the local humans learned how to put his skills to good use. They paid for his services with offerings of milk and honey and called on him to help steer their ships and protect them from the sea's icy grip and deliver them home safely to their children and wives. Playing in their nursery, Anna and Lijsbeth alternated the role of Stoom. One would burst through their bedding pillows, erupting in an explosion of feathers, a war cry warming her throat while the other cowered in the corner and begged for mercy. They played this game for weeks until their mother discovered them. She punished them for the destruction of the pillows by forcing them to sit still for hours and recite Bible verses. Although any further opportunities to indulge in the pantomime of male violence were curtailed, Anna never forgot the feeling of Stoom's power, running through her veins like snowmelt.

Catharina snaps the book shut.

'That's enough of Seneca,' she says, rubbing her temples. 'Come. I want to show you where I work, in case you need to find me there.'

The entrance to the studio in the west wing is through a carved door set into a wooden frame embossed with fat-cheeked cherubs and trailing vines. Walking under the arch, Anna feels as if she has entered the nave of an old-fashioned church. Although it occupies the footprint of two good-sized master bedrooms, the canvases stacked against the walls and shelves crowded with props and accoutrements compress the space. Swagged curtains let in shafts of light through four big windows. Their beams dissect dusty books and wax candlesticks, dried moths and beetles pinned to boards, ostrich feathers and glass goblets ranged shortest to tallest, some patterned with elaborate whorls, the others plain. The ceiling of Catharina's inner sanctum is decorated with scenes and symbols from Greek mythology. Craning back, Anna contemplates the logistics of painting so high. Does the woman possess wings?

When she asks Catharina this question, her mistress smiles grimly. 'No, but it would please me greatly. Imagine having such a gift! I would fly east each winter and I would not stop until I reached the tropics.' She points at the ceiling. 'You strap a rope around your waist and lash yourself to a platform like a baby tied to a swaddling board. Then you get another person to winch you up and hold the rope steady while you paint. Anyone could do it.'

'I couldn't,' Anna admits. 'Heights frighten me.'

Catharina nods. 'Fair. The last time I had Lotte do it, she nodded off and dropped the rope such that I almost fell. An unpleasant feeling it was, sailing through the air like that. I imagine it's how Icarus felt when his feathers singed and he could see the sea looming, the hungry waves ready to devour him whole. Griet was much better. *She* never let me fall.'

Anna's ears prick up at the mention of Catharina's apprentice. While sifting through Margriet's clothes this morning before she dressed, Anna searched for clues to the woman's disappearance, but the few skirts and kirtles told her nothing she didn't already know. She had more luck with the combs, managing to locate a few strands of long red hair that gleamed on her palm like freshly spun copper. Coiling the strands up, she tied them in a handkerchief and buried them in the bottom of the dresser under her mother's precious silk dress. She feels a little guilty for not informing Mrs Hartog about the dress's presence. It could probably be altered. Worn over a chemise, padded at the hips, and with the accompanying accessories of stockings, shoes and ornamental headwear, it might just be suitable enough to be seen at court. But why shouldn't she keep the knowledge of its existence to herself? If the dress is indeed a talisman, a way of warding off her own ill luck, she can't afford to dilute its potency or risk losing it to someone else. She needs every scrap of good fortune for herself.

On an easel is a portrait of a richly dressed couple. The woman is at least three decades younger than her husband. Her cheeks are flushed with youth and her lips, curved in a smile, are the same blushing shade as the posy of tulips in her arms. The husband affects a more serious pose, legs planted wide, chin raised imperiously, the golden chains roped about his neck conveying his superior status as one of the city's elite. In his left hand, he clasps a set of golden keys – the keys to the city, or his wife's heart, perhaps.

'I ought to finish it,' Catharina mutters, throwing the portrait a dark look. 'Crispijn will only bother me until I do. But I just cannot seem to summon up the will.'

'It looks finished to me,' Anna observes.

Catharina snorts in disbelief. 'Does it so? Look again. Can you not see how Lady Huysum's dress appears thin? I haven't worked up the colour. The dress is meant to be pink, not white. I've run out of poppyseed oil. Crispijn was supposed to bring me more back from Amsterdam. I suppose I should send you upstairs to ask him for it, but I cannot stand the thought of his gloating, thinking he's won and I am hard at work again. He should respect my wishes and support me, knowing how hard it has been to lose the one person I trusted above all others.'

Dropping her hands to her sides, Catharina leads Anna to a velvet curtain which conceals another painting hanging on the wall, a rope dangling beside it. Catharina picks up the rope.

'This is the most important piece in my collection,' she says. 'Before I show it to you, I need you to understand that it wasn't always this way. Crispijn and I used to be close. "Two cherries connected by one stem" – that's how my mother described us. She was called home to God just after our fifteenth birthday. Her death plunged me into the deepest melancholy I have ever experienced. Until that moment, I'd never truly believed that someone I loved could just disappear, that they could depart for Heaven without saying goodbye and leave nothing of themselves behind.'

Catharina's eyes shine. She pauses to press a hand against her stomach, and inhales a deep, steadying breath.

'I sought comfort in the usual places. I prayed, sometimes hourly, kneeling beside her grave. I tried so hard to eat, but the food refused to stay down and its reappearance left me weak and light-headed. I grew hopelessly thin. My father began to suspect I would wither away and die. He went so far as to purchase a grave slab within the local kerk next to Mother's, so that we might spend eternity in each other's company. Nobody understood my pain, except for Crispijn. He sat on my bed each day and read me stories and told me about the constellations, how stars die and are reborn. He was gentle and encouraging, never pushy. Ever so slowly, he convinced me there might be a reason to stay.' She sighs. 'When at last I recovered, I was shocked to discover almost a year had passed while I hovered between life and death. In less than a month, Crispijn and I would be sixteen. The house was still in mourning, the mirrors covered, the furniture draped with black crepe. But I felt somehow hopeful, filled with God's blessings. I was lucky to have a brother who cared enough about me that he'd fought death on my behalf. I was determined to mark his sacrifice. So I blew the dust off my brushes, removed the cobwebs from the ground pigments in their pots and set to work. I'd intended to paint us sitting together in the form of Apollo and Artemis, but as I was mixing the colours, an image of Crispijn materialised that was so strong and self-assured it was as if God had shot it directly into my mind. I painted it exactly as I saw it, working late into the night. The morning of our birthday, I presented it to him here in the studio, and here it has remained ever since, despite numerous offers from my father's friends and collectors to buy it.'

She tugs the rope, the curtains slide apart and Anna sees Crispijn's face, decades younger, leap out of the canvas. Catharina has painted him posing beside a globe on a wooden stand, the sphere engraved with animals from the Greek zodiac and sailing ships flying the red, white and blue banners of the Dutch Republic. The dark eye of a telescope lens glints in the light from a table lamp whose rays fall on the cover of the family Bible, the crest embossed in delicate gold leaf. A spray of flowers droops next to a grinning skull, offering the usual painterly reminders of impermanence and the futility of earthly pleasures.

'What is your opinion of it?' Catharina says.

Anna leans left then right, taking in all the angles. It's clear Catharina has captured Crispijn's boyish innocence, as well as his ability to put his friends and associates at ease. She recalls the way he questioned her over breakfast, his gently probing questions a stark contrast to his sister's brusque interrogation last night. Cornelis de Witt must have explained the circumstances that led to Anna's acceptance of the companion's role, yet Crispijn didn't make any reference to Lijsbeth's death. She can only assume he did so to spare her suffering. Perhaps her assumptions about his greed proved false. Perhaps he is as keen as Catharina to make his own way in the world.

'It's remarkable, Madam,' she says, hoping Catharina can hear the sincerity in her tone. 'It's perfect.'

'It's not perfect.' Catharina's forehead wrinkles as she folds her arms and leans forward to study the picture. 'This area here, you see? Near his neck and shoulders. It could be better painted. Up close, the lines appear soft and subtle, but if you step back, you can detect the unevenness, the lumps and contours where I applied the paint too thick. I wasn't as experienced then as I am now and the mistake bothers me. Of course, Crispijn has only the highest praise for it and refuses to let me retouch any part.' She sighs again. 'He has always spoken of my work in a positive manner, has always found something which pleases him, even in the paintings he doesn't like. He's a walking contradiction.

On one hand, he wants to harness my art for guilders and on the other, he claims the truth and purity of spirit that shine from my canvases are a divine gift which must not be squandered. I wish he'd make up his mind. And I wish I didn't love him, but he is all the family I have left and this painting is the physical bond which connects us. I could never part with it.'

Catharina points out a long chaise longue and two leather armchairs arranged at the back of the room. 'If – when – I resume my portrait sittings,' she says, 'it will be your duty to show the clients in and ensure they are comfortable. They may wish to speak to you or they might ignore you entirely. You must judge when it is appropriate to engage. Never forget you are representing the van Shurman name every time you open your mouth. Can you do that? Can you remember?'

Anna nods.

'Good.' As Catharina turns to pull the curtains closed over the portrait of her brother, her hip connects with a series of canvases stacked against the wall below. A pencil drawing slides out and floats to the floor. Anna scoops it up. The girl's face sketched on the paper is strangely familiar and Anna thinks back to last night's carriage ride, remembering the unsettling intimacy surrounding the image of the woman painted on the carriage walls, the wise owl watching keenly from its woodland perch. Although rendered in ink, it's possible to trace the same sensual tilt of the goddess's chin and this model, the glossy waterfall of her hair moving the same way the warrior's tresses tumbled out of the brass helmet. Small details are missing on the painted version – the dimpled chin, for instance, has not found its way onto the panelled carriage, and a constellation of freckles orbiting the girl's nose has disappeared somewhere between the first draft and the completed vision. But the two women are unmistakably the same.

'You've found Griet,' Catharina says. Plucking the sketch out of Anna's hands, she smooths a folded crease lovingly back with her thumb. 'I'd forgotten I'd made this. I must find a better place for it, away from my clients' prying eyes.'

Rolling up the sketch, she presses it into Anna's hands. 'Can I ask you to keep it safe for me? Hide it where nobody will find it. I can trust you, can't I?'

Her dark gaze bores deep into Anna's own. 'Of course,' Anna says. Fingers tingling, she accepts the proffered scroll and buries it deep in her pocket, her spirits lifted by this unexpected confidence.

The next few weeks pass slowly. Each day, Catharina rises early to read or respond to letters sent by writers, artists and thinkers wanting to either debate a point with her or seek advice for future placement of their work. Sometimes she dictates aloud, her thoughts filling the parchment so quickly Anna's hand cramps as she struggles to keep up. Catharina's familiarity with all aspects of classical philosophy is astonishing, her worldly knowledge of matters ethical and theological far outweighing the experience Anna gained from her father's books. At first, Anna is too busy scribing to register the names of Catharina's correspondents. They return to haunt her later, crowding into her bedroom like familiar figures materialising through the mist; *Birgitte Thott, Queen Christina of Sweden, Queen Elizabeth Stuart, Margaretha van Godewijk.* Female artists and noblewomen, translators of religious writings and classical works, people Anna would be afraid to approach, let alone confront the way Catharina does, demanding to know their reasons for choosing one philosophical path over another, or praising the merits of their education, but asking why they have not taken advantage of their elevated position to promote the interests of all women, regardless of status. In her letters, Catharina seems particularly uninhibited, her lively forcefulness channelled into elegant sentences and persuasive metaphors that drip from the nib of Anna's pen like shimmering droplets of water, reforming and condensing on the page and in her mind. Anna learns more in one week about the history of women's education on the Continent than she ever gleaned from years spent in her mother's company, being shown how to embroider cushions and manage the household affairs.

She learns that the key to all sciences – namely grammar, logic and rhetoric – are as valuable to women as they are to men, that theories pertaining to the practice of law, military discipline and oratory in the Church should not be excluded from the scholastic knowledge of the fairer sex but encouraged, for the contemplation of such subjects offers women the opportunity to pursue a higher degree of happiness which in turn promotes a love of God. When corresponding with male acquaintances, Catharina expresses her arguments in more subtle suggestions and promptings. She links her reasoning back to the classics and refers to herself often as their 'humble servant' and even once 'your good virgin'. The contrast between these two approaches is so obvious that, once recognised, Anna finds it difficult to ignore. A few times while she is scribing, she grows distracted and her pen wilts as she stares unseeing through the fog-edged window until Catharina recalls her.

'Whatever are you dreaming about?' her mistress says sharply.

Anna hesitates. 'I was only thinking,' she says, 'that it's clever, the way you present the different facets of yourself in order to achieve your ends.'

Catharina's mouth works. 'I don't understand,' she says and Anna is surprised to see fear cross her face, although the expression is quickly swallowed up by her trademark scowl.

'It's as if—' Anna wets her own lips, her pulse racing as she tries to corral her wandering thoughts. She feels stupid for opening her mouth. How does Catharina manage to sound both elegant and self-assured all the time? What can she, Anna, possibly add to the conversation? But she must try, even if what comes out bears only the slightest resemblance to what exists inside her head.

'My mother gave me a poppet when I was a child,' she says, speaking slowly so that she doesn't stumble over the words. 'An imitation of a *hofdame*; a young lady, wearing a golden silk dress, fringed with creamy lace. She had a beautiful face, sweet and smiling, but if you turned her over and pulled up her skirt, you found a very different woman. This woman's face looked older. Perhaps she was the girl's mother, that's what my sister always said. She wasn't smiling and her eyes were grave, as if she'd endured many things during her time under the fabric and she planned to tell you about them, even if you didn't want to listen. That's what I think about when I write out your letters, Madam. How there are two sides to you, the one sweet and simpering, the other strong and unyielding in her opinions. I meant no offence, only to compliment you on your deportment and tact.'

It is the longest speech Anna has ever made in Catharina's presence. She stares at the floor, afraid to meet the older woman's gaze. Catharina's silence could convey anything: fury, understanding, confusion. She may even have stopped listening, too caught up in her own internal dialogue to consider Anna's speech worth listening to. But then she appears in front of Anna, her fur-lined slippers unmistakable, embroidered with a trellis of green silk vines.

'I like your story,' she says. Looking up, Anna is relieved to find her smiling. It is perhaps the first genuine smile Anna has observed her make, aside from her reaction to the sketch of Griet which is now hidden upstairs in Anna's dresser, next to the coils of red hair and her mother's silk gown. 'You are correct,' Catharina goes on to say. 'I play to my audience, depending on who they are. In the circles I move in, it's wise to keep your cards close to your chest. Age and beauty can be both a hindrance and a blessing if you are a woman.' She tilts her head, her dark eyes watchful. 'You have hidden depths to you, Anna Tesseltje. Here I thought you were mindlessly scribing and now I find you have been listening and learning. You would make an admirable spy.'

Anna looks worried at the startling sentiment, which

makes Catharina laugh. She taps her foot on the rug.

'I think I will paint,' she says, suddenly. 'Leave the letter to Magdalena; we will return to it tomorrow. For now, I wish you to find Susanna and ask her to show you how to prep the studio. Then you can send a message to Abraham Beverwijck, informing him we will be ready to receive him later today for his first portrait sitting. You'll find his address in my ledger. I'll start the preliminary sketches now.'

Obediently, Anna lays down the pen, stoppers the ink and stands. She is halfway out the door when Catharina recalls her. She turns to find her mistress studying the portraits on the walls intently, as if to familiarise herself with her own talents.

'I owe you a debt of gratitude,' she says, seeming to address a painting of a woman wearing a wide lace ruff. 'I feel inspired after our brief conversation. Grief has a way of dulling the senses, and the cold doesn't help my moods. But you have reminded me my spirit is stronger than those of many men and my talent immense. What good is there in squandering it? After Griet left, I assumed I could never feel that way again – confident in my abilities, ready to employ the talents God in his great wisdom has seen fit to gift me. Yet here we are.' She sniffs, still eyeing the painting.

But she is talking to me, Anna thinks. She is thanking *me*. 'You're welcome,' she wants to say, but her boldness has evaporated so she nods and hurries away to do Catharina's bidding before the woman changes her mind.

Later that evening, they eat together in the lavish dining room overlooking Sterrenwijck's leafy drive. Crispijn joins them, as he does on nights when the weather storms and heavy rain clouds obscure a good view of the sky. His presence in the house is unpredictable. He seems to come and go as he pleases, presumably seeking business commissions on Catharina's behalf. Anna has seen him adding names to the little ledger he uses to record upcoming assignations. He hasn't raised the subject of the commissions again, at least not in Anna's presence, but he has clearly carried on arranging work, waiting for the day Catharina decides she is ready to resume her old career. From things Catharina has said, Anna has learned more about his interest in astronomy, the study of planets and stars, the laws of motion and gravity that influence the moon and the tides. His absorption in the movement of the Heavens came as something of a relief since it explained why he always rushed his evening meal, gulping down his food before excusing himself and hurrying back up to his attic that serves as both bedroom and observatory. The first night he did this, Anna wondered if she was the cause. She supposed – irrationally – that he could sense the ill luck she carried, poisoning her father's wits, cutting short her sister's life. It wasn't clear until Catharina rolled her eyes and said, 'My brother is full of celestial longing. It is a sickness with some people, I tell you. What is so wrong with God's earth that you must search for answers written in the sky?'

Tonight, Crispijn seems relaxed. He sips his soup slowly, pretending not to notice Lotte hovering at the edge of the room, waiting to clear away the bowls and implements ready for the next course. He calls for more wine and leans back in his chair, resting the heels of his boots on one of the braziers Mrs Hartog has positioned around the table to keep them all warm. Anna, too, feels at peace, buoyed by her success in encouraging Catharina to take up her paintbrush again.

'Are there many stars visible from Sterrenwijck, sir?' Anna asks.

Crispijn's expression is puzzled. 'Of course. Haven't you seen them?'

She shakes her head. She has been too exhausted each night to do anything but crawl into bed and let sleep claim her.

'You must come up to the attic one night,' Crispijn says. 'The view is very clear from up there and I have a telescope I can lend you. Several, actually. You may take your pick.'

'Crispijn has his own little business outside his art dealings,' Catharina interjects, her lip curling as she stirs the dregs of her cold soup. She makes it sound like a childish hobby and Anna tenses, remembering the siblings' ugly argument the morning after her arrival. But Crispijn only smiles.

'It's small,' he tells Anna. 'Six investors, at present. But I hope that interest in our project will grow as word spreads. We are inventing a new kind of telescope, one which may bring the stars closer to us than they have ever been before.' He goes on to tell her that his knowledge of the sky began when he was just a boy; looking through his bedroom window each night, he couldn't help wondering how God's great universe came into being and what role he could play in recording it. Observation, he tells Anna, is the key. 'If we could better map the planets and the stars, we might have greater insight into ourselves. The ocular lens I have been working on will allow me to see the details beyond the blurred images of Saturn we have now. Last year in Amsterdam, I met a very talented optician called Jan de Wijck. Together, we drew up plans for two new types of spherical lenses – one the eye and one the field. Jan will grind the glass for the lenses and I shall create a telescope casing to house them. Jan is confident it can be done. We just need time. And funds.'

'So you see, Miss Tesseltje,' Catharina interrupts, 'my brother is at the mercy of the winds of commerce, as much as I am with my art. There is some satisfaction in that, I confess. I could lend him the money, but it is better if he saves his own from the cut he takes from each commission. It's character-building. You must have finished your soup by now, brother. Or are you aiming to nurse it all through the winter?' She beckons Lotte forward to remove the empty bowls.

'Was that Abraham Beverwijck I saw leaving earlier in his carriage?' Crispijn says, as Lotte marches out with the bowls stacked up on her tray.

Catharina purses her lips primly. 'It was.'

Crispijn blinks, waiting for her to elaborate. When she stays mute, he turns to Anna.

'He came for his portrait sitting? Can it be true? The ice has thawed at last?'

Anna glances at her mistress. If she confirms the truth, will Catharina resent her? It cannot be kept secret for very long.

'It's true. I sent for him,' Catharina says. 'Miss Tesseltje and I had a – a talk earlier. And I realised I was wrong to squander the opportunities you've been so good as to arrange for me. We need the money, as unpalatable as that sounds.'

Crispijn's face breaks into a grin. Before anyone can stop him he jumps to his feet, folds his arms across his chest and begins to dance. Anna is so startled she leans back, almost toppling off her chair. Crispijn seizes her hand to arrest her fall, then scoops her into his arms and swings her around wildly, tapping his feet to the strains of some music only he can hear.

Catharina smiles.

'Put my companion down, you fool,' she says. 'Your behaviour is most unbecoming. Are you a peasant? Are you drunk?'

'I may be one or both or neither by the time this winter is over,' Crispijn says, releasing Anna gently, her head still spinning as she clings to the back of her chair, trying to catch her breath. 'You don't understand how happy this makes me. Our future secured and those of the servants. And Miss Tesseltje.'

Catharina smirks. 'Miss Tesseltje may never speak to you again after tonight,' she says. 'I would not blame her.' But Anna can tell she is pleased by his exuberant response. Catharina even goes so far as to tell him about a commission she has accepted: an urgent portrait of a court lady, part of Elizabeth Stuart – the Winter Queen's entourage. For once, Griet's presence does not haunt the conversation. The crystal sparkles, the cutlery shines and the ghost of Catharina's former apprentice stays in the shadows, where she belongs.

The next day Anna learns that the woman who is to have her portrait painted is the wife of a nobleman exiled from England for supporting the Royalist cause.

'You would not think, to look at her, that they fled London in the dead of night, taking nothing with them but a few fat purses and their best court attire,' Catharina says. They are waiting in the studio for Mrs Hartog to show the woman in. 'Her husband was stripped of his lands and titles. Now they must rely on the generosity of Queen Elizabeth Stuart. The Queen found roles for them within a month of their arrival. Lady Killigrew is a lady-in-waiting in Queen Elizabeth Stuart's retinue and her husband has been given a diplomatic posting to France. He's been away for months, but is due back any day now. This portrait is intended as a token of gratitude for the Queen, to thank her for her generosity.'

Anna tries not to stare as the Englishwoman is ushered into the studio. She retreats to the corner where she can safely observe Catharina sketching the woman's features onto canvas.

'Did you hear the news?' Lady Killigrew says, after ten minutes' quiet sketching have elapsed. She speaks from the corner of her mouth, her eyes fixed on an invisible point beyond Catharina's head. 'There's to be a masque tonight in Queen Elizabeth's rooms.'

Catharina pauses, her brush poised. 'Really? I wonder that the Queen has not issued me with an invitation. There's been nothing delivered, has there?' She glances at Anna who shakes her head.

'It was decided yesterday in haste,' Lady Killigrew says quickly, 'after the Queen's nephew arrived at court. He dis-guised himself as a pauper to throw the Englishparliamentarians off the scent. Her Majesty didn't recognise him until he was kneeling at her feet. Thinking he was a beggar, she prepared to toss him some *stuivers* when lo – he ripped away his cloak and unmasked himself. The masque is to be held in his honour. I've just come from Binnenhoff and I tell you, it is a sight calmer here. Everything there is chaos, performers reciting their lines, dancers bumping together . . . And the sets! Picture forty men winching set pieces through upper-storey windows while musicians mill about on the lawn, waiting for the stage to be built . . .' She grimaces. 'The theme is the storming of Neptune's Palace – it must be suitably vague in order to avoid any diplomatic complications. The Queen has chosen six gentlemen to be sailors. They will deliver romantic verses to Neptune's daughters. I heard one gentleman declare that he will need to ink the sonnets permanently on his wrists, in case he forgets. The Princess Mary and the Dowager, Amalia van Solms, are planning to attend, too, so we may expect fireworks, even if the masque itself disappoints.'

Catharina's hand had stilled. Now she resumes her sketching. Anna watches the shadowy shapes emerge onto the canvas like figures stepping out of the mist. 'And how did the Queen's nephew look?' Catharina asks. 'Did he appear to be in robust health?'

Lady Killigrew hesitates. 'Given what he's been through, I think Prince Charles seemed in excellent sprits. He's still handsome, although much thinner after so many months on the run. He told us about how he had to conceal himself inside a hollow oak tree for a whole day to evade Cromwell's brutes. That devilish pretender to the throne was offering a thousand pounds in exchange for his capture. Thankfully, the prince was in no danger of starving, his minders having planned ahead and supplied him with cheese and beer. Still, it must have been terrifying. I don't know how he passed the time without losing his nerve. The last time I saw him, he made me promise to dance a set with him. It's a great shame that his marriage to the Dowager's eldest daughter fell through. Now his mother will have to find him another bride.'

'Lucky that you yourself are safely married,' Catharina says, tossing back her fringe. 'No need to concern yourself with contracts and false promises and such. Your future is secure.'

Lady Killigrew's smile falters. 'Yes, well,' she says. 'I suppose you're right.'

Catharina sends Anna to fetch the timber heart. Carved from a lump of oak and painted red, the prop is destined for Lady Killigrew's slender hands. She will pose with it, paying homage to Queen Elizabeth's generosity.

'In England, they call Queen Elizabeth the Queen of Hearts,' Catharina explains. 'She was married to her husband, Count Palantine, on Valentine's Day many moons ago and London was lit up brighter than the Milky Way in her honour. That was before she moved to Prague – before the terrible uprising which saw her stripped of her Queenship and exiled here to the United Provinces. The exiled Queen has a much stronger constitution than anyone else gives her credit for. She is as strong as a mountain lioness. She gave birth inside a draughty castle while Catholic armies battled Protestant defenders on the doorstep. Amalia van Solms – we call her the Dowager now – helped deliver the boy safely before the women fled and sought sanctuary at last within

213

the Stadholder's household. Amalia was Elizabeth's lady-in-waiting till she married the Stadholder's half-brother. Now the two women are bitter rivals. There are three courts in The Hague – my lady Elizabeth's, the Dowager Amalia van Solms' and her daughter-in-law, the young Princess Mary, now sadly a widow. If it sounds confusing, that's because it is. One must choose where one's loyalty lies, but one must never betray one's true feelings in the matter.'

When Anna proffers the prop to Lady Killigrew, the woman ignores her. Anna has to clear her throat and, even then, the noblewoman refuses to look directly at her, adopting instead a thousand-yard stare that makes Anna feel invisible. At last, the noblewoman accepts the heart limply. She stays frozen as Catharina arranges a trailing swathe of golden silk around her shoulders and waist. Two potted orange trees positioned nearby give off the scent of summer, all sunshine and warm earth. Catharina fusses over them, arranging them either side of Lady Killigrew's chair before deciding only one is required. Anna heaves up the other plant and carries it out into the corridor. The greenhouse is located at the back of the house, near the entrance to the east wing, accessible via a long, winding gallery of paintings. Anna has taken ten steps in the greenhouse's direction when she encounters Crispijn leaving a room she knows to be his study, copper stars decorating the timber door.

'Oh,' she says, coming to an abrupt halt. 'Excuse me, sir.'

He waves away her apology. 'Here, let me help you.' The plant's weight evaporates as he takes the pot from her hands. They walk together along the corridor, observed by the paintings lining the walls. Most are Catharina's, but a few of them bear the hallmarks of other artists. Crispijn points them out as they walk along. There are artworks depicting market sellers and dusty cattle yards, tables groaning under giant horns spilling seeds and fruits. Anna stops to examine a large artwork of Saint Margaret of Antioch, depicted moments after freeing herself from the stomach of one of Lucifer's minions. The girl's expression of abject terror is well realised. She brandishes a wooden cross protectively above her head, her bare feet slipping on the beast's eel-like coils. The auburn hair spilling around her shoulders is the same shade as Griet's in the likeness Catharina captured of her on the carriage wall, but this model is a stranger. Anna absorbs the girl's face and stance thoughtfully. Saint Margaret is bravery personified. She has burst through the beast's belly and now she is running, running from the fate that threatens to ensnare her, running towards God's protection, his blessed holy light. *If only it were so easy*, Anna thinks.

'I rescued this painting the last time I visited London,' Crispijn tells her. 'I suspect it belonged to the former King but I can't be sure. A man in a leather apron was carrying it out of the banquet hall. When I stopped him, he told me he was a blacksmith who had stayed when London was besieged in order to fend off the Roundheads. He was planning to burn the painting in his blacksmith's forge, but I begged him to sell it to me and, after some haggling, he agreed. It's been here, safe at Sterrenwijck, ever since. If young Prince Charles ever regains his throne, I'll see it's returned to him.'

They resume their slow progress up the corridor,

Crispijn shifting the plant from right to left to relieve the pressure on his arms.

'What were you doing before?' Anna asks him. The question makes her feel bold and she follows it quickly with another, before she loses her nerve. 'When I encountered you?'

'I was on my way to find you, actually. Well, my sister, but you seem to be always together now. You are allowed some time for yourself, you know. You've already surpassed all my expectations. She's painting again, praise be to God, and I know I have you to thank for the improvement in her spirits. Is there nowhere you'd like to go? Into town, perhaps? I can ask Lotte to wait on my sister, if she needs some urgent thing.'

Anna smiles. 'I'm quite happy to be here. And I fear Lotte may do more harm than good. She means well but she's so young.'

He snorts softly. 'There can only be three or four years between you.'

'That's true,' she says. 'But she still has her family. She isn't all alone in the world with nobody to rely on except herself.'

The greenhouse is warmed by a well-banked fire that nourishes the plants during the winter months. Snow is piled against the windows and the panelled glass is webbed with sparkling frost. Crispijn sets the plant down in a corner, then dusts off his hands. Reaching into his pocket, he extracts a cream envelope.

'For you. An invitation to the masque tonight.'

The envelope is addressed in an elegant, sloping hand

to Madam Catharina and Master Crispijn van Shurman.

'Tell my sister to be ready by four,' Crispijn says. 'Henrick will drive the three of us in the carriage. He's preparing the horses now.'

Anna lowers the invitation. 'I'm invited, too?'

'Of course. You are Catharina's companion now, are you not? I hope you have something suitable to wear.' Noting her dismay, he adds, 'It needn't be the latest fashion. That's the point of a masque. Everyone gets to wear their old rags without suffering the indignity of not being able to afford new ones. All the exiled English courtiers will be dressed in last decade's fashions. You wait and see. I'm sure you have something.'

Anna thinks of her mother's dress. The skirt will need to be steamed over a hot iron until smooth and she will need Mrs Hartog's help to pin up the excess material and lace her into the bodice. When Arabella died, she was even slimmer than Anna is now, although she carried it better. Her mother was country-girl strong. Privation was a choice for her, not a punishment. Despite being so slender, she was capable of carrying a large porcelain vase brimming with water and tulips from the *voorhuis* to the front room. When Anna catches her own reflection in the vanity, she's always surprised at how gaunt she appears, as if someone has slashed her cheeks with a palette knife. She's seized by sudden panic. What if she makes a fool of herself? What if she embarrasses Catharina and Crispijn – not just in appearance, but by her actions? The manners required of a former Amsterdam merchant's daughter are nothing like those expected of a woman raised from birth for a life at court. Protocols that come naturally to the others will not occur to her. Even her mother's gown wouldn't be able to shield her from a damaging social misstep. She flushes hot then cold and has to lean against the wall to steady her nerves. When Crispijn asks her what's wrong, she's too overwhelmed to tell him anything except the truth.

His response surprises her. 'They're just people, Anna, not monsters. Under their silks and furs, they are subject to God's will just like us. The masks they wear are the faces they show the world, but they are no better than you or I.' He hesitates. 'In one of his letters, Cornelis de Witt mentioned you were renting rooms in Jodenbuurt before you arrived here. I have friends who live there, too. Poor craftsmen and glassmakers and bricklayers. They are not prosperous in any monetary sense, but they're far happier than many of the courtiers I have encountered after thirty-five years of attending court functions. It's not the clothes that make us, but the company we keep. I'm grateful to God for allowing me to keep my family close. It enables me to be grounded and to ward off the temptations of wealth and decadence, the overindulgence of which you will doubtless witness tonight. You are young, as I said earlier. New experiences can be frightening, but they can also be a gift. Now, you'd better get back to the studio and deliver that invitation before my sister suffers any further torment. I should speak to Henrick about the horses.'

Bowing, he continues off towards the kitchens. Anna watches him a long moment before turning away. Retracing her steps down the long corridor, she realises that her heart is lighter and the dizziness she felt at the thought of embarrassing her employers has dissipated, leaving her level-headed and clear-eyed. When she reaches the painting of St Margaret fleeing the dragon, she stands straighter. I will be brave, she thinks.

Her mother's dress will lend her courage.

By four o'clock, the sky has grown so dark it's almost black. Mrs Hartog sweeps out of Catharina's room, bringing with her a waft of Catharina's cloying floral perfume. Anna hovers in the doorway, watching Catharina tighten the leather straps on her iron pattens. Her mistress wears a richly embroidered riding habit of red-and-gold brocade and her hair falls loosely down her back, resembling a man's periwig. A starched lace cravat spills from her collar and Mrs Hartog has taken in the panels so the coat hugs her body's curves, accentuating her waspish waist. Anna exhales hard, testing the limits of the housekeeper's lacing skills on her own bodice, but the dress clings to her waist as if it were made for her, the extra ribbons and folds pinned away by the housekeeper's deft fingers. The gold fabric gleams; the gilt thread woven through the silk is star-spangled, radiating points of dazzling light where the candlelight strikes. Anna executes a subtle half-turn, admiring how the fabric skims the floor in a soft wave. It's so rare for her to feel this way – worthy of attention. She tries to imagine Crispijn's reaction, then bites her lip at her own foolish notions. He is being kind, that's all. Spying Anna lurking in the shadows, Catharina beckons her forward. A nervous sweat rises on Anna's skin as she submits toCatharina's inspection, a doll being evaluated by a particularly fussy craftsman. After a moment's deliberation, Catharina gives an approving nod.

'You'll do,' she says. 'That gown is exquisite. An

older style, but it suits you. If you were a duchess and asked to be painted in it, I would not try to convince you otherwise.' She frowns. 'Something is missing. Your ears and neck are unadorned. It makes the dress seem plainer than it needs to be. Here.'

She lifts the lid of a lacquered box and draws out two glimmering orbs.

'You wear them like this,' she says, holding them up either side of her face to demonstrate, then passing them to Anna who cradles the glass ornaments gingerly in her cupped hands. 'They're made of glass and vapour. Crispijn brought them back from Amsterdam, but I never wear them. They're too delicate for me, I prefer something more robust.'

Anna shakes her head. 'I'm sorry,' she says. 'I can't wear these.' She feels herself blushing. Her mother had the foresight to pierce her ears when she was just a child but she hasn't worn earrings for over a year now, ever since Lijsbeth sold the last pair in their mother's jewellery casket – a pair of heart-shaped amber stones set in gleaming gold.

A look of surprise crosses Catharina's face. It has not occurred to her that someone might lose all their worldly possessions in one fell swoop. 'You could pierce them again,' she suggests. 'I could help you. You must get used to wearing fine things if you accompany me to court. It will only hurt for a moment and I have some cream you can rub on it afterwards to take the pain away. Here.'

She holds up a glass hand mirror. Anna bites her lip, fingering her earlobes in the reflection. Locating the small lumpy scar, she draws in a deep breath and presses the long glass spike through the flesh. Pain, hot and searing, and then relief as the tip punches through. Anna repeats the process on the other ear, a little dizzy from the rush of blood to her head. The task done, she stands back and lifts her chin, trying to ignore the throbbing pain in her earlobes. Catharina beams her approval. Being careful not to tread on the hem of her skirt, Anna follows her down the stairs to where Crispijn is waiting, handsome in his velvet suit, a fur-lined cloak thrown across his broad shoulders. He stares openly, shocked at Anna's transformation from dowdy companion to court attendee, until a sharp jab from Catharina's elbow recalls him. Reluctantly, he turns his back on them to ask Henrick a question about the horses.

It's still me, Anna wants to say. I'm still the same person inside. But the truth is, she feels altogether different, as if she has shaken off the old Anna and slipped on this new, bolder version.

The drive to The Hague is mercifully short. It feels as though they've barely left Sterrenwijck when the coach begins to slow. Another vehicle ahead of them disgorges its passengers into the sleeting wet. In the light from the lanterns, tall figures bundled into winter overcoats are dancing under vaulted parasols and strange accents echo in the frigid air.

'In summer, you can sit for hours on the grassy lawn,' Catharina murmurs, peering out her window across the dark fields. 'The *Hofvijver* is a popular picnic spot. Queen Elizabeth likes to hold her court outdoors when the weather is fine. Constantijn Huygens arranged a musical soirée for her last season under the stars. It was a celestial triumph –'

'Until a stray pig ran through the stage, dragging half

the musicians' instruments with him,' Crispijn interrupts. He grins at Anna. 'The Hague isn't big. You could draw a thousand yard circle around it and capture all the most important buildings in one try. The only reason it was chosen as the seat of government was because the states couldn't stop bickering. So the choice was made for them. When the Stadholder died last year, the states began building a grand new meeting hall, encroaching on the residences of the Royal House. Naturally, the Dowager Amalia van Solms and her daughter-in-law, the Princess Mary, protested, but to no avail. The work is due to be finished within the next few years. Until then, Binnenhoff is still the centre of the universe and the foreign ambassadors and government representatives are as planets drawn into its powerful orbit.'

He falls silent as a gust of cold air from the open door blasts through the carriage, making them all shiver. Anna accepts Henrick's proffered hand. His skin is like ice and she feels sorry for him, exposed for hours to the wind and rain while they enjoy themselves inside the warm palace. He waves off her concern, though, pointing through the drizzling rain to a sheltered barn where a group of men – other servants, she guesses – are squatting around a blazing fire, warming their outstretched hands. It looks cosy and dry and Anna almost wishes she was staying, too, imagining the good-natured banter and easy gossip, the servants freed from their obligations, allowed for once to be their true selves.

Binnenhoff is lit up like a winter wonderland. The walls of ginger brickwork glow like spiced loaves. Potted fir trees strung with jewelled ropes nestle against the brick facade and the window drapes have been thrown wide to reveal a tableaux of tastefully furnished sitting rooms. A footman escorts them into a reception hall, with floorboards so highly polished they are like the canals back home, although these waterways reflect mahogany roof beams and oil paintings instead of blue summer skies. Anna drinks in the view, trying to suppress her sense of awe. A month in Catharina's company should have acclimatised her to this kind of wealthy pageantry, but the proliferation of colours and textures continues to astound. Milky chinaware crowding every surface reflects the sublime luminescence of the tooled-leather walls while the architecture seems, even to Anna's untrained eye, masterfully executed, a cut above the work of cheap draughtsmen designed to cram as many bodies as possible into an ill-fitting space.

Another party waits alongside them to be shown upstairs. The women hide their glances behind a scrim of lace fans, but Anna senses their interest all the same. They are scrambling to place her, longing to identify the young woman accompanying the famous artist Catharina van Shurman and her helpmate brother. Anna's cheeks begin to burn. She wishes there was something she could say to defend or justify her presence, but she remembers Catharina's warning on her first day not to speak unless addressed. To distract herself, she studies the paintings. Many are family portraits of solemn children posing on their parents' knees, although some are decidedly more heroic – male youths posing on horseback, leading a hunting party. The young Princes of Orange gaze adoringly at their mothers, their puffed cheeks and sausage arms reminiscent of fat cherubim.

The Bible has not been forgotten; there is Judas Iscariot, clutching his purse of purloined silver – a popular theme among biblical painters. The last wall holds a display of maritime scenes – *fluyts* and galleons decked out in the Republic's flags, their commitment to the mother-trade's transportation of grain and wood distilled forever in browns and greys. A large painting at the centre of the arrangement draws Anna's eye. In the foreground a single ship lists starboard, buffeted by a monstrous wave, spray surging over the tiny figures on deck while villagers kneel on a distant beach, their hands clasped in fervent prayer. Broken ship parts floating on the water's surface signal the storm's destructive power – timber planks, a scrap of sail, a man's jacket ripped away by the current. A scrolled cartouche at the bottom right quotes Ezekiel: 'I will cleanse you from all your impurities and from all your idols. I will give you a new heart and put a new spirit in you. I will remove from you your heart of stone and give you a heart of flesh.' Beneath that, the title and date, indelibly inked: *Texel Storm, Christmas, 1633.*

Anna's skin crawls. She peers closer, disbelieving, but there's no concealing the truth. Perhaps the artist learned the story from someone else or perhaps he was there the night of her birth, when the monstrous storm ripped Texel's anchorage apart and killed all those men. Coming so swiftly on the heels of her joy in wearing her mother's dress, the revelation feels like a bad omen, a reminder of her dark past. Black specks dance in her vision and she holds her breath, waiting for the dizziness to subside. From somewhere within the building's depths, an infant's startled cry is cut short by a nursemaid's hand.

'Anna?'

She spins, pulse racing.

'You were lost in that painting.' Crispijn is wearing a bemused smile, but catching sight of her expression, his face changes, becomes concerned. 'Is everything all right?'

She shakes herself. 'Yes. Yes, I'm fine.'

Avoiding glancing at the painting again, she follows him to the bottom of the staircase where Catharina waits, tapping her boot impatiently. The theatre upstairs is tightly packed with bodies. Padded chairs have been set out according to rank, but most of the courtiers mill about, talking or studying each other's clothes or picking at the food piled high on long tables pushed against the walls. At the front of the room, a painted castle on a makeshift stage towers over a musicians' gallery, the seated players cradling their lutes and viols like gentle lovers, plucking lightly at the strings. Elaborately carved thrones positioned closest to the action are occupied by three noblewomen – two old, one young. A phalanx of well-dressed attendants is settled on cushioned footstools at their feet and, although they are within speaking distance, the groups seem to be studiously ignoring each other. Three miniature courts, Anna muses. One for each sovereign. But which one holds the most power?

'There is my patroness, Queen Elizabeth Stuart,' Catharina whispers. Anna's eyes follow the direction of her gaze. The Queen's face is thin, her nose long and slightly crooked. She might once have been beautiful, but years of exile and loss have robbed her face of its youth. Although deep creases have formed at the corners of her eyes and lips, there is a regal stateliness about her expression – a self-assuredness borne from years of weathering storms. Anna remembers what Catharina told her about how the Queen's heart had been broken – first by her beloved brother, Henry, the Prince of Wales, who died unexpectedly at the age of eighteen, and then by her husband who succumbed to illness soon after their arrival in The Hague. Widowed and unable to return to either her native England or the kingdom of Bohemia where she'd expected to live out the rest of her life, the Queen focused her considerable energies on securing a stable future for her surviving children and her nephew, Prince Charles. She rebuilt herself from the ground up, becoming a patroness of the arts. She is known somewhat derisively as the Winter Queen because her reign over the Palantine lasted only one season.

The Queen's gaze falls on Catharina and she beckons her forward. Catharina drops into a low curtsey which Anna copies. As Anna raises her head, she spies a small creature peering out between the elbows and shoulders of a woman seated in the Queen's retinue. The animal is deformed, its body lumpish, its face patched with irregular tufts of black and white fur. The creature blinks its moon eyes, then utters an unearthly shriek and skitters over the attendant's shoulder. Swinging itself into the Queen's lap, it reclines on its back and half-closes its eyes, looking for all the world like a human infant. Anna's mouth drops open in surprise and the Queen laughs.

'This is Ferdinand,' she says. 'My pet monkey. All sweetness, you'll find, until he is denied a treat. Then his temper is beyond foul. And who, may we enquire, are you?'

'Your Majesty, this is Anna Tesseltje,' Catharina says. Her tone is meek, deferential, belonging to someone Anna doesn't recognise. 'Anna is my new lady's companion. My brother, Crispijn, procured her services as a favour to me.' She gestures at Crispijn, who has walked off and is now talking to a bearded man in a plumed hat. 'Anna comes to us from Amsterdam,' she goes on. 'She is the daughter of a shipping merchant whose family has fallen on hard times.'

'Tesseltje,' says the Queen. 'Unusual name.'

'It is an island, Your Majesty,' Anna says. 'Lying to the far north of here. I've never been there but my father's ships used the anchorage often. He often said Texel was the making of him . . .'

She trails off as tittering laughter erupts from the ladies-in-waiting. Catharina frowns and Anna realises she should not have babbled or spoken out of turn. Mercifully, the Queen seems not to notice.

'So you are a stranger here, Miss Tesseltje,' she says, stroking the monkey's back. 'As once I was. And what do you think of The Hague?'

Anna's heart gives a frightened gallop. If she casts her mind back to her arrival at Sterrenwijck, how might she find words to describe the sheer pleasure of sleeping on a soft featherbed, the relief that came from knowing she would not be plunging her bleeding hands into a vat of boiling water from noon till dusk? If she were permitted to speak the unadorned truth, she could explain how

227

uncomfortable she once felt in Catharina's presence, how she fretted over the woman's every word and gesture, until she realised Catharina had no intention of tossing her out onto the streets. Anna cannot say these things to the Queen though, so she dithers and her protracted silence takes on an awkward edge. Even the attendants stop their prattling to watch her squirm. Underneath her panic, Anna recognises one of the faces – it belongs to Lady Killigrew. It's unclear whether the woman recognises her from their earlier meeting. Her grey eyes are hard little pebbles and her mouth is a thin line, no trace of humour. In the end, it is the monkey who spares Anna from answering. Abandoning the Queen's lap, he darts towards her. Anna's first instinct is to draw back in fright, but she forces herself to stillness.

'Hold out your arm,' the Queen commands. The pads of the creature's agile feet grip Anna's sleeve as he climbs, wrapping his tail around her forearm for support. When he reaches her shoulder, he perches there, his fur crushed against her cheek. Someone has rubbed a fruity pomade through his pelt so the scent masks the worst of his musky odour.

The Queen beams. 'You are blessed, Anna Tesseltje. Ferdinand is a good judge of character. If you need anything during your stay at Sterrenwijck, you must ask us. I can already see the effect of your good influence on Lady van Shurman. The last time we spoke, she was suffering an imbalance of ill humours from which we feared she would not recover. Now she fairly glows with health. Isn't that so, ladies?' She looks to her attendants for confirmation and, after only a slight delay, the women chorus their agreement. Catharina looks pleased.

'We must speak to your brother about arranging another commission,' the Queen says. 'I'd like you to paint a portrait of myself with Ferdinand. He is the baby of the family. I have four more creatures just like him. Ferdinand sleeps at the bottom of my bed in a crib that once belonged to my son, Henry. Henry was my – my firstborn. He died when he was only fifteen, poor lad. Drowned crossing the Haarlemmermeer. It's a terrible place to get caught in a storm . . .' The Queen's cheerful expression slips, her gaze sliding out of focus. She coughs softly as if to mask a sob.

Lady Killigrew stands abruptly. Glaring at Anna as if she is responsible, she seizes the monkey and deposits him back in the Queen's lap. 'Your Majesty, your nephew has just arrived. Shall I tell the musicians to begin?'

Anna follows her gaze. A young man in a black cloak has just entered the room, surrounded by a throng of courtiers. Prince Charles' dark beard and tanned skin remind Anna of the Italian merchants her father entertained sometimes in his study, ushering them past his young daughters with an enigmatic wink. He always maintained he could out-manoeuvre the Italians in business matters, but later analysis of his books proved otherwise.

Queen Elizabeth brightens. 'Yes, Lady Killigrew. You may tell the actors to prepare themselves, now that the guest of honour has arrived.'

Lady Killigrew crosses the room and sinks into a low curtsey before the prince who takes her hand and kisses it, then draws her to her feet. They gaze into each other's eyes for such a long time that even Anna, who has never been in love, cannot mistake the look of intense intimacy that passes between them.

'Isn't she married?' she whispers to Catharina. Her mistress raises an eyebrow, but says nothing. Anna cannot really imagine how it must feel to be bonded to someone like that, whether married or not. Love is still a foreign concept to her, as difficult to define as the idea of true freedom and a life lived outside the shadows of her father's curse. But she isn't a complete fool. She caught enough of the maids' chatter when she was younger to unlock some of the mysteries that took place behind the curtained hangings of her parents' bed box. One of the young parlour maids who waited on them until Kikker came along referred to her mother as 'the mare'. Braying like a common cart horse, she huffed and puffed, crying Anna's father's name and rolling her eyes back until only the whites showed. The other servants guffawed and begged for more salacious details. Only Anna, sitting unnoticed in the *voorhuis*, her favourite book splayed on her knees, felt her guts liquefy with hot shame at this crude parody of her mother's conduct.

Prince Charles escorts Lady Killigrew to the musicians' gallery where the warning strains from the musicians' instruments send courtiers scrambling to claim their seats. Lady Killigrew stays by the Prince's side and they sit together, their heads bowed in conversation, her pale hair a contrast to his curling dark. Crispijn waves Anna over to the seats he has secured and she sinks into a chair beside Catharina as a troupe of actors dressed in sailors' garb emerges from the wings, hefting a board between them painted to represent a wooden galleon. The first scene is a terrible storm. Timber waves on pulleyed ropes surge back and forth, transforming the stage into a roiling, storm-struck sea. Cymbals crash, the floorboards shake, the ocean roars, the musicians saw frantically at their instruments. Above the din, the ship's captain urges the men forward. There is no way back through the storm, he declares; they must pray for Neptune's bride and her daughters to spare them from a watery grave. A great thunderclap echoing off-stage makes Anna jump. Half the footlights go dark, extinguished by unseen hands, and an eerie green light floods the stage, revealing the mossy grotto inside the underwater castle where Neptune's daughters live with their mother, the Sea Queen. Dressed in swathes of green and blue chiffon, the nymphs are gathered at the feet of the statuesque woman seated in a golden throne – an exact replica of the one in the audience from which Queen Elizabeth watches.

The Sea Queen's hair drips with glittering jewels and pearls and her beautiful, haughty face is half-concealed by a netted veil, fashioned from silver thread. Hearing the men's desperate cries, she orders her maidens to find the men and return them to her mermaid's court so that she might decide what is to be done. The nymphs fan out across the stage, their bare legs visible beneath the trailing gowns. One by one, the sailors are rescued and brought back to the Queen's court where they gasp like landed fish at her jewelled feet. When the last man has been deposited in the grotto, the Sea Queen declares she will give the men a choice: death by drowning, or a lifetime imprisoned as her underwater slaves. The Queen's daughters, who have fallen in love with the sailors, beseech their mother to have mercy. They writhe in torment, prostrating themselves over the stage as the men groan and the music swells to a feverish tempo.

'Spare us!' the men cry. 'We don't wish to drown! *L'amour! L'amour!* We love!'

Anna's mouth is dry. Her heart slows, blood thudding in her ears. She thinks of the painting she has just seen, the Texel ship flattened by the mighty sea, the men cowering helplessly, succumbing to their dark fate. Across the heads of the crowd, a young woman catches Anna's eye. She, too, seems caught up in the play's drama, biting the white knuckle raised to her lips. Her face is soft and beautiful and she cannot be older than fifteen. A tall, bearded man on her right leans across and whispers in her ear; her father, Anna guesses. The girl drops her gaze to her lap and doesn't raise her face again, not even when the Sea Queen declares her cold heart has been warmed by the men's plight and the masque ends with the sailors returning safely to the shore, clasping hands with the Queen's daughters, now dressed as human brides. The actors gather one last time before the audience to proclaim: *We serve you alone, Oh Gracious Queen of the Seas! Long live l'amour!*

Their bows are met by thunderous applause.

'Bravo!' Queen Elizabeth calls, tossing glittering coins over the heads of the crowd. The courtiers fall to their knees, snatching greedily like squabbling hens, tucking the coins into purses tied to their waists by long strings. Seeing Anna's shocked expression, Crispijn murmurs, 'They are all in debt. Well, most are. The ones who have the Queen's favour are

232

lucky enough to receive a stipend from Lord Craven and a few others who support the English court from afar. But there's still an expectation that they will gamble and host grand events like dinners and masques, such as you see tonight. There must always be a tipping point, though. One cannot live forever on promises and air.'

As if to drive home his point, Anna sees Lady Killigrew bending to retrieve a gold piece. She hands it to Prince Charles who pockets it coolly with no hint of shame or embarrassment. Making his way over to his aunt, the Prince drops to one knee and kisses her jewelled hand while the Queen beams at him, her former sadness over her lost son all but forgotten. With the masque over, the courtiers are free to talk again and the noise and heat builds steadily until Anna feels as if her body houses hundreds of living bees. She considers the wisdom of excusing herself and going in search of a quiet corner. Catharina has no need of her company, it seems, being now engaged in serious conversation with a thin, grey-haired man who gestures expansively as they talk, troubled by Catharina's constant stream of interruptions. Crispijn tells Anna quietly that the man's name is Sir Huygens. Anna has heard of him; her father mentioned him once or twice, always in connection with the court.

'He's a kingmaker, of sorts,' Crispijn says. 'Or a queenmaker, if you prefer. Amazing that such a thing is still possible in a place like Holland where we have no real need of monarchs or false prophets. He acts as an arbiter between the English and Dutch courts. They say he can procure anything for anyone, for the right price. Nothing happens here that he doesn't have a hand in or know about. He pays off the servants from the Orange and Stuart households to spy for him, but he is an excellent scholar and composer in his own right and a keen art dealer. I've come up against him once or twice in the auction halls. I've found it's always best to let him win. We need him on our side; everyone does. He's quite close to my sister, being a great friend of the Queen. They've spoken before about collaborating on a series of poems, set over the course of one winter's day. So far, nothing has come of it. Perhaps Catharina will broach the subject, now they finally have a chance to speak. But there, you see? The French ambassador has called him away. Another missed opportunity.'

He sighs as Sir Huygens offers Catharina a deep bow and moves off, chatting to a bearded man in a dark suit.

'There will be dancing now,' Crispijn says, as the musicians raise their instruments to their chins and liveried servants scurry forth to drag the heavy furniture into the corners. 'Do you dance?'

Anna shakes her head. 'We had a dancing master visit us once or twice. He was supposed to instruct my sister in the art of the waltz and even some ballet, but when my father sickened we could no longer afford his fees.'

She trails off as a woman dressed in a salmon gown pushes past them, her fan tickling Anna's cheek.

'I will have to,' Crispijn says, looking around. 'Catharina will not want any of the other men for dancing partners.'

'Is it strange?' Anna says. 'Living with just your sister? Did she never consider marriage?'

Crispijn frowns. 'I wouldn't describe it as strange.

234

You've lived with us for a month, though, so perhaps you have a different view. It's unconventional, perhaps. We've always been close. If she ever needed someone to speak up for her in support, she knew she could rely on me. I assume she's shown you the portrait she made when we turned sixteen?'

Anna nods.

'I've often told her she should paint another, one that reflects my advanced years. Marriage was expected by everyone, but Catharina was adamant she would not have it and my parents never tried very hard to persuade her. She was not expected to live long when she was born. It's common in twins for one to receive all the mother's goodness while the other withers. The midwife told our parents to say their goodbyes and deliver her soul into God's hands with open and willing hearts. But Catharina was always a fighter. She's stronger than people give her credit for, including Griet.'

'What happened to Griet?' Anna says.

'If I tell, you must promise never to mention it in my sister's company. It will be our secret, yes?' He pauses to consider his next words. 'Her family were unhappy. They disapproved of her desire to learn the painter's craft under Catharina's guidance. She struck a deal with them, promised to marry one of her rich cousins if they allowed her to undertake a year's apprenticeship first. A few months in, she wrote to inform them she'd changed her mind. She'd fallen in love and would not be coming home as planned. In response, her family sent some men to Sterrenwijck. They charged in around midnight and stole Griet away before anyone had a chance to stop them. I was in Antwerp at the time, but I understand from Catharina and Mrs Hartog that the experience was quite terrifying. The men were rough mercenaries, ex-VOC. No good would have come from confronting them. Henrick wanted to, but Catharina convinced him otherwise and I'm glad, for he's too old for such things and would likely have been killed.'

'God in Heaven,' Anna murmurs. She conjures the thump of men's boots on the stairs outside her bedroom, Catharina's frightened face illuminated by a guttering candle, a woman's muffled scream, trailing off into the dark.

'Indeed.' Crispijn touches his forehead, as if the memory pains him. 'We've no idea where they took her. She hasn't been seen in public since that night, not even in Delft where her family live. They refuse to answer any of my sister's enquiries. I feel partially responsible. When I introduced Margriet to my sister at a musical gathering a few years ago, I little thought they would become so attached to one another.'

He falls silent as Catharina approaches, holding two goblets. A third is tucked in the crook of her elbow.

'Here you are,' she says, handing them out. 'Dutch courage before we enter the fray.'

'Miss Tesseltje doesn't dance,' Crispijn says, taking a long sip of wine.

'That's fortunate,' Catharina says. 'Neither of us can claim that excuse. Come, brother.'

They drain their glasses and she threads her arm through Crispijn's and draws him towards the centre of the room. Anna watches the siblings take their place among the rows of dancers. Most of the guests seem happy to seize the opportunity to make merry, but a few, like Anna, drift instead to the sides of the room where they can observe the action undisturbed. As the dancers weave together, Anna glimpses the young woman she noticed earlier sitting beside an older male companion. The two are arguing. The man's hand is clamped around the woman's wrist and his face is contorted with rage. The girl seems to be hissing at him, defiant yet afraid. She tries to shake off his arm and, when that fails, rises up on the tips of her toes until they are roughly the same height. Anna cannot hear what she says, but the father looks shocked. He yanks the girl's arm, pulling her so hard she stumbles. Anna's heart lurches; she's about to cry out when an elderly man in a moth-eaten tailcoat too large for his frame blunders into her sightline. By the time he's moved off, the pair has disappeared.

Anna scans the faces of the crowd. On some level, she knows she should mind her own business, but she cannot rid herself of a terrible sense of foreboding. Right before she vanished, the girl's gaze had connected with Anna's. In that brief communion, Anna sensed a desperate cry for assistance, a longing for help. She's about to go off in search of them when two English courtiers stride over, blocking her path.

'You are Lady van Shurman's new companion,' one woman says, peering hungrily at Anna through bleary, bloodshot eyes. Her voice is slightly slurred. 'Is it true, what they say about her? That she is a . . . well. Don't pretend you haven't heard.'

Anna stares at her in confusion.

'She must be mute,' the other woman says loudly. 'I

had a dress like this once.' She pinches Anna's skirt without asking for permission. 'A fine fabric and cut . . . I couldn't wear it now, not with this waist.' She pats her rounded stomach. 'If this child doesn't make his appearance soon, I will have to trade the last of my gowns for food. God willing it is a son or all this sacrifice will be for nothing. There will be nobody to petition for our return once the Prince reclaims his throne. We might just as well have stayed in England. I wonder what Lady van Shurman thinks of this new pet.' She tips back her goblet, swaying, her throat swelling like a bullfrog's as she swallows. Wine dribbles down her chin and leaks into her bodice. Anna stares at the dark stain. That will be difficult to remove, she thinks. 'I heard it was the brother who arranged the hiring of her.'

Her companion sniggers. 'Maybe they share her.'

Anna glares at them, her cheeks burning, but the women make no attempt to cover their drunken laughter. They collapse in a fit of giggles, leaning against each other for support, the jewels adorning their clothes winking in the illumination from the wall sconces. Disgusted, she bobs a curtsey and walks away. Crispijn was right. These courtiers who place themselves high on gilded pedestals and parade themselves as paragons of good breeding and taste are no better than her or anyone else.

She passes two silent footmen guarding the entrance of the ballroom and turns left in the corridor, following a series of floral paintings down the hall, passing countless doorways leading into empty sitting rooms, each heated by its own private fire. Anna lingers as long as she dares in the entrance of a particularly grand parlour, drinking in the view. She cannot imagine owning even one of these rooms. The heating alone would cost more than she and Lijsbeth made over the course of one year. Catharina tells her that the Queen's private residence lies behind Binnenhoff's labyrinthine public corridors, and Anna imagines her rooms must be even more sumptuous than these mahogany-panelled sanctuaries, these islands of luxury where exiled English nobles can dance and make merry, pretending the outside world no longer exists.

The sound of muffled voices arrests her progress. She pauses outside a half-open door to listen to a series of guttural groans and soft whimpers. Perhaps a dog has wandered upstairs and got lost, she thinks. Or else it's a ghost.

'Hello?' she calls. The door squeaks as she shoves it open with the heels of her hands. At first, she assumes she has stumbled upon a private bedchamber. Her brain cannot comprehend what she's seeing – the girl, backed against a book-lined shelf, her arms tensed at her sides while her father stands before her, praying. Her tear-streaked face is flushed pink and her eyes bulge grotesquely, mimicking the slaughtered haddock that used to sit on the fish seller's block back home in Amsterdam. An unearthly gurgle issues from her gaping mouth as she struggles to breathe, choking on her own sour spit. Stupidly, Anna wonders why she doesn't just take a good, deep inhalation. And then she sees the source of the girl's distress. The older man is not praying with her; he is killing her. One hand is clenched around her throat; the other grips her waist forcefully. His knuckles are white. In a minute, maybe less, he will expunge her life completely. Even as Anna stands there, dumbstruck, the girl's eyes begin to roll back in her head. Her body shakes then slackens, as if her spirit is too tired to fight and has accepted the grim inevitability of death. The sharp scent of urine rises, transporting Anna to the rank heat of the laundry room. Her hands prickle. A shiver ripples through her chest.

'Stop!' she gasps.

The man turns and, in his shock at finding himself observed, releases the girl who crumples at his feet.

'Who on God's earth are you?' he says, wiping his mouth on his sleeve.

Anna is too unnerved to answer. She hurries to help the girl who has begun to cough and retch, her thin body racked with small shuddering sobs. The girl stares at Anna's outstretched hand as if she can't trust her own eyesight.

'Take it,' Anna urges and the girl obeys, allowing Anna to help her, wincing, to her feet. She weighs next to nothing. Anna can feel the small, bird-like bones in her fingers and see her collarbones shifting under the pale, translucent flesh at her chest. Once she's righted herself, she brushes Anna's hand away and begins to adjust her clothing, scooping up a fringed silk scarf from the floor and tying it around her neck to conceal the dark bruises there which have begun to ripen. Anna senses the man behind them, still watching, waiting to see what she will do, although when she glances back, he pretends to be examining the books on the shelves as if nothing untoward has occurred. Anna wants to draw the girl out into the corridor with her and urge her to run, to keep running, as far away as she can possibly go. She opens her mouth to speak but the girl, sensing her intentions, whispers in English, 'Say nothing or it will go much worse for me.'

'I'm Maarten Horst,' the gentleman says gruffly, looking at last in Anna's direction. 'I'm an officer with the VOC and this is my wife, Blanche. Thank you for assisting her. As you could see, I was doing my best to dislodge a sweetmeat she'd swallowed.'

The lie drips smoothly from his lips and Anna's dislike of him rises.

'How do you do?' Blanche says, hoarsely. Her Dutch is bad and she mangles the greeting. Maarten frowns.

'I'm afraid my wife is still learning our language,' he spits. 'It's been six weeks since we left England, but she's yet to master any long sentences or any of our customs.'

'I know who you are,' the girl says. 'You're Anna Tesseltje, Lady van Shurman's new companion. I overheard you speaking with the Queen. I heard her praising you for improving Lady van Shurman's spirits.'

'Van Shurman?' Maarten says, sharply.

'She's my employer,' Anna says. 'Along with Master Crispijn.'

Maarten sniffs and fiddles with his coat sleeves, his expression sour.

'And you, Mistress Horst?' Anna says, trying to lighten the mood. 'How did you come to Holland?'

Blanche darts a glance at her husband who gives a curt nod. When she begins speaking, Anna regrets asking. The essence of Blanche's story is there, buried beneath her bad Dutch. Blanche's parents, Lord and Lady Battenham, lost their titles and their lands during the English war and arranged a match between their daughter and Maarten Horst before fleeing England for France. Anna finds she

241

must concentrate hard though to understand the details. Blanche's voice rasps, she starts and stops, stumbling over the unfamiliar translation and Anna attuned to her heightened panic. Eventually, at a look from her husband, she falls silent and lifts her fingers to the silk scarf at her throat, as if she anticipates her punishment. In the awkward silence that follows, Anna is grateful she never married.

The Dutch East India Company dominates the global spice trade, controlling ports in Batavia, India, China and Japan, among others. Their reach is long, their wealth almost incalculable, piling up more swiftly than the many vessels that cross the sea bearing their flags. The vessels carry nutmeg and coffee, tobacco and cinnamon, priceless silk, finer even than the shining fabric used to create her mother's gown. If Maarten Horst is an officer, he's either worked his way up through the ranks or else his family are rich. They must have paid for his appointment, but if this is so, why didn't they have him promoted straight to Commander? Her father often talked about the *smalle burgerij* – a class of men and women who could afford to place their sons in high positions within the company's ranks. No such position ever exists for women. Women must marry into their good fortune, their ill luck assuaged by the exchange of guilders and the birth of heirs. Perhaps Maarten means to encourage her to think of the future. But his abhorrent conduct towards his young wife is enough to turn Anna against him forever.

'Did Catharina lend you that dress and those ornaments?' Maarten asks suddenly. 'She must have done, for how else could a maid afford such a gown? Six guilders per yard on the exchange.'

Anna blinks, thrown by his line of questioning. 'The dress was my mother's,' she murmurs. 'I brought it with me from Amsterdam.'

'And do you have plans to return?' His voice is commanding; she can tell he is used to being obeyed.

'I'm very happy living with the van Shurmans,' she says. 'My mistress has been painting again and fulfilling commissions. Master Crispijn seems pleased with her progress. I can't imagine living anywhere else now.'

Her answer seems to disappoint him. 'You ought not to sell yourself short. A good servant is worth their weight in gold, my mother always said.'

Anna stares. What does her employment with the van Shurmans have to do with him?

Footsteps echo in the hallway and Catharina appears in the doorway, Crispijn shadowing her.

'There you are,' she says, her brow wrinkled in irritation. She dabs her sweat-dampened forehead with an embroidered handkerchief. 'We've been looking everywhere. It's time to leave. The dancers have drunk themselves into a rotten stupor. They've set up gambling tables and their bets grow wilder by the second. I have no wish to lose all my money to some former English lord without a *stuiver* to his name.'

She takes one step into the room, then sees Maarten. A look of shock crosses her face, replaced swiftly by disgust. There is a terrible, awkward silence before Crispijn coughs and pushes past Catharina to stand between them, as if he half expects them to fly at each other, fists raised to strike.

'Good evening, Maarten,' he mutters, making the smallest of bows which Maarten doesn't return.

'You've met our new hireling,' Crispijn says, nodding at Anna. 'We're grateful to God for sending Miss Tesseltje to us.'

Although Maarten's gaze remains fixed on Catharina, he addresses the whole room. 'Yes, we've met. I've just finished thanking her for her assistance with Blanche. She was having a choking fit. If Miss Tesseltje hadn't come along, I fear my new wife might have suffered a terrible fate.'

'Your wife?' Catharina asks.

Seeming to remember herself, Blanche stumbles forward and sinks into a deep curtsey. Catharina stares down at her, eyebrows raised before folding her arms, looking scornful. 'When I saw you earlier, I assumed she was your niece. Nobody here would marry you so you cast your net wider, did you? Where did you find her? In England? Did you pick her up in one of those infamous parliamentarian fire sales, along with a glut of the King's paintings?'

'I'm an officer now, Madam,' Maarten says, stiffly. 'And my wife is a Lady, the daughter of a former Earl. You might show us some respect. The Governor has chosen me for a special assignment. I'm to manage his estate in Sumatra. It's a large plantation house, requiring good, hard-working staff as well as decoration. That's why I'm here. I was tasked with securing a wealth of artworks and furnishings from the estate sales of exiled nobles. I have the furnishings. Now I need only secure the staff and I can return.'

'And you thought you'd procure a wife along the way,

I see,' Catharina says. 'Like a piece of silverware.'

'Perhaps I should have asked for your advice,' Maarten counters coldly. 'Two lady's companions in quick succession. Let's pray you can keep this one a little longer than you managed to hold onto Margriet.'

Catharina's face drains of colour. Sensing her distress, Crispijn interrupts.

'This has gone far enough,' he says, briskly. 'Maarten, we offer you our most hearty congratulations on the occasion of your marriage. You will have to excuse us. My sister is tired and she has many commissions to fulfil over the coming months.'

Maarten pins Blanche to his side, his fingers pressed into her waist, and Anna shudders, thinking of the bruises under the cloth. 'I'd like to speak to you about a commission of my own. I'd like a painting. A marriage portrait. It will need to be completed before we leave, although I'm sure you can manage, Madam, now you've found a reason to renew your creative spirit. We could arrange for the sitting to be done at the Governor's chambers in Middleburg. I understand Margriet's family still live there. They've recently returned from their own tour of Antwerp and Ghent. Perhaps they could suggest someone to act as intermediary. A relative, perhaps?'

Catharina's cheeks redden. She opens her mouth to speak, but snaps it shut as Crispijn shoots her a warning look. She staggers a little as she turns, reaching for her brother's arm, and Anna follows in the siblings' wake as they cross the threshold. Her skin prickles and she feels the soft threads of destiny binding the two groups together. She fingers the skirt of her mother's dress for the protection it offers, a talisman against Maarten's dark, brooding energy and Blanche's awkwardness.

On their way back to Sterrenwijck, Catharina is restless. Twisting her hands together, she jostles her leg up and down and her gaze swivels from one window to the other, as if the darkness holds hidden worlds of possibilities only she can discern. Crispijn seems more concerned about the impression Maarten left on Anna than he does about Catharina's restlessness.

'I apologise for Maarten's behaviour. He makes everyone uncomfortable. We've known each other for years, ever since we were children. We used to play together until our families fell out over a disagreement. There was some talk of money, a loan gone horribly wrong. Our parents refused to have anything to do with Maarten's family after that.'

'I was so relieved when Father finally forbade them from visiting,' Catharina says. 'Maarten liked to sit on me. I was only small and I wasn't strong enough to push him off. I had to wait for Crispijn to come along and rescue me. Maarten always lied afterwards, saying he'd tripped and fallen, blaming me for being clumsy and getting in his way. Father would have been so angry if he'd known. He refused to hear any suggestion of Maarten marrying into the family. It was proposed by his family when I turned nineteen, but Father simply laughed it off and said he would as soon as make a deal with the devil than have anything to do with the Horsts.'

'I think he beats his wife,' Anna says, quietly. 'Maarten, I mean. I saw him choking her. He lied afterwards, said she was unwell, that he was trying to help her.'

Catharina stares from Anna's face to Crispijn's, open-mouthed. At last, she shakes her head. 'He's a tyrant. I would not have married him for all the spices in the Orient. I can't believe he even asked. But then he has never cared for anyone's opinion except his own. When I saw him sitting there tonight, I swear my blood ran cold. But I didn't want to acknowledge him nor give him the satisfaction of thinking I'd noticed. That poor girl.'

'What do we know about her family?' Crispijn asks. 'I've never heard of them, never seen them at court. It sounds as if they sold the girl to Maarten to absolve their debts and then abandoned her in a foreign place.'

'They wouldn't be the first family to do so,' Catharina murmurs. She is staring at the wall behind Anna's head, transfixed by the image of Griet as the warrior goddess.

'I wish we could help her,' Anna says.

'It's none of our business.' Crispijn raises a tired hand to rub his forehead. 'Where Maarten is concerned, it's best to be overly cautious. Leave him to sort out the Governor's affairs. He will return to sea soon enough and, if he is distracted by his business in Sumatra, all the better for us.'

'I'm considering Maarten's request for a portrait,' Catharina announces. 'There's just enough time to organise the initial sitting before they leave. I can fill in the details later, as I plan to do for Lady Killigrew.' She looks straight ahead, but Anna can see that her jaw is tightly clenched and her eyes are full of a steely determination.

There is a tense silence before Crispijn says, 'You cannot be serious.' His expression is one of horror mingled with confusion. 'Why would you even consider his request, after the stories we've just shared about his behaviour?'

Catharina's eyes flash brightly, lit up with sudden feverish excitement. 'Didn't you hear what he said, brother? Didn't you understand the import? He knows where Griet is. He was giving us a clue. Antwerp, he said, or maybe Ghent. She's still here! Why, she might only be a day's journey from Sterrenwijck.'

'You've gone mad,' Crispijn mutters. 'He's playing with you. He doesn't know where Griet is. Even if he did, he would never tell you.'

'He might,' his sister snaps. 'He only needs encouragement. We can help each other; he needs a portrait and I need to find Griet. To know that she's safe. And he will pay. You said yourself, we need the money.'

'Never his coin.' Crispijn's voice has taken on a hard edge. 'Remember Father's warning? With Maarten, there is always a hidden cost. You know that.'

Catharina bats the air. 'That was before. If Maarten knows where to find Griet, then we must make a temporary truce. Griet's life is at stake. Would you leave her to suffer? Is she to blame for the cruel way her family has behaved?'

'Perhaps she should not have written to them so rashly,' Crispijn says. 'Perhaps she should have waited until her safety was guaranteed.'

Catharina glares. 'How can you say that? There is no safety for women like Griet. You have always set yourself against us. I am doing this portrait, with or without your permission.' Crispijn begins to speak but his sister hunches away, cutting off further communication. Anna feels caught between them, exhausted by their constant fighting. She's glad when the carriage rattles to a stop outside the house and Henrick appears to guide her along the darkened pathway to Mrs Hartog, a glowing lantern casting a pool of light around her stocky figure, banishing the shadows on her creased face.

In the hallway, Catharina and Crispijn shed their cloaks in silence. Anna imagines them as children, coming in from the cold. She remembers Catharina describing how they used to skate together when the river froze. In typical fashion, Catharina always wanted to venture further, travelling up the river to finds its source.

'Praise be to God that Crispijn was there to pull me back,' she'd said. 'No doubt, I would have fallen in and drowned. If we were a windmill, I would be the sails, full of air, and Crispijn the millstone, anchoring me to the earth. He has always tethered me. We need each other, even if we do not always get along.'

Watching them now, Anna fears they will never mend their disagreement. What if they decide their life together is no longer tenable? What if they break up the household, leaving her and the other servants stranded?

Crispijn bids Anna a curt goodnight. Anna expects Catharina to sleep, too. But her mistress flings herself at the writing desk in the front room and draws a piece of parchment towards her. After writing on it and signing her name with a flourish, she stamps her letter with the family crest and hands it to Anna, asking her to ensure Henrick delivers it to Maarten's estate first thing in the morning.

'Make sure my brother doesn't see you,' she instructs, her eyes two dark warnings in her flushed face. 'You may keep the earrings, in exchange for your obedience. I have no use for them. I will soon possess a much greater treasure.'

Anna carries the letter upstairs with her, holding it gingerly as if the contents could explode at any second, killing them all. She props it carefully on the dresser and takes off her mother's silk gown. Folding it carefully away, she drags on her shift, crawls into bed and watches the flames dance in the fireplace, her thoughts creaking like set pieces drawn across a wooden stage. When at last she dreams, she sees Ferdinand's hairy monkey face transposed on the bloated body of an adolescent boy, his skin blue, cold to the touch. She sees Blanche standing on a beach wearing Anna's mother's dress, the silk unspooling in waves around her as if she's floating in air or water. Anna reaches for her but a shadow falls as the sun disappears behind a cloud and when, at last, the dream brightens, Anna is all alone again.

8

Jo

THE ARCHAEOLOGY FACILITY AT CASTRICUM WAS SET
inside a grey Brutalist-style building surrounded by a
miniature forest of needle-straight pines. A scrubby
garden choked with weeds stood baking in the sun to one side
of the carpark. A green banner flying from a rusted flagpole
bore the institution's name: Huis van Hilde.

The temperature inside the lobby was a few degrees
below arctic. I thought longingly of the woollen jumper I'd
left sitting on the bed at Gerrit's beach cottage. I'd intended
to throw it into the back of the car Gerrit had loaned me
before I left Texel, but an unexpected call from Marieke had
caught me off guard and I'd been so flustered afterwards,
I'd erased the jumper from my thoughts, only remembering
when the ferry docked at the marina in Den Hoorn.

Through an open doorway, I could see a circular room
lined with glass display cabinets full of broken plates and
iron-age tools, the artefacts illuminated by strategically
placed downlights. A set of lockable metal doors in the far
wall prevented visitors from accidentally wandering into
the conservation and research areas. That was where Liam
would be – up to his neck, I hoped, in revelations about the

gown's composition. I shivered, imagining the slipperiness of the floral silk draped over my hand, the pulse of it, like a living thing, waiting for us to decode its secret language.

A young woman in a crisp pantsuit emerged from behind a reception desk.

'Welcome to Huis van Hilde. Are you here to visit the museum?' Her tone was formal and distanced, and with her straight blonde hair and spotless nails, she appeared every bit the heritage professional. I must have looked like a scruffy backpacker standing beside her, my jeans rumpled from the drive, my grey T-shirt stained with cleaning solvents.

'Actually, I'm here to visit Doctor Pinney,' I said. 'I'm Jo Baaker.'

There was a stunned silence as the young woman took this in, then she grinned, holding out her hand. 'Doctor Baaker? I'm so sorry, I didn't recognise you. I'm Sara Van Dijk, a lab assistant here at the facility. Give me a minute to telephone down so I can let Doctor Pinney know we're on our way. You're welcome to look around while you wait.'

She waved me towards the display room, removed a slim black mobile from her pocket and began speaking into it. As I wandered around the exhibits, my gaze was drawn to a clear box the same size and shape as an oubliette. The box was filled with artificial sand, an assortment of blackened rib bones and a human skull which floated a few centimetres below the Perspex surface.

'That's Maja,' Sara said, coming up behind me. 'She was the first skeleton recovered by the team during a rescue operation on an archaeological dig in Oosterpoort. People used the place as a burial ground for thousands of years, but Maja is special. She was only twenty when she died. According to a leading anthropologist, she was some kind of Frisian warrior – there's evidence to suggest she sustained severe trauma to her chest and skull at some stage in her short life. She took a spear to the chest sometime between 1262 and 1270, probably fighting off the Hollanders during one of the first Frisian wars. Most unusually, whoever administered the mortuary rites made sure her sword was buried on her left-hand side. Since warriors generally wore their swords on the right, we can assume she was left-handed. If you go through there later,' Sara said, pointing towards a small antechamber, 'you can see what she might have looked like. An anthropologist from Utrecht made a complete facial reconstruction using her remains and an artist used the scans to build a full-body replica. It's really quite extraordinary.'

Swiping us through the double doors, she led the way down a short flight of stairs into the museum's climate-controlled basement. It was even colder down there than it had been upstairs in the public display area and the pungent scent of chemical agents and decomposition pervaded the corridor, despite the wintry blast from the air-conditioning vents overhead. We passed a few open doors – storage rooms, mostly, metal shelves crammed with archive boxes and trolleys and broken bollards, the kind of detritus found in every museum basement. Sara stopped in front of a white door, knocked loudly, then pushed it open. Inside the lab, long metal-topped workbenches reflected the clinical glare of electric ceiling lights and the warm glow of wall-mounted computer screens.

The archival box resting on the bench looked big enough to house a body or a full-length silk dress. It had a fitted lid that Liam was in the act of securing as we entered. I caught the sheen of silk as the lid came down, a rainbow arc like the flash of fish scales in a pond. Even this one tantalising glimpse was enough to reignite my excitement. Just knowing the dress was right there, within reach again, was enough to inspire a visceral reaction in me. I felt my shoulders stiffen and my stomach tense, as if I was somehow anticipating a blow to the abdomen. I fancied I could smell the fabric, the strange whiff of cinnamon and aniseed mingled with the briny scent of seawater.

A few times back in Sydney, I'd heard Marieke's gallery friends recounting the first time they'd seen a Rembrandt or Van Gogh or Picasso in the flesh. Some described it as a fever – chills and a dry throat and heavy, aching limbs. Some swore it was like falling in love, like coming face to face with the person you knew you were destined to be with forever. I've never felt that way about paintings. For me, it's always been clothes. I had to resist the urge to go over and prise off the lid just so I could bask in its reflected brilliance.

'There you are,' Liam said, stepping around the workbench to kiss my cheek. 'I was expecting you an hour ago. Everything okay?' He pushed a pair of oversized, gold-rimmed spectacles up his nose. He didn't need to wear them – his vision was perfect – but he felt they suited his style, which was a combination of relaxed vintage seventies attire and conservative academia, skinny ties and tweed blazers. 'Ted Hughes on acid' was how he'd once described it to me. I'd been trying to purge the disturbing comparison from my memory ever since.

'You can blame Marieke,' I said. 'She called to ask why I hadn't replied to her last email. Then we got into a fight about . . . something. And by the time she hung up, I'd missed the ferry. I had to hang around waiting for the next one to arrive.' I could feel my palms growing hot again, the frustration boiling over.

The conversation had started amicably enough, Marieke accepting my explanation of the delay – that I'd been too busy coordinating transportation of the dress to the mainland to respond to her email – with unusually good grace.

We'd chatted for a few minutes about the family who'd moved into the terrace next door. The woman had just given birth to twins and Marieke was enjoying playing the role of friendly neighbour, ordering the bewildered husband around, writing out shopping lists and shouting advice to him over the communal front fence. Apparently he seemed shell-shocked. He walked around wearing a worried frown and said very little when Marieke appeared on his doorstep with homemade herbal teas and a raft of criticisms. Knowing Marieke, I suspected the man's recalcitrance had less to do with his abrupt induction into fatherhood and more to do with working out how he could avoid her attentions in the future. I didn't voice this opinion aloud but maybe Marieke had an inkling because she said, 'Your mother swore an infusion of mint tea from the garden with a few drops of clove helped her regain her strength after she gave birth. She was back home with you within the week. She didn't like staying on the mainland. Said the hospital was full of people from the cities and one of them might steal her purse while she slept. I suppose you've been to see the house?'

'No,' I said, shortly.

There was silence on the other end of the phone line. A dog began to bark distantly, the sound conjuring the whirr of sprinklers and wide blue skies and Sydney's lingering summer heat seemingly trapped in the courtyard behind Marieke's house, necessitating the watering of delicate ferns and vulnerable herbs well into March.

'Did you forget the address?' Marieke said. 'It's number 6, Schilderweg—'

'I remember,' I interrupted.

'Well, then?' Marieke sounded annoyed. 'I thought the whole reason for your going there was to find closure. You can't just spend your whole life avoiding what happened. If you wanted to do that, you might as well have stayed here.'

'I'm not avoiding anything,' I snapped. 'I'm here for the dress, remember? I don't need to go searching for spooks just to bring up the past. You're the one who can't let it go. What's it to you if I can't remember some lullaby my parents supposedly sang me? It's probably all nonsense. Your memory isn't infallible. Maybe you dreamed it up or saw it in a television show years ago. You have no proof.'

'What about the shoes?' Marieke said. 'The shoes from the beach. Your mother kept them for years in an old chest in the attic. After they died I looked for the chest, but I couldn't find it, it wasn't in your parents' things.'

'That's because it didn't exist,' I said. 'You're delusional!

They have a term for this kind of thing. Gaslighting. You're just making excuses, projecting the image you've kept of them all these years onto a blank canvas. You're rewriting history. It's not fair. It's all part of the same theme: the lullaby, the shoes, the all-encompassing love. Why don't you believe me? Doesn't my opinion count at all?'

When Marieke spoke again, her voice was quiet, tinged with stubborn defiance. 'What about Gerrit? What did he say when you met him? Did he tell you anything interesting?'

I breathed deeply, trying to quell my natural instinct to shout. 'Not really. He said they'd been lovers. He apologised for breaking up the family. I forgave him. End of story.'

Marieke sighed. 'That's a shame. I was hoping he might know something.'

'Well, he didn't.' Anger pulsed in my gut. 'I have to go.'

I'd hung up before she could say another word. It was only later, as I was sitting on the ferry watching the waves vanish under the stern and the marina shrink in the distance to dollhouse proportions, that I thought about the photograph Gerrit had taken at the opening of the seal sanctuary. Small fragments of that day had begun to re-establish themselves in my mind, tiny slivers mostly, but they stirred in me a wistful nostalgia, a deep throbbing ache of sadness that not even my obsession with the dress could soothe. Thinking of that photograph now, I tasted buttery popcorn, felt the sticky condensation of a glass nursing bottle and smelled my mother's hand cream as she laid her soft palm against my cheek. Had I spun these experiences out of wishful longings or were they real memories? And was it possible that more were out there, waiting for me to find the courage to face them?

'Let me show you what I've discovered,' Liam said, break-ing into my thoughts.

He brought up a professional photograph of the dress on the screen, lit from above by warm halogens so the full spectrum of the fabric's luminous copper colour was displayed. A cataloguing number hovered in the top right corner.

'You've been busy,' I said. 'My pictures not good enough for you? Who took it?'

He shot me an unapologetic grin. 'Avril Svensson. She's the best. She's been down at the Mauritshuis finishing up some forensic photography work on the Rembrandts. I convinced her to come out here before going to the airport. She sent through the files this morning.' He flicked through the images Avril had taken, pausing on a close-up of the printed fabric. 'The detail is truly exquisite and I needed some high-quality shots to capture it properly. I thought the pattern in the brocade was flowers and black swans at first, but that doesn't fit the geography or the dates. Black swans don't crop up until at least the nineteenth century, so the bird is probably a peacock or a phoenix which fits my theory that the silk originated in Persia. It must have been imported into Holland sometime during the seventeenth century by an industrious silk merchant and sewn into a dress somewhere in Haarlem. The silk-weavers living there were extremely skilled. They would have known what was in fashion among the wealthy elites living in Amsterdam.'

He clicked through a series of close-ups, each shot capturing a different section of the dress – skirt, bodice, sleeves, hem. The final image had been taken from high above, giving an artistic, bird's-eye view of the sleeves and skirt spread to their fullest length. Viewed from that angle, the outstretched dress was reminiscent of a body in an old-fashioned anatomy lesson. I imagined the gown surrounded by a host of curious faces: the ghosts of the women who'd worn it and the eye-witnesses who'd admired the silky sheen of the copper fabric shimmering under the warm glow of tapered candles. Theirs were the voices we needed to hear, if only we could convince the dress to give up their stories. I wanted to say this to Liam, but he was already talking about what Avril's analysis of the fabric under UV light had revealed. 'Based on traces of iron mordant in the fabric seams, the dress was originally gold, not brownish copper. It probably oxidised at some stage – maybe an air bubble got through the layer of mud and sand and landed on the fabric. The damage spread from there. The laces on the bodice have taken the worst of it. They're so thin that they're almost falling apart. Chemical analysis of the fabric's composition showed a significant amount of gold thread woven through the silk. Given gold thread was so expensive, it's highly likely the dress belonged to Catharina van Shurman rather than her companion. And the glass earrings you found – the Dutch tears – were listed in an inventory of goods taken at Sterrenwijck by the housekeeper, Susanna Hartog, in 1645.

'I propose that Catharina's companion stole the gown,

and the book and earrings, too, sometime in the winter of 1652, and that's why she was let go. Her crime was discovered, but for whatever reason the goods weren't reclaimed. Instead of selling them, she held onto them and packed them in her belongings when she took up her new role as companion to Maarten Horst's wife. She probably intended to sell them later when she reached her new home in Sumatra. Your investigations into Catharina's lack of personal connections with Texel support the theory, so it's what I'll be telling the press. I've already informed the vice-chancellor of the Glasgow School of Art and the Noord-Holland government. And I'm planning to contact Peta Humphries at *The Guardian* while you email your editorial contact at *The New Yorker*. Maybe we can instigate some kind of pitching war between the two of them. Imagine it.'

'Hang on,' I said, raising my palm. 'Don't you think that's jumping the gun? We agreed to wait. I haven't finished following up all my leads yet. Just because there wasn't anything to connect Catharina to the island doesn't mean the dress didn't belong to Anna Tesseltje. I went digging into Catharina's oeuvre. Her paintings are scattered in galleries all over Europe, but the Rijksmuseum is hosting some of her less-famous artworks as part of an exhibition on seventeenth-century art dealers called "The Birth of the Art Market". There's a painting there I'd like to see – it's unfinished, but there's a suggestion Catharina's companion may have sat for it. The exhibition doesn't open for another few weeks so I'm hoping I can convince the curator to let me take a peek. Her name's Jeanette Hall; she was one of the senior art historians at the Courtauld gallery before she went freelance. I'm meeting her later this afternoon. I'm going to ask her if she thinks Anna might have borrowed the dress for the portrait sitting and forgotten to return it, or whether it's possible Catharina might have given it to her as a parting gift when she left the household. Either theory could work.'

Liam looked sceptical. Leaning back against the metal workbench, he folded his arms.

'You think so? You told me the companion was a laundress before she joined the van Shurmans. She was probably living in some rat-infested attic in one of the poorer districts in Amsterdam. If the dress was hers to begin with, why didn't she sell it? A dress like that would have been worth a lot, even back then. She could have lived on the proceeds for a year. Come on, Jo. Listen to your instincts. What are they telling you?'

'They're telling me we shouldn't rush any announcements,' I said, now sounding slightly exasperated. 'It's too soon. Besides, there are other factors to consider. Other stakeholders. The divers who found it, for instance. The Texel community. It would be good if they had a chance to see it before it disappears into some vault for years. The Texel Historical Society have their own museum and the funding to host a short exhibition of the dress and the artefacts. They asked for our help so I took the liberty of calling Rob Disijk this morning and discussing the matter with him. He sounded keen, especially since the funding is already in place and the Noord-Holland government won't have to provide any money. He's going to talk about loaning out the dress and the artefacts with the other councillors at a meeting later today. Bram and the divers have been so helpful providing information about the location of the wreck. With their help, Rob's hoping more shipwrecks might come to light. They're even thinking about establishing a permanent beachcombers' museum on Texel so there's a properly equipped facility to store anything valuable until it can be assessed.'

Liam's frown deepened. 'You contacted Rob without telling me?'

'I didn't think you'd object,' I said. 'It's a pretty harmless request, all things considered.'

'Well, you thought wrong. I have to be honest, Jo, I'm having second thoughts about getting the divers and the historical society on board. If we allow the community to get involved, don't we risk compromising our own scholarship? What if they refuse to give the dress back? And what about your book? Isn't this dress research supposed to be the basis of the final chapter? What if someone writes up the findings first?' He cleared his throat. 'And there's my own position to consider. Before all this nonsense happened with the vice-chancellor's niece, I was headed for tenure. I was just waiting for the ink to dry on the offer. Now it's all looking a bit uncertain. I promised the vice-chancellor that Glasgow School of Art would have first dibs on anything that came to light about the dress. He's really excited about the possibility it might have belonged to Catharina. Apparently, she was a pioneer of women's rights. He reckons the Me Too crowd are going to love her. I've already lined up a meeting with the director of

Glasgow School of Art's publishing arm. I can't just ring him now and say he'll have to wait because some senior citizen with an Ancestry account wants to show off.'

'That's a pretty harsh assessment,' I said, frustration burning inside my chest. I thought back to the Flemish tapestries and nightgowns project. I'd assumed at the time that the Dean had been the one pushing for the promotion of Liam's scholarship over mine. But what if it was Liam? Even the way he was standing right now bothered me: arms crossed, blocking my view of the dress in its archival sarcophagus, acting as if I was an assistant who needed to seek his permission to see it, not a peer whose years of experience and scholarship rivalled his own. A few years ago I might have taken the easy route, letting him have his way so as not to make a scene. But years of dealing with male archivists and museum directors who thought they knew everything had inured me to this type of intimidation. Besides, the dress didn't belong to Liam any more than it belonged to me or the divers or anyone else.

'The members of the historical society aren't like that,' I said. 'They could have broken the story already, but decided to wait so they could find out if the dress could be loaned for a few weeks. I don't think it's an unreasonable request. You'll just have to let the university know there's been a delay. They'll still get the story. It might be even better than the one you've sold them.'

We stared at each other for a long moment, neither of us willing to bend. If Sara hadn't coughed gently to remind us she was in the room, I suspect the stand-off might have gone on indefinitely.

'Fine,' Liam said, at last. He turned back to the computer and pulled up another of Avril's photographs and busied himself scribbling in a notepad.

I reiterated I'd like to see the dress, that I had a few queries about the seamed pocket that had once held the Dutch tears. 'I read the notes you sent over this morning about the chemical analysis of the seams,' I said. 'The majority of them appear to be French-made, constructed with that precious gold thread. But the secret pocket was sewn on separately in an altogether different yarn. The stitches are crooked and the plain crimson thread makes it look like a wisp of arterial blood. In any case, it was the chemicals in that seam that intrigued me. Don't you think the presence of harsh lye suggests the owner of the thread was familiar with washing methods of the day? I can't imagine Catharina would have known how to clean her own clothes, so I think we can safely assume Anna owned the dress, even if she never wore it herself.'

Liam shrugged. He didn't refute my claims so I asked Sara to take one corner of the lid while I lifted the other. The dress lay there, nestled among the tissue paper, an enigma spun from gossamer threads, the folds of the skirt spread like the delicate expanse of a butterfly's wings. I felt the hairs on the back of my neck prickle.

'Wow,' Sara breathed. Her eyes shone. 'I still can't get over how amazing it is. How on earth did it survive down there for so long?'

I couldn't answer. The true circumstances of the dress's miraculous survival were part of a tale that could not be illuminated by Liam's science or my investigations into the dress's provenance. Those who believed in luck or destiny might have had a better appreciation of how the dress came to be lying there for over three centuries and how its unique position, sandwiched between layers of oxygen-free mud, had prevented the material fibres from rotting, protecting it from ravenous shipworms and hungry currents. Was it just coincidence that Bram and his friends happened to be diving the day after the storm washed the sand away from the wreckage? Or was there something else at work that day, something that could not and would never be explained?

I didn't want to be late for my meeting with Jeanette so, after taking down some observations in my notebook, I sealed the dress back in its box and followed Sara out of the lab and back up the stairs into the exhibition space.

'Is he always like that?' she said, as the doors swung shut behind us.

'You mean Liam?' I felt my phone vibrate with a message. An email from Jeanette's secretary, confirming our appointment. *Please don't be late*, she'd written at the bottom. *Ms Hall's schedule is extremely busy this afternoon and I've only managed to allocate you half an hour. If you aren't on time, I'm afraid it won't be possible for her to see you until the exhibition is launched.*

'Yes,' Sara was saying. 'Doctor Pinney seems quite old-fashioned. He asked me to get his lunch for him a few times and call this hire-car place to see if there were any better vehicles. I laughed it off, but I'm not a hundred per cent sure he was joking. When I told my boyfriend, he said I must have misheard.'

'Liam can be difficult,' I said. 'He'll sulk now. I know what he's like. Just avoid him for the next few hours, if you can.'

Sara grinned. 'Noted.'

We crossed the room, heading back towards the lobby. As we passed an open doorway, Sara stopped abruptly.

'You never got to see Maja's reconstruction,' she said. 'You have to meet her. She's like our patron saint here in Castricum, a warrior for women's courage.'

She seemed so earnest, I found it impossible to refuse. Although aware of the mounting time pressure, I pushed through the beaded curtain and entered the small ante-chamber I'd seen earlier from the other side of the room where Maja's skeletal remains were housed in the oblong box. The lighting was different here. The clinical glare of white-tinted halogen globes showed up every pore and freckle on the face of the figure positioned at the centre of the room. If it weren't for the uncanny stillness, the mannequin could have been a real person. Crinkled blonde hair plaited into two braids hung either side of her face and her cheeks and nose were florid, as if burned by the wind or sun. Her blue gaze held me captive, burning with a fiery intensity. There was a certain wisdom in those eyes that seemed to be at odds with her extreme youth and reminded me strongly of Anneke.

A white, keloid scar over her left eyebrow was the only outward indication of any physical damage, but the story of her fate echoed inside my head. If I lifted her woollen tunic, would I find her celluloid skin peeled back, the soft flesh ruptured by the deadly tip of a spear? When she ran out onto that muddy battlefield for the last time, did she have any inkling what the future might bring? Did she pray to some higher power to grant her immortality, sensing that her remains would one day inspire this modern curio of plastic skin and teeth? Maja's bones had lain hidden for a thousand years until a team of people prised them out of the earth and set about piecing together the clues of her life and death. Anna Tesseltje and Catharina van Shurman died so long ago, their bones were nothing but dust. A silk dress was all that connected them to each other and to the world of seventeenth-century Holland. Liam might be happy with a premature media announcement, but Anna and Catharina deserved better. I was not ready to relinquish control of the project just to soothe Liam's wounded ego. We would simply have to keep digging for the truth.

9

Anna

AN HOUR BEFORE MAARTEN HORST AND HIS WIFE are due to arrive for the first portrait sitting, Crispijn stands up from the breakfast table and announces he is leaving.

'Where are you going? When will you return?' Catharina demands to know. She flicks back the bell-shaped sleeves of her painter's smock and rotates her wrists impatiently, peering through the open doorway of the breakfast room into the entrance corridor as if she can already hear voices.

'I'm destined for Amsterdam,' Crispijn says, pulling on his riding gloves. He turns to Anna. 'You may contact me there, if you need me. I'll be staying with my good friend Doctor Wijck. He is the night-sky enthusiast I told you about.'

'Playing with your telescopes again?' Catharina murmurs, although she sounds distracted, still gazing past him at the empty corridor.

Crispijn shakes his head. 'I've no wish to stay here and watch you debase yourself at Maarten's feet. Unless you've changed your mind?'

His words seem to snap Catharina from her reverie.

She glares at him as she stands, facing him so they are eye to eye. 'You are right to take your high morals elsewhere. I'm doing this for Griet – not for you, and certainly not for me. Maarten knows where she is. We must convince him to help us find her.'

Crispijn nods gravely, as if this is the answer he expected. With one last bow to Anna, he settles his wide-brimmed hat on his head and disappears into the corridor. The front door slams. There is the jingle of a horse's reins, then the clatter of hooves on the drive.

'We don't need him,' Catharina says, waving her hand dismissively. Sinking back into her chair, she picks at her bread, slicing it into halves then quarters before sitting back and leaving the food untouched. Anna stirs a spoon through her own rapidly cooling pottage. Since arriving at Sterrenwijck, she has eaten everything set down in front of her, but today her appetite has shrivelled to the size of a pea. Crispijn's unexpected departure has cast a pall over what should be a day of relief, the culmination of artistic negotiations between the van Shurman and Horst estates. The house already feels different without Crispijn, emptier and more sombre, like the aftermath of a funeral. Anna has grown used to spending time with him, chatting about the stars and Catharina's progress with the commissioned portraits.

The evening after they returned from the Winter Queen's masque, he invited her up to see the heavenly constellations. Viewing the stars through the telescope in his attic bedroom made her feel tiny and insignificant, a grain of sand on a vast celestial beach. It held at bay the worst of her fears about her father's curse, although she still found herself rising in the night and going to the dresser and fumbling about in the dark until she felt the cool silk of her mother's gown, reassuring in its constancy. The night before last, their hands connected as he adjusted the eyepiece and Anna felt the touch of his skin sear her fingers. She jerked her hand away, starting guiltily as if she'd burned it. Crispijn only smiled and held out the telescope, moving aside slightly so she could look through it to see the bright orb of Venus burning like a beacon in the darkness.

Lotte slips in to clear away the breakfast food as Catharina moves into the parlour to wait for the Horsts. Anna follows her, watching as she moves to stand beside the window, her eyes fixed on the drive, her gaze burning with a feverish intensity. Barely two weeks have expired since the Winter Queen's masque, but it feels to Anna as if a dozen years have passed. Each morning, Catharina wakes before the sun to pace the perimeter of her bedchamber. Like a restless ghost, she rattles the combs in their ivory cups, pokes about in her writing desk and tugs extravagant costumes from her dresser, holding them up against her body and muttering to herself before tossing them in a crumpled heap. Anna follows in her wake, yawning as she bends to scoop up discarded clothes and return them to the fold. She sets aside the ones that need cleaning and mending, fingering the stained collars and small holes in Catharina's damask silk waistcoats, thinking of the lye bath she will ask Mrs Hartog to prepare for them later.

If only she found the preparation of Catharina's canvases as satisfying as a clean gown. More than twice she has boiled and mixed the preparation to daub on the porous surface and although her first attempts were disasters, she has improved. The first time, she spilled the mixture on her skin and the foul scent of bubbling animal fat hung about her for a whole day like a bad omen. The second time, she did better, holding the cauldron between her feet while she dipped in the brush and smeared it across the expanse of cloth. When it was done, she stood back, panting, to admire her efforts. It was only when a frowning Catharina appeared at her shoulder that she saw the drips and runs, the uneven patches where the glue had dried in clumps. After a moment's silence, Catharina's displeasure seemed to dissipate.

'It matters not,' Anna heard her say, to herself. 'Griet will soon return and she knows how to prepare a canvas. She has a natural talent for such things.'

These words should have sent a cold shiver through Anna's heart. But her recent experiences with Crispijn have dulled her fear of being thrown out immediately, should Griet somehow return. There is a softness in the way Crispijn looks at her that makes her suspect he would retain her services and find a place for her within the staff even if Catharina no longer needed her companionship. She has tried to make herself useful, and now that the Horsts are due to sit for their portrait, there will be even more for her to do. There will be errands to run back and forth between the households, props to coordinate and purchase and paint. Catharina has also warned her she will be so occupied with painting that she will not have time to respond to the usual queries from clients wishing to pick up their completed works. Anna reassured her it would not be a problem. But of course, she was working on the assumption that Crispijn would be around to help. Disappointment churns in the base of her stomach at the thought of his leaving. She cannot speak to the wisdom of Catharina's taking on the portrait, but the decision has been made. Wouldn't it be best to get the sitting over with as quickly as possible? Then they can all move on with their lives. Catharina's obsession (there is no other word for it) with Griet disturbs Anna and she cannot exactly say why. But she remembers Cornelis de Witt saying that artists can be temperamental, that they can fall in love with the strangest things – a vase, a mood, a pretty insect. They are adept at maintaining their passion until something better comes along. Perhaps Griet and Catharina enjoyed a close friendship of the kind it is difficult to describe. Anna has never had any close friends – it was only ever her and Lijsbeth.

Crispijn is the first person outside the orbit of her own family whose opinion she has ever trusted. Given time, might it be possible for them to exchange even deeper confidences? She cannot imagine he would ever stoop to marry her. That is a fantasy even her overactive imagination cannot reliably conjure. But they could be friends, couldn't they? Perhaps one day he will marry and she might be employed to watch over his children and organise the household laundry. It's a harmless dream and one she has indulged in often of late. He would treat her kindly, just as he does the rest of the staff. She imagines his children – a girl and a boy, both sporting the van Shurmans' coppery mop and serious dark gaze, loose curls framing their solemn faces. When she tries to imagine her own children, she always draws a blank. It's as if her subconscious cannot conceive of a future beyond Sterrenwijck. But there's no time to brood any further, for she hears the sudden creak of wheels and spies Mrs Hartog hurrying past the room on her way to open the front door.

Catharina takes a long inhalation and shuts her eyes to compose herself as muffled voices echo in the hallway. A moment later, the housekeeper announces the visitors and Catharina's eyes fly open, her lips forming a bright, welcoming smile.

Maarten is dressed in his officer's uniform, a red sash tied across his chest, medals pinned to his collar. He accepts Catharina's greeting formally, bowing to her and then to Anna, who shifts from foot to foot, uncomfortable with the sudden attention. She is merely a servant, a nobody. Why should he bow? She turns her attention to Blanche, assisting the girl to shrug off her muddy cloak and passing it out to Lotte in the corridor who bears it away, holding it carefully.

Blanche seems even paler than the last time Anna saw her. She smiles wanly at Catharina's enquiries about her health and tells them in a soft voice that she's been confined to her bed with a bad cold. That is the reason, she says, for the delay arranging the portrait sitting. They could not come sooner, could not find the time between daily visits from the doctor and the hours where she felt too weak to even lift her head.

'But you feel better now?' Catharina says, playing anxiously with the cord she has wound around her smock to belt it in.

'I do,' Blanche says, after only a slight hesitation. 'I kept this day in the back of my mind. All through the fever dreams and the awful swelling, I thought of it as a reward, a prize I had to get better in order to claim. My husband plans to hang your portrait in the reception room of our new house, Lady van Shurman. It will be so hot in Sumatra. I have heard it is a place of extremes. Rains every afternoon like clockwork, but otherwise as dry as a desert.' She touched Maarten's arm tentatively. 'Maarten assures me there will be a degree of civility about the place. Servants and some homelike comforts. I hope the portrait will remind me of Holland where we might one day return.'

'That is a worthy sentiment,' Catharina says. Anna can tell she is impatient to begin the sitting; she has probably missed half of what Blanche said, too busy devising how she can extract the location of Griet's imprisonment from Maarten's silent lips. 'Everything is ready for you,' she says. 'Miss Tesseltje has been preparing canvases for days now and the portrait studio has been cleaned and dusted within an inch of its life. As we discussed, I'll paint you standing, Madam, by your husband's side. If you'll follow Miss Tesseltje, I'll meet you there in a matter of moments.'

Anna beckons them forward, glad Catharina omitted any reference to the first botched canvases. She hears Blanche take a step behind her, then falter. Looking back, she sees that Maarten hasn't moved. He holds himself stiffly and there is a sour expression on his face that even Catharina, buoyed by high spirits about Griet, cannot fail to misinterpret.

'Is something wrong?' she says.

'I've changed my mind. I would prefer you to paint us in the library. I remember the way – it's down that corridor and to the left. I remember hiding in the window seat when I was a child, waiting for your brother to come and find me.'

Catharina frowns. 'Father's library? But it's been shut up for years. And there's no fire in there. It would be most unsuitable, sir. Better you come to the studio where it's warm. I would hate Madam Horst's cold to return due to any neglect on my part.'

Maarten's jaw tenses. 'I insist,' he says. 'The library is the grandest room in the house. I do not want this to be like any other portrait you've painted before. I'm not paying you to create yet another version of something already hanging in a dozen other houses.'

Catharina's cheeks colour. She flicks an anxious look at Anna who bites her lip hard, grounding down on the soft flesh with her teeth. This meeting must go smoothly, she thinks. If they offend him, Maarten will surely withhold any knowledge he possesses. It crosses Anna's mind that he could be bluffing, pretending to know more than he really does. But Catharina is not willing to take the chance. Anna watches her struggle with her own pride. It is clearly an effort. At last, she summons a strained smile.

'Of course,' she says. 'It's for you, the patron, to say. I will ask Mrs Hartog to prepare the library now and have it cleaned. Anna, you help her. Go on, now. I will light the fire in there myself. I've done it before . . .'

She crosses to the firebox to scoop up an armful of fresh kindling and Anna catches Maarten's quick, triumphant smile.

* * *

The portrait sittings continue for the next month. Each morning, the Horsts arrive in their carriage and Mrs Hartog shows them into the library where Anna is tasked with ensuring they are comfortably seen to – that there is ample wine filling their crystal goblets, that the outfits they are to be painted in are pressed and clean, no untoward creases to distract Catharina as she sketches the figures into the scene. Blanche poses wearing a gown of silver gilt damask. It is the dress she was married in. She tells Anna that Maarten chose it for her, that it was one of the gifts he brought with him when he came to meet her father at the inn in Amsterdam where their family was staying after they fled to the Continent. Maarten was there to negotiate the terms of the arrangement. He obtained her measurements in advance from Blanche's mother and the silver dress arrived in its own carriage, as if it were a real person.

'Was it not a little presumptuous of him, Madam?' Anna says when they are alone. 'To arrange the outfit if the marriage wasn't already agreed upon?' They are standing in a small chamber that opens off the grand library and has been adapted as something of a makeshift dressing room. She tightens the laces on Blanche's bodice as gently as she can, avoiding the faded bruises on the girl's shoulders and back. At least there are no fresh ones. Since the sittings have begun, Anna has noticed no further injuries on Blanche's person and she has started to wonder if she imagined the abuse. Perhaps Maarten was right and Blanche was choking and he was trying to help her. Perhaps his cruelty does not extend to his wife, although he is driving them all mad with his demands about the portrait. Outside the door, she can hear him now, barking orders at Henrick. The poor manservant has been recruited to help Maarten into his costume since Maarten has no valet of his own. Henrick's fingers are gnarled and he struggles to pin Maarten's suit together. Anna hears him mumbling a string of apologies and Maarten's terse rejoinder. If Crispijn were here, she thinks, he would do a better job. But he would probably refuse to help. The servants have no power to do anything but follow Catharina's orders. Crispijn would not last a day in this tense atmosphere.

'Oh, we were very grateful that he considered me at all,' Blanche says. 'When we fled England, we left with nothing and disguised ourselves as peasants to escape the notice of Cromwell's soldiers. It would have been improper for me to be seen in the Oude Kerk wearing a shabby blouse and kirtle. Maarten tells me this gown is worth more than what an artist working in The Hague makes in one year and I think it is very fine.'

She touches the gown's sleeves delicately, a half-smile on her lips, and Anna wonders if Blanche missed the hidden sting in Maarten's boast, his belittling of Catharina's work.

'He bought me other things, too,' Blanche says. 'But later. A velvet purse and a set of wooden combs. I had nothing to my name when we married. Nothing. Now I am rich, with a husband who adores me. It's a situation many women would envy. That's why the other wives are not so friendly when we meet them at court. They're jealous of my good fortune.'

'I'm sure that's true, Madam,' Anna says. She fixes a band of seed pearls on Blanche's hair, tucking away the stray wisps under the fabric. Lijsbeth might have asked her to do this one day, she thinks. Instead, Anna dressed her corpse.

'I hope this portrait brings us luck,' Blanche continues. 'We could use some good fortune after such a tumultuous year. I pray every day for Maarten's health and my own, and that of my parents, too, wherever they are. But Maarten says a portrait is a symbol of unification between a husband and wife. It is like declaring our vows again before God, our intention to start a family . . .' She continues to chatter about babies and families and God, reminding Anna of a bird, a lark perhaps, singing the same tune over and over. Kneeling, Anna holds out the girl's stockings so she can slip her long, skinny legs into the fabric and, as she does, something Blanche has said finally catches her attention.

'Did you hear about Lady Killigrew?'

'No,' Anna says, straightening. 'What about her, Madam?'

Blanche stifles a giggle. 'I shouldn't gossip. Especially not to the help.'

Anna ignores this; she's heard worse descriptions of servitude.

Blanche continues, oblivious. 'Lady Killigrew is with child. The news is all over court. It must belong to Prince Charles. Lord Killigrew has been delayed in France for the past year. They are saying Lady Killigrew will have to be sent away until the infant is born. Queen Elizabeth is displeased with Lady Killigrew's indiscretion.'

Anna mulls the news over. It makes sense to her now why Lady Killigrew has not responded to any of Anna's entreaties to send one of her servants along to Sterrenwijck to collect the finished portrait Catharina painted of her on behalf of Queen Elizabeth. The Queen would not want a reminder of her nephew's bad judgement. But how unsurprising, to learn that Lady Killigrew is to be sent away to deal with the consequences. Imagine giving birth alone, she thinks, far from your friends and family. Utterly disgraced. Meanwhile, Prince Charles will no doubt find another paramour to lavish his attentions upon. The idea turns Anna's stomach. Why are women always the ones who must take responsibility for men's foolish actions? She cannot say this to Blanche. Although the girl is only a few years younger than herself, Anna feels the difference in their ages keenly. Blanche has also faced hardship – the loss of her family's estates and titles – but she has rebounded with a favourable marriage while Anna must rely on the connections she has made in The Hague to support her.

'There, Madam,' she says. 'You're dressed. And you look as elegant as always.'

She brushes down her apron and turns, preparing to call Catharina over and let her know the girl is ready for her sitting. She's taken aback when Blanche suddenly clasps her hand and draws her back towards the window. Blanche's palm is damp and clammy and Anna feels uneasy, knowing of the girl's illness a few weeks earlier.

'Miss Tesseltje, I have news. I believe I myself am expecting a child. Please don't say anything to your mistress. If I'm right, it's early. Maarten is the only other person I've told and, as you can imagine, he is beyond happy to think he will soon have an heir. There is nobody else to confide

279

in, and I feel closer to you after this past month than I do to any other woman in Holland.'

Anna doesn't know what to do with this news. She murmurs a blessing to the blushing Blanche and makes a move to push past the girl, hoping she will take the hint and release her hand. Blanche only grips her tighter.

'I wondered,' Blanche says, a little breathlessly, 'if you might consider leaving the van Shurmans and joining our household? Lady van Shurman's spirits seem so much restored now. She can surely spare you. And I would dearly love for you to become my maid. You can help with the baby, when he finally appears. You'd have to accompany us to Sumatra when we leave next month, but with you, a four-month journey across the seas would not feel like a burden.'

Anna's first instinct is to refuse. There is a difficult silence while she formulates and discards the harshest rejections. Imagine, she thinks, giving up Catharina and Crispijn for Maarten's manipulation and Blanche's clinginess. But the girl seems so moved by the idea that she finds it difficult to reject her outright.

She is saved from answering when Catharina pokes her head through the chamber door.

'Is she ready?' she says to Anna, who nods mutely, not trusting herself to speak.

Catharina gives Blanche a little push through the door, following her out into the library where Maarten is waiting in his uniform. He grasps his wife's arm possessively as she crosses the room to stand in the place Catharina has marked in chalk upon the floor.

'There you are,' he says. 'I was beginning to think you'd died.'

Catharina frowns at the unpleasant thought, but Blanche laughs, indulging her husband's taste for poor jokes. Anna retreats into the shadows at the back of the room behind the easel Catharina has set up. A canvas is propped on the timber frame and Anna can see the figures of the VOC officer and his young wife committed there in oils. Catharina had spent the first two weeks sketching the couple, drawing their arms and eyes and hands and clothes with a kind of fervour until Maarten grew annoyed and demanded to know why she didn't just start on the final portrait at once. Catharina's face had hardened and Anna knew she wanted to argue, but her desire to discover what Maarten knew about Griet proved stronger. A week ago she began working on the canvas which will eventually hold the finished portrait of the wedded couple. Her biggest challenge, of course, has been incorporating Maarten's shifting desires. He is a difficult model, moody and restless, often refusing to stay still for the required hour. Today, he seems even more annoying than usual. He puffs up his chest and walks around the room whenever he grows bored of standing by his wife's side.

When Catharina asks him to return, he pretends he hasn't heard. He looks around the room as if it is an empire he plans on conquering. His gaze falls on Anna.

'I want her in the portrait,' he says. Anna looks behind her, assuming he refers to somebody else.

'Who?' Catharina says.

Maarten points to Anna.

'What is the good of her hanging around if she cannot be useful? She can be a marriage witness or a servant hovering in the background.' Maarten waves his hand. 'I am a great art connoisseur, Madam. You'd know that if you had ever bothered to listen to me before it served your own interests to do so. Now that you need my money, you listen to every word with rapt attention. Eh?'

Catharina doesn't answer. Anna stays motionless where she is. Maarten, noticing, waves at her.

'Go and change,' he says. 'You can wear the dress you wore to the masque. Was it cream? Or gold? I can't remember, I don't pay attention to fashion. Hurry up now. My time is valuable.'

Anna exchanges a look with Catharina. She can tell Catharina doesn't want to submit to Maarten's demands.

'Griet would do it,' he says suddenly, into the empty air.

'Come upstairs with me,' Catharina says to Anna, quietly. She takes Anna's arm and guides her into the corridor. They walk together to Anna's bedroom. Catharina leans upon the wall next to her as Anna fumbles in the dresser for her mother's gown.

'I'm sorry,' she says, her face as white as chalk. 'I no more want to paint you than you want to model. But it's for the greater good, Anna. You understand.'

For the first time, Anna feels a small kindling of dislike for her mistress. If she were not so weak-willed . . . But then she thinks about Crispijn, her true friend. He's written twice since leaving for Amsterdam and his letters are full of news about recent construction work around the city and the polder which holds back the powerful waters of the IJ.

If he suddenly disappeared without explanation, she would also grieve his absence and she would want to know what became of him.

Catharina makes a sudden, gasping sound and bends down. In her efforts to extract the dress, Anna sees that she has disturbed the handkerchief in which she kept Griet's long red hairs. Catharina cradles them as if they are more precious than gold. Pocketing them, she helps Anna to put on her mother's gown.

'It does look well on you,' Catharina says, as she ties the last ribbon. 'No wonder my brother stared when he saw you. You look entirely different. Even the way you hold yourself. Thank you for agreeing.'

Her grateful compliment makes Anna blush.

They return to the library together. Maarten wants Anna to kneel at the couple's feet, her arms prostrate as if she is curtseying or bowing, a supplicant praying at a shrine of marital bliss. Thankfully, Catharina convinces him otherwise. She positions Anna behind the couple, stooping to gather the folds of Blanche's silver wedding gown. 'She looks more like a lady's attendant,' Catharina says. It confers a certain power on the couple, to know they can afford the services of a companion. Maarten grunts his approval.

After an hour in the same position, Anna's arms and back begin to ache. Catharina informs Maarten that the sitting is over and that the couple should return the day after tomorrow to continue. Catharina's face is grey with exhaustion and stress. Maarten says nothing about Griet as they part at the doorway and Anna feels Catharina's mounting despair at his lack of transparency. Anna returns to her bedchamber to take off her mother's dress. Folding up the silk, she replaces it in the drawer and her gaze catches on the sketch of Griet. She is beautiful, her neck long and elegant, her hair fiery perfection. Anna examines her own plain features in the looking glass, wondering whether Catharina will draw her the same way, with fondness, or whether the image of her on the Horsts' portrait will somehow capture the look of someone hunted, always glancing behind at the shadow of fate darkening her heels.

The next time the Horsts visit Sterrenwijck, Blanche confronts Anna again, choosing to speak to her while they are both trapped in the small dressing room where there is no possible chance of escape.

'Have you thought any more about my offer?' the woman says, as Anna rolls on Blanche's stockings. 'Maarten says he has almost finalised the staffing of the Governor's property in Sumatra. We will be leaving within the next month once the last arrangements are made.'

'I'm afraid I can't abandon my employers,' Anna says. She is wearing her own gold dress and stands carefully to avoid crushing the hem. 'It's a kind and generous offer, Madam, and I thank you for it. But Madam van Shurman suffered much after the loss of her assistant and friend. And now her brother has been called away to Amsterdam. I fear she might relapse into melancholy if I leave now.'

Blanche's young face falls. A faint flicker of anger crosses her expression and Anna steels herself for a fight. But the girl seems to rally. 'I understand, of course,' she says, a little stiffly. 'You may go and wait in the library. I will see to my own hair, thank you.'

Anna curtseys. She opens the door and goes to stand in the appointed place. Something about Blanche's attitude disturbs her. She has seen that expression before on Lijsbeth's features. An all-or-nothing look that never bodes well for the person on the receiving end.

Uneasily, she watches Blanche emerge from the closet and take Maarten's arm. Grasping the train of the silk gown, she bends her knee the better to balance, trying to find a pose she can comfortably hold since her body was sore after that previous sitting, her limbs stiff and frozen after hours stuck in the same position.

Catharina begins to paint. There are dark circles under her eyes and Anna can tell her patience with Maarten Horst and his endless demands is beginning to wear thin. Today, though, it is Blanche who surprises them by breaking away after half an hour has slipped by, eliciting a sigh from Catharina and a stern look from her husband that she, for once, ignores.

'Was Griet a good painter?' she asks, plucking a paperweight off a side table and hefting the glassy orb in her hand.

Catharina turns pale. 'She was an excellent apprentice,' she says in a small, choking voice. 'She would have gone on to be a master painter, I've no doubt about that, Madam.'

Maarten sniffs.

'I suppose you've heard nothing about her for months,' Blanche continues. Catharina's brush hovers over the canvas.

'No,' she says hoarsely.

'I would hate to lose a friend in such a way.' Blanche sets the paperweight down and rests her hands across her belly. 'I can tell you where she is.'

'Blanche!' Maarten's face is scarlet. He moves towards his wife, but Blanche darts away, towards the dusty curtains out of his grasp.

'She is being held in a convent to the south of here,' she says. 'It is a place run by Catholics somewhere between Antwerp and Ghent. I believe she would be very happy to see you. Maarten made enquiries weeks ago and I think it only right that you hear the truth from –'

Maarten seizes her arm and begins to drag her into the corridor outside. Blanche shrieks and gasps, trying unsuccessfully to fight him off. Catharina and Anna stare at each other, too shocked to move. Moments later, Maarten reappears, panting. There is a scratch near his left ear, a trickle of ruby blood. Blanche is not as submissive as she appears.

'I've asked your manservant to bring my carriage around. You are to ignore everything my wife says. She is not in her right mind. The malady she suffered a short time ago has obviously left some lasting damage. I expect you to continue painting my portrait, Madam van Shurman. In less than a month, my wife and I will board a ship destined for Sumatra. I want the portrait to be ready.'

Catharina blinks at him and Anna wonders if she has even heard a word he said. A glow of hope lights up her face like a lantern. She says nothing and, after a tense moment, Maarten grunts and leaves. As soon as he's gone, she collapses to the floor. Anna hurries over to help her.

With an effort, she pulls the artist to her feet and manages to push her into a velvet armchair. A cloud of dust rises as Catharina grips the armrests.

'Did you hear what she said? Or did I dream it?' she says softly.

'I heard.' Anna feels the silk of her dress puddle around her feet as she sinks to her knees beside the chair. 'If she speaks the truth, why would she tell us when it clearly upset her husband?'

Catharina purses her lips. 'That Maarten. I should never have trusted him.'

'He knew all along that you were trying to find her,' Anna says. 'I believe he would have gone on withholding what he knew until it was too late, and Griet either perished or he left for his new position in the East Indies, taking the secret with him.'

'Then why did Madam Horst confess it to us?'

Anna hesitates. 'I believe it was because of me,' she says, and when Catharina stares, she goes on. 'Madam Horst asked me to leave your household and join hers. She wants a companion of her own, to keep her in good spirits when she reaches Sumatra. Also, she is expecting a child and may need help from a trusted servant. I suspect she hoped Griet's return might hasten my decision.'

'Well, she cannot have you!' Catharina exclaims. She clutches Anna's hand; Anna feels the hard lumps of calluses and the many scars caused by Catharina's engraving stele slipping as she worked. 'You are one of us now,' her mistress says. 'You belong at Sterrenwijck. I hope you know that.'

'It's nice,' Anna admits, 'to hear you say it.'

'Crispijn and I, we are not so easy to live with. Even Griet grew tired of our fighting. She often went out walking on her own through the woods. But you have brought us together,' says Catharina. 'I owe you a debt. I intend to pay it, in good time. And now I must think what to do about Griet.'

They are still sitting there, hands clasped, when there is a sudden commotion at the door. Mrs Hartog hurries past, calling for Lotte, and Henrick lumbers behind, his back bowed under the weight of a large travelling trunk. A familiar footfall sounds in the corridor, causing Anna to startle. She stands awkwardly as Crispijn enters. His hair is frizzed and damp from travelling, but he seems renewed by his sojourn away. His gaze softens as he looks at Anna and she realises she is still wearing her mother's dress. She feels slightly foolish in it, as if she's been caught playing dress-up. But then he smiles and comes to kiss her hand and Catharina's cheek and every notion of embarrassment flees.

'What have I missed?' he says.

10

Jo

I WAS RELIEVED TO FIND JEANETTE HALL STILL WAITING when I raced into the café courtyard inside the Rijksmuseum's glass atrium. I'd forgotten how congested the traffic in Amsterdam could be during morning peak hour. All those one-way canal streets and swarms of cyclists had conspired against me, resulting in a delay of fifteen minutes past our allocated start time. She sat with her back to the museum's entrance, her white hair styled in an elegant chignon that glowed under a halo of autumn sunlight. Our eyes locked. I'd googled her of course. Her professional profile photos must have been taken during the 1980s when masculine power suits and sweaters with shoulder pads were considered the height of fashion. Apart from that, she didn't seem to have aged much at all. She had a long, thin nose, painted lips and a piercing blue gaze that held me captive.

'Doctor Baaker?' she said.

I nodded. 'I'm so sorry I'm late.'

She accepted the apology with good grace, but declined my offer of a fresh pot of tea. 'Let's keep this short. I've got a schedule as long as my arm. I shouldn't have taken the weekend off, but it was my partner's sixtieth birthday so we hired a houseboat with some friends. Things may have got a little messy.'

She shot me an impish smile and I found myself warming to her. Taking the chair opposite, I searched my pockets for the small journal I'd been carrying about with me for the past week. The notebook was filled with the research notes I'd taken from my earliest observations of the dress as well as the interviews I'd conducted with Bram and the other divers and Olivia at the historical society. But it was nowhere to be found. I assumed I'd left it in the hire car or perhaps back at Liam's lab in Castricum but there was no time to dwell on its absence. I'd have to call him later.

'I understand you're coordinating an exhibition on the birth of the art market,' I said.

'If you're here to beg for a pre-show ticket, I'm afraid the allocation has already been exhausted. There are at least twenty journalists ahead of you on the waiting list.'

'Oh, I'm not a journalist,' I said, quickly. 'I'm a textiles historian and a freelance curator. I'm trying to track down the owner of a dress.'

She smiled. 'Just one dress? Isn't that a little reductive?'

'It's an unusual artefact,' I said. 'Some Dutch friends of mine – divers – brought it up from a shipwreck at the bottom of the ocean.'

'And it survived the process?'

'Miraculously, yes. Preliminary chemical analysis of fabric samples suggest it dates back to the early seventeenth century and I have reason to believe it was owned and worn by either the Dutch artist Catharina van Shurman or her companion, Anna Tesseltje. I understand Catharina van Shurman is significantly featured in your exhibition and I was hoping to convince you to let me take a look at a few of her artworks. My colleague, Doctor Liam Pinney, is undertaking the technical lab procedures so I promised to follow up the tangential leads, which might provide some proof of ownership.'

'So what you're saying is, he's left you to do all the grunt work?'

'I hadn't thought about it in quite those terms.'

'Some men will always take the low road, if you let them. I once had a man sneak into one of my exhibitions before opening night to take photographs that he proceeded to sell to the press for an exorbitant fee. The paper ran a story he'd prepared which made me out to be some kind of nymphomaniac, suggesting the only way I could have possibly secured those artwork loans was to have conducted affairs with the collectors.'

'He sounds like a total loser.'

'He was my ex-husband, so yes, your character assessment is correct.'

'Well, I can assure you, Ms Hall, that my intentions are purely academic.'

'Which is not, in and of itself, completely altruistic.'

'That's true,' I admitted. 'But can any of us really claim to be operating purely from a love of art and history? I think the real reason I'm prepared to look past my colleague's laziness, if that's what it boils down to, is that chemical analysis and dates can't tell us everything about an artefact. They can provide clues, but they can't string a narrative together. I want to fill in those gaps, if I can. When someone stands in front of that gown, I want them to feel as if the person who wore it is still there in the room with them. Clothes are uniquely placed to teach us about the world and ourselves, don't you think?'

It was a gamble. I gazed down at my clasped hands. The splash of water from the nearby fountain and the throb of car engines coming from the street seemed like a distant melody. Striped tulips swayed in their planter boxes. When I finally gathered the courage to look up, I saw that Jeanette's playful expression had hardened into one of serious absorption. She stood and picked up her purse.

'I can give you fifteen minutes. Come with me.'

I followed her across the courtyard and through a side door in the museum's façade. After some hurried consultation with a uniformed guard and a few discreet phone calls, she waved me through a security barrier. 'It usually takes a lot longer to get clearance, but the director's away at a conference and the deputy director owes me a favour. I've told him you're an international historian at the top of your game working on a television series funded by the World Heritage Committee about trailblazing Dutch women artists.' She flashed me a grin. 'Never let the truth stand in the way of a convincing lie.'

She led the way down a series of twisted corridors, her heels clicking on the marble floors, until we reached a service lift. After riding it up a few floors, we emerged at last into the public reception foyer of an exhibition space that had been sectioned off from the main gallery by portable panels.

'Here we are.' Jeanette slung her handbag into a drawer inside a tall podium. 'Excuse the mess. Most of the paintings are already in position, but we've had some lighting issues to fix. I'm sure I don't have to tell you it's utter chaos right until the last second.'

'There's always so much to do,' I agreed. 'It feels like an impossible dream, like it can't possibly come together. And then it does.'

She smiled. 'And then it does.' She beckoned me forward into the first display area. 'Every room in the exhibition has been designed to reflect a different geographic location – Delft, Antwerp, Amsterdam, Leiden, Middleburg, The Hague. Art dealers didn't really exist in Europe until the sixteenth century, not in any way we would recognise today. Before then, fine art was indistinguishable from the craft market. Guilds did not differentiate, for example, between house painters and artists. They were considered competitors, on par with one another. The seventeenth century changed all that. You said you wanted to know more about Catharina van Shurman. Have you seen a self-portrait of her yet?'

She led me over to an illustrated artwork no bigger than an A4 sheet of paper. The parchment was faded and the piece had been damaged during its journey through the centuries. A careless brown splotch stained one corner and there were very faint creases, indicating the drawing had once been folded into thirds. Yet for all its flaws, the child's face staring out of the drawing was unmistakably vibrant. Dressed in a long-sleeved Dutch dress trimmed with a fussy lace collar, typical of the era, the little girl's gleeful expression invited the viewer to guess what – or who – might have amused her.

'Catharina sketched it for her twin brother's eighth birthday,' Jeanette said. 'They were inseparable. I've no doubt he was just out of frame, probably making funny faces. His name was Crispijn. He became an art dealer, one of the few who dared to go up against the likes of Hendrick van Ulyenburgh and Johannes de Renialme. He gave up his dream of becoming an inventor to sell his sister's artwork, which must have made financial sense because Catharina didn't just paint. She also carved wax miniatures and etched glass wine goblets. She was an incredibly gifted polymath with an immense intellect and capacity for remembering things. At age eleven, her father gave her a book by Seneca and paid for her to be tutored in Latin, which, as I'm sure you know, was unusual at the time. Girls weren't generally given what we would term a classical education. They most certainly weren't encouraged to read Seneca! Catharina was a great advocate for women's education and published, during her early twenties, a treatise about the importance of teaching young women to read and write. The pamphlet was hugely popular – and hugely controversial. In the end, her father and his high-powered friends rallied to support her. That was how things worked back then. You had to be endorsed by the fraternity in order to have any chance of succeeding professionally. They began calling her the Tenth Muse.'

'It sounds as if you adore her.'

'Oh, I do,' Jeanette said, playing with a small silver pendant around her throat. 'As someone who spent the first thirty years of her life trying to get the male-dominated departments of scholarly institutions to take me seriously, I can't even imagine how a woman like Catharina van Shurman – lacking precedent, with only her father and brother to support her application – even summoned the audacity to set foot into Leiden University, let alone attend classes there. I had no male allies – is that what you call them? – back when I was an undergraduate. It was cut-throat. Men would try to get you to sleep with them just to put you off your lectures the next day.'

I cleared my throat and she laughed.

'Look, their methods might have changed these days, but the goal hasn't: stay in your lane. That's what a lot of them would like us to do. Not all, of course. But if it wasn't for women like Catharina, it might have taken even longer for women to gain personal independence. That's why it's important to me to stage exhibitions like "The Birth of the Art Market". People like Catharina might have been celebrated during their lifetime, but they're largely unknown by the public now. I want to lift her achievements, ensure she becomes a household name.'

She led me to a gilt-framed oil painting of a pretty, three-storey brick mansion set on a riverbank surrounded by tall trees and green hedges.

'This is Sterrenwijck, a property outside The Hague where Catharina lived with her brother. They had a large staff when their parents were alive, but this was slowly reduced as the years wore on. Eventually it was whittled down to one housekeeper, her husband and a kitchen maid. Oh and there was a lady's companion, too. The one you mentioned, Anna Tesseltje. But she lived there less than a year and became more like part of the family, by all accounts, so I don't know if she can be classified as "staff".'

'I read she modelled for a painting Catharina started in 1652.'

'Yes. *The Marriage*.' Jeanette pointed at a large canvas hanging on the opposite wall. 'It was meant to be a wedding portrait. A man named Maarten Horst commissioned it for his new bride. He was an officer with the VOC. We have a copy of his signed contract in fact. It was customary for art dealers to issue legally binding work agreements, just like it is now, but for some reason this portrait remained unfinished. It's different to Catharina's other pieces. She was a fast painter, but she liked to work in a very deliberate manner. She approached each portrait commission as a real challenge even though she found the work quite unfulfilling – a means to a financial end.

'Look at how this portrait is much more chaotic. You see the smears of paint around the officer and his wife? Those are mistakes or changes Catharina made during the process. Some critics think it indicates a shift in style. They think the disordered application of brushstrokes represents Catharina's anguished indecision over her wish to sell Sterrenwijck and relocate to France. And, of course, this is the only portrait featuring Catharina's companion, Anna Tesseltje. There she is, playing the role of devoted bridal attendant.'

As Jeanette moved her hand aside, I leaned forward. My breath caught. There was Anna, stooping low, her fingers grasping the hem of the bride's silver train. She wore the silk gown, the damask now a familiar shape and pattern, although the colour was different to how I imagined.

'That's it,' I said, clutching Jeanette's arm. 'That's the dress!'

'Is it really?' Jeanette said, her eyes rounded in shock. 'How extraordinary. You're sure?'

I nodded, too excited and overwhelmed by emotion to speak. My heart had begun to thud and all the details of the room had become softly blurred so that only the dress stood out in vivid clarity, the centuries-old oils that had captured all those fine details in the fabric gleaming in the glow of the downlights. Jeanette and I stood for a moment longer in silent communion, staring at the painting that would never be completed. The dress itself was more of a pure gold, as Liam had suggested, rather than rich reddish-copper. It shone as brightly as freshly churned butter or like the sunlight that fell through a large casement window, casting its matrimonial blessing over the young couple standing in the centre of the wood-panelled library. There was a stiffness in Anna's posture, and her face, what I could see of it, wore a serious expression. Her downcast eyes were fixed stubbornly on the task at hand and wisps of dark hair spilled from the contours of her velvet cap. She had the glass earrings – the Dutch tears – threaded through her earlobes. Clearly, she had been dressed up to represent the wealth and power of the newly wedded couple – her future employers. Yet there was something unique in the way Catharina had painted her – a vibrancy and solidness, compared to the two washed-out figures at whose feet she knelt – that suggested her loyalty lay elsewhere. I kept waiting for her to raise her head and stare defiantly at us, but she remained static, just a varnished facsimile of a once living, breathing person.

'You know,' Jeanette said at last, 'there's a theory Catharina van Shurman was in love with a woman. Her name was Margriet Pieterson. There was some confusion in the early days of van Shurman scholarship over whether Griet was actually a man, but her gender has been pretty well established for a while now.'

'Catharina and Anna Tesseltje,' I said. 'There's nothing to suggest they were involved?'

Jeanette's brow crinkled. 'I highly doubt it. Catharina only painted Anna once. Whereas she made dozens of different sketches of Griet and used her as her model and muse for at least six paintings. When Griet left the van Shurmans' household suddenly – the circumstances around her departure are unclear – Catharina fell into deep despair. Her brother wrote to various physicians, asking their advice for treating a severe case of melancholia. These days we'd call it depression. And then he hired your Anna Tesseltje to be her companion and boost her spirits. When Anna left it must have hurt Catharina's feelings deeply. And then she died before they reconciled.'

'What about the brother?' I said.

'Crispijn.' Jeanette pointed to a portrait of a boy in his late teens, his dark eyes full of laughter. 'He died young, the same year as Anna actually. You can see how similar the twins were in looks and temperament. Catharina often said he was the anchor to her boat, the thing that pulled her back when she was at her lowest ebb. She didn't paint many other portraits of him either, but I've seen letters they wrote to each other which are full of fondness and affection. Griet seems to have been a bit of a sore point between them. There were heated exchanges back and forth. But underneath it all, they really loved each other. And that must have been something worth holding onto during a time when life was so precarious, when you could wake up with a cold and be dead by sunset.'

She nodded towards a painting on the far wall that I hadn't noticed. A funeral scene, depicting a coffin being carried out of an old Dutch church past two pale-haired children who wept openly, holding onto each other for support.

'Do you know why Catharina never finished the Horsts' wedding portrait?' I said.

'No. Perhaps it was something to do with money or payment. Considering what happened afterwards – Anna's defection to the Horsts, all those tragic deaths – I suppose everyone forgot about it. Or maybe Catharina just lost interest. She moved to France the following year after selling the house and dismissing the servants and declaring she was giving up painting for good. She did continue painting, as it turns out, but never sold her art for a profit again. She just gave them as gifts to close friends and people who'd shown her kindness. Interestingly, the figures she painted weren't royalty or wealthy merchants like the subjects of her earlier works but servants and ordinary people. Catharina depicted them going about their daily business – praying, gardening, reading, preparing a meal. The technique she used – luminous effects, it's called – makes it seem as if they're glowing, illuminated from within by a radiant goodness. The glaze is made from linseed oil applied in thin layers over a tempera base. Her subjects were almost always women.'

Jeanette glanced at her watch.

'We're going to have to leave it there,' she said. 'It's been a pleasure. I'm so glad you made contact and that you were able to confirm the owner of the dress. You must keep in touch and let me know if you discover anything else about Anna's wardrobe.'

'I still don't know that we can definitively claim that the gown was Anna's just because we have proof that she modelled it in one painting,' I said. 'But it's a very good start.'

I took one last, lingering look at the dress in the painting before allowing Jeanette to lead me back through the exhibition towards the podium. When she reached the desk, she paused and turned.

'There is a suggestion that Catharina painted one last image of Anna. I've never seen it – it's been held by the same family for generations. The owner's name is Johann de Witte. He's something of a recluse. He lives down south in a small township near Zeeland. I can give you the address. I've asked to visit him many times through the years and he's always refused a meeting. If you wanted to email him, I have those details, too. My emails have never bounced so I'm pretty sure he receives them. He just never replies.'

I tried calling Liam as soon as I left the Rijksmuseum. My mind raced. I needed to tell him about the wedding portrait and the presence of Anna's dress and the suggestion that

Catharina might have been in love with her apprentice. His mobile rang out so I left a message asking him to call me back. Getting in my hire car, I programmed Johann de Witte's address into the GPS system. I wasn't going to sit around and wait for an email that might not come. There were just enough hours in the day to make it down to Emmadorp and back before the last ferry to Texel left Den Hoorn at 8 p.m.. Far from satisfying my curiosity, my time with Jeanette Hall had only reinforced my determination to discover if Anna was indeed the dress's original owner. The sooner I had all the pieces of her tale, the sooner I could construct a story on which to hang the opening exhibition. Everything seemed more vibrant and alive as I navigated the winding Amsterdam streets that led onto the highway that would take me all the way down to Zeeland. The cherry trees shone with promise, the river water glinted in the canal and the sky was splashed with daubs of ultramarine blue.

I was on the verge of something, chasing down a woman who darted ahead, her silk dress catching the autumn light.

11

Anna

IT TAKES CATHARINA ANOTHER FORTNIGHT TO TRACK down the convent where Griet is living.

Anna is with Crispijn in the library when the letter arrives, delivered by Henrick into the mistress's eager hands. She appears in the doorway, looking half-wild, spirals of copper hair escaping from her woollen cap.

'I've found her,' she cries, waving the missive triumphantly.

'Who?' Crispijn says, but Anna can tell that, like her, he has already guessed. Even Catharina ignores the question. Crossing the library in three swift bounds, she falls at her brother's feet.

'Our Sacred Lady of Bruges.' Catharina wrinkles her nose. 'It's situated next to a swamp. An hour's journey from Antwerp. That's why it has been difficult to find any record of it. But I have it now. An old friend sent his manservant at my request to scour the area and report back. Griet is there, within the convent's walls. He saw her with his own eyes. She is alive, praise be to God.' Catharina exhales a long sigh, shuts her eyes and clasps the letter to her chest.

Crispijn clears his throat. He looks at Anna, who tucks

away under a cushion the book she has been reading to him. There will be no more reading today. Since his return to Sterrenwijck, he has complained of headaches and dizzy spells and, with Catharina busy searching for Griet, armed with the information Blanche Horst divulged during their last, fated sitting, Anna has been tasked with entertaining him and ensuring his needs are met. He claims his eyesight has been affected by the vast amount of snow he had to wade through up north, the frigid lakes stretching all the way to the cold North Sea. He can walk around on his own well enough, but occasionally, a sudden sharp head pain leading to a bout of dizziness will set in, meaning Anna has to stay nearby in order to offer him her arm and help him to a chair. He finds reading and writing difficult so she has taken over these tasks, too. Crispijn assures her the condition is temporary.

'Snow blindness,' he told her, his mouth twisted in a humourless smile. 'It's common among travellers. Doctor Wijck says it will go away on its own within a matter of weeks.'

Anna had no reason not to trust the good doctor's assessment – after all, he is a learned scholar and she is just a humble maid. But she can't shake off the fear that Crispijn's ailment may persist. What will become of his new telescope venture then? He brought back an early prototype with him from Amsterdam and asked Anna to use it to record a description of Saturn for him. She had never seen a planet up close before and the colours were a revelation – pinks and mauves, shot through with mustard yellow, patterned with whorls. It was a new way of seeing and she felt guilty that he could not appreciate the fruits of his research and invention. 'I'm only happy to see it being used,' he insisted, placing his hand over hers on the windowsill. Again, she felt the tenderness of his friendship envelop her. She felt her father's old curse drop away, her loneliness sinking beneath the calm surface of her life here at Sterrenwijck.

Perhaps, combined with the talisman of her mother's dress, Crispijn's affection for her can hold back her natural misfortune, as a polder repels the ocean tide. Catharina, for her part, has lavished Crispijn with all the comforts he might want. Mrs Hartog has been kept busy baking and stewing Crispijn's favourite childhood dishes. Lotte carries them out each night in a kind of formal procession – first soup, then meat and cheese and thick fresh bread slathered with butter. Crispijn was amused, at first.

'It's like we always planned,' he told Anna. 'When we were children, we used to imagine what kind of feasts we would hold when we were grown and our parents were no longer there to accuse us of being gluttons.'

But Anna has noticed that, for all his talk, he doesn't eat much and there is a thinness about his wrists, like canvas drawn over a timber frame, which reminds her of how her father looked in his final months. She has to push this thought away in order to smile when he asks her to read aloud, what-ever takes her fancy. Sometimes it's Virgil's *Eclogues*, where the story's bucolic setting soothes them both. Sometimes she reads him the English gardening pamphlets he'd brought back from one of his trips to London. If Catharina joins them – if she can tear herself away from searching for Griet – she reads them Descartes' *Meditations on First Philosophy*, translating passages from Latin to Dutch effortlessly. Catharina's appetite for both food and philosophy is robust. Most nights, she shovels in her supper before fleeing upstairs to write more letters. It's rare for Anna to see her walking to the studio to paint. The Horsts' marriage portrait has stalled. Maarten refuses to pay and Catharina, now that she has gained the knowledge he once held over her, has stopped. The last time Anna saw the unfinished portrait, it was propped against the studio wall next to a painting of Griet modelling a sea nymph's daughter. Anna had set down the wine goblets Catharina had asked her to clean and tilted her neck, taking the marriage portrait in sideways. What a strange feeling it gave her, to see herself mirrored on the canvas like that. She had the oddest sense of looking down through time, could see herself hanging on a wall somewhere in Sterrenwijck, watching the lives of the van Shurmans and their servants pass by.

Of the three figures in the painting, hers was the most substantially finished. Blanche's figure was ghost-like and Maarten was a series of smudges and mistakes redrawn – the consequence of all his fussy changes, Anna supposed. She is consumed by guilty thoughts that Blanche was probably being punished on her behalf. If she had agreed to take the position offered to her, perhaps the painting would have been finished. It might have healed the rift between the two families and made Blanche's life less of a torment. But there was Griet to consider, wasn't there? Before she met the Horsts, Anna sometimes dreamed that Griet was haunting her bedchamber, searching in the dresser for the sketch Catharina made and the stray hairs Anna had plucked from the combs. Now she knows Griet is alive and Catharina does, too, and this knowledge has changed everything in the household. It's almost a relief, she thinks, to hear that Catharina has tracked her down.

'What do you intend to do about it?' Crispijn says.

Catharina's smile fades. 'Well, we must go and fetch her,' she says stoutly.

'And what then?' Crispijn says. 'What do you propose we do with her? Do you suppose she will be able to return here? That her family won't try to reclaim her yet again? You think that they will give up control of her just because *you* have discovered where she is being kept? There is also the difficulty of helping her escape the convent, assuming she wants to leave . . .'

'Why would she want to stay there?' Catharina bursts out.

Crispijn shrugs. He looks weary, Anna thinks.

'I will ask Queen Elizabeth to find a situation for her,' Catharina says, her expression hard. 'Her Majesty will not refuse me. She is a generous patron and a kind friend. And she believes in friendship and love. Why else would they call her the Queen of Hearts?'

'It will need to be far,' Crispijn says. 'A different country. Somewhere her family cannot exert their influence and control. A foreign court.'

Catharina says nothing. In the stillness, Anna hears Mrs Hartog lecturing Lotte for letting the supper burn. The smell of burned potatoes taints the air like a sour omen.

'Would you be happy,' Crispijn says, softly, 'to let Griet go again?'

'Yes, if I knew she was safe,' Catharina says. 'If I knew she had gone there of her own free will, not forced in to it.' A small sob escapes her. 'She is my world, Crispijn. My soul cannot rest knowing that hers is suffering in bondage, trapped somewhere she has no desire to be.'

Crispijn holds his sister's gaze for a long time. And then he closes his eyes and rubs his temples. 'Very well,' he says. 'Then let me think.'

Two days later, they reach the slum-lined outskirts of Ghent. The private coach they are travelling in is old and smells of leather and sweat. An unfamiliar horseman tightens the reins and the creatures slow, the better to navigate the winding, twisted streets jammed with smoke-blackened shacks. Anna, wearing her mother's dress, leans forward to watch the hungry, doe-eyed children and nursing mothers who stare frostily back, the women's modesty barely preserved by an arrangement of ragged shawls.

There is a lump in Anna's throat. The sentence for impersonating a person of status in the Dutch Republic is imprisonment. Anna might once have laughed at the ludicrous notion of dressing in her mother's silk gown and presenting herself as the sister-in-law of someone she has never met. Now, after everything she has experienced this past year, it doesn't seem so far-fetched. But if things do not go well today, she might well end up one of these unfortunates, crushed by the wheel of life, unable to claw herself out of her own miserable circumstances. She doesn't know what the prisons are like here in Ghent, but in Amsterdam, parents and nursemaids use the *Spinhuis* as a threat to goad girls into good behaviour.

She rubs one damp palm nervously along her thigh, bunching the silk. Crispijn, sitting beside her, notices. Without asking, he picks up her hand and tucks it into the crook of his elbow. It's a brotherly gesture, an act of gentle kindness, but it makes her skin tingle and sends a thrill of exhilaration whooshing through her stomach into her chest.

'Careful. You'll ruin your fine dress,' he warns. 'It would fetch a good sum at the cloth market. The fabric alone must be worth thirty guilders.'

'I'll never sell it,' she says.

'You won't have to.'

Anna peers up at him curiously. But he has turned his face away and will not meet her gaze. Catharina, sitting opposite, pays them no attention. After all these months of nervous agitation, she seems finally to have found her inner calm. Her hands are clasped as if in prayer and the veiled hat she has chosen to wear disguises most of her face, leaving everything but her mouth and chin bathed in shadow.

The slums fall away as they near the heart of the city, replaced by peaked canal houses adorned with flourished scrolls and statues of heralds playing flutes and fiddles and rosy-cheeked cherubs flanked by outstretched angels' wings. The coachman guides the horses through the cobbled streets, slowing to let a man trundling a wagon piled high with bolts of shimmering cloth push past them to join a throng of others heading towards a vast, grey-stone building.

'That's the Lakenhalle,' Crispijn says. 'You can buy any fabrics you like there, anything your heart desires, and have it sewn into a gown fit for royalty.'

Anna wonders if her mother's dress came from a place like that. She never thought to question her mother or sister about its origins and now there is nobody left to ask. It feels as if the dress sprung fully-formed into her life when her sister passed away, but if Anna had tried to wear it years ago, the silk folds would have easily swallowed up her childish torso and limbs. I have grown up, she thinks, and the realisation is bittersweet.

When the coach stops at the resting place near the Town Hall, Catharina is the first to climb out. Anna follows her, stretching out her aching back and blinking in the watery light reflecting off the wide, curving river they have followed to arrive here at their destination. Anna looks about her, momentarily forgetting their purpose, awed by the sheer spectacle of the place. Ghent reminds her a little of Amsterdam with its stately architecture and its ringed canals mirroring the austere frontage of tall houses, but here the Catholic churches are not hidden in little side streets and alleyways. They are dazzling tributes to the divine, stained glass in every window, the saints' miraculous deeds flooded by warm sunlight. The trio make their way to the inn Crispijn has booked, a place called De Zwaan. Crispijn pays a boy to carry their bags upstairs, although they haven't brought much between them, just a change of clothes and one of Griet's old frocks. The room itself is sparse, lacking the warmth and character of Sterrenwijck's living quarters. Two lumpy mattresses propped on narrow cots are pressed against the walls and the ceiling is stained black. But it's clean enough for one night. Anna stands beside Catharina on the threadbare rug, worry gnawing at her gut.

'My room will be down the hall,' Crispijn tells them. He looks worn out by the long journey, dark shadows circling his eyes. Yet he draws himself up and glances at Anna. 'We should get going.'

Impulsively, Catharina springs forward and hugs first Anna and then her brother. Surprise crosses Crispijn's face and he returns her embrace awkwardly. But Anna thinks the gesture is pleasing to him. When they draw apart, he is smiling like his old self. 'We will find her,' he assures his sister. He offers Anna his arm.

'Mrs Pieterson?'

Anna hesitates, then grasps it. It's only acting, she thinks. Like the players at the Queen's masque. I am Mrs Pieterson, wife of Willem Pieterson, Margriet's sister-in-law. God will overlook this sin; He will understand I am doing this for the greater good.

'I never realised what a handsome pair you make,' Catharina says. She looks small and lonely, standing by herself in the centre of the drab room. Anna knows she longs to go with them, but they cannot risk taking her in case she is recognised. 'I'll pray for Griet's safe delivery and yours.'

The paintwork on the carriage Crispijn has arranged to take them out to the convent is a glossy black, even finer than the one they own back at Sterrenwijck. The coachman wears a tall hat and a suit made of fine black linen.

'I thought it best to choose something grand,' Crispijn says as they bump along, leaving the city of Ghent behind and heading out towards the marshes. 'Something that signifies our wealth.'

Anna swallows. 'Good,' she says. It comes out hoarser than she intends. Her guts are churning. She glances out the window at the vegetation rolling past, the tree-lined paths, the bushes clumped together in a long impenetrable wall. Thankfully, there is still a strip of road. The carriage clings to it, bucking wildly like a ship on a storm-tossed sea, jolting and juddering, throwing Anna and Crispijn together.

She mumbles an apology as their knees connect.

'Don't be sorry,' he says. Pulling himself upright, he extracts a handkerchief and dabs his forehead, the skin clammy and flushed pink. 'Do you think they make this road intolerable so that the isolation and deprivations of cloistered life are easier to bear?'

'Perhaps,' she says. 'A life devoted to God seems noble. But there are things I would miss.'

'What would you miss?'

'Oh, singing,' she says. 'Music. Art. Reading. And – it sounds foolish – clothes. Dresses and white petticoats. Ornaments. Shoes.'

They smile at each other.

'Animals, too,' she says, warming to her theme (if this is his way of distracting her from the task ahead, then it is working). 'I left a dog behind when I came to live with you. His name was Wolfert. He belonged to my sister, Lijsbeth, and myself. But Lijsbeth didn't care for him much so I think he saw me as his mistress. It was difficult to let him go.'

'I wish I'd known. I love animals,' says Crispijn. 'I would fill Sterrenwijck with them, if I could. Hounds and cats, all of them together. But their fur makes Catharina sneeze so I was never allowed a pet of any kind.'

'What would you miss?' Anna says as the carriage jolts.

His smile fades a little. 'I would miss my friends. My sister. My work. And you.'

He fixes her with his dark gaze. Anna feels the heat climb in her cheeks and a strange weightlessness ballooning through her limbs.

'Perhaps this is too forward,' he says. 'You are unchaperoned and an orphan. I am your employer. But I feel I must confess the truth or it will haunt me. I enjoy your company, Anna Tesseltje. It's rare to find someone that you look forward to seeing every day. Could you ever see yourself joining our family?'

Anna stares at him, shocked. She suddenly understands why he has spent the journey sweating nervously. It wasn't the dizzy spells nor the headaches. Her heart fills with sudden gladness. This is an offer she never dreamed of, the chance to start her own family and with a man she could learn to love, one who has shown her friendship and kindness beyond measure. She is on the verge of accepting, but then she remembers.

'I can't marry you,' she says.

His face falls. 'Why ever not?'

Anna looks down at her lap, at the patch of silk fabric shimmering under the cloak. 'When I was born, my father cursed me. He gave me the name Anna Tesseltje to remind everyone, especially me, that God takes away what we love most as a lesson in humility and pride. And his wish came true. Everyone I have loved has perished – my mother and father, my sister. It would be better for you if we do not become too attached. You have had enough misfortune in

312

your own life; you do not need mine.'

Tears sting her eyes, but once the words are out, she feels lighter, as if speaking them has purged her of a bitter poison.

Crispijn says nothing for a while. He stares at her, his brow wrinkled. At last, he takes her hand. 'I believe you are wrong,' he says. 'I don't think you're cursed. That's not what your father intended you to believe. I think instead you were his blessing and he wanted to remember how lucky he was to have you when everything else seemed so dark.'

Anna laughs humourlessly.

'I made you laugh,' he says. 'That is a good sign.'

Tears rolls down her cheeks and drop onto her gown. Crispijn hands her his handkerchief.

'They say tears are a good way to begin a marriage. You will live in comfort,' he adds. 'And we can travel. I will show you all the things that you in your life have not had a chance to experience. And Catharina will paint and she will be happy, knowing that Griet is safe. We can even visit Griet, once enough time has passed and it is deemed safe for us to do so.'

'What would Catharina think?' Anna imagines the artist looking shocked and then angry. 'She will not want to share you.'

'She already does,' he says, spreading his hands wide. 'She is fond of you. She's always wanted a sister. She used to pester our mother about it. Apparently my company was not enough.'

Anna nods. 'I will consider your offer carefully,' she says.

'Don't wait too long. I'm thirty-eight. An old man.

I might soon be in my grave.' He laughs and then his expression becomes sombre. 'I'm serious, Anna. There is nobody I would rather share my life with, good fortune or ill. We will make our own luck.' He holds her gaze for another moment and then glances out the window. 'I believe we are almost there.'

The carriage begins to slow. When it stops Crispijn helps Anna from the coach and she jumps down and shades her eyes, gazing around. The convent is set in a flat clearing, spiky trees rising up around the building like a crown. A makeshift garden divided by a dirt path is set before the small clapboard building. It is two – no three–storeys high. An attic window glints at the very top. Anna thinks she spies a white face behind the pane. She squints, but the face has vanished.

Crispijn takes her arm, linking it through his own. Together, they walk up the path, stopping when they reach a set of double doors, peeling and worn, the paint rubbed away by weather and time.

Crispijn knocks on the door, the sound falling short, absorbed by the oak.

Anna's legs prickle with nervous energy. She imagines turning around and fleeing, but Crispijn's arm on hers is steady and reassuring. They could be married in truth. For the first time, she allows herself to imagine the softness of his lips and all the other pleasures that marriage would bring. It will make their performance more convincing, she tells herself. As the door opens, she smiles.

'Yes?' says a young, frightened-looking nun, no older than eighteen. She surveys them with wide, blue eyes. Anna notices the way her gaze falls on her mother's silk dress and she hopes its beauty can convince the girl to trust them. 'Can I help you?'

'I hope so,' Crispijn says. 'I'm here for my sister. Her name is Margriet Pieterson. I understand she was brought here a few months ago to recover from an ailment. I have come to take her home with me. My wife and I have recently moved into our new residence in Middleburg. We have left our children in the care of a nursemaid, but it would be more prudent for Griet to return and work for us. That is the fate, after all, that awaits many spinsters and Griet is no exception.'

The young nun purses her lips and turns back to glance at the shadows. 'I'll need to consult with the Abbess,' she says, doubtfully. Opening the door, she ushers them into a cold, dark reception hall. Anna notices that the hem of her black robe is flecked with white housepaint. 'Wait here until I return.'

Anna watches her vanish down a corridor.

Crispijn drops his smile as soon as she is gone. Releasing Anna's arm, he removes his hat and worries the fabric nervously between his fingers.

Minutes pass and no one comes.

'The longer we wait, the more I fear discovery,' Crispijn says.

They gaze at each other. His eyes are dark pools Anna could drown in. What would he do if she leaned forward now and kissed him? Just a chaste peck, swift and sweet. She could stroke his jaw with her thumb, as she's seen real wives do. A small gesture of marital unity, a promise of a lifetime bound together. The temptation is overwhelming. If she did, some boundary would be crossed. A kiss is tantamount to acceptance. Who can even say whether she would ever want to find her way back?

Heavy footsteps can be heard suddenly, coming down the corridor, not the young nun's pattering footfalls. These shoes belong to the Abbess who appears in front of them, an old, heavy-set woman.

She nods to them.

'I'm sorry to have kept you waiting, sir. You've caught us at a busy time. We are restoring the walls in the east wing. If you'll accompany me to my study, we can sit and talk quietly there.'

She leads them along a dusty hallway and opens an arched door. The Abbess settles herself behind an ornate wooden desk, leaving Anna and Crispijn to sit in the chairs opposite.

'Sister Marie advises that you wish to remove your sister, Margriet, from our flock.' She pauses. 'I'm afraid you have travelled all this way for nothing. I cannot permit her to leave. Your sister is wilful. She must be tamed. And her assistance is needed with the restoration project. The exercise is good for her mind and soul. It is her duty to God.'

'Her duty is to me,' Crispijn interrupts. 'We are expecting her to return with us to help care for the children.'

He reaches for Anna's hand and squeezes it. The Abbess follows the direction of his gaze. Under the woman's intense scrutiny, Anna feels her cheeks grow pink.

'Margriet is good with children,' she says. 'We know she will take the lessons she has learned here with her and impress upon them the importance of faith and worship.'

The Abbess drums her fingers upon the table. She stands

suddenly and turns to fetch a ledger from a shelf. Letting it thud onto the desk, she flicks the pages with thick fingers.

'The problem, sir, is not only related to faith. It is financial.'

Anna can see dates recorded at the top, sums scratched in the column, set down in black ink. The old woman taps a page with a wrinkled thumb.

'When those men brought your sister to us on your mother's behalf, there was an agreement that we would keep her for a year until they could decide what was to be done with her. Now you tell me you would like to change this arrangement. So I must ask you, sir, what recompense will you offer in order to secure your sister's freedom? The total outstanding amount is one hundred guilders, less the thirty guilders still owing for this year. That covers her bed and board since the first instalment.'

Crispijn frowns and Anna can tell this is unexpected news. His plan to pluck Griet from the convent's grasp relied on manipulation and acting. He never considered the money.

The door opens suddenly and Griet appears, guided inside by Sister Marie. Anna is shocked to find herself in the room with a figure she has only ever seen in Catharina's sketches and paintings. In person, Griet's features are very different to those captured on canvas – her nose is long, her cheeks angular, the skin mottled with dark spots. Her pale eyes are deeply set and her head has been shaved. She is not at all the beautiful, ethereal creature of Catharina's paintings, but she is a real, living person. How strange love is, that it can blind even an artist of Catharina's calibre.

Griet shuffles past them, stares in confusion. Anna breaks the tense silence by standing up and crossing the room. Grasping Griet's shoulders, she embraces her.

'Dear sister,' she says. 'How I've missed you.'

Griet's body is thin and bony beneath the shapeless grey shift and she smells of body odour and unwashed hair.

'We've come to bring you home,' Anna says loudly. 'You belong with us.'

Aware of the Abbess watching them closely, she presses Griet to her even tighter.

'We can pay,' Crispijn says. He pulls out a purse, the coins inside chinking as he throws it onto the desk. 'Here is thirty. That's all I have brought with me and it will more than cover the costs owing for the remainder of the year. I will send you the rest when we return to Amsterdam. I'm willing to overlook your counting skills, Madam, as I know the work you are doing here is God's work.'

The Abbess' eyes flash greedily. Unknotting the bag, she tips the guilders out onto the desk, raking over them with gnarled fingers. The coins gleam in the sunlight breaking through the diamond-shaped window. With a last grunt, she nods.

'Take her then, and have done. We will not miss her dis-ruptive behaviour. I expect the rest of the fee to be sent within the month. Sister Marie will see you out.'

They leave her recounting the coins, preparing to record them in the open ledger.

Sister Marie asks Griet if she would like to go up and fetch her belongings. Griet shakes her head.

'I want nothing that reminds me of this place,' she mutters. Her voice has a nasal quality to it, as though she has a permanent cold. She takes a hesitant step through the open doorway and then seems to lost her balance. Anna grips one arm, Crispijn the other. Together they guide her up the dirt path to where the carriage and the horseman are waiting. They help Griet clamber into the carriage and, once she is safely inside, Crispijn offers Anna his arm. As she swings herself up into the body of the coach, he kisses her cheek, a light, soft gesture which so surprises her she cannot formulate a response.

Catharina is pacing the bedroom of the inn when Anna and Crispijn return at last. Afternoon sunlight, muted by its passage through the grubby windows, illuminates her wild hair. She has used her fingers to comb it, Anna sees, and tried to dress it as Mrs Hartog would have, pinning it in tight ringlets, but the effect is one of dishevelment. It seems to matter little. As Anna and Crispijn lead the exhausted Griet inside, Catharina shrieks and runs towards her.

'What have they done to you, my beauty?' she says, leaning forward to embrace her friend. Griet allows herself to be held for a long time. Eventually she pushes Catharina off her, wincing.

'You're suffocating me.'

Catharina looks chastened. 'Forgive me,' she says. She sits down on a chair, her eyes searching Griet's face hungrily. Griet accepts the scented washcloth Anna holds out and buries her face in the folds.

'It smells so clean,' she says, lifting her chin. She scratches her hip through the grey material of her shift. 'I will need new clothes. The bedding was infested with foul lice.'

'We brought them,' Catharina says, gesturing at Anna to fetch the clothes. Crispijn clears his throat, excusing himself.

'I'll be in my quarters if you need me,' he says.

Griet takes the fresh clothing, looking Anna up and down as if she has only just noticed her properly.

'Who are you?' she says, as she pulls off her grey shift and drops it on the floor. Anna blushes, averts her gaze, but not before she's glimpsed thin ribs jutting beneath small breasts, the flex of muscled forearms.

'This is Anna Tesseltje,' Catharina says. 'She's my companion. Crispijn arranged the hiring of her. She has become a friend. You can trust her. And Crispijn enjoys her company.'

Griet's mouth curves in a smile. 'So I see.' She takes Catharina's hand. 'So what's to become of me?'

Catharina hesitates. 'We can talk about that later.'

'I would rather discuss it now.'

Catharina sighs. 'You are to join the retinue of the Queen's daughter, Elisabeth, in France as one of her ladies-in-waiting. We have arranged your passage. A man and his wife are due to arrive here tomorrow morning to escort you.'

'France?' Griet sounds shocked.

'It must be far enough for your family not to find you,' Catharina says gently. 'Once you're safely within the Princess' fold, they cannot hope to extract you. They have no power at court.'

'But . . . so far away . . .' Griet lifts her hands to her face while Catharina puts a comforting arm around the woman's bony shoulders.

'We will come and visit you,' she says. 'Crispijn has promised. You will not be lonely.'

She kisses Griet's hand a little clumsily. After a moment, Griet returns the gesture. Anna feels as if she has intruded upon a private moment. Mumbling an excuse, she withdraws from the room and closes the door. The corridor of the inn is lit by smoky lanterns. There is nowhere else for her to go so she wanders down to the other end of the floor and raps gently on Crispijn's door. It opens after a long moment and Crispijn appears, stifling a yawn, his face careworn and exhausted.

'You caught me resting. Don't go,' he says, taking her arm as she begins to turn away and drawing her inside the room. 'Stay.'

The room is darker than the one she is to share with Catharina and Griet. A low fire burns in the grate.

'Sit down,' Crispijn says, rubbing his eyes and waving with his free hand towards a worn armchair. Anna perches primly on the seat, her heart thudding in her ears.

'How are you feeling?' she says. He has not complained of headaches much at all since they set out and she hopes that this means he is cured. But his next words send a shiver through her.

'I did not want to alarm you earlier, but I fear I'm losing the sight in my right eye.' He taps the tip of his finger. 'These past days it's been like a lantern flickering on and off. I'm afraid to ask the physician in case he tells me it bodes badly for the other.'

For the first time, he looks afraid. Anna cannot bear to see him so distressed. Standing, she takes his hand. 'I will be your eyes, then. I have thought about your offer all afternoon. You are a good person, Crispijn van Shurman. I would be lucky to spend my life with you.'

He searches her face, then nods. 'I'm glad,' he says. 'For I will take care of you as well as Catharina and anyone else who comes along.'

Anna has never been kissed. Her body tenses as Crispijn moves towards her, covering her lips with his own. His mouth is soft and he tastes of sweet wine. As he helps her ease the silk dress off her shoulders, unlacing the bodice, she imagines their bodies are water, moving together, the currents converging until they are one ocean. When she slips her hands inside his shirt, he does not resist.

12

Jo

THE TOWNSHIP OF EMMADORP WAS EVEN SMALLER than it had looked on the map. It was just a tiny strip of shops encompassing a service station, a café and grocery store, backing onto flat grassy fields filled with cows and sheep. The car's GPS struggled to pin down Johann de Witte's precise address and, when I picked up my phone to check Google Maps, I realised I didn't have any service. That probably explained why Liam hadn't called me back. I parked and went inside the café to ask for directions. The interior was decorated with vintage cuckoo clocks and peeling posters from the 1960s, advertising holidays in exotic destinations. A lady with dark hair appeared between two salon doors which swung inwards, like the ones in old-fashioned cowboy movies. 'Can I help you?'

'I'm looking for this address,' I said.

She squinted at the piece of paper in my hand.

'Sure, I know it. Mr de Witte is quite the collector,' she said. 'His family go way back. He lives in a farmhouse just a few minutes from here. He donated a lot of the vintage decor. Some of the pieces are quite valuable, but he always refuses to take any money for them. I'll write the directions down for you.'

She disappeared into the back room and returned holding a pen.

'Do you get many visitors here?' I said, looking around at the empty tables.

She shook her head. 'Not since they built the motorway. Things used to be better. People would drive out from the city on the weekends to go hiking in the nature reserve in Saeftinghe. It's over that ridge,' she said, pointing through the window at a green hillock rising in the distance.

Cold shock ran through me. I'd been so fixated on finding Johann that I'd failed to notice how close Emmadorp was to where my parents had died. I didn't really want to ask the woman for details, but I couldn't stop. It was like watching myself from a distance. All those years I'd avoided visiting and now, without even realising it, I'd found my way here.

'Do you remember a couple who drowned in the reserve?' I said. 'It would have been twenty years ago now.'

The woman looked grave. 'Oh yes. That poor couple. There've been no drowning cases since, but a few near misses. Tourists often don't realise how fast the water rises once the tide comes in. The council put up warning signs everywhere after it happened. There's a plaque, too, dedicated to the couple who passed away. A gentleman from up north arranged it. Came out once to see it for himself and stopped in here for lunch. He was a nice man. Said he worked in a seal sanctuary, told me to come say hi if I ever went up that way for a holiday.'

She handed me the directions to Johann's place.

'Oh, I should warn you that Johann is a bit of a crank. He often ignores strangers who come out to see him. He's had quite a few visitors over the years come to ask him about his collectables. Don't give up. Make sure you leave your name and number so he can contact you in case he changes his mind.'

I thanked her, returned to the car and followed the directions she'd given me. The whole time, I could feel Saeftinghe watching me, trying to pull me back like a current clawing the sand. A rusted gate came into view, framed by a stand of linden trees, and I pulled the car up beside a vast, three-storey farmhouse that looked as if it could hold twice as many paintings as Jeanette's exhibition. I knocked on the door.

'Mr de Witte?'

No answer came, but I thought I saw the upstairs curtains twitch. I waited a few minutes, then called out.

'Mr de Witte? My name is Jo Baaker. I'm a historian. I'm trying to track down the owner of a particularly fascinating dress that I believe might have once belonged to a woman who worked for the artist Catharina van Shurman. I was told you have one of her paintings in your possession and I'd love to see it. In return, I can tell you more about the discovery of the dress.'

I stood back, waiting. The wind tinkled through a set of brass chimes hanging beside the door. Nothing stirred from within the house. I waited five minutes, then ten, and then fifteen.

'All right,' I said, at last. 'You win. If you change your mind, please let me know.'

Suppressing my disappointment, I slipped my Texel

address and phone number under the door. Confirmation of Anna's ownership was so tantalisingly close and yet I could do nothing but hope the old gentleman might have a change of heart.

I reversed the car and drove back towards the motorway. When the turnoff to the Saeftinghe nature reserve appeared, it was as if my brain and my body were separate entities. One part of me continued driving, heading north towards Texel, and another, larger part of me turned the wheel and accelerated onto the off-ramp and entered Saeftinghe. I headed up a gentle slope and parked on a small verge, then got out and walked towards the guardrail that formed a snaking circle around the park. It was cold at that height with no trees to break the wind blowing across the saltgrass. I imagined my parents pulling up in their battered Skoda on the gravel where my hire car now sat. I saw my mother yawn and raise her arms over her head, stretching out her back. My father's fluoro windcheater flapped around him like a kite. Shivering, he drew the zipper up to his chin. After locking the car, they set off, shading their eyes against the sun's glare. I watched them disappear, two tall figures slowly swallowed up by the incoming tide.

At that moment, I heard someone singing. It was a woman's voice, strong and lilting, coming from the direction of the swamp. I froze and gripped the guardrail. The wind blew. The grasses shivered. And I stood there listening, every nerve in my body thrilling. I could have sworn the voice was my mother's, singing the lullaby Marieke had been pestering me about my entire adult life.

A sudden memory went off in my head like a flash of

lightning. I was in my childhood bedroom, tucked inside my bed. The inky blackness haunting the corners of the room held myriad terrors. I resisted the urge to scramble out and flee for the safety of the lighted hallway. But then a familiar figure appeared in the doorway and another behind it. My parents. I held out my arms, but my mother shook her head. She stayed where she was and sang, her sweet voice harmonising with my father's husky tones.

'Little Nod,' she said, when the song was over. 'Lie down and sleep now. Let the water carry you away!'

I closed my eyes, comforted, knowing I was safe. That no matter what darkness lay outside, my parents' love would protect me from it.

All these years, that memory had waited for me. Marieke had been telling the truth. The terrible yawning emptiness that had haunted me through late adolescence and into adulthood now seemed as distant and removed from reality as a sky full of alien stars. It was too late to tell my parents I now understood. Or was it? Clutching the guardrail, I hoisted myself over the fence, my shoes sinking into the mud. The atmosphere changed as soon as I started walking. I had some strange desire to keep walking until I reached the very heart of the reserve. I was sure that's where the sound was coming from. But I'd gone only ten metres or so when the singing stopped. All I could hear was the wind beating the air and the cry of birds swooping overhead, flapping their way towards the sea.

After waiting another minute, I turned and retraced my footsteps and swung myself back over the guardrail. A stone plinth had been erected halfway along the fence under a big warning sign advising hikers not to enter the swamp without a guide. Sunlight glanced off the bronze plaque, dazzling me. I saw my parents' names and the date of their deaths. Gerrit must have arranged it after the funeral. Underneath their names, he'd engraved:

They sailed off, into the night, on a river of crystal light, into a sea of dew.

The words sent another jolt of emotion rippling through me.

Their voices and faces cut clearly through that black river of memory, the tide of the present pushing against the past. Words and gestures came rushing back – a touch on the back of my hand, a gentle caress I hadn't noticed, too wrapped up in my friends and my diving to acknowledge any parental softness, however brief.

My parents loved me, to the best of their ability. And then I began, at last, to cry.

I drove all the way back to Den Hoorn without stopping. It was dark by the time I arrived and I hoped I hadn't missed the last ferry back. I'd felt my phone vibrate continuously with emails and texts, but kept my eyes on the road, refusing to allow myself the luxury of distraction until I was safely on board. As the ferry pulled out of the harbour, I locked my car and headed upstairs to the passenger seats, hoping to gather my thoughts and buy a cup of hot tea. I hadn't eaten since morning and the lack of food, combined with the day's excitement, had left me drained and exhausted.

When I pulled out my mobile, the hunger dissolved, overtaken by a cramping nausea.

There were fifteen messages, the first from Bram.

Feine, are you there? Everybody knows about the dress! Did you leak the story to the media already? I thought you were planning to hold out until Rob Disijk approved the exhibition and the return of the artefacts. Why didn't you tell me?! The pizza shop is going crazy. Everyone's here asking. Get back to me as soon as you can, OK?

I felt sick to my stomach.

The next few messages were from international journalists, each practically identical and *wanting to confirm some details around the significant textiles find Doctor Pinney had identified as belonging to Catharina van Shurman, the celebrated seventeenth-century artist and poet.* Doctor Pinney had mentioned my *brief assistance on his project* and they were wondering if there was anything I'd like to add?

The last message was from Monica Rosetti at Sydney University.

Jo, I just heard about the dress! What a find. No wonder you dashed off in such a hurry. I assume this means you've almost finished your book? Shame you weren't the lead researcher. A story like that could have been a springboard for your own documentary series or something! Anyway, the teaching offer still stands if you want it. Let me know when you'll be back. Cheers, Mon.

I groped blindly for a seat and sank into it. My chest hurt. Liam had gone public. Anger swept through me like a wave. I punched his number into my phone and pressed dial. When it rang out, I called Huis van Hilde.

Sara Van Dijk answered. 'Liam went back to his hotel

soon after you left. I haven't been able to contact him since. I saw the news, though. I thought you were going to announce the discovery together?'

My silence must have told her everything.

'Oh God,' she said. 'I'm so sorry. If I'd known, I would have tried to stop him.'

'There's nothing you could have done,' I said bleakly.

All that work for nothing. A week of obsessive research and this was the result. A premature media announcement that killed off the potential for any future deals for Bram and the Texel Historical Society to exhibit the dress, and destroyed any chance I might have had to tell people the truth about Anna's life. White rage flickered at the corners of my vision, making everything look as though I were seeing through a smudged camera lens. I began to pace back and forth between the plastic ferry seating, growing more and more agitated each second.

As I brought up Liam's number again, I could barely see clearly enough to stab the call button. It went straight to voicemail again, a disembodied recording urging the caller to leave a message and return number. As the recorded message beeped, I allowed my frustrations to erupt, full-force and let him have it.

I thought I'd feel better after venting my frustrations but instead I felt curiously drained.

As the ferry docked, I dragged myself to the lower deck to retrieve my car.

The phone buzzed in my pocket with a message and I pulled it out, half-expecting it to be Liam. Instead, I discovered an email from Rob Disijk.

I've just come out of a meeting with the other councillors. And I'm pleased to inform you that the Noord-Holland government has reviewed your proposal and given approval for the dress and the other artefacts to be displayed on Texel for a maximum of four weeks, assuming the historical society is still happy to pay for transport and conservation requirements. I hope this pleases you. I agree with your suggestion that it would be wise to keep the Texel community on our side in case any other significant discoveries are made in the area. I trust you'll let the society know? On another note, did you know the story about the find seems to have leaked out into the press? I just fielded a call from a journalist friend at De Telegraaf. *Did you send out a press release stating the dress was owned by Catharina van Shurman? I only ask because I would appreciate a little notice next time you're planning an announcement. I assumed you were going to wait until you could confirm the details. Or perhaps you've already done so. The government's position on the exhibition won't change, of course. We're still happy for the items to be returned to the island for a short time. But please keep me updated on the scholarship and the progress of the exhibition, so I can stay on top of the latest developments and avoid any nasty surprises.*

With my best regards,
Rob

I read the email three times. Each perusal generated different emotions – relief, embarrassment, rage. I was relieved that the Noord-Holland government had approved the historical society's request to host the exhibition. Imagining Olivia and Flora's excited faces when I relayed the good news to them filled me with an elation I hadn't felt in a long time. I had not been exaggerating when I told Liam how much it would mean to them for the items to be accessible to the Texel community who would treasure the opportunity to connect to this important embodiment of the island's past. I was mortified that Rob had been taken off guard by the premature announcement about the origins of the dress, especially since he had gone to all the trouble of pushing for the exhibition to be approved. If there was only some way to dial back the hours and warn him, I would have done it wholeheartedly. Lastly, I struggled to overcome the white rage which flickered and flared. Liam had so much to answer for. His interference and rash decision could have potentially ruined both Texel's chances at hosting the exhibition and any chance we had of discovering the identity of the true owner. But of course, as usual, Liam had been thinking only of himself.

The sky was dark as I navigated the twisted roads back to Gerrit's beach house. I wanted to hide under a blanket and never show my face again. As I pulled into his driveway, I saw a figure dart across the dunes, racing towards the cottage. My heart leaped. I'd experienced too many strange things today to cope with another one. But as I climbed out, the figure materialised into someone familiar.

Marieke, travel-weary and exhausted, clutching the

handle of her suitcase. I'd never been so glad to see her.

'I owe you an apology,' I whispered. 'You were right about everything.'

Marieke's face crumpled. Sniffing, she held out her arms and, after a moment, I let her hold me as if I were fifteen again, meeting her for the first time in my whole life.

13

Anna

CRISPIJN LEAVES FOR AMSTERDAM ON A WARM, spring day one month after Griet's rescue and a week after a note arrived from her, confirming she has safely reached France. He is dressed in a black doublet and a grey travelling cloak, and a bulging bag of instruments and equipment rests at his feet.

'I wish you didn't have to go,' Anna says. She touches his forehead with the back of her hand, searching for a trace of heat. But the headaches and fevers seem to have abated these past days and she must do what he is always telling her to do: relax.

Crispijn catches her fingers and kisses them lightly. 'Me, too. But Jan Wijck says the new lenses need adjusting and he cannot be responsible for that side of the business. His children have been ill, his wife, too. He's had to care for them and work on the telescope around his commitments to the eye clinic.'

'I will pray for your safe return,' she says.

They jump apart as Catharina enters the hallway. Anna blushes, waits for her to say something. Every night, she and Crispijn have been together, but he insists that they should wait to get married until Catharina has grieved Griet's departure to France. It is not so bad as before – she has not given up her painting this time, but still she is quiet and distracted. She often walks outside, even when it's bitterly cold, and returns home shivering, her lips pale. Anna sits with her beside the fire until she warms up and Crispijn, despite his own health troubles, sends for tonics and restoratives for her and stands over her, making sure she gulps them down.

'We won't be married until the summer,' Crispijn had told Anna one night as they lay secretly together inside the attic bedroom. 'The church is too cold. We don't want any of our guests freezing to their pews while we say our vows.'

Anna always smiles. She is content to wait. She has never felt so happy or safe, so far removed from her father's curse. She plans to be married in her mother's dress. It will be an omen of good fortune, a way of casting off the old Anna Tesseltje and inhabiting the new. She has sponged the dress since its adventure to the convent and replaced it in the dresser.

'Travel safely,' Catharina says vaguely, kissing her brother's cheek.

'Anna will look after you,' he says, as Henrick appears. He picks up his bag and doffs his hat. Anna and Catharina wave him goodbye, but as he is walking down the stairs to the waiting horse, a shadow falls and Anna squints up at the sky. Just a cloud, she thinks. Shaped like an anchor.

When she looks back, the horse has already reached the end of the drive.

Later that day, a forceful knock at the door makes Catharina and Anna look up. They are in the studio –

Catharina working on a series of engravings while Anna daydreams and cleans paintbrushes in jars of linseed oil. A man's voice echoes in the hall. A few moments later, Mrs Hartog appears in the doorway, a tall dark figure lurking behind.

'I'm sorry, Madam,' she says, looking worried. 'But he insisted.'

Maarten Horst doesn't wait for her to finish speaking. Brushing past her, he strides into the studio, not bothering to remove his hat.

'Maarten.' Catharina has gone rigid. She sets down her stele and stands up, glaring. 'I thought our business was concluded. I'm surprised you're still here.'

Maarten wears an angry expression. 'We were due to leave last week, but the Governor has some last-minute assignments for me. And we had some unfinished business in town. Didn't we, Blanche?' He glances behind him and Anna sees the pale English girl hiding in the shadows of the hall. At his rough summons, she sidles into the room, shooting Anna an apologetic look. There is a fresh bruise on her cheek, the colour of a ripe plum.

Maarten folds his arms. 'Since we were in the neighbourhood, I thought I would stop and ask for my painting.'

'It doesn't belong to you,' Catharina says, her tone frosty. 'You haven't paid for it.'

Maarten's cheeks turn red. 'I have paid for it a hundred times over, the amount of trouble you've given me and my kin. I demand it back. I will hang it in my new residence.'

'You can't. It's not finished.'

'Then I will find someone to finish it for me,' he says, his gaze roving around the room. 'Which is it?'

'I've painted over it,' Catharina lies. 'Haven't I, Anna?'

Anna hesitates, but at a look from her mistress, she nods slowly. 'Yes, Madam.'

Maarten explodes. 'How dare you?' he says. 'I will have you blacklisted from every good family in the Republic.'

'Go ahead,' Catharina says. 'If they are friends with you, then they are far from good citizens.'

Maarten glares at her before stalking out. Anna hears him a moment later in the hall, abusing Henrick and demanding he fetch their carriage. Catharina follows to save Henrick from the vile tide of Maarten's tongue and Blanche stays by Anna's side, wringing her hands.

'I didn't want to come,' she said, 'but he made me. And I wanted to warn you. He is in a foul mood.' Her gaze drops to the floor. 'I lost the baby,' she says, her voice breaking. She touches her cheek. 'Maarten says it is my fault. Now I am even more afraid of travelling to a distant country. Will you not reconsider coming with us?'

Anna thinks of Crispijn. She wishes she could tell Blanche about their secret union, but it isn't possible so she shakes her head.

'I must stay,' she says.

She assumes that Blanche will walk away now, out into the corridor to join her husband. But Blanche hesitates. 'You must be careful,' she says. 'If the Queen's court discovers the true nature of Catharina and Margriet's relationship, they may turn on her. Maarten would happily tell them. But perhaps if I tell him you are coming with us, to be my companion, he will not say a word. We could be great friends, Anna Tesseltje. I would see that you want for nothing once we reach our new home.'

Anna is torn. She has to trust that Crispijn will protect her and Catharina. That's what he promised. She will write to him, she thinks, and warn him of Maarten's threat. In a week, the Horsts will be on a ship bound for Sumatra.

'I'm sorry,' she says. Blanche's face falls. Hunching her shoulders, she turns away and scurries out.

14

'So, WHAT DO WE DO NOW?' BRAM SAID, HIS VOICE booming through the speaker of my phone that sat on the kitchen table of Gerrit's cottage. I could hear noisy laughter in the background, the chime of cutlery, Sem shouting something about a late order.

I rubbed my tired eyes.

'I'll keep trying to get Liam to talk,' I said. 'Although he blocked me after that last voicemail I left.' I suspected I'd solved the mystery of the missing notebook: Liam had either stolen it from me or found it after I left the lab. He'd used my notes to draft a media release arguing Catharina's ownership of the dress, conveniently leaving out the details about Anna's connection to Texel and the presence of caustic washer-woman's lye in the seams. Since he'd blocked my phone number, I'd sent off a furious email as soon as Marieke and I reached the cottage.

How could you! I'd written, my hands shaking so hard I could barely type. *After everything we've been through, I thought you'd at least have the decency to tell me you were planning to detonate our arrangement. Please know that despite your damaging announcement, the Noord-Holland*

339

government has agreed for the dress and the other artefacts to be returned here for a short display at the historical society's archives. I'll be in contact with Sara at Huis van Hilde to arrange transportation of the dress in two weeks' time. If you have any issues, feel free to take it up with Councillor Rob Disijk and the Provincial Government of Noord Holland.

'I think the best thing to do is just lie low for a while,' I said to Bram now. 'Things will blow over. In the meantime, I'll get to work on the exhibition. I'm hoping I can get Jeanette Hall to help us coordinate a small display of artworks connecting Anna and Catharina together.' Liam's absence would create a hole in the exhibition that I hoped Jeanette's scholarship could fill.

'You still think the dress belongs to the maid?' Bram said.

'I believe so,' I told him. 'There are still a few clues to follow up. I'd like to confirm exactly how the dress ended up here, for instance, and Anna's reasons for leaving Sterrenwijck.'

'Well, I can't complain about the business side of things,' Bram said. 'This is the busiest night we've had in ages! Everybody wants to speak to us, everybody is desperate to know everything about the dress and our 'amazing discovery'. It's so loud, I can hardly hear myself think. Call you tomorrow?'

'Sure.'

He hung up. I continued to sit with my face cradled in my hands. I felt worn down to my very core. When my stomach gurgled loudly, I remembered that in all the excitement and drama, I'd forgotten to eat.

'Can I get you anything?' Gerrit said gently, leaning

against the kitchen doorframe. I could make out Marieke's profile in the lounge room behind him, her sharp profile illuminated by the glow of a lamp. 'A cup of tea? Water?'

I shook my head. Marieke cleared her throat.

'Do you have any mugwort?' she called out. 'Any sandalwood? Herbs?'

Gerrit blinked at her, astonished.

'It's to clear the air,' she explained, rising off the couch and slipping into the doorway beside him. 'Wards off negative energy. This Liam fellow is like a bad stain. I can feel his terrible influence all over you, Jo.'

Gerrit bit his lip. 'I think I might have some dried lavender back at the house. Should I go get it?'

'Would you?' Marieke smiled at him sweetly.

When he was gone, she fussed around the lounge room, poking through cupboards, ostensibly searching for bedding.

'What am I going to do?' I murmured, more to myself than to her. She came over to stand beside me, a pillow over one arm.

'I know you, Josefeine Baaker, you'll pick yourself up and show this Liam character exactly what you're made of. You'll just have to present your own side of the story in the most compelling way you can. You have the contacts, I know you do. Haven't you told me often enough? And you know Bram and the divers better than anyone. If anybody can do it, you can.'

She gripped my arm tightly and after a long moment, I folded my hand over hers.

'I'm glad you're here.'

'Me, too. At least I can sort out your living space. As usual, you've left everything to chance. Not even a decent blanket on your bed! I saw a few things poking out of a chest in the spare room there. One of them may have been a blanket. I'm going to stickybeak and see if there's anything in there that's clean and dry.'

I didn't have the heart to stop her, but when, a few moments later, I heard a gasp, I shot to my feet and hurried into the brightly lit bedroom to find her bending over an open timber chest. The shoes in the timber chest were worn and threadbare, some of them – the leather ones – dusty with fungal blooms. I felt my breath catch as I held one shoe and then the next, remembering the wild excitement that had run through me as I had once dashed about madly on the beach, collecting them.

'They were here,' Marieke choked. 'All along. Why didn't I think to ask?'

She knelt beside me and, together, we sifted through the detritus of my childhood, the scent of the trapped sea rising around us like mist. Gerrit found us there when he returned, a few stems of bedraggled lavender clutched in one hand.

'I should have told you,' he said, his eyes downcast. 'I knew I should have asked before taking them the day of the funeral. I feel terrible.'

'Did you organise to have the plaque installed near Saeftinghe?' I asked.

Gerrit nodded.

'It was the least I could do, under the circumstances. It felt like closure.'

'Then I forgive you,' I said. 'It was kind of you.'

We were silent a moment longer.

'Maybe you could come out to the sanctuary with me tomorrow?' Gerrit suggested. 'It's a quiet day. Take some time off and come see the orphans. You come, too,' he said, handing Marieke the lavender.

The carpark of the seal sanctuary was deserted when we reached the facility at 10 a.m. Gerritt helped Marieke out of the car and led us over to a locked door.

'This entrance is for the staff,' he said. 'Visitors usually enter via the main gate near the gift shop. We don't open for another hour. But if I can't sneak in a few friends, then what's the point of all my years of dedicated service?' He smirked at Marieke who returned his smile. She looked pretty in her pale sweater and dungarees, her cheeks flushed from the walk she'd taken earlier across the dunes.

I'd spent the morning emailing my remaining contacts at every university and research lab I could think of, anyone who could back up my theory that the presence of soapy lye in the seams, in addition to Anna wearing the gown in not just one but possibly two paintings, meant it was more likely the dress belonged to her than to her former mistress. Jeanette Hall had scoffed when I told her what had happened with Liam.

'Oh, that bastard,' she said. 'Academia will get him, if karma doesn't. One bad turn, as they say. You can't hide your bad habits forever. Yes, I can help with the paintings. I can't lend out the originals, of course, but I know of some excellent reproductions and I'd be happy to write the foreword to the exhibition catalogue, if you're keen. Just say the word.'

She rang off, promising to email me later with the names

of a few galleries. Talking to Jeanette made me feel better and worse at the same time. On the one hand her reaction only strengthened my conviction that he'd betrayed me. But on the other, why had I trusted him in the first place? I'd kept trying to see the good in him long past the point he'd given me reason not to. At least Rob had given us permission for the exhibition go ahead. When I'd called Olivia to tell her the good news, she'd squealed excitedly in a decidedly un-Olivia fashion and started describing the plans she and Flora had made for a local carpenter to alter the upstairs exhibition space in the Texel Historical Society so it would be enough to accommodate a bigger crowd.

'There's a small storage closet we don't use,' Olivia told me. 'We're hoping the builder might be able to knock out a wall and whitewash the board so they match the rest of the room. We could call the exhibition: *De Jurk*. The Dress. The gown is the hero, after all. Or heroine, if you prefer. The space could be ready in two weeks. What about the other artefacts – the book cover and the purse, the earrings and comb? How long would you need to arrange for them to be returned? How can we ensure we display them properly when they arrive?'

'Leave that to me,' I assured her. 'I'll contact Marien at Leiden University this afternoon. She might be Liam's contact, but she has to do what the Noord-Holland government say since they are the official owners. Besides, Marien's a professional. She has to maintain a certain level of impartiality to preserve her reputation.'

A little wave of bitterness washed through me. Liam was supposed to be a professional, too, but that hadn't stopped him putting his own career before everything and everyone else.

'Before I let you go,' Olivia said, 'I wanted to let you know I found something in the archives that might shed some light on Catharina van Shurman's connection to Texel. Catharina appears to have made a substantial donation to the Texel children's orphanage fund in the winter of 1652.'

'Really?' I said, a prickle of excitement tingling at the base of my skull. 'Why would she do that?'

'I'm not sure. But it's possible she struck up a friendship with one of the Abbesses in charge of the orphanage. The Abbesses were very persistent – they often wrote to anyone famous or successful, begging for donations to feed and house and clothe their young charges. They saw it as part of their calling. Next time you're free, I can show you where the old orphanage used to stand. The building's all gone, of course. We started a petition to save the old stone well. That's all that's left of the orphanage now.'

She hung up, leaving me to contemplate the connection between Catharina and the Texel orphanage. I'd have to investigate Olivia's suggestion of the Abbess who might have befriended such a famous artist. She must have been charismatic, I thought. Or had something else which appealed to Catharina's prickly nature. Why else would the artist have parted with her money so willingly? People had probably written to her all the time asking for funds. What made Texel so special?

I'd called Nico next and asked to speak Anneke.

'What's up?' Anneke said, sighing down the phone as if my call was a grave imposition that had interrupted some extremely important event. But I knew better than to let her attitude bother me. I had once possessed a similar nature, after all.

'I've been given approval to help coordinate the exhibition of the dress and the other artefacts brought up from *La Dragon*,' I told her. 'I want you to help me. Olivia and Flora will be doing most of the legwork on the exhibition space but there's promotional material to coordinate and I need someone to field phone calls from the media and send out invitations. Oh, and I'll need you standing by to assist when the other artefacts arrive from the mainland. I'll need a commitment from you of a few hours a week. You could do the work after school. I'll pay you, of course. What do you say? Are you in?'

Anneke made a hmm-ing sound then allowed the silence to stretch. I waited patiently.

'OK,' she said, at last. 'I'm in.'

'Come on,' Gerrit said. 'I want to show you something.'

He led us through a deserted staff room and outside to the seal enclosures.

A young man hosing down an empty tank waved hello as we passed.

Gerrit waved back. 'Hey, Greg. How are my girls today?'

Greg shrugged. 'Pretty good. Martha was in there earlier, checking on them. They're waiting for their breakfast. You know what they're like.'

We followed Gerrit to a concrete basin, a few metres tall and filled with water.

Dark shapes swam beneath the surface. As we approached, the seals swam up to greet us. Their dark eyes were haunting. They looked like hungry orphans.

'Oh,' Marieke breathed. 'They're so small.'

346

'These three are all rescues,' Gerrit said. 'Adolescents who've got lost or been separated from their families. Once they've been here for a little while and built up some resilience, we'll release them back into the wild. You stay here and get to know each other. I'll be back in a minute.'

He disappeared into a small brick shed, returning with a bucket of fish. Handing us some gloves, he held out the bucket. Marieke wrinkled her nose, but she picked up a fish all the same. The orphaned seals swam closer, until we could almost reach out and touch them. I picked up a shining body, tossed it to the nearest seal who caught it in her maw, gulped it down and swam a joyful half-circle before returning to beg for more.

Gerrit laughed. 'They've got a good appetite on them. Like most teenagers.'

'They're gorgeous.' Marieke's face shone. She squealed as one of the seals flicked up her flipper, spraying us with water.

'This one's new,' Gerrit said, pointing to the seal who had splashed us. 'You can name her,' he said to me. 'Every seal has to have a name, at least for recording purposes.'

I thought about it for two seconds. 'Let's call her Anna.'

After we'd finished feeding the seals, Gerrit dropped Marieke and me over at Bram's pizza shop. Bram was standing at the counter when we got there, helping Sem take orders, and waved us over.

'Nico was just here,' he said, dusting off his flour-coated hands. 'You missed him.'

'Why didn't he stick around?'

Bram waved a hand. 'Something about Anneke. You know what she's like.'

'Did something happen?'

His forehead creased. 'She heard from her mother.'

'Oh, no.'

He sighed. 'From what Nico said, Anneke managed to track Tess down this morning. She wanted to invite her back to Texel – something about the dress exhibition. Tess must have refused and the rejection upset her. Don't worry, though, Nico will sort Anneke out.'

His words made me uneasy. As we discussed the forthcoming exhibition, I found myself distracted by the idea of Anneke, hiding out there somewhere, hurt and alone. After the conversation we'd had earlier, I felt as if she might have turned a corner, the exhibition providing a distraction from the issues surrounding her relationship with her mother. Bram was, of course, as excited as Olivia and Flora that the Noord-Holland government had agreed to allow the artefacts to return, albeit for a short time. Bram wanted one of the Texel divers to be present every day during the exhibition so that they could answer questions from the public about the artefacts and their retrieval.

'Hopefully, we'll have a sample of the exhibition notes to show our guests, too,' he said.

I promised that I would have something to show him next week, even if Tess' rejection tipped Anneke into such a deep depression again and I could no longer rely on her help.

'The exhibition might be busier than expected,' I warned. 'Now the local media has got word.'

Bram looked pleased. 'Is that a bad thing?'

* * *

I dropped Marieke back at the cottage to rest then I drove out to Nico's bookshop. The sign read CLOSED, although it was only midday. When I knocked on the door, nobody answered. I started to feel anxious and was about to call him again when I heard my name.

I turned to find Nico in his orange ute, looking worried.

'Have you seen her?' he said.

'Who?'

'Anneke. She took off an hour ago and I haven't been able to find her. I've been driving around in circles like a lunatic.' He was panicking.

'Slow down,' I said. 'Where would she have gone?'

He shook his head. 'I've looked everywhere.'

I thought about the first time we'd met. Her blue hair in the morning light, the beer cans rattling around in the dirt.

'I think I know where she is.'

We reached the clubhouse in record time. The engine was still running when Nico leaped from the ute, leaving me to shift the gear into park. The door of the clubhouse was ajar. He ran inside and I followed. The change room lights were off and, at first, I thought I'd made a mistake. Anneke might be anywhere. She could be hiding out with a friend.

Then I heard a sniffle coming from the corner.

Nico flicked on the lights.

She was wearing her wetsuit, but she hadn't been able to fit the tank on herself. Nico marched over to her and seized her arm.

'What were you thinking?'

She shook him off, her face angry.

'I just wanted to do something for myself. You're always ignoring me. You don't pay any attention. And then hearing from Mum. I was upset.'

He was breathing hard, fighting to control his temper.

'We'll go together,' he said. 'I promise, I will take you diving. But you're not to go out on your own. It's insanely dangerous.'

Anneke looked across at me. 'I want Jo to come,' she said.

Nico looked surprised. 'That's up to Jo.'

Anneke held my gaze. I felt the warmth of connection flow between us. I, too, had been misunderstood – or so I thought. If I'd had an older friend – a female role model to emulate and look up to – it was perhaps possible I might never have misinterpreted things as badly as I had.

'I'd love to come,' I said and was rewarded with Anneke's grateful smile.

15

Anna

ANNA IS HELPING LOTTE REARRANGE THE STUDIO FOR the next client when she hears Catharina scream. The young girl's eyes widen in alarm.

'Stay here,' Anna says.

She reaches the entrance hall at the same time as Mrs Hartog, her footsteps flying along the marble. Catharina is bent, broken, weeping, a crumpled letter clutched in her hand. Doubled over on the floor, she can't or won't get up. Mrs Hartog tries to comfort her, but Catharina turns, a savage look on her face, and the housekeeper falls back.

Anna is afraid to go near, but she thinks of Crispijn – how he would want her to care for his sister – and this gives her courage.

'What has happened?' she says, forgetting to address Catharina as she should, as the mistress who wields her fortunes.

Catharina's face is haggard, her mouth a dark hole. Wordlessly, she holds out the letter and Anna takes it, smoothing out the folds. There are blotches where Catharina's tears have caused the ink to run, but she can just make out the words, written in a cramped hand. She makes it to the second paragraph before a wave of dizziness overcomes her.

351

The words blur, their meaning lost among the dark stick shapes of the letters.

She hears Mrs Hartog demanding to know. She forces herself to straighten, imagines a mask dropping over her features.

'It's from Master Wijck,' Anna says. 'He writes to say that Crispijn fell ill a week ago. His headaches returned and he was suffering a fever, seeing things that weren't there. He died yesterday.'

The words are ashes on her tongue. She coughs, swallows, continues.

'Master Wicjk's maid died, too. He says the plague has returned to Amsterdam and that we should stay away. He will ensure Crispijn is buried in a proper cemetery where his grave can be visited in some future time.'

Anna stops reading, unable to see through the shaking. Catharina's weeping echoes around the hall, a skirl of misery and pain, the loss of a sibling still a wound in Anna's heart too.

She thinks of Crispijn's kind face, his gentle hands on her hips. Of late, she has felt a kind of fluttering in her belly and begun to suspect a life grows there. Crispijn's child. She drops to her knees, seeing nothing, lost inside a vortex of pain.

Her grief over the next week is a torment and she takes to her bed. Trays of food are brought and taken away by a sniffling Lotte. Anna's absence is barely noted; Catharina has abandoned them all. She locks herself in her studio and forbids anyone to enter. Every night, Anna is haunted by Crispijn's death. She saves him a dozen different ways, sees him die in a variety of poses, eyes open, arms flung wide to the sky. Waves of nausea assail her, forcing her awake, and she wraps her arms around her stomach and wishes for death.

One morning, she wakes to a dead fire. Shivering, she dresses herself and goes to visit Catharina. She knocks on the door, gently and then more urgently. When there is still no answer, she pushes open the door.

Catharina looks awful, her hair oily and flat, her clothes rumpled as if she has not slept for days. She looks at Anna as if she is a ghost.

'Can I fetch you anything?' Anna says.

Catharina doesn't answer.

'You need to eat,' Anna says. 'Let me fetch some of Mrs Hartog's broth for you. Or a slice of bread.'

She turns to the door, trying not to sob.

'I'm leaving,' Catharina says. Anna turns back.

'What?'

'I'm going to France to find Griet.' Catharina holds out a letter, her expression dull.

'When were you going to tell me?' Anna says.

Catharina shakes her head. 'It doesn't matter. None of it matters now that he's gone, don't you understand?' Her eyes flash. 'He was everything to me,' she says. 'I am half a person. Half of me is in the grave. I cannot feel, I cannot think. I certainly cannot eat. If I go to France, at least I can escape this house and all the memories here.'

'But what will become of us?' Anna says, growing angry. It is so typical of Catharina, she thinks, to care only about her own grief. 'I don't want to leave Sterrenwijck. It is the only place I have felt safe these past few years.'

'You will find a new position elsewhere,' Catharina says. 'I will write you a reference.'

'I want to stay with you,' Anna says. Tell her about the child, she thinks. But the words are frozen on her tongue. She can't reveal an infant who has no father living. The authorities will throw her onto the streets. She is not Lady Killigrew, able to be pensioned off, her baby born in secrecy.

Catharina shakes her head. 'Impossible. My spirit is dead and I'm sure it will not be long until my body follows. I thought it died once and Crispijn brought it back to life. But without him, it is impossible.' She looks away, as if the very sight of Anna standing there offends her. 'Leave now. Take your belongings and go.'

Anna waits for her to change her mind, but Catharina grows suddenly angry. Sobbing now, she throws a bolster that bounces off Anna's chest.

'Go!' she says.

Anna flees. Crying, she runs upstairs and begins to throw her things inside the trunk she brought with her. The strings of an apron snare her hand; she shakes herself free, sobbing. Reaching into the drawer, she touches silk and pauses. Her mother's dress. She draws it out. It shines dully in the light from the window. Holding it to her, she inhales the faded scent of sweat and perfume. She thinks of the night at the masque when Crispijn was so kind. Her eyes fly open. She bundles up the dress, shoves it into the trunk. Then, fumbling in the bottom drawer, she pulls out the Dutch tears Catharina gave her and wraps them in a handkerchief. There. She is done. She arrived with nothing but hope and now she is leaving with a child in her womb. Unmarried, she will have no choice but to give up. There is only one place she can go.

On her last night in The Hague, Anna checks that she has packed everything she plans to take with her to her new life. Unwrapping the Dutch tears from the handkerchief, she rolls them in her hands, closing her eyes as the cool glass kisses the skin of her palms. Their beauty makes her nervous. When she arrived on the Horsts' doorstep three weeks ago and begged Maarten to take her in, he smirked before accepting her offer and outlining the terms of her employment, one of which is the master's right to ownership. A maid may reasonably possess a few worthless trinkets – buttons, a lice-comb, a needle and thread – for how else can she perform her duty otherwise and keep herself neat and tidy? Anything more valuable must be declared. Maarten knows about the silk dress – she cannot hope to hide that, but she cannot bear to think of Catharina's gift being leered and pawed at by greedy Maarten.

While Blanche is preoccupied in the kitchen overseeing the packing of the best china plates, Anna hurriedly sews a secret pocket inside her mother's silk dress. She uses the thread she brought with her all the way from Amsterdam – it once fell into a bucket of caustic lye and Lijsbeth fished it out, exclaiming at Anna's carelessness. Now the red thread feels like it is binding her old life to her new one. She squeezes the Dutch tears into the opening then stitches the corners tightly shut. When Blanche returns a few moments later, the tears are safe and Anna plasters on a smile to match her new mistress' enthusiasm, although she can still feel the tears cocooned in their tiny, silk world, a grief she cannot forget.

It has been decided that she and Blanche will travel to Texel by boat and then take a larger vessel to the east. Urgent business will keep Maarten in The Hague a little longer but he has promised to join them at the next port.

The morning of their departure, Blanche comes to see her.

'How are you feeling?' she says, squeezing Anna's hand.

'A little unwell,' Anna says. She had to tell Blanche about the child. Blanche has agreed to raise the child as her own.

A small ship carries the women out to Texel, depositing them at the anchorage on a bitterly grey afternoon.

A storm is brewing on the horizon, dark clouds skimming along the water, reflected in its glassy surface. Blanche accompanies Anna along the beach that runs alongside the anchorage. The sand is gritty and dark and stings Anna's eyes as the two women walk across the dunes. Although the wind is unpleasant, it is at least cool. Anna cannot stand the close quarters of the inn where they are staying for the night. An oarsman from *La Dragon* will row them out the next morning.

As they walk along the narrow rocky ledge, Anna sees a group of children tramping after an old figure in a tattered dress. The children stop to let them pass first. Although they look hungrier than the saddest dogs she has seen skulking in Amsterdam's backstreets, they smile at Anna and Blanche. Blanche asks Anna to procure their packed lunch and hand the bread to the children. The children look to the old woman for permission and, when she nods her blessing, they break it into seven equal pieces – enough for all of them to share.

'How kind you are,' the old woman says to them. 'These

are Texel's orphans. They will cherish your goodness for years to come. May God's blessing find you.'

A fierce wind whips the woman's dress. Anna thinks she looks like a storm crow, a weathered portent of fortune, of change. Rain begins to fall, lightning forks the sky.

Grasping Blanche's hand, Anna drags her mistress towards the inn. When they reach the safety of the porch, she looks back to see the small figures of the orphans like ants in the distance, filing into an old cottage.

The storm has died down a little when she rises early the next morning. The child in her womb flutters incessantly and she has to use her chamber pot three times before she feels comfortable enough to clamber into the rowboat that will take them out to *La Dragon*. The man rowing them across the water is a grizzled-looking thing. He says nothing to them and, when they at last climb onto the deck, he points them to their quarters and disappears without a word.

'He's scared,' Blanche says. 'Maarten says the sailors don't like having women aboard. It's bad luck, even for paying passengers.'

In the cabin, they pass the time by playing cards. Blanche loses twice then, by some fluke, wins a hand which sends her whooping around the room. Anna laughs – a good feeling. She hasn't laughed in months, not since she learned of Crispijn's death. The thought sobers her. She touches her belly, feels the tightening pang like a band wrapped around her middle, squeezing. What will she do when this strange gift makes its presence known to the world?

The next storm arrives all at once. It flings itself upon the anchorage like a beast, battering the sails, beating the masts. The vessel rocks, throwing Anna and Blanche against each other. They stumble together, right themselves, fall again. Anna tries to clamber out onto the deck, seeking help, but the wind pushes her back. An enormous wave breaks over the bow of the ship, washes down into their cabin. Blanche is like a drowned rat, her hair soaked. The next big wave knocks her into the bed. She cannot climb out and screams at Anna for assistance. Anna stumbles across to her, but then another sudden, drenching wave cascades down through the open hatch, deluging them both. A great scream of rending wood fills Anna's ears. Blood pounds in her head. She can hear nothing, not even Blanche's desperate cries. As the cabin fills with water, she kicks, thinking of nothing but her own breath. Somewhere behind her, Blanche has gone quiet. Anna knows she is already gone, pinned to the bed by the great weight of water descending on them. The guilt of her death is one Anna will carry with her always. She kicks, kicks. Fights the water with every ounce of strength. The sun is like a moon, white and iridescent. She strives towards it, as if the world of water is one of air.

16

Jo

Flora was waiting outside the Texel Historical Society's archives when Marieke and I arrived. Cristof was standing with her but as we approached, he kissed her brusquely on the cheek and walked off up the main street.

'He's headed for the tavern,' she said. 'I told him this is secret women's business and he's not wanted, at least for a few hours.'

'Won't he be offended?' I said.

She laughed. 'Have you met Cristof? Water off a duck's back. He's impervious to offence. That's why I married him.'

The reception hall was a buzz of activity since the exhibition was due to take place in three days' time. Builders and removalists carried out their duties with ruthless precision, hammering frames into place, heaving archival boxes onto trolleys and testing the temperature-controlled large glass display case in the centre of the exhibition space that would house the silk dress for the entirety of its stay on Texel. The climate-controlled case, paid out of Eva Van de Berg's generous donation, reminded me of Snow White's glass coffin. In a few days, the dress would be sealed inside, protected by invisible layers of nitrogen gas injected into the atmosphere. The nitrogen would prevent further oxidisation of the fabric and also prevent potentially harmful pests infiltrating the exhibit. Special alarm sensors were installed at the base to prevent anyone slipping into the building at night and stealing the dress away. In addition to these protections, Rob Disijk had helpfully provided a security guard, paid for by the Noord-Holland government. The divers and I had arranged a video call to thank him personally for the government's generosity.

'No problem,' he'd said, his blue eyes sparkling. 'Can't have anyone running off with our most precious asset, can we?'

He'd agreed with Bram's suggestion to allow one of the divers to be present at all times during the exhibition to provide information on the discovery of the artefacts. Bram had been training the others up as unofficial tour guides. I spied him as Marieke, Flora and I entered the room. He was standing beside the dress' display case, in deep discussion with Nico. The two men paused their conversation to wave at me and I smiled back, glad to see the return of their easy companionship. Things had been slightly strained, the push-pull of new and old relationships threatening to drive a wedge between the three of us. But we'd worked it out together over drinks a few nights ago at Texel's local pub. Bram had needed a little reassurance that the memories we'd created and shared as children were not at risk of being forgotten and cast into the shadows by the warm blaze of my new friendship with Nico and Anneke. And Nico had been able to reassure him that their friendship as divers and peers remained unchanged.

The night had ended messily but I was glad we'd broached the subject. It would make things much smoother in the long run and the exhibition had a greater chance of success if there was no tension between the divers and myself.

Flora led us past a row of Catharina's paintings hanging on the wall in their glass frames. Jeanette had generously sent the reproductions a few days ago. *The Marriage* was there, as well as Catharina's portrait of her brother Crispijn. The ultimate prize, of course, would be having Catharina's missing painting hung in the place of honour beside the dress. I had emailed Johann de Witte three times last week to tell him about the exhibition. I was hoping he might be tempted by the idea of seeing the silk dress in person and I had begged shamelessly for a chance to speak to him about the van Shurman painting I believed he had in his possession. There had been nothing but silence, though, and I'd all but given up hope of hearing from him. It was a disappointment I would simply have to bear.

'Olivia said you wanted to know more about the Texel orphanage and its connection to Catharina,' Flora said, turning to Marieke and myself. 'Why don't we go upstairs and take a look?' She led us up into the archival area and after rummaging in a drawer, pulled out a pile of facsimiles.

'These aren't original,' she said. 'But they were copied before the old letters fell to bits. They're from the first nuns who took care of orphans on the island. The children used to sell the well water to the sailors. It had special properties. It was tainted with iron so it kept for much longer than normal water. Men could go to sea for months and never need to stop in at a port for fresh water supplies. Anyway,

I thought you might find these interesting.'

I flicked through the letters. There had been two Abbesses during Anna's time. One was a woman called Yolente. Yolente had written to the local landowners, begging for alms for her young orphans. Then her letters petered out. The next ones were written by someone called Agneta Corrin who had taken over from Yolente after her death. Continuing to shuffle through, I saw a letter from Agneta addressed directly to Catharina van Shurman. I pounced on it, scanning the contents greedily. It had been sent via an emissary to Catharina van Shurman's address in France, the postal date recorded as 1658, a few years after Anna's death.

Dear Mistress van Shurman,
Please accept our humblest thanks for this great bounty. We will use the funds to repair the orphanage these poor children so badly require. There is a child here we would love you to meet. Her name is Brechtje, and she is a most precious star among the celestial currents, a comfort to all who know her. She would make a good model or muse for one of your paintings, if you could ever convince her to sit still. Please visit us, if you can ever spare the time. We pray that your heart is light and your paintbrush swift and true.
Ever yours,
Agneta Corrin

I sat back, my head spinning with visions of stars, silk dresses and cold glass tears. Agneta's letter had fired my imagination. Had the two women eventually met? Why had Catharina taken a sudden interest in the Texel orphans? I could only assume she had felt some kind of connection to Texel after Anna's death. The truth was that, unless more correspondence came to light, we would probably never know the truth. And maybe that was OK. It was those cracks within the past that let in the light of possibility, small tears in the fabric of the past.

17

Anna

NNA WAKES AND SLEEPS. WAKES AND SLEEPS. SHE cannot seem to keep her head above the water. She struggles, feels a cool hand on her forehead. Sleeps again. Fire races through her body in a vengeful arc, then departs without warning, leaving her clammy and cold as a pebble in the rain. She is chasing Lijsbeth through the meat hall, her nose full of the butcher's stink, the sour tang of raw flesh and bloody entrails. Lijsbeth laughs, throws a teasing glance over her shoulder, deliberately slows her pace until they are close enough to touch. Anna stretches out her hand, grasps only air. The scene shifts and she is sitting beside Crispijn in the lush, green gardens at Sterrenwijck. The taste of strawberries on her tongue. Looking down, she sees the fruit is full of maggots. She screams, spits the mouthful out, claws at her tongue.

'Hush.' A soft voice in the darkness. Anna swims towards it, surfaces, gasping for blessed air. Liquid trickles down her chin. Warm broth.

She looks around, wide-eyed. She is sitting in a small room, its windows patched with rags. There is a strong stench in the room of butcher's meat and the waft of it makes her nauseous. She gags.

'Hush.' It's night-time. An old woman's face appears in the blackness, lit from below by a guttering flame. Anna squints at her in the gloom. Do they know each other? It's the woman from the beach, she realises. Outside, rain hammers the roof, pelting down in icy blasts.

She tries to sit up, but her legs are wet, coated with viscous fluid. The woman pushes her back gently. A circling pain sears her insides. She cries out in terror. A hand finds hers, the skin hard and work-worn. The pain subsides and then returns. Anna screams and her scream is like the wind, a deep, elemental shriek. She is drowning. Crispijn's child is slipping away, she is losing him. He is rushing out of her like the tide. All she can do is clutch the woman's hand, her lifeline in a stormy sea.

Anna wakes to find the storm has passed. She raises herself to her elbows, looking around in confusion. Someone has dressed her in a coarse cotton shift and she is lying on a hard cot in a small room. Grey light falls through an uncurtained window onto the sparse furnishings, just the bed and a chair. Outside, she can see the dark boughs of trees twisted across the sky. Recollection returns in a cold rush. Heart thumping, she runs both hands over the small swelling in her pelvis where she knows her child has been growing – still grows, assuming he survived her near-drowning in that terrible storm. From somewhere down the hallway she hears lilting voices raised in prayer. Her own prayer to her child is silent. She speaks the words aloud in her head. *Please, let him live.* She waits, holding her breath, listening for that faint drumbeat, the moth-like fluttering which had only just begun to make itself known, that soft but insistent rhythm. *I am here, I am here.* She weeps when the knocking inside her comes, tears tracking down her chin into the scratchy blanket as she imagines the small stirring of her baby's tiny limbs, green shoots breaking the earth's crust. Six more months and he will be a real child, someone she can hold, a connection to Crispijn and Catharina and her own past.

A moment later, the knocking becomes real.

'My name is Yolente,' Anna's saviour says, standing in the doorframe, lowering her hand as she assesses Anna with dark, intelligent eyes. Yolente is a thin, wiry-haired woman, dressed entirely in black. Storm crow, Anna thinks. Harbinger of destiny. An image of Blanche's face, wide-eyed, bloated, swims up, unbidden. Anna groans and clutches her stomach, squeezing her eyes shut as a wave of nausea forces its way up her body. Yolente darts forward with a bucket and when Anna has finished vomiting, helps ease her back onto the cot.

'I thought you'd lose that child,' the old woman remarks, touching Anna's belly through the shift. 'I did everything I could to save her. In the end, I prayed. God sent me a message this morning telling me he had spared you and your child for a reason. You'll need to eat and rest and build up your strength to carry that girl to term.'

'You think it's a girl,' Anna says.

'Oh I know so.'

When Yolente smiles, Anna senses the woman's youth peering through the wrinkled creases like a dusty painting restored to its former glory.

'God said so. He also told me you must stay here until she is born. He intended for us to meet, perhaps not in such

366

dramatic circumstances. But His ways are mysterious to everyone but Him. I will fetch you something to eat. Sit and rest and let your soul be at ease.'

Anna obeys the old woman's directives. She closes her eyes and allows sleep to carry her away. When Yolente returns later, carrying a bowl of warm barley groats sweetened with softened apple, she tells Anna that she is the last of the nuns who swore to care for the island's orphans, the ones nobody wanted or could afford to take in.

'We were once so many and now it's only me left,' she says. 'All my sisters have gone to God. Now they are living in Paradise. I would like to join them but there are the children to think of. Who will look after them once I pass? I have been praying for God to send me an answer. To give me a sign. And he has sent me you. You have no family, nothing and no one to return to. Here on Texel, you can be anything. You can take another name, if you desire, as I did. Before I was Yolente, I was a broken woman, living in sin with a married man who beat me every night. I ran away, hid myself on a ship destined for the east. But something, some calling, drew me off the boat before it could set sail. And I found my way here. I will help you raise your daughter, when she is born. She will thrive in the company of the other children, she will be safe and happy even without a father's care.'

Later, when Yolente has shuffled from the room again, Anna thinks about her offer. Touching her stomach, she wonders how the woman knows so much. Perhaps in her delusion she let things slip. Or perhaps God does speak to Yolente. Who is Anna to say? Perhaps fate intended her to end up here all along.

Six months later, after a short but violent labour in which she felt she would be torn apart, Anna is holding her daughter at last, and dawn has broken in the sky outside the window. The terrible storm that snatched Blanche's life and those of a hundred sailors whose names she will never know is but a distant memory, and she realises that her choice to stay on Texel was the right one.

'What will you call her?' Yolente says, stroking the hair off the baby's forehead. Anna has never seen such a perfect pearl of a child, with pale, unblemished skin, rosebud lips and Crispijn's sombre grey eyes.

'I will name her Brechtje,' Anna says, kissing the soft skin on her baby's cheek. 'It means light.'

Nestling Brechtje against her chest, she watches the light move across the wall of the room that has become her sanctuary now, her own little piece of home. The light is always best after a storm, she thinks. It is cleansing and pure and capable of washing away sin. There are a few regrets she still harbours. Over the last six months following Blanche's death, Anna intended to write to Maarten and tell him of her own survival. He might want to know about Blanche's last moments. It might bring him comfort. But for some reason, she could not bring herself to do so. Every day, she woke with the intention of asking Yolente for paper and pen. Every day, she spent so much time caring for the orphans – feeding and bathing them and keeping them warm – that the letter never eventuated.

There are seven orphans who share the rundown cottage with Yolente as their teacher and protector. At first, they were stunted, underfed. Anna longed for the funds to feed them up but she had nothing worth selling except her mother's silk dress and the beautiful Dutch tears Catharina gave her, which are now resting together at the bottom of the ocean. There was only one course of action she could think of and so, a month after her delusions pass and she could once again think clearly, she summoned the courage to write to Catharina for help. She signed herself Agneta Corrin. A new name for the new person she has become. She wanted to forget Anna Tesseltje ever existed.

For five months, nothing came. Anna worked in the garden, pulling vegetables, stocking the parlour against the coming winter frosts, her belly swelling to the size of a ripe melon. She supervised the orphans selling the water from the well to the sailors. Occasionally she overheard bits of gossip. In this way, she learned that Maarten remarried, that he and his new wife moved to the west. She felt sorry for the woman who has taken Blanche's fate, but grateful that God has delivered her this second chance. Sometimes she dreamed of the silk dress at the bottom of the ocean, imagines swimming out there and retrieving it, selling it to one of the cloth merchants. But it is surely dust now, broken down by the powerful tide.

On the morning she walks into Yolente's room to find the woman has passed away in her sleep, a package arrives, brought by a boy on a cart. It is a painting wrapped in cloth. There is a pouch, too, filled with coins, although the coins are wrapped individually to ward off the temptation of theft. There is a letter, with an apology for the delay. Anna uses the coins to buy supplies for the winter. She waits until night has fallen to unwrap the canvas.

And then she weeps.

18

Jo

'YOU REMEMBER WHERE THE OCCY GOES?' NICO said.

Anneke nodded. She clipped the neon yellow tube into the safety catch, her blue hair sparkling in the water's reflection. Gentle waves rocked the boat and the three of us – Nico, Anneke and me – clung to each other. It was early morning, the sun low in the sky, the air mild. Winter would soon be on its way and it would turn the island into a different kind of place, but for now, it was the perfect weather for diving. It was perfect weather, too, for the exhibition taking place tonight.

In an excited voice, Anneke had reminded me this morning that over fifty guests had sent confirmations saying they were planning to come, including Jeanette.

'I wouldn't miss it,' she'd declared when she phoned me last night. 'I'm quite busy of course and I'll have to stay overnight. But I plan to make the effort for you and for Catharina. When else will I get the chance to see a dress connected to the famous Catharina van Shurman?' Her voice dropped an octave. 'By the way, how did things go

370

with your male colleague? Did he ever apologise or try to make amends?'

I explained that Liam had called one afternoon a few weeks after our falling-out. In a move that shouldn't have surprised me as much as it did, he'd launched into a mumbled half-apology before boldly requesting my help.

'Jo! I was wondering if you could send over that paper you wrote for the Flemish nightgowns? The one we never used? A friend at the BBC wants to run an interview on the link between women's textiles and the art market. I'd really appreciate the help.'

'Are you serious?' My voice rasped and my cheeks burned. 'Why on earth would I help you?'

'Because we're friends?'

'If we're friends, why did you block my number? You must have unblocked it just so you could call me now and ask for help. Friends don't treat each other the way you treated me, Liam. Nor do research partners.'

'I apologised, didn't I? You know how it is. I'm sorry I couldn't wait, but my career was on the line and I really needed to secure my tenure. You wouldn't listen. Besides, you seem to have handled it fine. The dress will be going back to Texel for the exhibition and there's been no significant damage to your work prospects. You're a freelancer, Jo. You'll always find another project. It's not quite the same for me, is it? I just wish you'd appreciate my position a bit more.'

'Your position?' I was shouting. 'Not only did you betray my trust by stealing my notes, you knowingly launched the discovery with the media without bothering to establish the truth. It's a grubby approach to scholarship, Liam. And a pretty low thing to do to someone you're supposed to be working with.'

'You'll have your chance to tell your version when the exhibition goes live and you publish your book.'

'No thanks to you,' I said, icily. 'I'll be lucky to get that job at Sydney University now you've made me look completely foolish. I had no idea what to say to those journalists. You didn't even have the decency to warn me first.'

'Would you have listened?'

'I guess we'll never know.'

I hung up before he could reply.

When Nico called last night to ask if I'd go diving early with Anneke, I'd said yes. No hesitations and no regrets. After edging onto the diving platform, I put the regulator in my mouth and slipped backwards into the waves. I felt the pull of the current, trying to separate me from the others. A swirl of bubbles hit my face, gentle as a kiss. I breathed long and deep, shutting my eyes against the deep, intoxicating blue. Two hands found mine. I opened my eyes to see Anneke and Nico holding onto me, drawing me into the future, away from the past.

'There you are.' I turned around to find Nico smiling down at me. He looked handsome in his grey suit. He kissed my cheek while Anneke, walking a few paces behind, looked disgusted. She brightened, though, as she came closer, and her eyes widened as she took in the spectacle of the exhibition space and sensed the excited atmosphere inside. In her short black dress, she looked older than her fifteen years and happier than I'd ever seen her. Working on the exhibition had given her a sense of purpose. I was proud of her commitment and I told her so now, pretending to ignore the blush of pleasure which spread across her cheeks.

'I can't believe how different she looks,' Nico whispered in my ear. 'She's like a different person.'

'She's the same person,' I assured him. 'She's just found her calling.'

I led them both inside and we walked over to where the dress was displayed inside its glass case. It looked magnificent under the strategically placed downlights, the interplay of brightness and shade suggesting it was still underwater. My very own time-traveller, or Anna's, if my theories were right. I'd chosen to wear a golden, silk dress, hoping to pay homage to Anna's tragic journey. Marieke was handing out programs. Printed on glossy paper, the information inside was an amalgam of fact and supposition although the most arresting page was the front cover which was a full-colour photograph of Anna's silk dress. A banner across the top of the program read 'De Jurk'. The Dress.

'It reads well,' she said, passing one to Nico. 'Your daughter did a fantastic job.'

Anneke flushed with pleasure.

As the night wore on, it was clear that the opening of the exhibition was a grand success. Bram had written a speech, thanking the community for their warm response to the artefact's discovery and praising the historical society for the generous use of their exhibition space. When he singled Rob Disijk out for his valuable contribution to the artefact's return, the councillor raised his arm to wave away the praise.

'Ah, it was nothing,' he called out, but it was obvious from the way he beamed at the colleagues who'd accompanied him to Texel that he appreciated Bram's gesture. The tension between the mainland government and the local community had been mended by the successful return of the dress and Bram, Nico, Sem and Cristof were already planning to meet up with Emerens and his team of Defence divers to explore some of the other wrecks which had sunk so many years ago, taking their secrets with them.

A smattering of applause from the audience seemed to indicate that Bram's speech was over. I turned away to get another drink but when Bram resumed speaking, his amplified voice ringing out across the room, I looked back.

'Of course, we can't forget Jo,' Bram said, squinting at me through the crowd. Spying me beside the drinks table, he beckoned me forward. 'Jo, come on up here.' The crowd parted and I moved forward, feeling self-conscious. When I reached the small platform, I took the arm Bram offered me and allowed him to pull me up.

It was warm under the downlights and I felt sweat prickle on my back. 'Doctor Jo Baaker was the first person we called when we made the discovery,' Bram was saying. 'She's a Texeller, through and through. It doesn't matter that she's spent half her life in other places. We knew she'd come back one day. What the sea gives, the finder keeps. And we don't plan on letting her go any time soon!'

He pulled me into a one-armed hug as the crowd applauded. I felt my cheeks burn. Tears stung my eyes. Now I knew how Anneke had felt when Marieke praised her so enthusiastically. I let Bram embrace me for another moment, then excused myself and climbed off the platform to rejoin Nico. The crowd dispersed, breaking apart to study the reproductions of Catharina's paintings and take their turns examining the silk dress in its glass case. Flora stood in front of the dress for so long, weeping, that Cristof and Olivia had to lead her away into a quiet corner so she could compose herself. On the back of the catalogue, I had included a sketch of the orphanage I'd found in the archives that Agneta must have made at some stage when she was designing the improvements to the orphanage. The building had stood proudly, a testament to her resilience and determination.

I walked back over to Marieke who was talking animatedly to Gerrit and his assistant, Marta.

'What are your plans, Doctor Baaker?' Marta said, as I interrupted the trio to hand Marieke a fresh glass of wine. 'Will you be taking the long flight back tomorrow?'

'I'm thinking of staying here a while, actually. I've finished writing my book. The manuscript is currently sitting with a publisher at Sydney University Press. I'm waiting to hear back. In the meantime, Rob tells me the Noord-Holland government is searching for a museum director for a beachcomber's museum on Texel. They want to fund it properly so that anything the divers find can be processed quickly and the less valuable items can be displayed in a way that honours their history. They've offered me an interview next week. The position comes with an extended visa sponsorship.'

'I think it's a wonderful idea,' said Marieke, squeezing my arm. Her cheeks were flushed and her eyes bright as if she'd drunk one too many glasses of wine but when she hugged me, her grip was firm and steady and I knew she was releasing me.

At the end of the night, as people were beginning to clear out, I spied a man I'd never seen before standing in front of Anna's dress. He was staring up at it, his gaze drinking in the fabric. His face was animated, an array of emotions sweeping across his features.

When I greeted him, he looked startled; he'd been a million miles away.

'You must be Doctor Baaker.' He was tall, thin and his choice of clothes was unusual: an old-fashioned cravat over a velvet suit. We must have looked a pair, like something out of an antiquated painting. 'Allow me to introduce myself. I'm Johann de Witte.'

I almost dropped my glass, but managed to recover myself in time. 'Mr de Witte,' I said. 'I didn't think you were coming.'

'That was quite a speech you made at my house,' he said. 'I apologise for never emailing you. I intended to come to Texel earlier, but there were complications and I didn't want to disturb you or take the focus off this magnificent find.'

He pulled out a handkerchief and dabbed his eyes.

'You've shown me something tonight that I never thought I'd get to see,' he said. 'My great-grandfather, give or take six generations, was an engraver in Amsterdam. He bought the painting off a friend – he never said who, but I assumed it was Catharina herself. I must admit, I became a little obsessed with her. The painting you referred to in your email was made by her sometime in 1652. It was her last and it's special to me. I don't like sharing my things, I suppose I am old-fashioned that way. But – for you – well. I thought you should see.' He turned towards the exit and I followed him into the carpark. The moon lit up the street and fairy lights danced in the trees.

The car boot creaked as he opened it.

Inside was a painting, half in shadow.

I held my breath. There she was – a woman wearing a golden, silk dress, her hands wrapped around a red-cheeked infant. Catharina stood beside her, linking arms. They were on a beach, lapped by waves. Above them all, a perfect blue sky.

'Do you like it?'

'Oh, yes.' I was overcome. I wanted to cry. Here was the proof all along that Anna had not perished. The dress had belonged to her after all. 'I'm staying in town,' Johann said. 'You can come and see it again tomorrow, if you like. It belongs here. Perhaps we can discuss where it will go?'

I nodded, unable to find the words to thank him.

He closed the boot carefully, said goodbye and left me standing there.

The next morning, I woke early and drove to the place where Anna must have crawled along the sand after the storm blew through. I walked through the breakers, watched the sun dancing on the waves and felt the warmth and protection of my parents' love encircling me. Somewhere out beyond the swell, Hilde, my mother's seal, was surging through the water, a wild creature, free but connected to the place where she had found herself reborn.

EPILOGUE

1653

A GNETA CORRIN IS WALKING ALONG THE BEACH, thinking of the past. Ships of all sizes dot the harbour, their flags billowing like clouds against the bright blue sky. It is a good day, she thinks. No storm clouds on the horizon, only ships. One ship in particular catches Agneta's eye. The flag it flies is a French one; it has carried its passengers all the way from Calais. They will be tired when they arrive, they will need food and shelter and to see the faces of their friends. The orphanage is not the grandest accommodation, but Agneta has prepared a bedroom for her guest. She has told the children and the people in the village that she is expecting a visit from her sister. The villagers raised their eyes. Agneta has a sister? They wanted to know about her, how she came to live in France, why Agneta has never spoken of her before. Agneta pushed away their enquiries with her trademark smile. She is a woman of many secrets. Like a well-made dress, she keeps them tucked within the boundaries of her person. Soon, people had forgotten that she had even mentioned it and now, when they see her, they raise their hands in greeting which she returns.

She throws a stick for Wolfert, smiling as he races along the sand to retrieve it. Her dog is a scrappy thing, grey-haired and of little pedigree. She found him one day sheltering in an alcove of the orphanage, whimpering as a storm blew past overhead. She dragged him out and took him indoors and fed him nourishing broths until he regained his strength. Now his loyalty is unwavering. He grabs the stick between his teeth, trots back to her and drops the damp wood at her feet. Agneta leans down to pick it up, but before she can reach it, a small hand belonging to a three-year-old darts out and seizes it. The child is steady on her feet and she laughs as Wolfert waits patiently for her to toss it, his tail twitching eagerly.

'Go on, Brechtje,' Agneta says.

The small girl draws back her hand as far as she can and throws. Agneta scoops her up, laughing. Together they make their way down to the marina and the ship that has just docked, bringing the woman who changed Anna's life all those years ago. Beyond the forest of masts, the sea draws a breath and sighs and Anna hears in it all the longing and desire of a life well lived, the memories trapped beneath its glassy surface. She smiles at Catharina who tears her gaze away at last from the child with the golden curls and the sombre eyes to smile back, her expression full of wonder and hope.

ACKNOWLEDGEMENTS

T HANK YOU TO THE SIMON & SCHUSTER
publishing team – Dan Ruffino, Cass Di Bello,
Michelle Swainson, Anna O'Grady and the
wonderful sales reps – for getting this book to print
and into my reader's hands. Thanks also to Roberta
Ivers, Vanessa Lanaway and Jo Lyons for their sound
editing advice.

Alec Ewing, Head Conservator at the Kaap Skil museum
in Texel, provided an incredible amount of knowledge
about Dutch history and I'm indebted to him, as well as to
Corina Hordijk, Kaap Skil's Director, for answering endless
questions about the Palmwood Wreck and for trading
theories about the dress's mysterious provenance. Thank
you to the Texel Diving Club for sharing their incredible
diving experiences with me and for introducing me to a
world of sunken shipwrecks, beachcombing and forgotten
treasures.

I'm grateful to dress historian Hilary Davidson for
allowing me to interview her about the history of textiles and
clothing (and patiently answering my follow-up questions).

A generous grant from the Neilma Sidney Literary Travel Fund in 2019 enabled me to travel to the Netherlands to conduct research and interviews.

Rosie Scott was a talented Australian writer who sadly passed away in 2017 – thank you to her husband Danny Vendramini for allowing me to write part of this novel in her beautiful Blue Mountains studio in early 2020. Thanks to my wonderful writing friends, particularly Sandra Leigh Price and James Bradley, for providing companionship and much-needed laughter as well as editorial advice.

Thank you to my agent Tara Wynne for her guidance.

My greatest thanks is reserved for my family – my parents for always believing in me, my husband Michael for his love and support and my children for always keeping me grounded. You are more valuable to me than any treasure.

Thank you to my wonderful UK publisher Allison and Busby particularly Lesley Crooks (Publishing Manager) and Susie Dunlop (Publishing Director) for their faith in The Winter Dress and for giving it such a beautiful new cover.

In 2018 LAUREN CHATER was awarded a grant by the Neilma Sidney Literary Fund to travel to the Netherlands to research The Winter Dress. Her debut novel was The Lace Weaver and she is currently completing her Masters of Cultural Heritage through Deakin University in Victoria, Australia.

laurenchater.com